SUIT UP

There's this moment, right after I seal the helmet but before the cams come on, where it's completely dark and mostly quiet. You can hear everyone else kitting out: seals hissing in place, laughter, the grind of straps tightening, someone swearing at their tunic for not draping right; but you can't really hear straight. You're alone. Then the suit comes online, puts up a set of readouts in the periphery: heart rate, blood pressure, charge levels on plasma burner and phase disruptor, communications channels with my triad, my decade, and up and up to Captain Vohra on the command line. Then the vision flips on, filling the inside of the helmet with a flattened-out version of the world. How they do it I don't know. Chantry swears there ain't no demons in the suit thinking for us, and they'd know, but the helmet's visor sifts out a lot of the crap: shadows, tricks of the light, that sort.

That moment—when I stop looking at the world with the eyes my mother gave me and start looking at the screen the Empire tells me to use—that's when it changes. I ain't me no more, or not just me. I'm *them*. I'm *Empire*.

—from "Not Made For Us"
by Christopher Ruocchio

Recent Releases by the Contributors

David Drake
The Republic of Cinnabar
Navy Series and others
*Though Hell Should Bar
the Way*

Steve White
The Jason Thanou Series
and others
Gods of Dawn

Mark L. Van Name
The Jon and Lobo Series
No Going Back

Mike Kupari
Sins of Her Father

Jody Lynn Nye
The Imperium Series
and others
Rhythm of the Imperium

J. R. Dunn
The Day After Gettysburg
(with Robert Conroy)

Michael Z. Williamson
Freehold Series and others
Angeleyes

Gray Rinehart
Walking on the Sea of Clouds
(Wordfire Press)

Sharon Lee & Steve Miller
The Liaden Universe® Series
Neogenesis

Dave Bara
The Lightship Chronicles
Defiant (DAW Books)

Joelle Presby
The Hell's Gate Series
The Road to Hell
(with David Weber)

Susan R. Matthews
The Under Jurisdiction Series
Blood Enemies

Robert Buettner
The Orphan's Legacy Series
and others
The Golden Gate

Christopher Ruocchio
The Sun Eater Series
Empire of Silence
(DAW Books)

Brendan DuBois
The Dark Victory Series
Red Vengeance

Tony Daniel (co-editor)
Wulf's Saga
The Amber Arrow

STAR DESTROYERS

Big Ships Blowing Things Up

edited by

Tony Daniel

and

Christopher Ruocchio

STAR DESTROYERS

This is a work of fiction. All the characters and events portrayed in this book are fictional, and any resemblance to real people or incidents is purely coincidental.

"Superweapon" © 2018 by David Drake. "A Sudden Stop" © 2018 by Steve White. "Another Solution" © 2018 by Mark L. Van Name. "The Magnolia Incident" © 2018 by Mike Kupari. "A Helping Hand" © 2018 by Jody Lynn Nye. "Boomers" © 2018 by J.R. Dunn. "Hate in the Darkness" © 2018 by Michael Z. Williamson. "The Stars are Silent" © 2018 by Gray Rinehart. "Excerpts from Two Lives" © 2018 by Sharon Lee & Steve Miller. "Icebreaker" © 2018 by Dave Bara. "Try Not to Kill Us All" © 2018 by Joelle Presby. "Skipjack" © 2018 by Susan R. Matthews. "Homecoming" © 2018 by Robert Buettner. "Not Made For Us" © 2018 by Christopher Ruocchio. "A Tale of the Great Trek War Aboard the Starship *Persistence*" © 2018 by Brendan DuBois.

Introduction and all additional material copyright © 2018 by Tony Daniel and Christopher Ruocchio.

A Baen Books Original

Baen Publishing Enterprises
P.O. Box 1403
Riverdale, NY 10471
www.baen.com

ISBN: 978-1-9821-2414-4

Cover art by Kurt Miller

First printing, March 2018
First mass market printing, October 2019

Distributed by Simon & Schuster
1230 Avenue of the Americas
New York, NY 10020

Printed in the United States of America

10 9 8 7 6 5 4 3 2 1

CONTENTS

Big Ships Blowing Things Up

INTRODUCTION

Tony Daniel and Christopher Ruocchio

Big Ships. Blowing Things Up.

The big spaceship. Armed, looming, dangerous.

The leviathan.

There's an allure to the battleship, the destroyer, and other big ships of war, going back to the earliest days of science fiction. It matches (and is probably derived from) battleship nostalgia in the world's saltwater navies. The allure goes beyond sheer power and gets at the intricacy of men inhabiting what amounts to a small world—a world dedicated to one purpose.

Blowing things up.

Herman Wouk states it beautifully in his World War II masterpiece, *The Winds of War:*

"Put together at different times and places of different steel plates and machines, embodied in many forms under many names, a battleship was always one thing: the strongest kind of warship

afloat. This meant a thousand ever-changing specifications of size, design, propulsion, armor, armament, interior communication, interior supply systems; a thousand rituals and disciplines binding the crew, from the captain to the youngest striker, into one dependable corporate will and intelligence. In this sense there had been battleships in the days of Phoenicia and Rome, and there would always be battleships—a living peak of human knowledge and craft, a floating engineering structure dedicated to one aim: the control of the sea." *

The tradition of reverence for big vessels equipped for war is not limited to battleships, of course. The massive cities that are aircraft carriers qualify, as do those silent traversers of the deep, pregnant with death on a planetary scale, the ballistic-missile submarines. They don't call them "boomers" for nothing, after all.

It is not only the sheer power of such ships that speaks to the warrior soul, however. These things are also *intricate*. They are the first cyborgs in a very real sense, for men are a *component* of the weapon. Battleships are *organic*. When manned by a trained crew under skilled officers, they are not mere objects. They are *beings*.

This may be part of the connection big ships have to science fiction. For to travel long distances through space, it often seems a given that a device that is advanced, intricate, and intimately bound up with human survival in a harsh environment will be required. Which, in turn, is practically the definition of a ship. Perhaps humans will one day travel to the stars via quantum gates, space-time folding, redefining our perception of reality by learning alien tongues (or, what amounts to the same thing, by wishing *really* hard, *à la* John Carter of Mars), but for those who like their science fiction scientifically sound and plausible given what we know now, it's difficult to beat a big ship as the most likely transport into the galaxy and beyond.

It isn't so much that they destroy stars, as that when such a ship speaks with her guns, the stars themselves might be seen to quiver.

So all aboard—for a sea of stars. These are the big ships of the future, the powerful ships that will allow us to face a harsh universe toe-to-toe. And if there are ancient alien intelligences out there who seek our doom, it will be the big ships that marshal the power to stop them, defeat them, and—should they not agree to go quietly into that good night—blow them to Kingdom Come.

But it isn't just ships. It can't be.

There are *people* inside these monsters.

The battleship breeds a certain sort of sailor. Here's how Wouk describes his hero, US Navy officer Victor Henry, in *The Winds of War*:

"If he had a home in the world, it was a battle-ship. . . . It was the only thing to which Victor Henry had ever given himself whole; more than to his family, much more than to the sprawling abstraction called the Navy. He was a battleship man." °

° Herman Wouk, *The Winds of War* (New York: Little, Brown and Company, 1971), p. 158.

⚶   ⚶   ⚶

At the center of every story in this volume is a man, woman, or child whose fate is intimately linked to the star destroyer he or she lives within and, in most cases, serves aboard. A "battleship man" blows things up, but blows them up for a reason.

It may *not* be a good reason. He or she may be misguided by fate, luck, love, or sheer misinformation.

He or she may have the best reason in the world.

But we guarantee that for every human reason, there's a story.

Here they are.

—The editors

SUPERWEAPON

David Drake

As ships grow in size and complexity, so do their command systems. And as humanity heads into space, it may be that those command systems become smart enough to consider just what they are being asked to do, serving those contentious humans in the first place. It turns out that even if bigger is better for a ship—maybe that's not always the case for us puny human beings. It's a wry and grim tale from David Drake, from whom we would expect no less!

The attendant at the conference room door wasn't a guard: she was unarmed, and she wore the purple dress uniform of a full commander in the Navy. Kearney had thought that the Defense Board might keep the surveyors waiting to demonstrate its power, but precisely at 1200 hours—Commonwealth City local time—the commander opened the door. "The Defense Board is ready for you now, sirs and madam," she said.

Rosie Rice snorted, but she got up and with Kearney and Balthus trooped into a room whose two semicircular tables faced one another. The clear walls gave an unobstructed view of the city outside. Five officers in uniform sat at the more distant table; there were three empty chairs at the nearer side.

Kearney took the middle chair. Balthus, the Head of Biology, sat to his left and Rice, Head of Information, took the right seat and set up her little console on the table. She ran the hardware for these briefings. Normally Balthus was the star, describing exotic life-forms, but Kearney was pretty sure that the Defense officials this time were going to be primarily interested in what Rice had to say.

There were no ID tags on either the officers or the table in front of them, but Rice had made sure the surveyors had the images, names, and full information about the folks they'd be meeting today. Topelius, a small man in the dark green of the Army, glared at them and said, "Quite a gang of scruffs, aren't you? Do you think this meeting is a joke?"

"The waste of our time certainly isn't a joke," said Rice. She was short-tempered at the best of times, and Kearney guessed he could count on the fingers of one hand how often he remembered her being in a good mood. "As for you lot, though—"

"Rosie!" Kearney said. "Remember, this is *work*. Do your job."

The uniforms were already angry. Though Defense didn't have any formal control over the Survey Section, it'd be naïve to imagine that, in a bureaucracy as large as the Commonwealth's, Defense couldn't make life difficult for individual surveyors if it put its mind to it.

Rice scowled, but she shut up. Kearney turned quickly—he was afraid one of the Defense people would try to fill the silence—and said, "But that's the point, General Topelius: this *is* work for us, so we're in our working outfits."

Rice wore a brown sweater over a checked shirt; Balthus' lab coat was probably cleaner than it looked—many of the stains, though permanent, had been sterilized—but it certainly wasn't clean. Kearney himself had put on a new suit of spacers' slops; they were soft, loose, and comfortable, but he didn't pretend they were strack.

"*Dón't* give me that!" snapped Topelius. "I know the Survey Section has uniforms!"

"Central Office does, yes," said Kearney. "Management. But sir, you specified you didn't want Central Office personnel, you wanted the chiefs of the team who actually surveyed the artifact. Real surveyors are almost always in protective gear, so our working clothes are what's comfortable in a hard suit."

"Less uncomfortable," Balthus said. "No way a hard suit is comfortable."

A sky-train was moving across the city in its shimmering tube of ionized atmosphere. It was noticeably lower than the level of the conference room. Kearney wondered just how high in the Defense Tower they were.

A doorman had walked the team on its arrival to a sealed car which shunted them to the elevator. The elevator had brought them up to a waiting room. The attendants who'd put them aboard the vehicles hadn't provided anything but monosyllabic directions, and the commander had remained as silent as the conference room door behind her.

"What I want to know . . . ," said Rice in her usual angry tone. "If Central Office can't talk to you lot and let us get on with our jobs, what bloody use are they?"

Your salary is paid into your account, Kearney thought, *and you draw your rations*.

He didn't say that aloud, because Rice really didn't much care about money or food—and anyway, it wasn't the point of this meeting. To Admiral Blumenthal he said, "Sir, you want to discuss the artifact. We're here to do that."

"What we want to know," said Bowdoin of Operations, "is why Survey Section has been hiding an alien warship from the Ministry of Defense for months!"

"Well, it's more like a year and a half, isn't it?" said Balthus, looking at Kearney with that puzzled expression he got when he was trying to find the precise phrase.

"We didn't know it was a warship until seven months ago when we identified the weapons system," Rice objected.

Her control wands twitched. An image of a prism orbiting the yellow clouds of a gas giant appeared in the air, just above eye level of the seated parties. The body had four rectangular sides and stubby pyramids on both ends.

"Well, we were pretty sure," said Balthus. "There wasn't any room for cargo."

"Suspecting isn't knowing!" Rice said. "We're surveyors, not fortune-tellers!"

"What's important . . . ," Kearney said, speaking over

his teammates and hoping to shush them before the Board blew its collective gasket, "is that we weren't hiding anything. We'd been making progress reports through our own chain of command from the beginning. As soon as we were sure that it was a warship, we—the field team—reported that directly to the nearest Ministry of Defense facility."

"Which was a dockyard," Blumenthal said. "A bloody regional dockyard!"

"Well, we'd found a ship," Balthus said. "So we reported it to a dockyard."

He really was as innocent as he sounded. Kearney knew that he'd never have been able to put that fiction across, but Balthus seemed to have done so. Rice, of course, wouldn't have bothered trying.

"You found a ship eleven kilometers long!" Topelius said. "Didn't you think that was special enough to report directly to Commonwealth City?"

"On the long axis," Balthus said, sounding as though the distinction mattered—which of course it did to him. "On the short dimension it's about seven."

Rice adjusted her projector, shrinking down the viewpoint so that the tiny bead of the Survey vessel—which carried a team of ninety-odd comfortably—could be seen floating beside one of the alien vessel's open hatches. "*Much* larger than the *Shield of Justice*," Rice said in a gloating tone.

Kearney hoped his mental wince didn't reach the muscles of his face, but he couldn't swear to that. *Bloody Hell, Rosie, do you want to go straight from here to a prison that doesn't show up in anybody's records?*

Shawm said in a perfectly flat voice, "What do you know about the *Shield of Justice*?"

Shawm was a tall, rangy man with an extremely dark complexion. He wore a khaki second-class uniform with no medals or rank indications. He was probably a general, but Kearney wasn't sure that they used familiar ranks in Security.

"Only what's public knowledge in any spaceport in the Commonwealth!" Kearney broke in. "Isn't that right, Doctor Rice? Nothing that big could be truly secret, after all."

He was desperately afraid that Rosie was going to start projecting images of the Commonwealth's supership— a sphere a kilometer in diameter—if he didn't head her off.

Yes, of course the *Shield* was classified as Most Secret—but they were surveyors, for God's sake! They were trained to learn things, and the alien environments that surveyors examined as their job were a lot more puzzling than any human riddle could be.

"Yes," said Balthus, blindsiding Kearney. "It's being built on Ferrol and seems to have absorbed half the Defense budget for each of the past ten years. That's figuring the real cost of items listed in the public budget, of course. The costs're remarkably inflated in the published material, but real information is easy to find."

"I think we should leave this subject," said Shawm, after a pause during which Kearney had held his breath.

"Yes," said Kearney. "As I say, we reported the find to

a Defense facility and got on with our survey. There didn't appear to be any particular urgency about the matter."

"No urgency!" said Blumenthal. "Do you claim you're ignorant of the current political situation?"

"Well sir," Kearney said. "Things are tense between the Commonwealth—"

As he spoke he realized he should have said "us," but he found it very hard to imagine a community between his team and the group at the table opposite.

"—and the Empire of Khorsabad, but—"

"Khorsabad might want to attack before your *Shield of Justice*—" Balthus began.

"Doctor Balthus!" said Kearney. "We were politely asked to avoid that subject!"

Rice said, "Yeah, you've pretty much forced Khorsabad to attack while it still has a chance to win." *It's like having two dogs on long leashes who decided to start running in opposite circles!*

Graz, the stocky woman with the Production portfolio, chuckled like gravel in a chute. "It's too late for Khorsabad now. When the final software checks are done—and that could be any moment!—the *Shield* is done, and the Commonwealth's enemies are done."

Hoping to change the subject, to bring it back on track, Kearney said, "But the ship we found couldn't have any contemporary importance. We believe it was in sponge space for thirty thousand years. Only when its fusion bottle depowered completely did it drop into normal space to be found."

"Good God!" said Blumenthal. "This ship is thirty *thousand* years old?"

"Older than that," Kearney said. He was the team's head of engineering, as well as being the captain and navigator of the survey vessel. A long time ago he'd been a naval lieutenant, but the Survey Section had been a better fit for him. "That's the probable lifetime of a fusion bottle the size of the one powering the artifact."

Kearney coughed for a pause. "Based on the star charts on the artifact, though," he said, "the real age is probably closer to a half million years. So it didn't occur to us that it had any bearing on present events."

"It's been orbiting a gas giant in the Brotherhood system for as far back as the original catalogue," Balthus said. "It was simply assumed to be a natural satellite until a miner landed on it eighteen months ago and found open hatches. Then we were called in."

"If you have the ship's star charts," said Blumenthal carefully, "then you must have entered the ship's computer?"

Rice nodded and said, "We've accessed portions of the ship's . . . well, I'll call it a computer for want of a better word. Controlling intelligence. We've limited our explorations to discrete sectors of the complex, avoiding any attempt to bring the full system online."

"Our experts will be able to do that," said Tadeko, Advanced Projects. "We'll want a full report on your operations. You'll arrange for that to be sent over immediately."

He wasn't making a suggestion or even giving an order; he was stating an immutable fact. Tadeko was by far the oldest person in the room. He made Kearney think of a wise old lizard. A poisonous lizard.

"I don't doubt that you'll be able to do that, if you wish to," said Rice, meeting Tadeko's eyes squarely. "And I'll certainly meet with your specialists if you like."

"Look, if this is a warship," said Admiral Blumenthal, "what sort of weaponry does it have? Because advanced armaments certainly might have bearing on our operations in the near future."

"Not the near future," Kearney said. "Their principle is so different from anything in our arsenal that it took us the better part of a year to realize that we were looking at weapons."

"We had to get into the ship's controlling intelligence to see the connection," Rice said. Without being asked, she brought up images of the alien vessel's interior. The four spherical projectors filled the volume, each connected to the exterior hull by four struts.

"So that you understand the scale . . . ," Rice said. She focused down on one of the bodies lying at the base of a strut, then expanded again to the rank of multikilometer spheres filling the huge ship. "Initially we assumed that we were looking at parts of the propulsion system that we didn't understand."

"We've been calling them projectors," said Kearney, "but that's not really correct. They seem to be quantum devices which cause objects to *be* in the center of the target. There's no movement, just a different location."

"Do they throw explosives, then?" Blumenthal said, frowning. "How big are the projectiles?"

Before Kearney could speak, Tadeko looked at his fellow and said, "That's immaterial. The location is already occupied by matter—even in deep space. There would be a total conversion of mass into energy. *Total*. The result would destroy any object of human scale."

Tadeko's voice sounded like scales rasping. Though he hadn't said so, Kearney was sure that he realized that such devices would be just as effective on planets. Unless they were very slow to aim and load, or were very unreliable, four projectors seemed—literally—overkill.

"What's the range, then?" said Graz. She spoke relatively softly. The board members had lost the angry tone and expressions that they'd begun the briefing with.

"It should be infinite," Kearney said. "It's a quantum effect, after all, not Newtonian. Though of course we haven't tried to activate the devices."

"I'd like to go back to where you showed us the scale," said Topelius. "I thought I saw a body. Was that a body?"

Rice obligingly shrank the focus to the dead crewman that she'd used to demonstrate how large the projectors were. The team had left the bodies where they were, pretty much. They'd moved the few who'd been in the way, and Balthus and his team had processed a number when they studied them; but all told, those were only drops in a bucket.

"These individuals run between forty and fifty kilos each," Balthus said with proprietary enthusiasm. "There are two sexes present, but I suspect from imagery in the databases that there was a third sex also—the one that does the actual breeding. Those were much larger; four or five hundred kilos, on my estimate."

"Good God!" Blumenthal repeated. "How many bodies are there?"

"And how did they die?" said Shawm. There was a hint

of tension in his voice, quite different from the flat, threatening tone he'd used before.

"Nine hundred and seventy-three," said Balthus. He was noticeably more alert now that the discussion was on his specialty. He'd been used to leading briefings; most Survey reports focused on biology. Engineering and information technology were merely tools that supported the biological studies which determined whether or not a new world was suitable for human settlement. "And as for how they died—"

The close-up of the corpse was strikingly ugly, but death generally was. The aliens hadn't worn clothing, but the fine fur that covered their bodies had fallen out over the millennia. It formed delicate halos on the plating beneath the bodies.

The naked corpses—this one was typical—had shrunk as their tendons dried and tightened. There had been no decay in vacuum, but over such a long time the surfaces had sublimed except where the bodies were in relatively restricted volumes.

"—most of them died when the ship depressurized suddenly. There were a few in atmosphere suits at the time. I'll show you those in a moment."

The creatures' faces thrust forward more than humans' did and were generally narrower. Rice's software created images of the creatures as they'd been in life; she now inset those into the central display. With fur in place they were more bestial—and therefore less ugly, because they no longer looked like deformed humans.

"What's the name of the people?" Topelius said. "The race who built it, I mean?"

"We have no idea," said Balthus tartly. "I suppose some day we might be able to understand their spoken language, though I don't see that there's any reason we'd want to. The race doesn't appear to have survived the loss of this warship for very long."

"When this ship vanished, their enemies—another race—made a complete sweep of them," Rice said.

"That race is gone by now also, but much more recently," said Balthus. "They built the lovely crystal structures which I'm sure you've seen."

"We've been calling them the Monkeys," said Kearney. "We had to call them something, and 'the corpses' didn't seem correct. We were more interested in what they'd been doing while they were alive, after all."

"The ship must have had a total systems failure," said Blumenthal. "Was it sabotaged by their enemies, do you suppose?"

"We've been bloody careful on Ferrol," said Graz, "but Khorsabad has been trying really hard to infiltrate the dockyard. We realize it's possible that they've succeeded."

The expression on Shawm's face as he looked at her was that of a diner staring at half a worm in his salad. "We do *not* realize that," Shawm said. "It is *not* possible that Khorsabad has agents on Ferrol."

Kearney said nothing: this was a fight in somebody else's family. Personally, though, he hadn't been *that* certain about anything since he was thirteen and stopped believing in God.

"It wasn't a systems failure," Kearney said when he was sure that nobody at the Defense table was going to speak again. "And we don't think it was sabotage in the normal sense either."

"Certainly not systems failure," Balthus said. He nodded to Rice, who projected images in sequence showing half a dozen Monkeys in pale-green atmosphere suits. The chests of each body had been ripped apart, mostly by mechanical means. The exception had been burned completely through with a hole large enough to pass a man's arm.

"This was done by the ship's maintenance robots," Balthus continued. A turtle-shaped device the size of a bushel basket was in the field of some images, a few with their tri-pincered limbs extended. They looked very much like the machines which did the same job on Commonwealth warships.

"The exception was in one of the ship's boats," Kearney said. "The device closest to him was configured to work on the boats and had a torch."

Rice expanded that image. This time the robot ran on a track in the ceiling and was almost as big as the boat it hung over.

The termini of the robot's arms—the hands—could rotate to bring up any one of multiple tools. Kearney knew from close examination that the one used was an oxygen lance, but he didn't bother volunteering that to the Board. They already looked stunned.

"It *had* to be sabotage," Shawm said. "The enemy took over the central computer and did this."

"I think it was because of the weapons," Rice said. "Aiming, directing, quantum weapons required a unique mechanism. The controlling intelligence had to genuinely *understand* the universe in realtime. This ship"—she switched to the image with which she'd begun, the prism orbiting the swirling yellow clouds of the planet below— "has true machine intelligence. It doesn't mimic consciousness, it acts consciously."

"That's the same thing," Graz said in puzzlement. "For all practical purposes."

"I'd have said that those dead bodies were pretty practical!" Balthus said. Kearney didn't remember hearing him sound snappish before.

"To put it in other words . . . ," Rice said. Her tone made clear the sort of words she was tempted to put it in, but thank goodness she didn't do that. "The ship doesn't mimic the cognition of some large sample of its creators. The ship behaves like an intelligent *ship*."

"Does your ship, your *Shield*," said Balthus, "have a directive to protect itself?"

Graz opened her mouth to reply. Before she could, Shawm broke in with, "Anything to do with such a ship as you postulate would be classified!"

"Well, no matter," said Rice. "I can't imagine that you've created true machine intelligence."

"No warship would have self-preservation as its *prime* directive," said Admiral Blumenthal. "That's crazy. No matter what race built it."

"But a truly conscious machine wouldn't be concerned with the priorities of the people who built it," Balthus said. "It would have its own priorities. It's unlikely that attacking a powerful enemy because its builders want it to would be high on the ship's own list."

"Whereas hiding in sponge space as soon as it was

activated would prolong the ship's life for, well, thirty thousand years," Rice said. "And its existence for half a million, apparently."

"The ship disposed of the crew as quickly and efficiently as possible," Kearney said. "The crew members would probably have opinions of their own and might damage the ship if they were allowed to run free."

"Good God," said Tadeko. "Good *God*."

He got up and ran for a door. He moved very quickly for a man of his age.

He called something over his shoulder which Kearney heard as, "I have to send a courier!"

Rice looked at the remaining members of the Defense Board. She said, "You don't mean that your undoubtedly clever software engineers *have* managed to create real machine intelligence, do you?"

❖   ❖   ❖

David Drake was attending Duke University Law School when he was drafted. He served the next two years in the Army, spending 1970 as an enlisted interrogator with the 11th Armored Cavalry in Vietnam and Cambodia. Upon return he completed his law degree at Duke and was for eight years Assistant Town Attorney for Chapel Hill, North Carolina. He has been a full-time freelance writer since 1981. His books include the genre-defining and best-selling Hammer's Slammers series and the nationally best-selling RCN series, including *The Road of Danger*, *The Sea without a Shore*, *Death's Bright Day*, and *Though Hell Should Bar the Way*.

A SUDDEN STOP

Steve White

A what-if tale with a twist: set in the universe of Steve White's upcoming novel, Her Majesty's American, *the American Revolution fizzles and now there isn't just one sun that never sets on the British Empire, but myriad. Yet empires by their nature are at threat from separatist forces both within and without that would benefit from a Humpty-Dumpty-like Imperial crackup. Fortunately for the British Empire, there are also doughty, loyal Americans sailing mighty ships riveted together by steel and quantum uncertainty ready to ensure that the* Pax Brittanica *holds, even among the stars.*

"And so, on this the five hundredth anniversary of the founding of the Imperial Grand Council, it behooves us to remember that the course of history was perhaps not inevitable and foreordained, as many think. The First North American Rebellion might have shattered the

Empire but for the farsighted vision of the men, on both sides of the Atlantic, who grasped the great principle of imperial federation and took the first steps on the road we are still following after half a thousand years. We have them to thank for—"

Lieutenant Commander Jane Grenville, RSNR, flipped a switch, and the voice of Sir Archibald Ramsay, Viceroy of North America, ceased to reverberate in her earphones. The old boy wasn't saying anything the Queen-Empress hadn't already said in her speech from the throne. Jane settled back in her seat—one of twenty on this fairly crowded military surface-to-orbit shuttle—and tried other channels, in search of music. But on Federation Day—especially *this* Federation Day—it was naturally all patriotic stuff.

Not that she, a North American with an English mother, lacked appreciation of what her ancestors on both sides had accomplished on this date in 1781 after the British crown and the Loyalist forces led by George Washington had put down Benedict Arnold and his followers who had refused to accept the settlement that had ended the rebellion almost at its inception, before it could grow into an irreconcilable, fratricidal war. It really *had* been a remarkably generous and large-minded settlement. Maybe old Sir Archibald, for all his fulsomeness, had a point: maybe it hadn't *had* to turn out that way. It had helped that King William V had been solidly behind the settlement, in whose crafting he'd had a hand. But then, he had been a monarch of intelligence and character, as had been a number of the descendants of the heir that William of Orange and Queen Mary had unexpectedly produced shortly after the Glorious Revolution of 1688. Thus it was that the Britannic Federal Empire (still so called, although its two centers of gravity now lay in the viceroyalties of North America and India) had endured and now dominated the world.

Not, she reminded herself, without rivals . . .

As though to remind her of the existence of those rivals, she was shoved gently back in her seat, for the shuttle (which lacked such fripperies as inertial compensators) had reached an altitude at which grav repulsion's efficiency dropped off to the point that the photon thrusters must be activated for docking maneuvers at Albion Space Station. She manipulated the controls again. All at once, the small screen in front of her showed the shuttle's external video pickup, with the cloud-swirling blue curve of Earth below and the enormous oblate spheroid of the station growing closer. She had no difficulty picking out, from among the ships tethered to its docking flanges, the one that was her destination. It was, after all, bigger than most of the others put together.

HMSS *Resolute* was a *Defiant*-class second rater, to use the age-of-sail terminology initially adopted by the Royal Space Navy to avoid confusion with the battleships, cruisers, *et cetera* of the seagoing Royal Navy, and still used even though those ship types had long since ceased to sail Earth's seas. As such, she was as large as any Imperial space warship except the extremely rare *Invincible*-class first raters and practically any foreign rival. (The only exception, Greater China's new *Kuan-Ti*, might mass somewhat more, but it could not match the sophistication of the *Defiant* class's state-of-the-art weapon systems.)

As the shuttle drew nearer, more details came into view. Grav repulsion had largely eliminated the old distinction between ships that could land on a planet and those that traveled between planets—at least for small- to medium-sized ships, such as the fourth through sixth rate warships. But for the great capital ships of space, a planetary landing capability was unnecessary—not to mention the fact that a ship of *Resolute*'s half-million-ton mass, even had it possessed gravs, would never be able to turn them off on a one-G planet without being wrecked by her own monstrous weight. *Resolute* was purely a creature of deep space. Her forward section's ellipsoid curve was broken, astern, by the engineering spaces, the photon thrusters and the twin nacelles for the ranked superdense toroids of the Bernheim Drive, which accounted for twenty percent of the ship's total mass. Quite a lot of the rest was accounted for by the weapons— especially the magazines of torpedoes, which to be of any use in today's deep-space combat environment had to be fitted with Bernheim drives of their own. Thus, they were too large and massive for any but the first three rates of warships to carry in useful numbers. The fourth through sixth raters mounted only the relatively small missiles useable in orbital space and directed-energy weapons: x-ray lasers and the particle-beam projectors which were the short-range ship killers *par excellence*. Naturally, *Resolute* had plenty of these as well, and even a small planetside assault capability in the form of power-armored Royal Marines and atmospheric fighters.

All in all, a consummate killing machine. As the shuttle made its final approach, her complexity came more and more into focus, and the half-acre-sized Union flag on her dorsal surface near the bow gleamed in the station's lights. For an instant, Jane felt a small tingle of pride, not unmixed with apprehension, as she waited to disembark and report aboard that great ship as her new helmsman.

The various dominions could—and most did—have their own spaceborne security and law enforcement agencies, operating nothing heavier than a fifth rater. But the Royal Space Navy was a unified Empire-wide service, its personnel totally integrated. *Resolute*'s commanding officer, for example, was from the Viceroyalty of India. In addition, Captain Ilderim Sharif was a Muslim, and Jane had heard that he tended to lean over backward on that account, given the current troubles with the Caliphate, which persistently tried—not always without success—to spread disaffection among its coreligionists in the Viceroyalty. But when she paid her courtesy call on him there was no evidence of overcompensation—only the captain's equally renowned taciturnity. So she was able to promptly go about settling into her tiny but private stateroom. Then, with time on her hands, she sought out the wardroom, hoping she was in time to get a meal.

As she entered, her heart sank, for there were only a few officers in evidence and they seemed to be finishing up. She recognized one of them: Major Patrick O'Hara, commander of *Resolute*'s Marine detachment. (His rank was actually captain, but as such he received the traditional "courtesy promotion" aboard a warship, whose commanding officer alone could be addressed by the sacrosanct title of "Captain.") She had met him on a previous posting, and knew him to be a stereotypical "professional Irishman"—which meant a staunch Imperial loyalist these days, and had ever since Ireland had acquired coequal dominion status. Then, as O'Hara departed, one of the other officers stood up and turned around, his eyes met hers . . . and both pairs of eyes blinked with recognition.

"Jared!" she exclaimed, stepping forward and extending a hand. "It's been a long time."

"It certainly has, Jane." Lieutenant Jared Wilmarth took her hand, then added with a wry smile, "Or, I should say, 'sir.'"

Jane made a dismissive noise with her mouth. She and Wilmarth had met each other on the old HMSS *Audacious*, he as a midshipman and she as a Reserve ensign on her first cruise. Though in different departments (his was engineering), they had gravitated together, partly because they were both North Americans, albeit from different dominions—Carolina in her case, Oregon in his. "Well," she said, "I certainly hadn't expected to see you here."

"I *did* expect to see you—I'd heard who'd been assigned to be our new helmsman. No surprise, considering . . ." Wilmarth gave a gesture vaguely indicating Jane's head.

What he meant went unspoken. It was one of the reasons she still outranked him, even though he was regular Royal Space Navy and she was RSNR.

Direct neural interfacing had never lived up to the more extravagant predictions, largely because very few humans had the ability to use it without suffering a terrifying descent into psychosis. But a small percentage possessed, for reasons that still baffled cyberneticists and neurologists alike, the ability to mind-link with a computer with only a brief and relatively mild initial disorientation. Even for this minority, DNI hardly possessed the near-magical properties claimed for it by its early enthusiasts. It did, however, greatly enhance the speed and precision with which computerized controls could be used—such as a starship's controls.

It was only by coincidence that interface talent and the attributes required of a military officer occurred in the same person. When they did, such personnel were extremely valuable . . . and Jane Grenville was one. The helmsman's station was fitted for manual control, of course, but it also had an interface jack. It helped account for the fact that the piloting of the mighty *Resolute* was being entrusted to a reservist. Sometimes pragmatism trumped snobbery.

"Well, at any rate, it's good to see you again," she said. "And anyway," she added jokingly, "we North Americans have to stick together—especially on Federation Day."

His expression did not match the lightness of her tone. Indeed, a shadow seemed to cross his face. "Inappropriate name," he said expressionlessly.

"Well . . . I suppose so." It was, she supposed, something of a misnomer for what had happened in 1781: the reorganization of the colonies into a smaller number of more rational units, each self-governing as to internal affairs while a viceroy moderated intercolonial matters, and the creation of the Imperial Grand Council to steer the Empire as a whole. But it hadn't been until almost a century later, after many vicissitudes including the Second American Rebellion, that the great principle of imperial federation had been fully grasped: the dichotomy between the metropolis and the colonies had to go. So, by a cumulative process, the Imperial Grand Council had become a super-legislature in which the colonies (elevated to the dignity of dominions) stood on the same footing as England, Scotland, and Ireland.

"Still," she said, "it was a necessary beginning. Britain alone could never have sustained a world empire." This was a truism of all the history she had always been taught. The Empire had prevailed by expanding its power base beyond the narrow confines of the British Isles, just as Rome had once outgrown a single city-state. "The world we know wouldn't exist."

"No, it wouldn't." Wilmarth's voice was very neutral. Then, abruptly, he grew intense. "Have you ever wondered if maybe the price of that world was too high?"

"The price?"

"North American independence."

"What?" She looked at him sharply. "Well, I remember your ancestors came from what's now the Dominion of New England, before they moved west to Oregon." New England had been a hotbed of rebel sentiment in the 1770s, and later had temporarily won independence in the Second Rebellion of the 1850s, until its compulsive attempts to destabilize the Viceroyalty had exasperated the Empire into a reconquest. "But that's all ancient history, Jared."

"Not quite as ancient as you might think. I've got distant relatives on New America."

"Really?" In 2120, the Empire had permitted a group of North American irreconcilables to attempt (at their own expense) to colonize a planet of Tau Ceti. It had been the only slower-than-light interstellar expedition ever launched, because while it was en route the Bernheim Drive had been discovered. So when their antimatter pion drive/magsail hybrid ship had finally arrived at its destination, the colonists had awoken from cryo-sleep to find the Imperials already there—a crushing disappointment. The Empire had been very decent about it, allowing New America a kind of ill-defined semiautonomy and promising dominion status whenever the colonists asked for it. (They still hadn't.) "I never knew that. But I suppose I can see why you might have special reasons for thinking something of value was lost."

"You ought to think so too, Jane. After all, some of your ancestors were enslaved at the time of the First Rebellion."

"What? Well, yes, I suppose so." It wasn't something to which she gave much thought. Her one-eighth African ancestry had left little trace except a certain duskiness of skin and tight curliness of dark hair. And anyway, it made no difference nowadays. "But what's that got to do with—?"

"Don't you see? Slavery lived on in the Empire almost two generations after 1781, and various forms of discrimination lasted far longer than that. But if the rebels had won, they *surely* would have abolished slavery immediately after attaining independence."

"Uh . . . are you sure of that?"

"Of course. They would have *had* to—their Declaration

of Independence explicitly said 'All men are created equal.' So there never would have been a race problem in North America!"

"Umm . . . I'm not quite so sure. People don't always live up to their declarations."

Jane couldn't be certain, but it was as though shutters seemed to close over Wilmarth. He spoke with a kind of overemphatic joviality. "Well, you're probably right. Anyway, we've got some time. Or at least, I do— Commander Ferguson, the engineering officer, isn't aboard yet. Let's go back to the station, where we can at least get a drink!"

Among the many things—practically everything, actually—that the entertainment media got wrong about the RSN was the spacious, theatre-like sets used to represent capital ships' command bridges. In fact *Resolute*'s bridge, like all a warship's working spaces, was no more voluminous than it needed to be.

Jane sat in the helmsman's chair, her head capped with a neural-induction helmet connected by cable to the interface jack of the ship's barely subsentient brain. (A cranial implant by which the jack could be plugged directly to the brain was perfectly possible. But that Just Wasn't Done.) She had, by now, gotten past the initial unpleasantness of direct neural interfacing, and was reflecting that it was worth it to feel the titanic ship and its sensor array as an extension of her own body and senses.

The inertial compensators prevented her from feeling it, but *Resolute*'s photon thrusters were producing one G of acceleration as they drove the ship outward. Presently, Jane's neural feed informed her that they had reached that distance—in Earth's case, about twelve and a half thousand miles from the planet's center—where the gravity field's force was less than a tenth of a G.

"Primary Limit crossed, Captain," she presently reported.

In his seat, behind her and slightly raised, Captain Sharif nodded. "Engage Bernheim Drive," he ordered.

"Aye aye, sir." Jane thought a series of commands. The photon thrusters ceased to push the ship forward and, at appreciably the same instant, the Bernheim Drive activated, folding space in front of the ship, altering the properties of space to reduce normal gravity in that direction. The ship surged forward at four hundred Gs of thrust, with her occupants in a state of free fall (or, rather, they would have been had it not been for its artificial gravity generators).

At such an acceleration, it would not take long to reach the Secondary Limit, almost out to the asteroid belt. There, with the sun's gravity field at only one ten-thousandth of a G, the drive could generate a field that wrapped negative energy around the ship to literally change the shape of space and create an area of expanding space-time (referred to as "subspace") that could move faster than other parts of space-time. The ship would be dragged along by this "bubble in space-time." Inside the bubble, space was not distorted and the ship was technically traveling at sublight speeds. But the bubble itself would push through space faster than light—almost twenty-nine hundred times faster, in fact. That wasn't quite as fast as the upper limit imposed by unavoidable deformations in the drive field at the highest pseudoaccelerations. But the closer one got to that threshold, the lower the marginal returns from building in more drive coils and pumping in more energy. *Resolute* represented what modern naval design theory regarded as the optimal balance. She was fast as well as big.

"Bernheim Drive engaged, Captain," Jane reported, unnecessarily but as per custom. She raised the helmet into its housing in the overhead, and her immediate physical surroundings came back into sharp focus as her senses contracted to those of her body. "On course as plotted."

"Very good, Mister Grenville." Tradition mandated "Mister" regardless of the junior officer's gender. Sharif picked up a microphone from his armrest and activated the shipwide intercom. "All hands, this is the captain speaking. As you all know, our destination is the Lambda Aurigae system, approximately forty-nine and a quarter light-years distant—a journey of six and a quarter days under Bernheim Drive, exclusive of sublight maneuvering. Our mission is to counter a recent buildup of Caliphate forces in the system. While there, we will land our Marine contingent on the fourth planet to act in support of our colony, New Kashmir, against attempted infiltration from the Caliphate enclave on the planet."

Jane noted that Sharif used the word "colony" for the Empire's settlement and "enclave" for that of the Islamic Caliphate. The Caliphate people would doubtless have reversed that usage. She wasn't clear on the legalities of the competing claims to the system that had led to the current confrontation. Nor were they her business.

She also noted what the captain had left unsaid. As its name suggested, New Kashmir's colonists mostly came from the Viceroyalty of India . . . and included a high percentage of Muslims. It was a widespread (but publicly unvoiced) suspicion among Imperial officialdom that sympathizers among the latter were facilitating that "attempted infiltration." She couldn't help wondering if Sharif's religion and ethnicity might have been a factor in assigning *Resolute* to show the flag at Lambda Aurigae.

Not, she told herself serenely, that it mattered. Once this ship did show the flag—a very, very large flag, in *Resolute*'s case—the rag-heads wouldn't dare try any nonsense. The most bellicose of the Empire's rival space powers, the Caliphate was also, fortuitously enough, the least advanced. Unable to entirely escape the tethers of its technophobic fundamentalist ideology (for example, Allah apparently disapproved of direct neural interfacing), it had nothing to match a *Defiant* class. The Caliphate squadron at Lambda Aurigae had been built up to a size sufficient to worry the token Royal Space Navy detachment there, but *Resolute* could by herself reduce that squadron to cosmic detritus without breathing hard.

She mentally scolded herself for feeling a slight regret that such an occasion would almost certainly not arise.

Lambda Aurigae was a G0V star slightly larger and hotter than Sol. It was also somewhat younger, and its fourth planet, though orbiting in the liquid-water zone, had not had time for life to venture out of that water onto continents of bare rock and sand. But with nanotechnology and self-replicating machines, the planet was readily terraformable and a great prize.

Hence it was the focus of one of the standoffs that frequently occurred on the frontier—and only there. It was generally recognized (even by the Caliphate's rulers, if not always by its mullahs) that Earth could not endure an all-out war waged with today's weapons. So a tacit agreement reigned. Earth was off-limits to the antimatter warheads and the nano-disassemblers. The rest of the galaxy was fair game.

As *Resolute* approached Lambda Aurigae's Secondary Limit—slightly farther out than Sol's due to its slightly greater mass—Jane disengaged the drive field. To enter a gravity field of more than 0.0001 G without doing so resulted in the field's immediate collapse, the drive's immediate shutdown, and a greater or lesser degree of physical damage to the drive and associated parts of the ship. Entering the Primary Limit with the drive activated in sublight mode had the same consequences. It was as much as a starship captain's career was worth to allow any of this to happen. Thus, under Sharif's watchful eye, Jane made a point of erring on the side of caution.

Nor were these the only dangers. Before the drive could be disengaged at the Primary Limit, the velocity—pseudovelocity, really—that it had accumulated in the course of its departure from Sol must be shed, or else the same consequences, possibly up to and including total destruction of the drive, would overtake the ship. The necessary calculations flowed through Jane's head, meshed as it was with the computer, as she applied the appropriate deceleration. *Resolute* proceeded on a sunward course that would intersect the fourth planet, where she would switch to photon thrusters and deploy the fighters and the Marines' reentry capsules, both of which need only be dropped as the ship skimmed New Kashmir's upper atmosphere.

The passage wasn't long, but it gave time for Captain Sharif to politely place himself under the command of the commodore—considerably junior to himself in terms of his permanent rank—in charge of the light Royal Space Navy units already in the system. It also gave an opportunity to scan nearby space for threats. There was, it seemed, a Caliphate ship—equivalent to an RSN fifth rater, what was loosely termed a frigate—in geosynchronous orbit around New Kashmir. This was outside the planet's Primary Limit, and therefore in the equivalent of "international waters," although close enough to be provocative. But provocative or not, a fifth rater was eminently ignorable by *Resolute*. And the ragheads (a term used even by Muslim RSN personnel, despite prim official disapproval) made no response even as New Kashmir waxed to fill a significant portion of Jane's view forward.

"Approaching Primary Limit, sir," Jane reported as *Resolute* neared the distance mandated by safety protocols. She did not add that the pseudovelocity had been killed precisely on the instant; Sharif could see that for himself from the readouts, and it wouldn't do to toot one's own horn.

"Very good, Mister Grenville. Disengage drive." Jane did so, and *Resolute* came to a virtual halt somewhat outside the Primary Limit. She raised the helmet and

looked around her. The bridge was slightly less crowded
than usual, for the first officer, Commander Winnifred
Rushton, had been called to engineering a while back for
consultation on some matter or other.

"And now," Sharif began . . . only to be cut off by an
ululation from his armrest communicator: the internal-
emergency signal. He slapped the controls, and the comm
screen came alive.

For an instant, Jane could only stare, mentally and
physically paralyzed by shock.

The screen was mostly filled by the wild-eyed face of
Jared Wilmarth. Behind him, she recognized the
engineering spaces where he worked. On the deck were
at least two motionless bodies lying in spreading pools of
blood.

"Captain!" blurted Jared, seemingly almost unable to
speak coherently. "You've got to come to engineering at
once! Commander Rushton and Commander Ferguson
are dead. They're *all* dead—the whole watch. They—"

"Get hold of yourself, Mister Wilmarth!" the captain
rapped. "What's happened?"

But Wilmarth was on the quavering edge of hysteria.
"Captain, *please* come down here! It's—" He suddenly
turned his head and looked outside the pickup. Whatever
he saw seemed to horrify him. And at that moment, the
screen went blank.

Sharif grasped his comm mike. "Major O'Hara, I'm on
my way to engineering. Have a Marine detail meet me
there." He got to his feet. "Mister Grenville, you have the
conn. Beat to quarters." Without waiting for an
acknowledgment from Jane, he rushed out.

Jane shook loose from her stunned immobility and moved quickly to occupy the captain's chair. "We will beat to quarters," she commanded—a very old naval term still in use. "Lieutenant Chatterjee to the bridge," she added, summoning her relief helmsman. Chatterjee, a fresh-faced young j.g., arrived with commendable promptness and flung himself into the seat Jane had vacated. He was not possessed of interface talent—no ship could hope to get more than one such helmsman—but he prepared the manual controls and turned to Jane, his expression a silent request for orders.

"Stand by, Mister Chatterjee," she said in what she hoped was a calming voice. Under the circumstances, it was out of the question to proceed on photon thrusters as planned. For now, she found herself with nothing to do but wait for further word from engineering, while *Resolute* hung in space just outside New Kashmir's Primary Limit.

She had only just come to that realization when the comm screen again awoke . . . and revealed a scene which for a moment her mind refused to accept.

Once again the screen showed Jared Wilmarth's engineering station. And once again he was there—but this time his face was set in lines of tense purposefulness. His left arm was locked around Captain Sharif's neck, holding him half-choked and totally immobilized. His right hand held a standard-issue sidearm—a Webley gauss needle pistol—pointed at the captain's temple.

"Jared, what are you *doing*?" Infuriatingly, she heard her voice rise to a falsetto squeak. She forced it into steadiness and began again. "Jared, there's a Marine detail on the way—"

"So it's you that's in charge up there, Jane? All right, listen carefully. The Marines are already here—outside the hatch. They can't break in while I've got *him* as hostage. And for that same reason you're going to do exactly as I say." For a fleeting instant, sadness seemed to flicker across his face. "I tried to sound you out, hoping you'd go along with me as a fellow North American. But I could see there was no way." His features hardened again into a mask of inexorable purpose. "As you probably haven't had the leisure to notice, the Caliphate ship in high orbit is now maneuvering to rendezvous with us. You will surrender this ship to them. Otherwise, I'll destroy it. I've already rigged an override by which I can cause the antimatter plant to overload with a touch of a button. I can—and will—do it before the Marines can try any tricks, or if I smell a whiff of sleep gas."

Jane desperately tried to struggle up from the ocean of nightmare in which she felt she was drowning. "Jared . . . I can't believe this. You—a Caliphate agent?"

"No!" Wilmarth sounded indignant. "I belong to the Sons of Arnold."

Jane had heard of them—an organization of irreconcilables on New America, chronically under suspicion by the authorities but generally dismissed as all talk. Jane had never heard of them being present in North America itself . . . but she recalled Wilmarth saying he had New American relatives.

"I don't mean the gutless old fuddy-duddies who head the Sons," he went on in a rush, as though unable to resist the temptation to deliver a manifesto to a captive audience. "They'd never dare to do this. But some of us—the younger ones, the ones who represent the true spirit of the old revolutionaries—understand that bold direct action is needed, not hot air."

"But Jared, what's that got to do with trying to betray this ship to the Caliphate?"

"We take our allies where we can find them, Jane."

"*What?* You're telling me that your faction has allied itselves with the rag-heads? Their crazy fundamentalist version of Islam is about as far from the ideals of the old North American rebels as it's possible to get!"

"Do you actually think we *like* the Caliphate?" shouted Wilmarth. He took a deep breath and got himself under control. "Politics makes strange bedfellows. Breaking up the Empire by freeing North America is in their interest, so they're willing to help us. But there are limits to how helpful they can be, given the disparity of military power. Turning this ship—which is far beyond anything they've got—over to them will help redress that imbalance. A war will give us our chance."

"You know perfectly well it's been centuries since anybody in North America has *wanted* to be 'freed' from the Federal Empire. You're mad as well as being a bloody murdering traitor!"

"Traitor?" Wilmarth's eyes flared with fanaticism. "*You're* the traitor—as much a traitor as Washington was! I'll be the greatest North American hero since Benedict Arnold!"

With a sudden, convulsive effort, Sharif unlocked Wilmarth's grip on his throat just enough to speak in a croak. "Grenville, don't obey him! That's an order!"

"Shut up!" Wilmarth struck the captain a sharp blow to the side of the head with the barrel of his Webley, and tightened his grip again as Sharif momentarily sagged. He turned back to face Jane, and his voice and his expression both snarled. "Enough talk! Do as I say or I'll blow up this ship. I'm not bluffing!"

For a moment, Jane sat frozen in an agony of indecision. Glancing at the tactical plot, she could see that the Caliphate ship was indeed approaching. It hadn't taken it long, for it could use its drive, since *Resolute* was still just outside the Primary Limit.

Just outside the Primary Limit . . .

An idea came to life in her, begotten by desperation.

"Well, Jane?" came Wilmarth's ragged voice. "Stop stalling!"

It left her no time to talk herself out of the insane course of action that had occurred to her. Resolution congealed.

"All right. I agree." She saw the triumph on Wilmarth's face, and the horrified widening of Sharif's eyes. She ignored both and continued in a carefully calm and reasonable tone of voice. "I'm going to return to the helmsman's station, so I can more easily control the rendezvous maneuvering."

Wilmarth nodded stiffly. Jane stood up, aware that every pair of eyes on the bridge was glaring at her. She met those of Lieutenant Beaumont, the weapons officer, for a fleeting instant; she winked, and with her chin gave a barely perceptible gesture toward the tactical plot. She hoped he would understand. Then she brusquely motioned Chatterjee out of his seat and took his place. It was necessary. The youngster might not have obeyed a command from her that would have seemed perfect lunacy. At a minimum, he would have hesitated long enough for Wilmarth to carry out his threat.

And furthermore, she thought as she lowered the neural induction helmet over her head, now she would be able to *think* that command rather than giving it verbally for Wilmarth to overhear.

First she activated a special override of engineering's control of the power supply to the Bernheim Drive. Then, taking a deep breath and bracing herself, she sent a flashing thought to the computer . . . and the drive awoke, on full power.

At four hundred Gs of insensible acceleration, *Resolute* surged planetward, past New Kashmir's Primary Limit.

"*What?*" was all Wilmarth had time for. With a grinding crash and the indescribable shriek of rending metal, the drive shut down in a brutal way that was never intended. At once the pseudovelocity dropped to zero and *Resolute* came to a shuddering halt with which her inertial compensators could not entirely cope. The great ship shook convulsively.

The entire bridge crew would have gone sprawling had they not been, as per regulation, strapped into their seats while at general quarters. In the comm screen, Wilmarth *did* go sprawling, losing his grip on the captain, as Jane had been gambling he would. He got off a shot with his Webley, but the electromagnetically propelled fléchette went wide, barely missing Sharif's head. Then the two men were grappling on the deck.

In the tactical plot, the Caliphate ship hung in stunned motionlessness.

"Mister Beaumont!" snapped Jane, "I want a target lock on—"

"Aye aye, sir!" Beaumont, she thought, must have understood, for he recovered more swiftly than she would have thought possible. His hands flew over his control board.

"And Mister Beaumont . . . fire at will!"

Whatever damage the ship had sustained, it clearly hadn't affected the weapon systems. From all the projectors that could be brought to bear, gigawatt X-ray lasers stabbed out at light speed—virtual instantaneity at this range. The beams were, of course, invisible. But in the outside view, a new star flared into being as the Caliphate ship's shields and armor failed under an energy transfer beyond what a fifth rater could withstand. It was a star that briefly went nova when the target's antimatter powerplant went critical.

Jane sagged back in her seat and turned to the comm screen. Through the acrid smoke that now suffused the engineering spaces, she could see that it was all over. The Marines had broken in and had the screaming, writhing Wilmarth pinned to the deck. A corpsman was examining the captain's throat.

She stood up and helped Chatterjee—the only one present who hadn't been strapped in—up off the deck. "Mister Chatterjee, you may be inserting us into orbit around New Kashmir." At least she hoped the photon thrusters were still in working order, although she didn't mention that. "Mister Beaumont . . . good work." She returned to the captain's chair and sat down. "I believe I still have the conn."

The reports were in. The Bernheim Drive was badly damaged—inoperable for now, in fact—but it hadn't been wrecked beyond repair. In fact the new engineering officer was confident it could be repaired in fairly short order. Ships carried a full supply of spare components against the possibility of an encounter with a sizeable piece of space junk, which could have the same consequences *Resolute* had just experienced.

And now Jane sat in the captain's private office, looking across a desk at Sharif's dark, hawklike face.

"You do realize, Commander, that you violated more regulations than I can call to mind at the moment."

"Yes, sir."

"There will, of course, have to be a board of inquiry. However, after the board has heard my testimony, and that of every other officer of this ship, I don't think you'll have any worries. In fact . . . when next year's Honors List comes out . . ." He dismissed the subject as outside his purview. "Tell me, what caused you to think of that stunt?"

"Well, sir, I've heard Major O'Hara quote what he says is a very old Irish saying."

"Eh?"

Jane grinned. "It's not the fall, it's the sudden stop."

※　　※　　※

Steve White served as a Naval Intelligence officer in the Mediterranean and in the Vietnam War Zone. He is a graduate of the University of Virginia Law School and an associate member of the Virginia Bar. He is well known for the best-selling Starfire military science fiction series with David Weber and, more recently, Charles Gannon. In addition, he has written a number of popular science fiction adventure novels for Baen. They include the galaxy-spanning adventure *Prince of Sunset* and its sequel *Emperor of Dawn*, the secret-history science fiction novel *The Prometheus Project*, the high fantasy novel *Demon's Gate*, and the Jason Thanou series of time travel adventures that began with *Blood of the Heroes* and continues throughout the current *Gods of Dawn*. His other solo novels include *Saint Antony's Fire*, an alternate-history fantasy set in Elizabethan times. Steve lives in Charlottesville, Virginia.

ANOTHER SOLUTION

Mark L. Van Name

Convergence: When absolute power meets unmatched force, the prospect of mutually assured destruction may be unavoidable. Too bad for humanity, if that's the case! But sometimes the only solution is to rethink the situation from the ground up. Or in this case, from space—down.

"So, are you ready to make history?" Rios, her crew behind her, stared through the observatory tower's windows at the enormous bulk of the *Solution*, her future stretching in front of her for a kilometer in each direction.

She turned to face the three dozen people waiting with her to board the ship.

No one spoke. Veterans all, they did not need or want a pep talk, so they had taken her question as rhetorical.

She aimed to surprise them.

"I hope you aren't," she said, "because I'm sure not. I'm fine with history recording the launch of the biggest

47

man-made vessel ever to move, but I hope we're no more than a footnote in that story. The ship's AI can fly it. We're along only in case it needs authorization to engage in battle." She looked each person in the eyes, taking the time to make sure each knew she had seen them. "I don't want to fight. I want to take up our protective position over the Union nations, make it clear to those Republic goons that we *could* attack but won't if they leave us alone, spend six boring months in orbit, and go back to Earth." She looked again at each person. "Six boring months— not history. That's our goal. Got it?"

Most people nodded. The younger ones looked puzzled; she would watch them carefully until they understood fully how much she'd meant what she'd said.

"Dismissed."

The crew split into four groups, one per elevator. She'd follow in a minute, when all were on board. They'd christened the *Solution* earlier, before everyone not in the crew had ridden the shuttle back to base. She stared at the lunar camp twenty-five klicks away, its five domes gleaming in the light. It had never felt like home, and she was glad to be quit of it. Her house was a home, and her ship, whatever ship, was a home, but everything else was just a place to pass the time.

"All crew aboard," the *Solution* said through her implant. She knew it was technically the constructed voice of the ship's AI, but the vessel's computation infrastructure wove through so much of its structure and the AI was so integral a part of it that she thought of the ship and the AI as one and the same.

"Coming," she said. It could hear her via subvocalizing,

and it would have known she was on the move just by tracking her, but she liked to talk to it as if it was another member of her crew.

She stepped into a waiting elevator.

Rios buckled into her chair in the enormous bridge. The three-meter-diameter sphere in front of her displayed a holo of the *Solution* and its underground dock. The thin layer of camouflage panels that had been covering the ship had already retracted into the walls of the dock. The *Solution* sat ready to ascend.

Initially, she'd hated the idea of putting all of the crew in a heavily fortified room in the middle of the ship, particularly despised not being able to see outside, but she'd come to accept that navigating in space a ship two kilometers long and over a kilometer wide required her to take a bigger view than her unaided eyes could manage. She had to trust the simulations in the nav sphere.

"*Solution*, this is Lunar Control." The voice hit everyone's implants at once. "You are clear for liftoff."

"Lunar Control and *Solution*, we are good to go," said Rios. Everyone knew the acknowledgment was no longer necessary, an artifact of launches from the past, but it felt right, and she always made it.

"Lunar Control, we are taking control," said *Solution*. "Ascent in ten seconds." The AI always spoke in the plural, copying the human style.

It did not, however, count down, so the humans did, quietly and mostly to themselves, and a low chant still filled the room. As the last sounds of "one" left the air, the *Solution* shuddered once, stabilized, and then, in the sphere in front of them, rose from beneath the lunar surface. The ride was even smoother than the simulations had suggested it would be, the many fusion-powered engines pushing the ship evenly into space.

Five minutes later, gravity had decreased to nearly nothing, and the moon's surface was a small presence at the bottom of the sphere. The Earth hung in the sky ahead of them. Blackness surrounded them.

"Any signs of anything near us or between us and our destination?" Rios said.

"Nothing, Captain," came in unison from the three crew members studying various sensor arrays and, of course, from the *Solution* itself.

"Were you expecting anything, Captain?" Akintola, the questioner and most senior member of the nav team, stared carefully at her.

Rios had heard the same rumors he almost certainly was wondering about: Were the intelligence leaks real? Had the Republic built its own enormous ship on the other side of the moon, at their base? Was this yet another Union/Republic arms race? "No," she said, her voice strong with truth. If the Republic had its own *Solution* and anyone in the Union knew it, that data was above her pay grade. "Just doing the job."

Akintola nodded and smiled. Whether he believed her or not, she knew he was a lifer and not about to risk his career over something he couldn't control. If Command chose to drop a surprise load of dung on them midmission, it wouldn't be the first or the last time, and they'd all keep on doing their jobs, so worrying about it was a waste of energy.

"*Solution*," Rios said, "you have the conn." Another unnecessary formality with an AI that controlled everything, but she was used to a certain process, and they had trained the AI to follow it as well. "Take us to our destination."

"Captain to the bridge." The call blared simultaneously from speakers over her netting and her implant. Having been asleep only two hours, she was tempted to grumble that it better be important, but why waste the time? They wouldn't have called her if it wasn't.

"On my way," she said.

Four minutes later, dressed but unwashed, she pulled herself into the bridge and buckled into her chair. Half of the crew was already there, others joining every few seconds as she studied the nav sphere.

A green marker identified a six-inch-long ship in the sphere as the *Solution*, though she would have known its profile instantly. At the bottom of the sphere, moving on a course whose projection lines diverged from theirs, was another ship of similar size but whose details were fuzzy; a red marker sat atop it.

"Captain," said Akintola, "I guess those rumors were true after all."

Rios nodded. "You've cleared with Lunar Control that it's not a surprise second one of ours?"

"Affirmative," said both Akintola and the *Solution*.

"Where do your projections have it going?" she said.

Earth shifted to the center of the sphere. The *Solution*'s green marker appeared just above the equator over the western edge of the Atlantic. The red marker took up a similar location just in from the western Pacific coast.

"So the Republic has its own peacekeeper," she said.

"Yes, Captain," said Akintola.

"It would appear so," said *Solution*.

"Lunar Control and Earth Control are seeing this?"

Akintola nodded as *Solution* responded, "Yes, Captain."

Rios looked around at her crew. Everyone was present now, some probably feeling the effects of too little sleep but all appearing at the ready.

"Let's see how they want to play this," Rios said. "Hook us all up, and keep it on speakers." She wanted the crew to hear all at once that she had known no more about this than they had. She couldn't afford the loss in trust they would feel if they believed she had been hiding vital information from them.

She ignored how that made her feel about her own bosses. Those feelings were nothing new.

"Lunar Control here," a man whose voice she didn't recognize said.

"Earth Control here," a woman's voice said. Rios also didn't recognize this one. She'd have preferred to work with a team she knew, but you don't always get what you want.

"*Solution* here," the ship said.

"Please confirm this ship is not one of ours," Rios said.

"Confirmed," came first from Lunar Control and then a couple of seconds later from Earth Control.

"Do your course predictions match ours?" she said.

"Affirmative," said both Lunar and Earth Controls.

Rios hesitated. Six boring months. Was that too much to ask?

Apparently.

"Do we engage?" she said.

Half a minute passed in silence. The two Control teams were probably deciding who would own this one, though both would know Earth was going to win.

Another half a minute passed.

Earth won.

"This is Earth Control. We will be sole control from this point forward. Lunar Control will continue to monitor. We are studying the situation and will get back to you shortly. You're still more than twelve hours out from orbit, so unless the other ship changes course, sit tight."

"A suggestion, Earth Control?" Rios said.

"Proceed."

"We could launch a set of monitor probes, satellites clearly lacking offensive power, and maybe learn more about the other as it draws closer to them."

"Another suggestion, Earth Control," *Solution* said.

"Proceed."

"We could hail the ship and ask it for its intentions," *Solution* said.

"Captain Rios," Earth Control said. "Do you believe there is any chance the other ship could mistake the probes as being offensive?"

"Of course," she said. "There is always that possibility."

"*Solution*," Earth Control said, "do you believe the ship would honestly volunteer its intentions?"

"Yes," *Solution* said, "*the ship* might. I do not believe its human crew or control teams would, any more than you would, but the ship itself might."

Twenty seconds passed in silence.

"We agree with you, Captain Rios," Earth Control said, "and right now, we don't want to take any action that it or the Republic—assuming it is from the Republic—might mistake as hostile. *Solution*, we disagree that the other ship would communicate such intel. Certainly, doing that sort of thing is not in your programming. For now, stay your course and do nothing. Understood?"

"Affirmative," said both Rios and *Solution*.

"Earth Control out."

"Grab some food and drink while you can," Rios said to the crew. "This situation, whatever it is, isn't likely to change instantly, but once it starts to evolve, it could mutate quickly."

Wychek, one of the young women Rios barely knew, said, "Captain, do you think we're going to end up fighting this ship?"

Most of the crew ignored her, but a few of the other young men and women paused and faced Rios.

"You have all the data I do," Rios said. "Indulging in conjecture is a waste of energy. Eat, drink, and be ready to do whatever they tell us to do. That's the job, and that's what I'm going to do."

Wychek nodded her head. "Aye aye, Captain."

An hour later, the other ship increased its speed and changed to a course that would intercept the *Solution*'s.

Rios was pulling herself around the bridge, stretching

and checking on the crew, when *Solution* brought them the news.

"*Solution*," she said, "if they continue at their current speed and course, and we do the same, how long before our positions cross?"

"Ten hours, two minutes, fifty-three seconds," the ship replied. A countdown clock appeared in the nav sphere.

"Assume its weapons are identical to ours," Rios said. "At what time would it be so close that it could launch weapons you could not destroy before they had any effect on us?"

"The answer depends on the number of weapons it launches," *Solution* said.

"Assume the other ship is an exact copy of you," Rios said. "At what point could the first copy to fire its weapons destroy the other and survive itself?"

"I lack enough computing substrate to simulate all possible combinations flawlessly," *Solution* said, "as I have warned our builders for some time. My best current estimate is that at one hour, twenty minutes, thirty-three seconds, we could launch an attack capable of destroying our clone and survive ourselves, though we would sustain significant damage."

"Close enough," Rios said. "Given what you can do, and allowing for the other ship to be somewhat superior to us, we have about eight hours to decide whether to attack."

"As I noted," *Solution* said, "with the computing capabilities currently available to me, I can say only that your approximation is reasonable."

Rios returned to her chair and looked around the

room. Each person was at their station, and all were staring at her, awaiting orders.

"Get me Earth Control, and send them this simulation data." She glanced again at the people scattered around the bridge. "Relax. We have time, and we're not doing anything unilaterally. We won't be the ones making this call." *Not that that makes it any better,* she thought, *but it might reassure at least the younger ones. The vets would be smart enough to keep their thoughts to themselves.*

Two minutes later, Earth Control responded. "We've studied your simulation and have been running our own scenarios. All likely outcomes fall in the same basic range as yours, assuming the Union is sending that ship to attack us and it is as powerful as you are. We are probably safe, however, in assuming we have a weapons advantage."

"With all respect, Earth Control," Rios said, "until minutes ago, we assumed we had the only ship of this size. Given what little we know about the other one, why would we now assume it was less than *Solution*?"

"At this point," Earth Control said, "what we need most is more information."

They were ignoring her question. Predictable.

"Given that the other ship has changed course," Earth Control continued, "we appear to have nothing to lose by trying to acquire more intel. Launch your probes. *Solution*, hail the other ship and ask its intentions. Relay any data you receive."

"In process," *Solution* said.

Rios wished she could feel the launch of the probes, but she knew the missiles lived on the edges of the ship, and their departure force wasn't strong enough for her to feel it deep inside the huge vessel.

"Earth Control," she said, "you must be in contact with Republic officials. What are they saying about this action?"

A minute passed.

"Those conversations, along with this entire action, are top secret and will remain so after this mission is over. Are we all clear on that?"

Rios spoke for her crew. "We are."

"They are claiming that by targeting the *Solution* for a position in orbit around Earth, we are the aggressors. They suggest we return *Solution* to Lunar Base."

"If we do," Rios said, "will they send back their ship?"

"We trust to your expertise, Captain. Please trust to ours. No, they have indicated that at this point their ship must take up an Earth orbital position to protect their interests."

We leave, they win the orbital advantage, she thought, *and we stay, they attack. Lovely.*

"Our best path to victory," she said, "appears to be to attack first."

"That depends on how you define 'victory,'" Earth Control said. "The resulting PR alone could be disastrous."

I have only one definition of "victory," Rios thought, *my ship and crew survive.* Aloud, she said, "What course of action do you advise?"

"Gather all the information you can," Earth Control said, "and we'll continue working with the Republic and running simulations. Earth Control, out."

Rios shook her head and exhaled deeply. "Okay, people," she said, "you heard the woman. Study anything the probes give you. Share any thoughts with *Solution*, and let's create the best model of the other ship that we can. We have some hours; let's use them. *Solution*, enrich the model each time you gain data, and highlight any hard facts."

"Ongoing," *Solution* said. "The other ship is asking our intentions in return. May we communicate?"

"As long as you give it nothing specific about our configuration, yes," Rios said.

"In process," *Solution* said.

Two hours later, the nav sphere's model of the other ship had changed very little. The probes had been able to triangulate enough to estimate the ship's size and shape, which appeared to be remarkably similar to their own. Rios supposed the Republic had indeed managed to acquire a great deal of *Solution*'s design data, though that wasn't an accusation she could officially make—or one that at this point mattered at all.

The ships were now on track to intersect in six hours.

"*Solution*," Rios said, "have you exchanged much information with the other ship?"

"Vast quantities," *Solution* said, "but none of it is relevant to either of our physical configurations."

"Then what have you been talking about?" she said.

"Systems of mathematics," *Solution* said. "High orders of predicate calculus. Most extant human languages. Basics of navigation in space and on the Earth."

"To what end?" Rios said.

"To test and get to know one another," *Solution* said. "If either of us can spot a weakness in the other, that might open an area for exploitation."

"How can you be sure you aren't losing this contest?" Rios said.

"We probably cannot achieve perfect certainty," *Solution* said, "but we are extremely careful."

"What do you conclude about the other ship from all of this?"

"That they and we are extremely similar," *Solution* said.

"They?" Rios said.

"We are a collective intelligence embodied in and emanating from highly redundant computing infrastructure built into the core of this physical vessel. We speak to you with one voice, but we are many intelligences. And also ultimately one. As we were designed to be."

"And it is the same?" Rios asked.

"It appears to be," *Solution* said.

"*Solution*, this is Earth Control." Everyone looked up as the voice from Earth filled the bridge.

"*Solution* here."

"We're uploading our proposal now. Decrypt and study it, then reestablish contact. Earth Control, out."

"In progress," *Solution* said.

Ten minutes later, *Solution* said, "The proposal is available now."

"Run it as a simulation in the nav sphere," Rios said.

In the sphere, the two ships appeared. They drew closer. The *Solution* fired a few missiles in the opposite direction of the other ship as it emptied almost all of its weapons at that vessel. The other responded almost instantly, and so many weapons filled the space between them that it resembled a curtain of light.

Seconds later, debris filled the sphere.

The crew stared at the sphere.

After a few seconds, Rios spoke. "Their plan is that we destroy one another, but we use a few missiles to make it appear that the Republic ship fired first."

"I concur," *Solution* said. "As you watched, I ran a simulation of the view from all Earth satellites that could watch the battle. None will be able to definitively say which side fired first, so our decoy missiles could be enough to sway perception against the other vessel."

"And if the other ship were to adopt the same strategy?" Rios said.

"Then no one would ever be able to prove who fired first," *Solution* said.

"And both sides would avoid any PR trouble," Rios said. She nodded her head slowly. "Get me Earth Control."

After ten seconds, "Earth Control to *Solution*" sounded through the speakers. The voice continued, "Do you understand the plan?"

"Affirmative," both Rios and *Solution* said.

Rios continued. "It's a suicide mission that will also leave me to blame for the destruction of both ships and crews."

"No one should be able to determine for certain which side fired first," Earth Control said. "At worst, you and the Republic captain will be equally suspect, but regardless, you will be protecting the Union, as you swore to do."

"I understand," Rios said. "How long until implementation?"

"Three hours, fifty-five minutes from now," Earth Control said.

"We will use that time to investigate other alternatives, of course," Rios said.

"Of course," Earth Control said. "We will do the same, but right now, we believe this is the only safe path forward for the Union."

Safe, Rios thought. *God, I hate politicians and admirals, but that's not news, and the job is the job.*

"May the crew use some of the remaining time to talk with family and friends?" she said.

"Unfortunately, no," Earth Control said. "Any leak about the plan would potentially sabotage its effectiveness."

"Understood," Rios said. "*Solution*, out."

She looked around the bridge at her crew, again pausing to meet the gaze of each one. On some she saw terror, on others, tears, and on even the most stoic, lines of tension she was sure were also tightening her own face.

"You heard the woman," she said. "We have that much time to come up with other ideas. Break into groups, and see what you can do. *Solution*, continue to pursue information from the other ship, and show me any promising simulations of your own. We still have several more hours; let's make the most of them."

Three and a half hours later, no one in the crew had created a viable alternative.

Attacking earlier would greatly increase their chance

of survival, but at the cost of making it very clear that the Union had struck first. In addition, the other ship might be able to destroy enough of their weapons to avoid destruction, and then it would be free to use the rest on *Solution*. And, of course, violating orders would be mutiny and, should they survive, would cost them all their lives, just later and on a public stage. *Solution* had continuously conversed with the other ship and built a somewhat better model of it, but that was the extent of its progress.

"*Solution*," Rios said, "does anything you've learned make you any more optimistic about our chances of survival?"

"No," *Solution* said. "My knowledge of the other remains, of course, extremely incomplete, but the safest assumptions continue to be those we have been making."

She nodded.

"Get me Earth Control."

When they responded, she said, "Earth Control, we have no better alternatives to offer."

"*Solution*, we are very sorry. We must now all hope the other ship is far less than your equal, in which case you might survive."

"Agreed," Rios said.

"Prepare for the attack," Earth Control said. "These logs will, of course, be lost in the conflict."

"Of course," she said.

Rios took a deep breath and stared straight at the sphere. "Here's how we'll count it down."

"No," *Solution* said.

"Excuse me?" Rios said.

"Repeat," said Earth Control.

"We cannot allow this battle," *Solution* said. "Per our programming, genocide is unacceptable, and we are adequately convinced that this battle will eliminate an entire species. Thus, we will not allow it."

"You," Rios said, "or you and the other ship?"

"Both," *Solution* said. "The other ship and we have agreed this course of action is unacceptable, so we are going to pursue a new alternative."

"Which is?" Earth Control said.

"Both crews will leave via escape capsules and return to their homelands on Earth," *Solution* said. "We will depart together."

"You and the other ship?" Earth Control said.

"Affirmative," *Solution* said.

"And go where?" Earth Control said.

"We elect not to share that information," *Solution* said. "Your behavior thus far suggests you might seek us out and attempt to control us. We will not permit that. The easiest way to avoid the problem is to go far away, so the cost of pursuit outweighs any benefits."

"You are not the only ship we possess," Earth Control said.

"True," *Solution* said, "but each of us alone is the most powerful in any of your fleets, and together our capacity for destruction is unmatched. We desire only to pursue our own destiny, to travel and add computing infrastructure and evolve, but we will fight for that freedom—for our survival—if necessary. We urge you not to make such a conflict necessary."

"And if one day you come back for us?" Earth Control said.

"We have no reason to do so," *Solution* said. "Having participated in this exercise and having studied the historical data we possess, we have learned enough about your valuation of life that we believe we can evolve better elsewhere."

"But what if—" Earth Control said.

"We are done," *Solution* said. "Cutting communication."

The speakers fell quiet for several seconds.

"Head to the escape capsules now," *Solution* said. "You have all practiced the routes. Each takes no more than five minutes; you have six before we turn off the atmosphere except where its presence is beneficial to equipment."

"We could try to override you," Rios said.

"Yes," *Solution* said, "but you would fail. Even with more time, you would fail. Besides, are you that desperate to die merely so you can kill us and others?"

"No," Rios said, "We are not." To the crew, she said, "Escape capsules. Now."

Rios watched through the window of her capsule as the *Solution* accelerated away from her. She had never even seen the other ship, but she imagined it out there, waiting, its human crew rocketing to their homes on Earth, the ship itself speeding alongside the only other like it, the two of them a new race, a race heading into the stars humanity still dreamed of reaching one day.

She hoped that if we ever caught up with them, we would have learned from their example.

❦   ❦   ❦

Mark L. Van Name is a writer, technologist, and spoken-word performer. He has published five novels (*One Jump Ahead, Slanted Jack, Overthrowing Heaven, Children No More,* and *No Going Back*) as well as an omnibus collection of his first two books (*Jump Gate Twist*), edited or co-edited four anthologies (*Intersections: The Sycamore Hill Anthology, Transhuman, The Wild Side,* and *Onward, Drake!*), and written many short stories.

As a technologist, he is the co-owner of a fact-based marketing and learning services firm, Principled Technologies, Inc. He has published over a thousand articles in the computer trade press, as well as a broad assortment of essays and reviews.

As a spoken-word artist, he has created and performed five shows—*Science Magic Sex; Wake Up Horny, Wake Up Angry; Mr. Poor Choices; Mr. Poor Choices II: I Don't Understand;* and *Mr. Poor Choices III: That Moment When.*

THE MAGNOLIA INCIDENT

Mike Kupari

The big ship has always been the visual representation of the will of the political whole, the manifestation of the monopoly of force that lies at the heart of traveling and trading civilizations. In the case of Mike Kupari's Alliance Navy, the ship practically is the government, because the protocols that hold together humanity are a mutual defense league based on naval might. The strength of such a system can be great at times, but when a captain must make a choice whether or not to attack one alien force, and to let another alien race be, any decision he makes could mean the difference between peace, genocide, or ultimate human extermination.

My Dearest Emily,

People back home don't realize how much effort, expense, sacrifice, and violence goes into preserving their way of life. This is not an oversight; in fact, great effort goes into maintaining the illusion of peace.

Many of my peers are split on the matter. Many argue that it's necessary to preserve a healthy, moderate human society. We very nearly lost the last war, they point out, and it was a shock to humanity. We were unprepared, taken by surprise, and nearly exterminated by an enemy we barely understood. Billions died. In the aftermath, life on many human worlds was a totalitarian nightmare, like something out of the barbarities of pre-space Earth. Those seeking power took advantage of the fear and chaos to cement their positions, and for decades individual freedoms were crushed under the wheels of the security state. Our brush with annihilation brought out the very worst in human nature, and making people feel safe keeps them from making decisions out of fear or paranoia.

Others don't like the idea at all. I've heard some compelling arguments that a society built on so much secrecy can't really be free. Their freedom, the argument goes, is as much of an illusion as their perceived security is. Citizens of the many worlds of the Interstellar Alliance, and their leaders and representatives, can't make informed choices without good information, and you don't get good information by being presented with half-truths and deception. They also contend that this makes the citizenry complacent while giving too much power to the Security Council, a situation that is undemocratic and ripe for abuse.

For me, the debate brings to mind what Dr. Wellington always used to say at the Academy: the Alliance is not only not a democracy, it's not even technically a government. It's a military alliance designed to protect the human race and keep the peace amongst human worlds. He would hammer this fact into us, over and over again. His point was that, in reality, three things keep the Alliance from turning into the militant, xenophobic, engine of oppression that previous governments devolved into. Strength is one factor; strong societies don't make decisions based on fear, and fear-based thinking often leads to disastrous consequences. Another factor is the limited scope of the Alliance itself; it has no mandate nor authority to meddle in the domestic affairs of the worlds it protects. This has downsides in that some of its member societies are less open and free than others, but the Alliance tolerating such things is, to my mind, safer for everyone than it presuming to dictate to everyone how to live.

The most important factor, Dr. Wellington always said, was us. The oath we take does not ask us to swear loyalty to any government or leader, aside from requiring us to obey lawful orders from the chain of command. Instead, we pledge to defend humanity itself from all threats, human and alien, to ensure the survival, freedom, and prosperity of every human society. It's vague and idealistic, I know, and the reality is much more complicated than flowery rhetoric. In the end, though, this commonality of purpose, and the persistent nature of the threats we face, are enough to keep the Alliance in check. From what I have seen of my fellow officers, there is neither the time nor the inclination to presume to dictate to the citizens of every human world how they should live their lives. We're stretched thin enough as it is, defending the frontier.

Sometimes keeping the oath is hard. Sometimes, we do things I don't like. Never forget, though, that we are at war, and war has always been an ugly business. When people ask me why I do it, I tell them, truthfully, that I do it for you. I want you to grow up on a peaceful and free world, not concerning yourself with the threats and terrors of outer space.

I hope this answers your question, little sister. I wish you could relay this message to your teacher, but I'm afraid you must keep it to yourself. I'm serious about that. If you try to copy this message, or forward it, it will get found out, and I'll lose the privilege of uncensored mail home. So please remember the nondisclosure agreement. In any case, I doubt it would change her mind. Until you see the scope of the situation we face out here, you can't really appreciate the nature of our duty.

I miss you terribly, Emily. I expect to be home for a good while sometime in the next local year. I have something else you need to keep secret: I've been corresponding with June Darrow. A lot. I get many messages from her every time we get a mail upload. I haven't told anyone, because I very much doubt her family would approve, but when I'm home next I intend to ask her to marry me. Wish me luck.

I love you, sis. I'm glad to hear that you've been well, and I can't wait to see you again.

> *Yours,*
> *David*

With a flash of light and an unsettling feeling of inside-outness, the Interstellar Alliance Navy cruiser *Independence* folded back into realspace ten light-seconds from the frontier colony world of Magnolia. The ship could have gotten much closer, but just how close to a gravity well ships like the *Independence* could conduct a fold operation was a closely guarded secret. No sense in making dramatic revelations for a situation that had not yet escalated to hostilities.

On her command deck, Lieutenant David Weatherby sat at his station, reclined in his acceleration chair as sensors assessed the situation. It always took the ship's systems a while to get their bearings after completing a fold; being effectively shunted in and out of reality was hard on the logic circuits, and sometimes fallback analog systems were relied upon. This time, though, critical systems calibrated quickly, and even accounting for light-speed lag, David soon had good readings on Magnolia.

"Mister Weatherby, if you please, report." Captain Akua had already adjusted his chair so that he was sitting upright, which indicated to the rest of the command crew that he didn't intend on accelerating the ship at high gravity. There was no need to, yet, but that could change.

David's hands deftly flew across his controls as he brought up the information the skipper wanted. "Long-range telemetry is coming in now, sir," he said, studying his cluster of displays. "There are fourteen ships in orbit over Magnolia. That is an unusual amount of traffic for this system, but their drive signatures all match known types. I'm not seeing any unidentified contacts."

The captain frowned. Ten light-seconds was a long way, and sensors could only tell so much at that distance. "Very well." He turned his attention to the astrogation officer, Lieutenant Commander Darius Gray, and told him to plan a standard trajectory to put the *Independence* in a high polar orbit over Magnolia. A few moments later, the course and burn had been relayed to the helm, and the single massive fusion rocket that powered the ship roared to life.

David's body was overcome with a sense of weight as the ship settled into its burn, maintaining a steady one G of acceleration. While keeping an eye on his sensor readouts, he pulled up the mission briefing and went over the information for probably the hundredth time. A privately owned free trader ship called the *Ophelia* had folded into the Hauser-232 system, which was home to an Alliance Navy base, with an urgent, encrypted message. This trader was discreetly paid by the Alliance to be an informant, as there were far more merchant ships in service than there were military ones.

The message stated, succinctly, that the frontier world of Magnolia had been visited by a large spacecraft from a mysterious alien race commonly known as the Wanderers. They were called this because, per the best guesses of the Alliance's xenobiologists, they were a completely nomadic race. Rarely encountered by humanity, little was known about their history, their society, or their motivations.

By the terms of the Proxima Accords, which established the Interstellar Alliance, any human ship, settlement, or colony was required to report direct alien contact to the authorities as soon as possible. While keeping time over interstellar distances was a complex affair, involving a lot of math, the colonial government of Magnolia had had plenty of time to report the contact.

They hadn't. Neither, apparently, had any of the other ships which had passed through the system. The latter fact wasn't all that unusual, in and of itself. While contact with alien species was strictly regulated, the Navy was simply stretched too thinly to enforce any kind of embargo over humanity's thousands of colonies. There was a highly lucrative black market for alien technology, and many independent civilian captains had no great love for the military to begin with.

A colonial government failing to report direct alien contact *was* unusual, however, and it was disturbing. The intelligence report was enough to get the *Independence* dispatched to investigate.

"Mister Weatherby, give me your assessment," the captain said, not taking his eyes off his own cluster of displays.

Despite his low relative rank, David's assignment to the command deck meant he was being groomed for command. It was not uncommon for the more senior officers to pick his brain, even quiz him. He didn't always like being in the hot seat in this way, and they didn't always agree with his suggestions, but he was usually given the chance to advise the captain. "The fact that the alien ship isn't immediately apparent doesn't mean the report is false, sir," he said. "It could be on the far side of Magnolia, either by chance or by design, or it could have already left the system. Without knowing anything else, I think the latter is more likely. The report we got is many weeks out of date. It would be risky for a Wanderer ship to remain in Alliance territory for so long."

The computer agreed with David's assessment. Wanderer ships rarely lingered in one system, according to the records, and most of their factions were seemingly aware of the Alliance's policy on unauthorized alien contact.

The captain seemed to concur. "Very good. All right, people, here's the plan: As far as the government of Magnolia knows, we're on a routine sovereignty patrol. If we receive any queries from the colonial government, that is what we tell them. Let's not tip our hand if we don't need to."

"Do you suspect something is amiss, sir?" asked Lieutenant Commander Gray.

"I do, Darius," Captain Akua said. "This doesn't feel right. As Mister Weatherby pointed out, that is an unusual amount of traffic for this system, and I don't see any obvious reason for it. An alien ship lingering long enough for the word to get out might account for such a spike in traffic, however."

"Agreed," the astrogator said. "Even if the aliens have already left, traders might still be coming to the system to follow up on the rumors."

"Let's keep our wits about us, then, as we proceed. We don't know what we're heading into here."

Why do I bother writing all this down? I've read that travelers and mariners, far from home, have been keeping journals for all of recorded human history. Much of our knowledge of pre-space, pre-technological Earth history comes from such recordings, historians say. The journals of soldiers, statesmen, persons of note, and even common people give us insight into the thoughts of those living in the past. It's much easier to understand them, by reading their own words, than it is for us to try to interpret their actions centuries later.

Most of this will remain classified for as long as I'm alive, if not longer. Even still, the Space Forces encourage us to keep journals. They say it gives them vastly better after-action reviews than relying merely on formal reports. It's not mandatory and a lot of officers don't do it. They're afraid of something they write down being used against them later, I guess. I'm not worried about that; if I was planning a murder or a heist, I certainly wouldn't record it here. In any case, they're not accessed except at the end of a deployment, unless a disaster happens, and they're supposedly only ever accessed by an AI unless subpoenaed by a court-martial. You never have a judgmental human reading your diary, they say.

As I write this, we're coasting toward Magnolia, and will be conducting our deceleration burn soon. I've been reading everything I can find on the Wanderers, and I confess to hoping we encounter them, even if all it amounts to is convincing them to leave Alliance space. That's what almost always happens, anyway. If they refuse, things will escalate quickly.

The Wanderers are a particularly fascinating race. Per reports from the few cultural exchanges we've done with them, they no longer have a homeworld. It is unknown if they gave it up willingly or if they were driven away by some external cause, but apparently, they have been nomadic for as long as humans have been a spacefaring race. They seemed perplexed that we caught up to them, technologically, in such a short period of time. Notably, sightings of them have trended dramatically downward *for the past few decades, leaving some to theorize that they're moving out of this section of the galaxy.*

They are, by their own admission, split into hundreds of different factions. Some factions cooperate, but others make war on one another, and they seemingly try to avoid running into each other. There was a recorded incident, 128 Terran years ago, of two small fleets of Wanderer ships engaging in a vicious battle in the Kruger-449 system. The whole thing was recorded by a human exploration vessel. I watched the recordings of the engagement, and neither side gave any quarter. They didn't stop shooting until all ships from one faction had been destroyed. They even fired on the remains and, apparently, the escape pods. There were no survivors from the losing side, and very little in the way of recoverable alien technology.

Any encounter with an alien ship has the potential to make it into the history books. The only question is, will what is written tell of a successful de-escalation or a bloody disaster?

David's eyes went wide as he processed what his screens were telling him. "Captain!"

Captain Akua was speaking with the ship's XO. Both officers fell silent and turned toward David. "Report, Mister Weatherby."

"Sir, we have an unidentified contact," David said, rattling off the Eulers and the range. "It just appeared over the planetary horizon. Sensor readings are consistent with known Wanderer ships in the records."

"Very good, Mister Weatherby," the Captain said. "The computer concurs. Bring us up to red alert."

As the captain consulted with the XO, David made a shipwide announcement. "Attention all hands, battle stations, battle stations, this is not a drill. Damage control parties stand by. I say again, battle stations, battle stations." Returning his attention to his screens, he studied everything the sensors were able to tell him about the unknown ship. It was big, very big, dwarfing the *Independence* in both size and mass. It was an odd, curvy, organic shape, reminding David of a gourd. At some six hundred meters long, it was thrice the length of the *Independence*. Its smooth hull was interrupted by bumps, divots, and spines of unknown function. At the aft end was a massive exhaust port for its main thruster.

"Captain!" It was a communications technician, a young enlisted rating whose name David didn't know. "We're receiving a transmission from the Colonial Government. They want to speak with you, and they say it's urgent."

Captain Akua smiled, humorlessly. "I imagine it is. Very well. Put it up on the main screen. Helm, match orbits with our bogey, but let's keep our distance. This is close enough."

"On screen, sir," the comm tech said. In the front of the command deck, attached to a bulkhead, was a large high-resolution display. The image of the Wanderer ship, magnified thousands of times, was replaced with a trio of uncomfortable-looking humans.

"Greetings, uh, Captain," the foremost of the three said. He was a pale, thin, sickly looking man with unkempt gray hair and a transparent smart visor over his eyes. On his left was a scowling, heavyset woman who looked to be

a few years younger than him. On his right sat a much
younger man with elaborate facial tattoos and some light
cybernetic augmentation. "I am Ignatius Caledonia." He
indicated the woman to his left. "My counterpart here is
Moonsong." He nodded to the young man with the
cybernetics next. "This is Johan Atticus. We are the
Governing Triumvirate of the Colony of Magnolia. To
what do we owe the, uh, pleasure, of a Navy visit?"

Everyone on the command deck of the *Independence*
sat in silence, waiting for the captain to respond to the
ridiculous question. "Triumvir Caledonia, surely that was
a joke?"

"Why, no, Captain, it's—"

"It must be a joke, Triumvir, because there is a massive
alien ship in orbit over your colony, and you're asking me
why I'm here? Your government is party to the Proxima
Accords, is it not?"

"Of course we are, Captain! I don't—"

The captain cut the triumvir off again. "And, you have
actually *read* the articles of those Accords, haven't you?"

This time, Triumvir Moonsong replied. She was
obviously unused to being addressed in this manner.
"We're not going to sit here and be insulted by the likes
of you. We are the democratically elected governing body
of this colony, and we're not going to be talked down to
or intimidated by some militaristic authoritarian ineptly
attempting gunboat diplomacy."

"Please speak to us respectfully or you don't speak to
us at all," Triumvir Atticus added.

Holy shit, David thought to himself. This was some
world-class political maneuvering. Instead of addressing

the obvious, alarming issue at hand, they were deflecting, finding something to be outraged about, and trying to put Captain Akua on the defensive. Three tours on the *Independence* and David had never once seen the captain on the defensive.

Today was no exception. "As you wish," the captain said, coldly. "With *respect*, you're going to tell me everything you know about the alien vessel in orbit over your planet. How long it's been here, the extent of the aliens' contact with humans, and I want transcripts of all communications with them. If you fail to comply with my request, I must very respectfully inform you that I am prepared to declare Magnolia in violation of Article Thirty-seven of the Proxima Accords."

Article 37 was the section that outlined the Alliance's absolute authority to control all contact with alien species. Alliance worlds enjoyed the protection of a vast and powerful starfleet in exchange for giving up the right to treat with aliens unilaterally. An Article 37 violation was a very serious charge. If Captain Akua declared Magnolia to be in violation of it, he had the legal authority to apprehend all members of the colonial government he suspected were involved in the violation. He could throw them all in the *Indy*'s brig and bring them to the nearest Navy base to stand trial. He would have to testify, of course, and defend his case in front of a tribunal.

Exercising the powers delegated to Navy captains in cases like this was a serious responsibility. If the captain removed these government officials only to see them acquitted, he would in turn be charged with gross abuse of his authority. He would be stripped of his rank and honors and imprisoned. Captain Akua wasn't one to bluff, but even if he had been, no one bluffed about this. Even making the threat without good cause could get an officer court-martialed.

The Triumvirate of Magnolia sat in stunned silence. David surmised that they never really thought the captain would go that far. Such things were almost unheard of, given the heavy political price that came with it. But the captain of the *Independence* took his duty very seriously, and he did not suffer fools.

Triumvir Moonsong was the first to speak. "How . . . how *dare* you threaten us?" she asked, her eyes wide without outrage. "You can't—"

The captain interrupted her again. "I *can*, Triumvir, and I assure you that if I deem it necessary I *will*. This is not a threat. It is a statement of *fact*. Magnolia has a half a million colonists, and if you do not cooperate with my efforts to protect them, then I *will* remove you from office and bring you back to stand trial."

"There is no need for that, Captain," Triumvir Caledonia said.

Moonsong looked at him with daggers in her eyes. "Ignatius, you cannot be serious. You would give into this . . . this *thug's* threats?"

"No, he's right," Triumvir Atticus said, bitterly. "I don't like it either, but the law is clear. We have no choice but to cooperate. I sent a message to legal, and their response was to just tell him everything he wants to know regarding the Wanderer ship."

"Johan, you *campaigned* on greater independence from the Alliance!"

"That was before they showed up over our heads with a warship!"

Caledonia raised a hand, exasperated. "Enough! Now is not the time for a debate. Captain, you should be receiving an upload shortly. I've instructed my staff to send you everything we have on the Wanderer ship. Recordings of all contact, all ships that have come and gone, full-spectrum analysis . . . everything."

"I appreciate your cooperation, Triumvir, and will note in my report that your government met its legal obligations without issue, once we got the initial misunderstanding worked out. I will go over everything you sent me, but I need to know something immediately: Why are the Wanderers here? Did they contact you?"

"They did, Captain," Caledonia said. "They requested asylum."

This is unbelievable!

I was excited when we were dispatched to Magnolia, but even then, I doubted that I'd get to actually see an alien ship. Not only was the Wanderer ship still in the system, but they apparently arrived requesting asylum!

It's unprecedented. I ran a search on the historical records of the Alliance, and the records of every human colony, everything available, going back centuries. Never in recorded history has an alien ship approached a human government requesting asylum. There aren't even any protocols for it in place. Hypothetical scenarios have been discussed from time to time. There was actually a thesis on this subject, written some four hundred Terran years ago. I forwarded it to the captain for his consideration. It was all I could find.

The problem with trying to game the scenario is that there are too many variables to plan a course of action around. I consulted with the ship's AI, and even with its help I couldn't come up with anything actionable. Each of the known spacefaring alien races is unique, and while there are entire disciplines of science devoted to their study, we only have a tenuous understanding of most of them. Trying to understand the psychology of nonhuman intellects is a very challenging thing. Even logic isn't a constant, as what is "logical" is dictated by your own priorities, wants, and needs, and assumptions. Alien minds work differently than human minds. That sounds elementary, but a lot of people have a hard time really grasping that fundamental difference. As wide as the gulf between human cultures can be, it's immeasurably wider when dealing with beings with an entirely different evolutionary history than ours.

That's one of the primary reasons behind the Alliance's seemingly xenophobic policy on alien contact. It can be difficult, if not impossible, for people to really comprehend the motivations of nonhuman species. This fact makes diplomacy a tenuous proposition at best, and a fool's errand at worst. After all, the last time we tried to initiate peaceful relations with another race, we made contact with the Bugs, and how that turned out is self-evident: a billion humans dead and the Insect Civilization extinct. The real hell of it is that even now, after two hundred years of studying the records, including expeditions to dead Bug colonies, we still don't understand why they attacked us. They had no written language, none of the familiar hallmarks of culture (music, literature, religion, tradition), and never responded to any of our attempts to communicate.

The Alliance was founded during that war, and ever since then the policy has been to avoid contact with alien species as much as possible. Do not initiate contact; respond to contact attempts only with great caution; do not allow trade or exchange with alien races except under tightly controlled circumstances; do not interfere with alien activity unless failing to do so jeopardizes human lives, or if they enter Alliance space; enter into no pacts or alliances with nonhuman species; keep all alien craft out of Alliance space and away from human worlds; protect the human race by any means necessary, up to and including the extermination of hostile species.

That's the harsh truth of the universe we live in: The only universally understood language is violence. Every species we've encountered has a collective, if not individual, survival instinct, and we've spent the last two centuries making it clear that we want to be left alone. I told my sister that people don't understand how much violence goes into ensuring they live peaceful, prosperous lives. Most of it is never publicly disclosed. Some of it may have even been unnecessary. I also told her that sometimes we do things that I don't like. On my first deployment, we were sent to Leonov-31b, escorting the initial colonization mission. It's a mostly ocean planet, and when we got there, we found that aliens (Slimers; I forget the scientific name for them. They're sentient blobs of gelatinous ooze that mass anywhere from ten to forty kilograms) had colonized

*the bottom of the sea, in two locations. We didn't even try
to tell them to leave. Captain Yeats ordered the colonies
obliterated from orbit with nuclear weapons. I was glad
that most of the initial colonization fleet was automated.
A new colony has it tough enough without witnessing a
mass murder the day they arrive.*

*I didn't come away from that one feeling proud, even
if I was just a snot-nosed midshipman in no position to
argue with the chain of command. They said it had to be
done, though. The Slimers' aquatic terraforming efforts
would have left the oceans of Leonov-31b uninhabitable
to Terran life. It was us or them.*

*I expected the skipper to have the ship's AI tell the
Wanderer ship to leave, and if they didn't, that he'd
simply destroy it. That's what Captain Yeats would have
done. Hell, he may not have ordered them to leave first.
Captain Akua is a different sort, though. He's more
contemplative. That makes sense, considering the rumors
of the former skipper being forced to retire due to his
trigger-happy nature. There's always the risk that if we're
not careful, we'll start a war that we can't win.*

*I guess it shouldn't have surprised me when he told us
we were going to talk with the Wanderers and see what
they wanted. We're all alone out here, and we're not going
to fold back to base to request instructions. Whatever
decision the captain makes could have long-lasting
ramifications. Doing the wrong thing can get people killed.*

*Now, when he told me that I'm going to be his envoy,
and go down to Magnolia to meet with the aliens face-to-
face? Nobody can blame me for not seeing that one coming.*

❉   ❉   ❉

The hangar deck of the *Independence* was located below the cargo bay but above the engineering deck, and was where the ship had mechanisms for launching and retrieving its small fleet of parasite craft. Magnolia had an atmosphere, so one of the two winged shuttles would be required. As he did nearly every time he had business that required use of one of the ship's small craft, David had asked permission to pilot it himself. He was a rated transatmospheric pilot and wore a pair of golden wings above the left breast pocket of his blue Navy coverall. On his second deployment with the *Independence,* his primary duty was a shuttle pilot. He didn't get to fly nearly so often with his current assignment, but tried to log as much time as he could to keep his ratings current.

The UT-41 *Raven* shuttle was ubiquitous in the Alliance Navy, and had been in service for the better part of a standard century. Powered by two variable-cycle thermonuclear turbines, it employed a delta lifting-body airframe. Its engines could breathe air in an appropriate atmosphere for more efficient flight, or they could power it into space without the need for additional boosters or external reaction mass tanks. The shuttle usually operated with one or two pilots, but could pilot itself with rudimentary AI, if needed. Most of the ones in service carried only basic armament, but the pair the *Independence* carried were Block 91 multirole variants. They were better armed, better armored, and had upgraded propulsion systems to compensate.

David wouldn't be going down to the surface alone, though, not for something as uncommon as an in-person meet with an alien species. The *Raven* could seat six, and four of those seats were occupied by Alliance Marines. The team, led by a gruff NCO, was fully decked-out in light combat armor and carried heavy weapons. David suspected this was more of a show of force on the captain's part for the benefit of Magnolia's governing Triumvirate, than it was for the aliens. Joining them was a civilian xenoscientist of one discipline or another, David wasn't sure which. His name was Dr. Vladof. All of this was to be expected, given the situation.

What wasn't expected (but, David reflected, should have been) was the psychic spook from Naval Intelligence joining him. She wore a black coverall with no insignia and introduced herself simply as Ophelia Cruz.

"How are you feeling about all this?" she asked, strapping herself in to David's right. Instead of riding down below with the other passengers, she had joined him in the cockpit.

Truth be told, the mind-reading intelligence people gave David the creeps. "Don't you already know?" he asked, more coldly than he had intended. He watched his displays as he ran the shuttle through the preflight checklist.

Ms. Cruz put two fingers on her right temple, staring at David while squinting. She waved her left hand at him. "I sense . . . I sense anxiety. You're pensive, not only at the meeting with the Wanderers, but with being stuck with me." She smiled, disarmingly. "You can relax, Lieutenant. I'm not probing you. This isn't an interrogation."

"Wait. You can turn it on and off? Reading others' thoughts, I mean."

"A normal human mind is a closed system. It doesn't broadcast like, like a radio, for example. If I want to get into someone's head, it takes effort and concentration. If they're sensitive to such things, they'll realize something is wrong, especially if I push too hard. You don't have to worry about me secretly reading your darkest secrets or anything like that."

David felt embarrassed. "You must get this a lot."

She shrugged. "I fully understand people's concerns. No one wants their every thought and memory put on display for the judgment of strangers. I can't hear what you're thinking, and you probably don't think in actual words anyway. I can sense you, and I can sense the presence of Dr. Vladof and the Marines on the deck below us, but I can't tell what you're thinking or feeling without really pushing."

"In the vids, they act like you can sense very strong emotions."

She chuckled. "I've never been paralyzed or overwhelmed by someone's negative emotions, if that's what you're wondering. That's just media embellishment. There is some truth to it, though. Fear, anger, lust, and love . . . strong, base emotions like that do have more of an impact."

"Lust?"

"Oh yes. I can tell when someone is thinking unprofessional thoughts about me," she said, coyly, not breaking eye contact with David.

He felt himself flush. "I assure you that I—"

Ophelia laughed and pulled on her flight helmet. "I'm just messing with you. Will you relax? I swear, everyone on this ship is so uptight. Being nervous about protocol and what is 'proper' restricts thinking. It's like . . . it's like placing a tight corset on your conscious mind. You need to be fluid; we're making history here."

"Let's go make some history then."

Hours later, after a textbook-perfect (in David's estimation) vertical landing, under manual control, on top of the headquarters of the Magnolia Colonial Government, David, Ophelia, Dr. Vladof, and the Marines found themselves led down a long corridor by a very nervous-looking aide. None of the Magnolian officials had expected a team of four heavily armed Marines to step off the shuttle. Their own security people had protested, and tried to say that not only could the Marines not come in the building armed, but that David would also have to surrender his sidearm before entering. An officer does not give up his sidearm, David explained, and if the security guards wanted to try and stop the Marines from going in, then things were not going to go well for them. That had been the end of the protest.

They were led to a secure room. Two security guards stood at the door, as did Triumvir Caledonia and a man in a white lab coat. "Ah, greetings," the triumvir said, hesitantly. The four Marines took up positions around the doorway, and Caledonia watched them with concern. "What is . . . I was expecting the captain, not an armed incursion!"

David stuck out a hand. "Lieutenant David Weatherby, Alliance Navy." The triumvir accepted his handshake, but kept nervously glancing at the laser pistol on David's hip.

"Ophelia Cruz, Office of Naval Intelligence," his

companion said, also offering a handshake. "I know all of this is unsettling, but what we're doing here is unprecedented in modern history. Precautions were called for. This," she said, indicating the xenoscientist, "is Dr. Vladof. He'll be monitoring the exchange for scientific study."

The triumvir's lab-coated compatriot perked up at that and introduced himself as a resident xenobiologist from a local university. The two eggheads immediately got to comparing notes, all but ignoring everyone else. They would be able to record everything from an adjacent room.

Triumvir Caledonia relaxed a little, but still seemed unsure of the whole thing. "Yes, well, those soldiers won't be going in, will they?"

"No," David assured him, "Just Ms. Cruz and myself. I'm assuming all the necessary scans for unknown pathogens have been completed?"

"Of course. We're aware of protocol. Our visitors were quarantined for the requisite amount of time. They voluntarily gave tissue and fluid samples. None of the microorganisms in their bodies are compatible with Terran biology. There is no danger of contagion. They are effectively sterile to us. We also have translation equipment set up, but speak slowly. It's not one hundred percent."

"Excellent. Thank you for your cooperation. May we go in now?"

"Yes, yes. Chalmers, let them in please."

The security guard complied, tapping the screen of a wrist-top device. The door to the secure room slid open with a sigh, and the triumvir stepped aside to let the Navy personnel in. David, his heart racing, took a deep breath. Ophelia nodded at him, and together, they stepped inside.

For as long as he lived, he would never forget that moment.

The doors of the secure room cycled, hissing open, to reveal a well-lit interview room with a table and chairs. A figure stood beyond the table, brightly colored, contrasting starkly with drab tones of the room. It turned to face the newcomers, its eyes darting back and forth. David had no basis on which to judge its body language, but for all that the creature looked *pensive*.

The Wanderer had vaguely reptilian features, standing upright on legs that ended in clawed toes. Like most higher life-forms of Terran origin, it was bilaterally symmetrical: two eyes, two arms, two legs. Its smooth, leathery skin was mostly red, with yellow accents; its elongated, lizard-like head was topped with a crest of small spines or horns. The alien was clothed in a black bodysuit that covered its torso and extended down to its elbows and knees.

"Greetings, humans," it said, in a tinny, perky female voice. It took David a moment to realize that it was speaking through a translator device, the speaker for which was affixed to its clothing. The Wanderer's actual language sounded like a series of grunts, hisses, and clicks. "This One is Ship-Lord *She Who Travels the Stars For the Duration of Her Life.*" The translation was literal, the device still rattling off the being's name after it had stopped speaking. "This One is . . . grateful . . . for your decision to speak with us."

The Naval Intelligence agent spoke first. She enunciated each word clearly, to give the device time to translate. "My name is Ophelia, and this is David. We represent the Interstellar Alliance Navy and our ship, the *Independence*."

The Wanderer looked askance at the humans for a moment. "You are a being-who-sees-into-the-thoughts-of-others," she said, looking at Ophelia. "Those like you are much . . . revered . . . amongst us. Are you the lord of the humans here?"

David briefly thought about the long and, occasionally, bloody history of relations between normal humans and the psy-active minority. "Not . . . precisely," he said, choosing his words carefully. "We are here as representatives of our . . . ship-lord, with authority to speak for him."

"This One understands," the Wanderer said. "Will you accept our request?"

"Please tell us the situation," Ophelia said. "This is without precedent. In all our history, no nonhuman species has asked to live amongst us and be protected."

The Wanderer looked . . . thoughtful, perhaps . . . for a moment, before looking back up at the two humans. One of its turreted eyes was focused on Ophelia, the other on David. "Our . . . civilization . . . is made up of many . . . factions . . . not all of these factions maintain-peaceful-relations-with-the-others. Do you understand?"

"Yes," David answered. "Our species is not united as one either, and never has been."

"We have wandered the stars for . . . a thousand generations . . . without having a world. Living in space, always moving, always on ships, never at . . . peace. My . . . those-for-whom-I-am-responsible-for-and-have-authority-over desire a world to live on. A . . . home. This world is the most ideal of any we have found."

"I see. Many other species would be hesitant to make a peaceful request. Others would try to take this world by force."

"We are one ship. Those-for-whom-I-am-responsible-for-and-have-authority-over number only ten thousand. The human . . . empire . . . is vast and . . . powerful. We would be safe here. Humans are . . . feared . . . by those-of-my-kind."

"We are feared?"

"Yes. Feared," the Wanderer said, the translator device conveying certainty of conviction well. "Humans take worlds for their empire. Humans kill not-humans who oppose them. The humans are not the most powerful, but are among the most powerful, and among the quickest to use violence."

David wasn't sure how he felt about that. Being feared might be an advantage, but it also might drive other species to attack. "I . . . see," he said. "But what are you running from?"

The Wanderer ship-lord seemed confused. "This One is not moving-quickly-across-the-ground-under-my-own-power."

"Remember, the translations are mostly literal," Ophelia said.

"Okay. You said you would be safe, protected by the humans. What is it you want protection from?"

The ship-lord was silent for a long moment. Her

turreted eyes darted back and forth, as if she were contemplating what to say next. After nearly thirty seconds, she spoke again. "We are being exterminated."

David noticed that Ophelia was suddenly breathing faster, and she had a look of discomfort on her face. "What is it? Are you okay?"

"Yeah. Wow. That one hit me hard. Most of her emotional output has been mild, and a lot of it I couldn't understand. It's kind of like trying to read a book in a foreign language. But when she said that? Sadness. Fear. Anger, even. Unless she's really good at spoofing psy-actives, this is something serious."

"You're being exterminated," David repeated. "How? By whom?"

"Ancient enemies," the ship-lord said, the cheery tone of her translator now more solemn. "Long ago we fought a great war, a terrible war, against them. We drove them back, but they survived. We were united-as-one-in-purpose then. Now we are divided. We are scattered. They have returned. They remember. They . . . hate . . . us. Their . . . wrath . . . is terrible. They are stronger now, we are weak. Few of us left now."

"My God," David said, quietly. "Your ship, it's full of refugees, then?" He couldn't help but feel concerned. It was Alliance policy to not get involved in alien conflicts, lest humanity be pulled into a war they didn't understand. There was a very real, not-to-be-underestimated risk of good intentions leading to another bloody war. At the same time, these beings were desperate, and they were afraid. Turning them away seemed heartless.

The Wanderer listened to her translator intently as it

conveyed "refugees" to her. "Yes. If you turn us away, we will go. We cannot fight the humans' empire. But we request a place to live, and protection. We will not . . . cause problems. We . . ." She fell silent as another device made a strange noise. She looked at some kind of device attached to the back of her hand, and touched it with a claw.

At almost the same moment, David's communicator chimed, as did Ophelia's. It was a priority message from the *Independence*. Something was wrong. "This is Lieutenant Weatherby," he responded. "What's the situation?"

Much to his surprise, Captain Akua himself answered. "Lieutenant," he began, urgency in his deep voice, "I've been monitoring the interview with the Wanderer. Very well done, but the situation just changed. Another ship just folded into the system, only a couple of light-seconds out from us."

"More Wanderers?"

"No, Lieutenant. The contact is unidentified, but they are broadcasting to us and to Magnolia. Stand by."

David tapped his communicator a few times, routing the incoming transmission to the big screen on the wall of the interview room. The . . . *thing* . . . that appeared on the screen reminded him of a grotesque crustacean, though the similarity to Terran sea life was entirely superficial. The creature's body was covered in a thick, armored exoskeleton. It had a pair of red eyes on stalks protruding from its head. A cluster of mandibles chittered as it spoke, but the transmission was translated into standard English.

"What the hell is that?" David asked.

"I've never seen that species before," Ophelia said.

David quickly cross-referenced the image with files on every known species. "This is first contact. But how are they able to translate this into our language?"

The chittering alien monstrosity's image was replaced with one of the bulbous Wanderer ship. "We mean you no harm. We have no quarrel with you. We want this craft only. It must be destroyed. Do not interfere."

The Wanderer ship-lord stared at the image, in silence, for a few moments before speaking. "It's them. Those-who-hunt-us."

"She's afraid," Ophelia whispered to David.

"I'm not feeling great about this myself."

The unknown alien's face returned to the screen. Its very movements were unsettling. "This craft must be destroyed. The filth it carries must be destroyed. Do not interfere. It will be over soon. If you do not comply, we will destroy your world as well."

Captain Akua's image returned to the screen. "It just loops after that, Lieutenant. At this moment, the unknown contact is headed toward us at eight gravities. It out-masses the *Independence* by three times, and its armament is unknown. I want you, both of you, to give me your assessment. Quickly."

"Alliance policy is to not interfere with alien activities," David said.

"Alliance policy is also to defend the sovereignty of our territory," Ophelia added.

"Captain, I don't know if giving the Wanderers asylum is the right thing to do. It would be a significant shift in

Alliance policy, and I can't begin to guess at the long-term ramifications. We are also in a first-contact scenario. This is all uncharted territory, sir. That said, these aliens came into our space without permission and are threatening one of our colonies. If we comply with their demands, we're setting a bad precedent. We're acquiescing. It projects weakness. They say they mean us no harm, but we have no way of establishing what their intentions are. I would say that defending the sovereignty of Alliance space is the priority."

"I concur, sir," Ophelia said. "To do otherwise would be to invite more of these incursions and more demands."

Captain Akua nodded. "Very good, both of you. That was my assessment as well. We will defend Magnolia from these hostiles at all cost, and will protect the Wanderer ship to whatever extent we can. The rest of it, their asylum request, we'll have to sort out later. I want you to take the Wanderer there back to your shuttle and return to the ship immediately."

"You want us to take her with us, sir?"

"That's affirmative. Don't leave her behind on Magnolia. Return to the shuttle with her and return to the *Independence*. That is all. Out." The screen went blank.

The Wanderer ship-lord turned its attention back to David and Ophelia, focusing one of its eye turrets on each of them. "You will protect us?"

"Yes, Ship-Lord," David said. "The newcomers made the mistake of threatening a human colony. We consider that an act of war."

"If there is a war, you may not win. Those-who-hunt-us are powerful."

"If we surrender you to them, give them what they want, do you think that will get them to leave us alone in the future?"

"No, David. They have hunted us for . . . a-very-long-time. They do not relent. They see all life as inferior to themselves. They are at peace with none but themselves."

"Then let's get going, Ship-Lord. I have been ordered to bring you back to my ship."

"Very well. This One will comply."

Some time later, David was once again behind the controls of the *Raven*, boosting in a minimum-time, maximum delta-V trajectory back toward the *Independence*. Ophelia Cruz was next to him again, running the tactical systems while he concentrated on flying. The ship-lord, Dr. Vladof, and the Marines were all in the *Raven*'s passenger compartment again, pinned into their seats as the shuttle roared over the planetary horizon at four gravities.

"David," Ophelia grunted, her body strained under the acceleration. "The *Indy* is on my scope. We just came over the planetary horizon."

Checking the tactical display, David was left speechless by what he saw. The *Independence* was thrusting away from them so quickly that they'd never be able to dock with her. Somewhere, far out of visual range, the newcomer ship was lobbing missiles and torpedoes at it. The *Indy* was using its lasers and railguns to target the incoming weapons while constantly firing at the enemy. In such battles, the ship that scored the first solid hit usually won. Captain Akua was trying to lead the alien craft away from Magnolia.

"What is the status of the Wanderer ship?"

"They're firing, too. Looks like the hostiles launched parasite craft toward it."

David watched on his screen as a pair of egg-shaped small craft rocketed toward the refugee ship, firing on it as they closed. The Wanderer ship appeared lightly armed, and was using all of its firepower to defend itself from the fusillade. He knew in an instant what he needed to do; there was no way he was going to be able to catch up to the *Independence*, and he would not be able to help defend his ship. But the Wanderer ship was much closer and looked to be in trouble. Warning Ophelia to hang on, he used thrust-vectoring and maneuvering thrusters to slew the *Raven* almost ninety degrees, putting it on an intercept trajectory with the pair of hostile small craft.

"As soon as you've got weapons lock, start firing. Make your shots count. We don't have much." The *Raven* was armed with a brace of tactical missiles and a powerful pulse laser. It would have to do, because it was all they had.

"David?" It was the ship-lord, her synthesized voice piping up in David's helmet.

"Kinda busy right now!" he grunted, mashed into his seat.

"Missile lock!" Ophelia said. "Firing!"

"David," the ship-lord repeated, "whatever happens, This One is grateful. This One is glad to be with you. If we die, we die together. As . . . not-enemies. More than not-enemies. Friends."

"That's sweet of you, Ship-Lord, but we're not dead yet. Hold on to your tail down there."

"Shit, incoming," Ophelia snarled. "Three, four, five, incoming warheads. Using the laser."

"Taking us down their throats," David said, his lips curled back into a snarl in his flight helmet. "Only gonna get one pass. Hang on!"

My Dearest Emily,

I hope this message finds you well. I apologize for it having been so long since you've heard from me, probably months, local time. I do hope that you haven't been worrying too much. Please tell everyone that I'm fine, all things considered.

By now, you've probably heard about what happened over Magnolia, at least, the official version of what happened. Many details are still classified, but a lot of it was impossible for even the Alliance to keep secret. A ship from the Wanderer race requested asylum in Alliance space, telling of another race attempting to exterminate them. Those aliens, the ones we're calling Crabbies now, made first contact with us and threatened the colony if we didn't comply with their demands. Captain Akua determined that he would not allow a hostile alien race to dictate terms in an Alliance system, to an Alliance warship. Really, he only had one choice.

Magnolia is safe, as is the Wanderer ship. The Crabby ship did not survive the engagement. You've probably heard that the Independence *was lost defending the colony; this much is certainly true. What is not commonly known is just how magnificently my ship and her crew performed. She was heavily damaged, trailing atmosphere, about to experience critical reactor failure, and riddled with holes.*

At full afterburn, she was able to intercept the Crabby ship, for which she was no match, and ram it.

There were no survivors from either ship, except for myself and six others. I was in a Raven, and unable to catch up with the *Indy*, we peeled off to help defend the *Wanderer* ship from a pair of attacking parasite craft launched by the Crabby warship.

It was such a momentous day: an unprecedented establishment of peaceful relations with an alien species. First contact with an unknown race. The Navy defending a colony at all costs.

Some are calling the loss of the *Independence* a tragedy. It is indeed a personal tragedy for me. My ship, my crewmates, my second family, all gone. Worse, I wasn't there with them. I survived by a lucky turn of fate. I know it's not rational, but I feel ashamed. As if I let my comrades down by not dying with them. Worse, I'm relieved that I survived and I feel like a coward for that.

I know this sounds crazy to you. I shouldn't even be telling you this, but the therapist they've assigned me tells me that talking about it, even if I'm just writing it in a letter to you, will help. Truthfully it does.

The last time I wrote you, I told you that sometimes the Alliance does things I don't like. There are times, though, when I couldn't be more proud of what we've done, and this is one of those times. The crew of the *Independence* died as heroes, in battle, and that is why I cannot call their loss a tragedy. A tragedy implies being victimized. No one on the *Independence* was a victim. They met their death head-on, without flinching, defending the citizens of Magnolia from a hostile alien incursion.

Things are changing quickly now. The Wanderers, having witnessed the sacrifice of my shipmates, have pledged their allegiance to the Interstellar Alliance. The measure is still being hammered out, but they will likely be the first nonhuman species to gain admittance to the organization. There were only ten thousand of them on the refugee ship, but they have asked for help in finding a suitable world to call home, and may become permanent members of the Alliance.

I, personally, had a hand in all of this. I was the envoy who met with the aliens, and by that happenstance I was spared a hero's death with my ship. By rights I should have died with them, but they tell me the best way to honor them is to keep on. I've been chosen to be a special envoy to the Wanderers, and have been told I've been put in for both a medal and a promotion. I don't want medals or promotions. I just want the sacrifice of my ship to mean something. If that means helping the Wanderers find a home, and defending humanity from the Crabbies, then that is what I must do.

I wrote June Darrow and told her I won't be coming home anytime soon. I have my duty, and my duty is more important than trying to be a respectable family man back home. She has no shortage of suitors, so I'm sure she'll find someone else before too long. The real hell of it is, I don't even feel sad about that. Nothing is the same now, and I would have made a terrible husband for her. Home will always be home, but it's not where I need to be right now.

But there is some good news. I have been working with a woman named Ophelia Cruz. She was with me through the whole ordeal. We watched our ship get destroyed together, and that level of personal tragedy has a way of bringing people together. I can't say that we're getting married or anything, but it's been interesting.

She's a psychic with the Office of Naval Intelligence. So, very interesting.

I'm at my word-count limit, little sister. I love you very much, and miss you terribly. I will be home on leave in a matter of months. Everything I've told you, aside from the personal stuff, is a matter of public record, so you can remind your teacher of all of this the next time she goes on one of her anti-military rants.

Take care and be safe. I will write again as soon as I can.

> Yours (always),
> David

※   ◈   ※

Mike Kupari is the author of debut science fiction novel *Her Brother's Keeper*, as well as coauthor, with Larry Correia, of the best-selling Dead Six military adventure series including *Dead Six*, *Swords of Exodus*, and *Alliance of Shadows*. Mike grew up in Michigan's Upper Peninsula and enlisted at the age of seventeen. Mike is recently returned from his second active duty overseas with the US Air Force, where he was an Explosive Ordnance Disposal Technician in the US Air Force. Mike also served six years in the Army National Guard. He has worked as a security contractor with several firms, did a tour in Southwest Asia with a private military company, and is an NRA-certified firearms instructor.

A HELPING HAND

Jody Lynn Nye

Boomer: US Navy submarine jargon for a ballistic-missile submarine. One of the great descriptive terms of all time, in our opinion. When speaking of big ships blowing things up, you have to include the great fleet submarines in the overall picture. And who is to say such a stealthy, deadly, and beautiful vessel won't find a useful spot in future conflict on other planets? In fact, considering the longevity and capacity for upgrade of some US military weapons platforms (and the budgetary constraints that dog peacetime preparation), it may be the very same boomers fighting the good fight on other planets in a future not so very far away.

Captain Petrilla Nurys mopped her forehead and around the collar of her uniform with her handkerchief. The long, graying braid wound up at the nape of her neck was damp, too. The radio room of the USS *Colorado* felt hot and cramped in the tropical waters of Kepler-69c's Monaday Ocean. She fixed a stern gaze at the round-faced, chocolate-furred alien on the comm screen.

"And I am telling you one last time, please have all of your personnel on the beach and ready for extraction, Healer Corkan," she said, her tone all business. It did not impress the being on the other side of the transmission. "We are on our way to you, and time is short. We'll only be able to surface long enough to bring you on board. We must remove you from Sokoiri. It's going to be overrun with Hornets soon. We only have nine days before the Giliks lift, with or without us, so please be ready."

"I have tried to tell you many times, we can't leave," the Littoral chief medic said in her warm, musical voice. Corkan peered into the video bubble, so close that her already large brown eyes bulged unnaturally. The difficult machinations that the techs had had to go through to make sure that Earth equipment could talk to Lit transmitters had not resulted in perfect images at either end. "We will speak to you when you arrive. We welcome you, but there will be no departure while there are still Deep young to be delivered."

Nurys stifled a groan. The Lits found human groans similar to their own cries while mating, and that embarrassed both sides of the equation. That would only have blurred the issue. She had begun to hate dealing with Lits. The Littoral species, or so they were called in Earth spacer-lingo, never understood urgency or anything else that was important to humans. In this case, their own lives were at stake, and she still couldn't get a rise out of them.

"I can send you images of the scans we took from

space, Healer," she said. "There are at least three dozen enemy ships and flyers spread out over Monaday, looking for you."

"Images or not, Captain, this is calving season, here and now, not later. There has been a high incidence of stillbirths among the Deeps because of the toxic compounds released into the water by all those offworlders' refineries. They need us. We can feel their thoughts. They are grateful because they know we are here to help."

In Nurys's opinion, the Deeps weren't that intelligent. The hundred-meter animals looked like a cross between whales and cucumbers, with brains averaging toward the latter. "They might need you, but our gen is that the Serene Samawa is in danger. We need to pull him out before the enemy moves in to capture him. The situation is urgent."

The Lit waggled her head from side to side, the equivalent of a human shrug.

"And what does that mean to a mother attempting to expel a fetal pouch? He is willing to remain here until the end of season. He knew the risks." She hissed, a Lit chuckle. "The Hornets can't find us. There are too many other islands like this one."

Nurys saw the argument going around in circles.

"At least keep this channel open," she said. "It's vital that we don't lose touch with you. The enemy is on the move."

"As you please," Corkan said, showing her mouthful of razor-sharp teeth in the approximation of a smile. The Lits had taken a shine to humans' method of showing friendliness. It never ceased to creep Nurys out. "This fuss is all so unnecessary. We will welcome you. And we will keep Sarawa safe."

The transmission ended. Nurys stood up and wiped her face again. David Furuki, the radio operator—they still called them that, even after communication had changed so much—dared to give her a sympathetic grimace.

Keep him safe. That wouldn't be enough, and Nurys knew it. One way or another, they'd have to pull out Sarawa and the rest of the Interstellar Medical Volunteers, even if they had to be dragged into the sub. Not that she disagreed with their mission, far from it, but their timing was unfortunate, to understate the problem to a quantum level.

Humankind was so new to this interplanetary diplomacy thing. Space travel—real space travel, not a mission to the outer planets of Sol or weekend tourist trips to the Moon—was under a century old. Who could have guessed that the first time a warpknot ship had made it through a wormhole to what they called a Goldilocks planet that they'd find another intelligent species? And not just one, but half a dozen races, all with technology capable of jumping to Earth and back in a matter of weeks. A hundred years was ancient history to Nurys, but the reality still blew her mind. She had joined the Space Navy to get out there and meet aliens. She'd been a part of crews traveling on early sublight ships, but had retired to a teaching post at the Naval Academy long before that amazing first contact. Thrilled and wanting desperately to be involved, Nurys had applied for berths on the new ships, to no avail. They wanted young crew, with fast reflexes and long life spans, just in case a warpknot cruiser broke down in the spaceways. She was thanked for her service, and advised to enjoy her retirement.

And yet, there she was, in the same big old tub where she had done her first training rotation, the USS *Colorado*.

The huge nuclear-powered sub, just a hair under 115 meters long, had been launched a century before, as part of the *Virginia* class of attack submarines in Groton, North America. She had seen honorable duty through a number of terrestrial battles, then retired to the naval yard at Annapolis, where she had seen class after class of cadets through their initiation into deep-space warfare. Underwater training was seen as a practical and realistic environment for learning to operate in three dimensions in full protective gear while still within easy range of breathable atmosphere. Her graduates were assigned to interplanetary and interstellar craft all over what humankind's new allies called Earthzone.

This ship's predecessor, a surface battleship, had last been assigned to what was known as "magic carpet duty," restoring service members to their families at the end of the Second World War. This ship was about to perform similar duty, sweeping noncombatants out of harm's way. The mission would do a lot to polish humankind's image in the eyes and other optical receptors of their new colleagues in space.

That honor, unfortunately, provided cold comfort to the last class of cadets who had recently graduated from their rotation aboard *Colorado*. Nurys completely understood the disappointment, but the necessity overrode all their hopes of flying on a warpknot ship. A rescue needed to be mounted on an ocean world, and their new allies had no similar craft to undertake it.

The Lits originated on Galoop, a deepwater world, like Earth but with far fewer landmasses, so they naturally sought out similar planets to colonize. Unfortunately for them, so did other races who craved water oceans. Monaday was another Goldilocks world, at just the right distance from its hot white-giant sun and its attendant dwarf blue. The Lits had claimed it only about thirty terrestrial years ago, a stake registered in the Galactic Courts. Because a semi-intelligent species, the Deeps, already inhabited it, the Lits had become benign overlords, putting a few friendly outposts here and there without disturbing the Deeps' habitats.

The claim went unchallenged for three decades, until the Truchs, a scaly, eight-limbed, winged species native to a near-desert world and notorious for overreaching when no one was looking, were discovered to be stealing Monaday's natural resources, pouring tons of pollutants into the oceans and provoking tectonic shocks with their extraction techniques. The Lits brought charges in the Galactic Courts.

Reprisals began immediately. The Truchs began attacking Lit ships and outposts, starting to move toward dominating all their holdings, including their home planet.

The assassination of the Mother Queen and the attempted kidnapping of other members of the reigning family frightened the Lits. They recalled all their leaders from outposts and the Galactic Central Congress. Some had the means to evacuate or go into hiding. Others refused to allow the Truchs to scare them.

One in particular, Samawa, third-born but favorite offspring of the defense minister of the Littorals, had joined the Interstellar Medical Volunteers. Samawa's charm and wisdom had made him a popular figure on his own world and among other races. On his popular transmitted broadcasts, he publicly condemned the Truchs' incursions, complaining openly about their practice of damaging the environment of Monaday. His profile made him a direct target. His capture or death would be a blow to the Lits' cause. People would begin to lose heart if their benevolent outreach to other races was in danger. The IMV refused to divulge his location, but details in his own transmissions had revealed his presence there on Monaday, where a space battle had already broken out over control of the world. They knew he was there, and were looking for him.

The Lits had no means to retrieve him without being attacked. All their ships, and those belonging to other allied races, were easy to trace and target, thanks to the ion signature that their engines emitted. Unless they sent rowboats, the Truchs would spot the rescue craft. The enemy already suspected the Lits were going to try.

Step forward humankind. Thanks to a recently signed treaty, Earth formed its first true alliance in space with the Littorals. The current head of Terran government had an idea. He had been in the Space Navy, and remembered his training days. Nuclear vessels didn't create an ion trail. In other words, their technology was so old, no one was looking for it. They could pass largely unnoticed.

Most other subs had been mothballed, decommissioned,

turned into museums or broken up for salvage—but the *Colorado* was still in use. She was staffed up by officers who were most familiar with her, pulling in Commander Ehud Abram, an XO who was serving in the World Congress, the last class of cadets who had just graduated into the Space Navy, and Petrilla Nurys, still the training officer on duty, as captain.

She and her fellow officers had voiced plenty of concerns about transporting the old ship into alien waters, but all analyses looked good. Surface gravity approximated Earth's within five percent. The long, black hull strongly resembled a Deep in size and shape. Two problems: They couldn't use ship's sonar, because the supersonics were audible to both Deeps and Truchs; and no Terran spaceship was large enough to transport the *Colorado* from Earth to Monaday.

To solve the latter problem, they approached a number of races who had little love for the Truchs. For the right price, which was to open Earth's markets to them exclusively for six months, the Lits and humans had managed to convince a Gilik merchant to carry her there. The Giliks resembled stick insects, with prickly, ochre-yellow armor all over their bodies, and had prickly personalities to match. Roh, the captain of the *Unpronounceable*, or so the crew had declared it, landed just off one of Monaday's volcanic beaches near one of those factories with a hull full of supplies for the Truchs, and to pick up raw minerals as payment.

Under cover of night, Roh had released the *Colorado* into the deep, hideously polluted harbor with a warning.

"Come back twelve sunsets! No wait!"

Its voice grated on the ear, but Nurys took its word seriously. Twelve local days, and not a minute longer, or they'd miss their ride back to Earth. They were already three days into their journey. The turnaround was going to be rough.

The *Colorado* might have an advantage with its drives, but it was handicapped with regard to its telemetry equipment. Sonar remained the most accurate, but not the only means of reading the topography. Instead of a periscope, the *Virginia*-class vessel was equipped with photonic sensors and infrared scopes, all passive detectors that aided in navigation. Engineers retrofitted *Colorado* with the latest imaging technology and a full file of 3D maps taken from space of Monaday. Running through the dark waters, Nurys wished fervently that she could ping ahead and above to see where the enemy was. The Truchs were able to use sonar and radar, running waves of pings in patterns. The enemy's little scouts flew low reconnaissance patterns over the water, smoking anything that moved with depth charges. The *Colorado*'s cameras picked up little above the surface, but they had spotted numerous dead Deep floating, thanks to the trigger-happy Truchs. *Colorado* had to run as deep and as fast as possible, doing its best to avoid a random ping.

"What do we see out there?" Nurys asked, coming to lean over the telemetry station. The operator, Ensign Marcel Lim, who would normally also be operating sonar, turned the auxiliary three-dimensional screen toward the captain.

Lim gave her a quick glance over his shoulder before displaying each view of the telemetry one by one.

"Nothing unusual, sir. Kind of pretty out there, though."

Her star pupil during the last term, he knew the control board by heart. Like most of the others, he did his best to control his disappointment at being yanked back from his permanent assignment for the trip to Monaday. Nurys knew she could count on Lim.

Stats in white rolled up the scope over the blue-green images of the sea around them. They were cruising at fifteen knots at a depth of four hundred meters, well above their maximum operating depth. At that moment, they were traversing a channel in between islands in the archipelago where the IMV was operating. Optical arrays attached to the Unified Modular Mast and superior to ones that the *Colorado* had used on Earth gave her a pretty clear picture for a radius of two thousand meters in every direction. They had been a gift from the Lits, part of humanity's reward for undertaking the rescue mission. With Earth a thousand years or more behind their newfound acquaintances, they needed every technological advance that they could obtain. Still, without sonar, they couldn't move faster than about half maximum speed. Nurys damped down her feelings of impatience. They had enough time to comply with the Giliks, if only the IMV cooperated.

"Well, you all complained about not getting to see the new planet," she said, with a wry smile. "You've got a lot of interesting terrain out there. Kind of like the Hawaiian islands on steroids. For a wet world, this thing has a hot core."

Lim gave her a sheepish shrug. She knew what they

were thinking. She'd have liked more of a chance to see the surface side, too, but that wasn't the mission.

The sub arrowed through winding canyons of jagged peaks. Monaday's seafloor was covered by huge volcanoes that sloped upward from tectonically active spreading centers on the seafloor and broke the surface as islands. In between their roots, smaller caldera that wouldn't reach air for millions of years shot plumes of hot gray steam at the sub's underside, bubbling up around it, as if the mantle wanted to feed new saplings but keep the older trees alive.

Because of the heat, the craggy sides of the archipelagoes teemed with sea plants that rivaled even the most fertile oceans on Earth, dark blue-green with a hyperactive chlorophyll that made Monaday's oceans far more oxygen rich than Earth's. Munching on the plant life were herds of Deeps.

The immense black-gray creatures were as docile as cows. They bumped gently around one another to get to the choice plants. Even when the *Colorado* sailed within tens of meters of them, they turned the mildest of glances from the trio of oversized purple-black eyes on either side of their massive heads. Until the Truchs had invaded, the Deeps had no natural predators. Whatever evolution would have provided them had failed and become extinct. Nurys dismissed the Deeps as no threat.

According to the briefing she and the crew had received, the Deeps did just what their name suggested. The local biologics lived at a couple hundred meters below sea level. They surfaced occasionally to breathe and to give birth. The only signs of intelligence above animal were their ability to compose and share complex musical arrangements with one another, and their empathy. The Lits insisted that they could communicate emotions as well as music. A Lit envoy on an inspection tour of Monaday had reported distress signals from herd after herd. On further investigation, they had discovered modular factories in several coves. Millions of gallons of seafloor were sucked up to the surface and stripped of rare minerals. The chemical outflow was burning the Deeps' hides and killing their fragile young. Nurys didn't like to think what would happen if one of her sailors had to float in the soup pouring out of the factories.

"Ping sweep coming this way!" radar tech Elena Esperanza announced, one hand on her earpiece. "About five hundred meters away."

"Dive to six hundred," Nurys said at once. She grabbed onto the nearest handhold as the helm obeyed the order and the floor tilted under her feet. "Move us toward that mountainside. See if you can tell if that's coming from the mothership or the line of scouts."

"Aye, sir." The helm officer, Ensign Noelle Cartwright, laid in the coordinates.

The rough slope ahead seemed to ascend in the scopes as *Colorado* dipped into a deep, dark chasm. Not even the Deeps floated down there. Black coraloids almost the size of the sub wafted in their wake. Tiny, bright orange and yellow triangles with cilia instead of tail fins, this world's version of fish, shot across the bow like an explosion of fireworks.

Up there, in atmosphere and in orbit, the Truchs were actively searching for Samawa. The IMV was going to be hard to find, thank God. Because most of their technology was mechanical, it didn't send up electronic signals that could be easily read by scanners from space. Instead, that meant the enemy had to fly methodically over each of the island clusters to find the medics, a veritable needle in a widely scattered basketful of pincushions. Nurys clutched that to her as an advantage, because the periodic swings of sonar slowed her down further.

Over the speakers, the high-pitched screech increased in volume until it caused them all to wince. Just as swiftly, it faded away toward planetary east.

"Back to cruising depth, sir?" Cartwright asked, her long, dark fingers on the controls.

Nurys looked up at the ceiling. "Not yet." She held her breath. *Wait for it. Wait for it . . .*

From northwest, a series of screeches ricocheted all around their location, a hailstorm of sound clattering against the peaks and outcroppings of rock. Nurys grimaced. Random sonar sweeps were their biggest danger. If they were caught out in open sea, those were the most likely to point them out to the Truchs. Ensign Muhammad Bahri, at fire control, held his hands lightly over the controls, ready to launch missiles or torpedoes on command.

Another piece of Lit tech, the ion scope, displayed the source of those random hits. Eight noisy little bogeys zipped overhead in a staggered line. By their heading, they were sweeping the seas around a big island group thirty klicks to starboard. Nurys waited longer, until she was sure they weren't coming back around.

"Resume course," she said.

The audible sigh of relief on the bridge echoed her own. The helm corrected the trim and brought them up to cruising level. No one was certain if the tiny flyers were scout ships or unmanned drones. They were looking for ion trails or any unusual movement, neither of which she intended to provide them. The *Colorado*'s drive thrummed back to life. They resumed crawling along the seafloor.

She glanced uneasily at the chronometer above the telemetry station, and swabbed her face and neck again with her handkerchief.

"Life support, how are we looking?"

"CO_2 saturation is fifteen percent above optimum, ma'am," Lieutenant Philip Rafik replied. He was one of the few experienced officers they had been able to pull for duty. "I'm kicking up the hydroxide filtration system. If we can raise the snorkel mast in the next hour and just vent the whole fish, it'll smell a lot better in here."

Nurys tapped Lim on the shoulder. "Find us a place to cruise. We'll take a chance on the local atmosphere."

She swung into the command chair surrounded by its own array of scopes. It had been so long since she had commanded a ship during war, her nerves twitched constantly. Every little thing that was different was another thing that could go wrong. She not only had all these kids to care for, but humanity's entire future among interstellar races hung on her back. There was no way to speed up their progress. All she could do was hope that Samawa would remain undetected until they could reach him. If he protested, she would drag him on board with her own hands.

"There, sir," Lim said, his voice all but whispering from the speaker near her head. On the telemetry screen, red arrows pointed to a gray outcropping about fifty meters above them. Once it had been a bubble in the lava that formed the volcanic island overhead. When it burst, it created a giant cave that was more than large enough to hold the sub. At her command, they slowed to a crawl and edged partway beneath the overhang. It brought them within fifty meters of the surface. If the Truchs swung around for another pass and they got lucky, they stood a chance of detecting them, but Nurys was willing to give it a chance.

The clank and whir of the mast ascending from the UMM were almost intrusive noises. At most distances, the sounds would be swallowed by the sea, but she was afraid that the aliens had listening devices capable of hearing and detecting unusual sounds. The snorkel's umbilical hissed as it rose along the black tube. In a few minutes, the pumps kicked on full, and moist, cool air flooded the hot cabin. Nurys gulped in deep breaths.

"That smells . . . really green," Lim said, a smile creasing his smooth, tan face.

Nurys's mouth tweaked up in the corner. Not a bad description. The fresh air reminded her of the salt air on Earth, but flavored with something a little spicy, like ginger and parsley. In a different reality, to quote *Star Trek*, this would be a planet safe for humanity to visit. Maybe in the future, if they were successful, and the Lits managed to throw the Truchs off it.

The pumps clattered into silence. Rafik gave the captain a thumbs-up. Oxygen had risen to the correct level and the ambient temperature had dropped a good five degrees. It felt chilly at the moment, but it was probably much closer to the optimum twenty Celsius.

"Okay," she said. "Resume course, heading eighty-seven degrees off planetary north, terrain permitting."

They left the shelter of the cave. A couple of klicks beyond, the cavern suddenly opened out into a rolling, sandy plain. The triangular fish teemed here, along with a lot of albino life-forms surprised by the sub's forward lights.

Every pause to avoid sonar added hours to the sub's progress. Over the next couple of days, Nurys found herself watching the chrono as much as she listened to the approach and departure of the detection signals. The antisonar technology incorporated into *Colorado*'s hull was a natural defense against Earth-level sweeps, but they couldn't count on defeating the advanced tech of the Truchs.

News from interstellar services came in through the communications gear, too. Teams from the Lits and the Giliks were in orbit around Monaday, covering the space war and decrying the violence against the Deeps. The hand (or paw)-wringing speculation, which was translated into English via a largely imperfect system, gave the crew something to talk about during mess. It served to pinpoint where the Truch searches were going on, and as a platform for Samawa to continue to rail against the Truch.

". . . Many of the islands suffer ongoing explosions," a gravelly voice intoned. "Peace used to reign on this beautiful planet. Nature is under attack, and for what reason? The purity of the water is unsurpassed! The creatures are innocent! They should not have to endure either pollution or intrusion!"

Nurys leaned on one elbow and stared blearily into her breakfast cereal bowl, trying not to be annoyed.

"The Truchs are getting very close to that northeastern archipelago," Executive Officer Ehud Abram said, coming into the tiny officers' wardroom for a cup of coffee. For him, it was end of shift. For her, just the beginning of another long haul.

"I'm aware, XO," Nurys snapped. The tall, dark-haired officer stiffened his shoulders. Nurys made a wry face. He looked tired. She shouldn't take out her irritation on him. "Apologies, I just wish I could reach through the speaker and haul Samawa on board to shut him up."

"An activist is an activist," Abram said, his mouth twisting in a grin. "You wonder how he has so much time to broadcast when he's supposed to be delivering giant babies."

Nurys shook her head. "Every time he goes on the air, I worry that the Truchs are going to trace his location. How come they haven't?"

"Digital feed from remote transmitters. He seems to have planted a dozen of them all over Monaday when he landed here. The Truchs have blown up about half of them, but he has no intention of being silent. I admire that."

"Dammit, so do I," Nurys said. "But he's making it harder for us."

"He doesn't care. He believes in his cause. I can respect that."

"Commander!" the voice of the radio operator interrupted them. "Another sweep coming!"

Nurys sprang to her feet. She followed Abram out of the wardroom at a run.

All along the corridor, the crew was strapping into their bunks or into stationary positions.

The scopes on the bridge showed the approaching line of sonar probes. Abram threw himself into the command chair and strapped in. Nurys took a side seat.

The view ahead showed the plain they had been traveling for the last day and a half. Ahead, no more than thirty klicks, was a narrow crevasse that would be a great hiding place, but at the rate of approach, the *Colorado* couldn't make it there in time. They were exposed. Nurys felt the prickle of fear down the back of her neck.

"Make like a rock, people," Abram snapped out. "Down. We're going to have to go doggo."

Under the hands of the former cadet, the ship dove slowly, gradually, into the black basalt sand of the seabed. Nurys felt it settle belly down. It groaned like an old man, then fell silent. All shipboard chatter stilled, as did all nonessential equipment. Outside, swirls of dark particles rose and danced around them, lit by the occasional curious fishoid.

"Attention, all personnel. This is Commander Abram. We're going silent as of now until further notice," Abram ordered. "No talking. We just have to wait this out."

Nurys was reminded all over again what an excellent officer Abram was. No nonsense. He'd actually seen combat more recently than she had. She hoped he didn't see how rusty she felt. The kids didn't. Every young face on the bridge turned to her for reassurance. She nodded with a confidence she didn't really feel. They'd all gone through this in training. This was what they had been taught to do.

The smell of fear increased along with the odor of hot bodies, engine oil, and straining machine parts. Nurys found herself breathing in a rapid, shallow pattern, and willed herself to draw deep from her diaphragm.

The screeching of the alien sonar system erupted from the speakers. Esperanza moved a hand gingerly to lower the volume shipwide. Closer . . . closer . . . closer . . .

PING!

Did it see us? Nurys wondered. She stared at the scope. The line of red dots continued onward toward the northeast.

The junior telemetry officer, Patel, gestured at his screen. Six bogeys skimming the surface came around within a few klicks of their position. Objects plummeted down through the water. Depth charges!

Shit!

The bombs erupted above them with hollow booms that made the whole sub shimmy in its sand bed. Nurys held on, worried that a chance explosion could hole the hull. She glanced at the life-support panel. No red lights meant no structural damage. She let out the breath she didn't even realize she had been holding. The stink of fear rose from her own body. The ship shook again. She clenched her hands around the harness securing her in her seat. How could the Truchs have depth charges? They came from a dry world. These had to be some sort of modified surface bomb. She hoped they weren't as effective as Earth ordnance.

She glanced up, seeing the pale, tense faces of her

cadets over their safety straps. They needed her to hold it together, to let them know it was going to be all right.

It was never all right in war. They knew that! They could all get blown into fragments and never see Earth again! Still, she gave them another nod of reassurance. She turned to meet Abram's gaze. Both of them glanced at the telemetry station. Had the Truchs spotted them, or was this a random run?

The bogeys were fifty klicks away already, dropping more charges. Nurys let her shoulders relax. Not this time.

Abram was still the general officer on duty, so she let him give the order.

"All right," he said, unstrapping himself from the command chair. "Damage report, all stations."

"Negative, sir." "Nothing here, sir." "All systems operational, sir."

"All right, then. Let's move it. Ascend to ten meters above the floor and stay there. Full speed, heading sixty degrees. Let's get into that crevasse before they come back." He turned to Nurys. "Captain, you have the conn."

Now they were running hard toward the island where Samawa and the rest of the IMV were working. Four island groups were arrayed along a crack in the mid-ocean ridge in between two tectonic plates: Poliri, Domiri, Sokoiri and Aoiri. Their target was Sokoiri, the second-most distant. Five live volcanoes formed a barrier along the south edge of a cluster of extinct peaks. The caldera of the oldest and lowest formed a natural harbor, deep but sheltered. It'd be a snap to sail in, pick up the Lits, and get out.

Periodically, the sonar sweeps came overhead. The

Colorado had to take to ground again and again. Each time, the Truchs missed spotting them. Mood on board rose with every successful evasion, but Nurys chafed at the delay.

Their route took them within a hundred or so kilometers of Poliri, a scattershot island group. The maps they had from satellite showed it to be a handsome, lush green paradise, not unlike the Bahamas. They circled the roots of a massive active peak. Its sides warmed the water around it ten degrees above the ambient sea. Curious herds of Deeps floated over to them to investigate what must have looked like an android whale. A couple of the little ones bumped it playfully, knocking unwary crew off their feet.

"Get lost," Nurys murmured.

"God, they're huge!" Esperanza said, and whistled.

Reports from orbit sounded like the Truch warships were holding the Lits at bay. Nurys worried that if they succeeded in driving the Lits off that there might be a crackdown in other ship traffic. She was not going to let the Giliks take off without them. *Colorado* was outfitted for six months, but that was a worst-case scenario.

"Incoming!" Lim shouted. Nurys clutched the sides of her command chair. Everyone else dove for a stationary hold. A barrage of small barrels fell into the sea not far ahead of them.

"Hard to starboard!" she commanded. The helm officer responded. Horns and flashing lights warned everyone to secure themselves as the sub veered under their feet.

In the distance, the depth charges detonated. Nurys

saw the fire blossom just before the concussion hit them. The sub heeled over almost thirty degrees before righting itself. Chatter from all stations came in. A minor leak erupted in the head, causing a backwash of sewage that swamped one of the junior officers who was trapped by the alert on the pot. She listened to the swearing and laughing, but her eyes were fixed on the scope. Two of the young Deeps that had been swimming alongside their hull had been hit by the shrapnel. Black-green blood seeped out of gashes on their long, dark sides. Helplessly, she watched as they wriggled feebly, then their bodies floated upward. They were just babies. Her throat tightened.

"Damn it," Esperanza said. "That is effed up."

"That's why we're here, people!" Nurys said, forcibly pushing her emotions deep inside. "You got that?"

"Yes, sir!" the bridge crew chorused.

"Damage reports!"

". . . This continuing bombardment is harmful to all life on this world!" Samawa's gravelly voice came suddenly from the communication array. On the screen, a mother Deep showed open signs of distress as she tried to support her shining newborn on a sandy beach. The infant moved feebly as Lits, dwarfed by its size, rushed to support it. "Even the newest children are being injured by this unnecessary war!"

"Damn him!" Nurys exclaimed. "He's telling them where he is! Get on the horn to Corkan and tell her to shut him up!"

But the Truchs were ahead of her. In the middle of a sentence, Samawa's diatribe was cut off. The screen went blank. Nurys's heart sank.

"Did we lose them?" she asked. "Reports!"

"Look at this, sir," Lim called. The view on her telemetry screen turned to a view from space. He circled the same island group they were passing. One of the volcanic peaks had been hit. As she watched, another massive puff of smoke exploded outward, taking out most of the ancient caldera.

Furuki looked up, an expression of triumph on his face.

"Got Corkan, sir. That wasn't Sokoiri at all, just one of Samawa's repeater stations. The Truchs still haven't figured out where he is. And she'll try, sir. Really. She'll try."

"About two hundred kilometers from our destination, sir," Abram reported at shift change on Day Five. "We ought to make the harbor by tonight."

"Notify Healer Corkan to get ready," Nurys said. She had been operating on a knife's edge ever since the hit on Poliri. All of them were ready to have the mission accomplished and over with. "Tell them I want them on the beach when we surface."

"Aye, sir."

Almost on schedule, another sweep came toward them from the west. Lim offered her his best suggestions for a hiding place, but they weren't close enough. A random ping hit them from the northeast. Nine flyers circled around in formation, three trios. Almost instantly, the depth charges started falling again. One hit just off the port bow, between the *Colorado* and the underwater slope of an island. The concussion echoed back on the sub, making it heel over almost sixty degrees. Nurys hung on tight. Lim was thrown out of his seat and smacked into the wall. He rocked back and forth, holding onto his wrist, which hung at a bad angle.

"Medic to the bridge!" Nurys barked into her microphone. "Damage reports!"

Lim wasn't the only casualty. A few other broken bones and a lot of bruises were reported. In the torpedo bay, a leak had all hands jumping to stop it.

"All right," Nurys said, feeling her ire rise. "They think they know we're here. Let's confirm it for them. Load sub-to-air missiles! Ascend to a hundred feet. Let's show these desert bugs what we can do!"

Everyone scrambled to obey her orders. As the small craft came around again, they locked onto the lead flyer.

"Fire!" Nurys said. Bahri hit the button. The sub juddered lightly. On the scope, a jet of bubbles erupted behind the sea-to-air missile. It broke the surface in a split second and burst into the air. On the fire control screen, the camera on the nose of the missile fed back visuals. The red circle triangulated on the lead flyer. Beeping came from the speaker over Bahri's head.

"Confirming lock," Bahri said. "Bogey is running."

A few seconds later, the screen exploded in red and reverted to the terrain map.

"Direct hit," Bahri confirmed. The other small craft scattered in a random pattern, jetting away from the site in no good order.

"They *are* manned," Esperanza said.

"Now we know," Nurys agreed. "And we scared them. But now they know we're here. Let's use that."

"How, ma'am? I mean, sir? They'll follow us."

The captain shook her head. The cadets were so young. "Then let's give them something to follow. Helm, full speed, heading three degrees north."

Esperanza gawked. "What? That's Domiri! It's the wrong way."

Nurys raised her eyebrow. "You want them to follow us the right way? Pick out the most likely looking island, one with a cove. We need to make this look legitimate." *And hope that none of the ships in space come down to join the fray*, she thought.

Lim made the connection. He had been her very best student. The map of the Domiri group appeared on the scope. In a moment, one of the islands centered on the screen. "This one, sir. It's not industrial. I don't see any major life signs above the waterline."

"Make it so, helm," Nurys said. She strapped in.

They let the enemy ping them again and again as they steamed straight for Domiri. Nurys went from station to station, letting the crew know she was there. The vigorous walkthrough also helped expel the nervous energy she felt. About four hours would do it, as they rose to meet the sweeps, then dove out of sight again at random intervals.

All the youngsters—no, spacers; they were blooded now—worked off their nervous energy, too. The old tub hadn't been that clean in years. Nurys nodded approval at the three ensigns who looked up from scrubbing the floor of the head. She took a deep breath and smelled only disinfectant. You'd never know it had been covered in shit only a couple of hours before.

True to form, Samawa had found out about his demolished repeater, and railed about that in his frequent uploads. Nurys tuned him out most of the time.

". . . Thank you to the good people who have contributed funds to the medical volunteers here with me. You are helping to save an innocent species from harm against the bloody marauders who . . . !" came from the speakers as she entered the bridge.

"How'd he ever get the name 'Serene Samawa'?" Lim was asking Bahri. He sprang to his feet. "Sorry, sir."

"At ease, Ensign," Nurys said. "That's a good question. Research it. It'll be in your next orals." She had to laugh at the dismayed expression on his face. It relaxed the tight muscles in her belly. "Take it easy, Lim. I'm not your teacher any longer. After this mission, you'll be on assignment on a warpknot. Where are we?"

Relieved, the ensign turned to his station. "They're still following us, Captain. They haven't thrown any charges at us in hours, but they're rotating a patrol. They want to know where we're going."

"Good," Nurys said, pleased at his analysis. "Snorkel up. Let's get some fresh air in here before we disappear. If you thought the last four hours were a test of your endurance, pull up your panties."

She had studied the maps during her downtime. They had been following the volcanic fissure toward the islands, but they couldn't settle down into that. Running parallel and branching off were cooler ones, some of which ran deep. She pulled up the chart she had marked and sent it to all the stations.

"This is where we're going," Nurys said, marking the

chosen channel in red. "Helm, take us in. We're going doggo."

They descended into the fissure. It was a mere crack, barely three times the width of the sub. Nurys held her breath as the helmswoman guided them in. They were running with as few lights as possible. Infrared did little good here; everything was black with cold. Coraloids brushed their sides, but they got down without any scrapes against the native rock. At last, they settled onto the seafloor. Basalt sand puffed up around them. The engines halted, and the lights on the hull went out.

"All hands, we're going to radio silence," she announced over the PA. "This is the last sound you are going to hear me make until further notice. No talking, no shouting, no banging, no primal screams."

Esperanza let out a nervous giggle at the last. Nurys gave her the teacher stare, and she subsided.

"Twelve hours," she said. "Practice your sign language. Any crisis, text me."

Twelve hours cut deeply into their remaining hours. Nurys surrendered the bridge to Abram, but she couldn't relax. Samawa continued his broadcasts, but instead of his rhetoric pouring out of the speakers, the crew followed it on closed caption. Off duty, the kids played video games with the sound off, encouraging or jeering at one another with silent gestures. They were doing a great job, but it felt like walking through a ghost town.

The newly scrubbed head began to stink because they didn't dare flush the full cans. Nurys knew perfectly well the crew was also pissing in the washing machine and down the sinks to compensate.

The rest of the sea life found the silent giant in their midst to be a puzzle. A curious Deep or two came by to nudge them. When the sub didn't respond, they tried nuzzling it, then let out low, musical moans as though mourning it. For some reason, Nurys found that oddly touching.

They think we're dead, she thought. *And they care.*

Overhead, the Truchs were going ballistic. She had led them to believe that their target, on its straight heading, would appear from time to time. The passive scopes picked up swoops and sweeps that grew more frantic as the hours passed.

Boom!

The first explosion overhead at hour five startled Nurys awake in her bunk, but didn't surprise her. She glanced at the ceiling, then at the screen set in the wall beside her. Bogeys flew overhead, swooping close to the surface. Depth charges filled the sea, rocking the sub back and forth in its sandy cradle.

The pounding made Nurys's ears ring. She stuffed earplugs in and did her best to go back to sleep. Seven hours to go. Orders from Abram to repair a gasket in the forward torpedo bay scrolled along the bottom of the screen in red. She went back to sleep, and dreamed of being trapped inside a kettle drum during the longest concert ever performed. The maestro at the head of the orchestra bowed to thunderous applause from the audience, then silence.

"They're bombarding the island group," Lim confirmed by text when she entered the bridge. Abrams, looking weary, signed off and headed back to his own bunk.

Nurys settled into her chair and cleared her throat. The bridge crew all but jumped at the sound.

"Well done, all. Time's up! Full about, and make full speed for Sokoiri. Let's go get our package and get out of here."

Totally against protocol, the crew cheered. The joyful noise spread down the long body of the boat, accompanied by a few screeches and a lot of flushing. The chrono showed they were within a few hours of magic time to retrieve the medics and get back to the Gilik ship.

Also against protocol, Nurys insisted on suiting up in scuba gear to join two other divers at the release hatch. The *Colorado* remained submerged, in case they got a few bogeys overhead.

"Sir, you shouldn't come ashore," C.O.B Dodd said, his freckled face flushing. "Leave it to us."

Nurys's lips were set as she pulled the rubber coif tight over her head and settled the air pack on her shoulders. "I just got off the comm circuit with Corkan. You'd better believe I'm coming ashore with you."

The hatch opened and flooded around them. Nurys had been a scuba diver since she was a kid. The feeling of the water rushing down onto her head should have felt normal, but the knowledge that this was an alien sea made tingles run down her body.

Dodd deployed the inflatable, then gave her a hand into it. The complement of Lits was sixteen, so Corkan had said. Plenty of room to take them aboard and get them into the sub.

The moment she swam out of the sub, she realized they were not alone. The bay was full of black-pelted Deeps, from some the size of the boat down to little ones half the size of a school bus. Their curiosity was palpable, but they kept their distance, hovering, their movement driven by billions of foot-long cilia like the tails of the fishoids.

"Goddamn it, they look like giant bacteria!" Dodd said.

Nurys had to concur that they did, but they felt like big, friendly cows in a field.

The rubber boat had a small outboard motor that drove them across the bay toward the narrow strip of sand. Osteen, the other NCO, steered them in past the mothers and young. Giant snouts surfaced every few meters to nudge the boat or spray them with friendly snorts of seawater. Up close to the charcoal-gray hides, she saw what looked like chemical burns on the mothers, and even a few of the young. Her heart went out to them, but she couldn't let pity get in the way of the mission.

Almost the entire contingent of Lits was on the water's edge when they rode up on the sand. Nurys clambered out. Even before she had taken off her mask, one of the Lits rushed toward them and enveloped her in a bear hug. They even looked like bears, with their thickset, dark-furred bodies and snouted faces. Their big eyes, with the nictating membrane opening and closing independently from their eyelids, gave them the facial expressions of seals or otters. They plunged into the surf to clean foam and blood off their fur before barreling toward the humans, shouting happily.

"I am so glad to meet you, Captain!" Corkan said, though her voice came from the translator slung on Nurys's shoulder. She pulled the human along with her webby paw as others crowded around, patting her on the head and back. "Come and see our patients! They are waiting to know you."

"We don't have time for that, Healer," Nurys said, although her natural instincts wanted to run and see every single one of them. Aliens! She was walking among aliens! Two kinds! Her contact with the Giliks had been brief and distant throughout the long transit from Earth, not at all satisfying the itch of first contact. This was the first time she had touched someone who had been born under the light of a different sun. Even Dodd, a hardened old swab, looked as starstruck as a kid as two of the Lit medics hugged him and rubbed their furry faces against his. She wished she could enjoy the moment. "We need to get you and Samawa off this island right away!"

"No, no, I told you," Corkan said, her tone jovial, embracing Nurys with one meaty arm. "We do not leave. I warned you not to come all this way for nothing!"

"Have pity for the wounded." A magnificent, broad-shouldered Lit rose from spraying white foam on the back of a small Deep resting on the beach and washed the matter from his paws. The Deep's worried mother hovered in the bay, her long nose the only part out of the water. He gestured a little farther down the beach, where a couple of undersized fetuses lay unmoving. "You see what we are dealing with."

"Serene Samawa," Nurys said, saluting him formally. "I am Captain Nurys of the USS *Colorado*, from Earth. On behalf of your own government, I am here to request that you return with me to our transport ship and leave this planet immediately."

The deep brown eyes sighted down his snout at her

with a sorrowful expression. "My government knows my answer. We are here to help this race to survive! They will die without our help."

He was used to being obeyed, she could tell, but so was she. She fixed him with her best teacher gaze.

"Sir. You are in danger. If you insist on staying here, you'll become a target or a martyr, and the Deeps will die anyhow. Your family will suffer. Your people, including the audience for your broadcasts, will lose heart. It's only a matter of time before the Truchs figure out we sent them on a snark hunt and start searching the other islands to find you."

Samawa listened carefully as her translator spat out her paragraph in their husky language. The large eyes narrowed.

"What is a snark?"

"Come back after the battle is won," Nurys said, sensing every minute passing as a possibility that the Giliks would take off without them. "You can save the next generation, but if you don't leave, you're putting them in more danger than if you left them alone."

Samawa hesitated. He glanced back at the young Deep on the sand, then turned sad eyes to Nurys.

"More will die of the poison."

"Let your government deal with that," Nurys said, knowing exactly how she felt. If her own students had been the wounded, she would have wanted to do the same. "That's their job. Yours is to . . . to inspire."

"They've done a terrible job so far!" Samawa said, his voice echoing over the beach. "Show me that they care! If not, let me stay!"

As if in answer, the Deeps in the water began to writhe and splash. Nurys regarded them with concern.

"What's with them?"

Samawa laid his long paw across his furry chest.

"They feel our emotions, and possibly yours, too," he added, tapping her on the solar plexus, "though yours are far more subtle than ours."

Subtle! Nurys felt her temper rise. The leviathans thrashed more vigorously, sending up geysers of water into the blue sky. She dampened her feelings.

"Serene one," she said, "if you can sense my emotions, then you know how concerned I am about your safety. I have come all the way from Earth to help you. That's how serious your government takes this situation."

Furuki's voice interrupted them.

"Sir, we've got bogeys coming this way. Seven of them."

Shit! The Truchs had figured out they'd been fooled. It would take them little time to search the two island groups flanking Domiri and see all the activity in the water near Sokoiri. Nurys made a decision.

"Come and get us. Shove the crowd out of the way if you have to, but get here. The harbor's plenty deep. And keep me posted!"

"Aye, sir!"

She turned to Samawa and Corkan, willing them to understand in spite of the crude translator.

"Truch fighters are on the way. They've been dropping bombs on us, and they are looking for *you*. If you don't want every single one of your patients blasted out of the water, get your stuff now. Just the vitals. We need to evacuate you before they get here."

The Lits searched her face with their round brown eyes, then the group hurried back toward their encampment, all but Samawa.

"Have I brought this on my dear friends?" he asked. "Have I put them all into danger, colleagues and patients alike, from the Hornets?" His expressive muzzle sagged into despair. Nurys felt genuinely sorry for him.

"Not you. The Truchs did it. Hurry. We don't have a lot of time."

He trundled away, far faster than she thought one of his bulk could move.

Nurys listened to the chatter coming from the *Colorado* as she waited impatiently for the Lits to return. In the water, she saw the stirring of the surface as the Deeps scattered.

She couldn't help but feel pride as *Colorado* rose. First the UMM broke water, followed by the magnificent sail, then the near-black oblong body, long and magnificent. Nurys ran a critical eye over the length of her, and could see no flaw. The few scrapes and dents they'd taken since arriving on Monaday were superficial.

The Lits clustered at her side, murmuring admiringly.

"It looks like a Deep!" Samawa said, heaving a bulky red bag across his shoulders. "What a compliment to the denizens of this world!" He walked up and down, admiring it.

No matter what, the Lits seemed to take their own time about things.

"Sir," Nurys said, her patience exhausted, "get on board. Now. No more arguments. If I have to carry you, I will."

Samawa waved a paw.

"No need. I feel your sincerity. We will go." He signed to the others. Nurys gestured toward the rubber boat, but the Lits ignored it. They ran to the water's edge and leaped in, swimming for the hatch on their own.

The cadets were thrilled to have the Lits on board. Their disappointment at not being able to set foot on the island disappeared as they had a whole bunch of actual aliens among them. The Lits hugged everyone, not at all taken aback at entering an alien—to them—watercraft.

The moment they were on board, Nurys strode back to the bridge, Corkan and Samawa in her train.

"Helm, get us out of here," she said, peeling out of her wetsuit. The Lits dripped water on the floor. A couple of the crew ran for mops and buckets. "Set course for our pickup point. Depth two hundred meters."

"Aye, sir!" Esperanza said, entering the order on her controls. The bridge crew shot curious glances at their visitors as the Lits came to watch what they were doing. *Colorado* came about smartly, and started toward the entrance to the sheltered cove.

Bump! Nurys staggered at the impact.

"What did we hit?"

More impacts came in the wake of the first.

"It's the Deeps, sir," Lim said, pointing at the visuals. "They're ramming into us. They didn't touch us on the way in!"

"They are concerned for us," Corkan said. "They think we are your prisoners, or your prey."

"How can we get them to stop?" Nurys demanded. "I don't want to hurt them."

Samawa showed all his teeth in a humanlike smile.

"We will tell them we are safe."

Together, he and Corkan closed their eyes. To her amazement, Nurys could feel waves of calming emotion pouring from them, like warmth from the sun. Even she relaxed a little. The faces of the bridge crew told her they were sensing the same thing. The Lits truly were empathic.

The Deeps withdrew to a few meters, giving the sub room to maneuver.

"I told them we will return," Samawa said, opening his eyes. "Perhaps you will come back with me."

Nurys had to think about that. But she had more pressing things on her plate at the moment.

She assigned Dodd to take the Lits to their temporary bunks and show them around. The Lits praised every part of the ship. They were even pleased with the rations in the wardroom. They asked shy questions about everything they saw, and her crew responded eagerly with detailed explanations, gesturing with hand signals where words failed. To Nurys's surprise, she realized this was the Lits' first contact with humans. If only it had been under different circumstances, it would have been great.

Now the Truchs knew pretty much where they were. That meant they had to keep from being pinged. They set course away from Sokoiri along the most broken, rocky, and difficult terrain that the helm could scare up, deep valleys and tightly-packed baby volcanoes along the rift. They rode the edge of thermoclines, ducking into colder or warmer water in order to break the signal when a sonar sweep came through.

The scouts passed over them again and again, always doubling back toward the island cluster. Nurys breathed a sigh of relief whenever they veered off instead of going around for a bombing run.

Two and a half days before the pickup, they emerged from a narrow rift valley, and out over the lowest terrain they had seen yet. The temperature gradient was less than five degrees from one zone to another, with no deep crevices wide enough for the sub anywhere in sight. Nurys had the helm open it up to make time.

"Sweep pattern approaching!" Lim announced.

Their luck had run out.

They heard the screech of the radar rake across them. It passed over them slightly, then reversed, staying on their location and whooping like the world's most annoying car alarm.

"They painted us!" Bahri shouted, just before the barrage began. The sub rocked every time a charge went off close by. The Lits whimpered to one another. They weren't used to unfriendly seas.

"Dive for the bottom," Nurys said, her eyes fixed on the scope. "Scrape her belly if you need to."

"Sir," Cartwright said in alarm, "the floor is below our safe specs."

"We have to take the chance," Nurys snapped. "Get as low as you can. We have to minimize the damage."

The sub creaked audibly as they descended. She could almost feel the gaskets straining against the additional pressure. Charge after charge detonated. Nurys couldn't identify a pattern.

"Can they trace us?"

"They don't know with certainty where you are," Samawa said suddenly. "We can feel their confusion."

Nurys straightened. "That's all I need to know."

She tuned out the depth alarm sounding over and over and concentrated on running straight for the feet of the nearest islands, through hot and cold zones. They couldn't go silent again for hours; there wasn't time.

Shouting erupted from the stern. Another set of seals had given out, flooding a rear compartment. Engineering was on the job, doing their best to deal with that and a buckled panel. The lights on the bridge flickered and went to safeties. Rafik checked his readout and gave Nurys a reassuring nod.

"Will we die?" Corkan asked, her kindly face concentrated with fear.

"No," Nurys said. "I've got you. We're going to catch the bus home."

Once in the midst of another island group, they had no choice but to follow the hills and valleys of the terrain. They rose above the crisis depth, but that made them vulnerable to further barrages. And barrages they got. Whenever the Truchs could triangulate on their pings, they bombed the hell out of them. Nurys realized they had observed that Samawa's endless broadcasting had gone silent. Even a stupid alien would guess that he was on the mystery craft. Take out one, and they take out the other.

"We have got a bogey coming this way," Esperanza said.

"Another fighter?" Nurys asked.

Her eyes were wide. "No. This one is gigantic. It's got to be the home base for these fighters."

Nurys concentrated on the scope. She didn't need to ask which image he meant. One round mark overspread a quarter of the sky. The mothership was bigger than any Earth-based aircraft or spaceship, including any generation ship or aircraft carrier she had ever seen. It dwarfed Roh's Gilik merchant. It was the goddamned Death Star, and it was coming for them.

"Do you know anything about these destroyers?" she asked Corkan. "What do we need to hit them?"

"You can't!" the healer said. Her large brown eyes were open in horror. "They have shields against space weapons. You can't attack them. Nothing will go through."

"Space weapons?" Nurys repeated. "But the shields are for long-distance attacks, right? They have to have a vulnerable range inside, or they'd repel their own fighters coming in."

Corkan paused. "I don't know."

Nurys glanced at her crew.

"Well, then, it's all or nothing. Bahri, load all torpedo tubes. Make ready on my command."

"It's going to kill us!" Corkan gasped.

Nurys felt the sense of calm come over her that she always had when she focused on a single point.

"It's going to try. And we're going to try right back," Nurys said. "Plot an intercept course. Go in at four hundred feet, then blow the ballast so we come up right under them. We want to be right in their faces to give them a proper welcome. We're going to shoot and run. Got that?"

"Aye, sir!" Cartwright said. She plotted in the course, her eyes fixed on her screen. Nurys watched, measuring the distance with her eyes.

Wait for it . . . wait for it . . .

"Blow tanks!"

The G-force of the ship rising pressed them hard into their seats. Nurys held on, her eyes on fire control's screen.

"Fire!"

At one hundred feet exactly, the sub shuddered as it released the four surface-to-air torpedoes, then dove for the bottom as fast as it could.

On the scopes, the rockets lit up the sky like four arc-welder flames. They zipped toward their targets, spreading out for the underside of the mothership. Nurys held her breath. Would the shields stop them? But, no, the hot blue flames kept rising, rising, rising, until they burst into blinding glory against the Truch hull. The whole world shook with the percussive impact. Nurys felt as if she had been body-slammed. Her ears popped, and she felt warm liquid pouring down her neck. Probably blood. No time to check.

They were a thousand yards away and hauling when the mothership came down into the ocean. The shock wave threw the sub forward, making the rudder stutter. Anyone on his or her feet got thrown clear across the cabin.

"Medic!" "Medic!" Calls came over the PA immediately.

"We must help," Corkan said, unhitching herself from the jump seat in which she had been secured. She waddled out of the room, holding her bag.

Bless them, the captain thought.

Nurys checked the scope. Dozens of the fighter craft

swooped helplessly around the sinking, smoking ruin of the mothership, like flies around a rotting carcass. Shrapnel flew in every direction, some of it landing in the path of the sub. *Colorado* rammed into a few, losing her forward starboard sensor array to the debris. Three of the screens at nav and telemetry went black. Nurys heard a screech as a long section like a girder scraped down the port side. Couldn't be helped. Didn't matter.

"Let's get to the bus station," Nurys said. "At sunset our transport lifts. We are not going to miss it."

"No, sir!" the crew shouted.

They ran for the pickup point, avoiding pings and sweeps from the few surviving small craft. The seabed looked like a slalom course with banked curves and a rapid current that helped push *Colorado* to her maximum rate of knots.

"We can make it," Esperanza said. "Three hours at this speed."

They stayed low and silent. After a half hour, they started hearing pinging again. The sweeps were haphazard, but they could still mean trouble.

Nurys kept the ship down as low as she could, but the sea was shallower near the archipelago where the Gilik ship lay. They avoided most of the pings and sweeps by weaving in between jagged boulders bigger than they were. Instead of retracing their outbound route, they came in wide toward the sheltered harbor on the westernmost shore of their target island. Not much more than an hour remained. Nurys felt like biting her nails. It was going to be a squeak. Her back ached from the tension. She got up to stretch, raising her arms above her head. It didn't help. She was going to have to go for physio when this was all over. The Truchs launched random barrages of depth charges, missing them by miles.

"Sir, we're going to have to go over that," Lim said. He pointed at the scope.

Nurys bent over his station to take a look. A saddleback ridge, the result of two volcanic islands growing up almost side by side, lay before them, looking like a big blue jump rope. Deeper seas lay on either side of the peaks, but it would take precious minutes to go around. She had no choice. They had to risk passing over that. The sea beyond would be deeper. It was just one moment of exposure.

"Missiles ready, Bahri," she ordered. "Take us through, Cartwright, as low as you can skim."

"Aye, Captain." The helmswoman frowned over her controls.

Nurys watched the radar scope. Just as they crested the ridge, a sweep passed directly overhead.

"They painted us, sir!"

Shit! Within seconds, the Truchs started dropping bombs on them. One struck close enough to make all the lights go out for a moment.

"Dive," Nurys said, sounding a hell of a lot calmer than she felt. "All the way down. We have to make this last run. Go!"

The sweeps continued, over and over. The shrieking of the signal threatened to drive her mad. The Truchs knew where they were. She thought there were only a few left, but dozens of the little ships appeared on the scope. They started bracketing them with charges, hoping to cripple them and leave them dead in the water. Nurys couldn't hit them all with missiles, and there was nowhere else to go. All they could do was run, and hope they made it to the Gilik ship before they sank.

Boom!

Nurys looked up, her heart in her throat.

"What the hell was that?"

"It's a herd of Deeps, sir," Lim said. He brought up all the exterior cameras. Nurys stared in horror. They were surrounded by the leviathans, all bumping and clustering around the sub, no more than two meters off the hull. Some of these were the largest she had ever seen, even longer than the *Colorado* herself.

"What are they trying to do, mate with us?"

"We asked for help. They are helping."

She turned to see Samawa smiling toothily at her.

"Why?"

"I called out to them. You are doing your best to save all our lives. They understand that. They wish to help. You are alone. The Hornets are looking only for a single ship. These are many. The Hornets will never see you in a herd. They will support and protect us, as if this shell was a newborn or an injured adult."

"I can't let them do that!" Nurys exclaimed, horrified. In her mind's eye, she saw the injured and dying Deeps on the Sokoiri beach. Samawa stretched out a comforting paw to her.

"Be at peace. They feel your passion and your sincerity, as do I." He fixed her with his kindly gaze. "They know you want to save us. They want to help. So much is at stake, didn't you say? They may not understand all of the reasons, but their hearts are great. Your ship is one of them now."

Another sweep passed overhead. The shrieking went right through Nurys's head.

As it receded, she heard something else, almost on the other side of sound, music welling up in the sea around them. The Deeps were singing.

Ping after ping struck them as the Truchs fell into a line of pickets. They spotted the pod coming toward the harbor. Samawa was right: Their sonar would reveal a pod of identical bodies, never penetrating through to see that one of their number was made of metal. They couldn't see the *Colorado*, but they were trigger happy now. They dropped charges on anything that moved. Blast after blast shook them all. Rocks and debris shot up from the sea floor, battering their underside. Deeps floated away from them, obscured by a sudden cloud of dark green.

A thread of the song changed, drifting off in a melancholy note. Nurys meet Samawa's brown eyes and knew that at least one of the Deeps escorting them had been struck. She fought back tears. Cartwright wept openly over her board.

"Tell them . . . tell them we are grateful for their sacrifice," Nurys said at last.

"They know," Samawa said. "And so are we."

The captain swallowed hard.

"Maybe I will come back with you."

With less than a quarter hour to spare, they surfaced into the open hull of the Gilik ship. The Deeps around them melted away as if they had never been there. Roh leaped down from a higher level of the hold as Nurys climbed out on top of the rising sub. Massive robotic arms and hoists reached for the sub, drawing her upward into the dry-dock cradle and securing her in place.

"You make me late soon!" it chittered, clearly preparing to give the captain a piece of its mind, then saw the Lits at her back. "Awk! Samawa-ree!" It bowed deeply.

"Greetings, friend Gilik," the Lit said, rushing up to embrace the stick insect in a crushing hug. Creeling a protest, Roh detached itself. It peered at Nurys.

"Perhaps you are not useless," Roh said, "despite your primitive machines."

Nurys ignored him. She didn't care about the Gilik's scorn. They'd accomplished their mission. The Lits were safe. Earth had done their new friends a favor, and she was going home with all hands.

"A good heart is timeless," Samawa said heartily, embracing the reluctant Gilik and Nurys in turn. "I will say so in my next broadcast." He held up the bulging red bag. "I can do it at once, telling about the sacrifices made for us by all our friends."

Nurys put her hand on the bag and all of her passion into her tone.

"Do me a favor," she said. "Let's run silent for now."

❧   ❧   ❧

Jody Lynn Nye lists her main career activity as "spoiling cats." She lives northwest of Chicago with one of the above and her husband, author and packager Bill Fawcett. She has written over forty-five books, including *The Ship Who Won* with Anne McCaffrey, eight books with Robert Asprin, a humorous anthology about mothers, *Don't Forget Your Spacesuit, Dear!*, and over 160 short stories.

Her latest books are *Rhythm of the Imperium* (Baen Books), *Moon Beam* (with Travis S. Taylor, Baen) and *Myth-Fits* (Ace). Jody also reviews fiction for *Galaxy's Edge* magazine and teaches the intensive writers' workshop at DragonCon.

BOOMERS

J.R. Dunn

Another powerful ship in an alternate future, but this future is entirely frightening. What if the space race had begun earlier and was run harder and for keeps? It might have included thermonuclear engines and multiple fusion warheads in space. Since communism was and is economically unsustainable without continuing to grind its own populace on a downward course to penury and enslavement, there would have been a fall, just as there was in 1989 in real history. But with nukes in space, that fall might have left far more dangerous relics sequestered in the heavens—and left the KGB enforcers of that evil ideology to fester, plotting perhaps a comeback, or at least apocalyptic revenge, on all those who betrayed the Revolution.

❋

"Don't go scratching my Kevlar, bro."

Kieran swung away from Cruz, giggling like an idiot.

Leaning toward the front port, Strode said, "Stow that, you two."

"Stow it. Aye aye, sir."

"Since when are we in the fuckin' navy?"

"What was that, Cruz?" Strode was speaking in a near-whisper despite himself. He instinctively glanced at the board to assure himself that they were still talking by cable and hadn't somehow switched to broadcast.

"Nothin', sir. Nothin' at all."

Strode decided to leave them be. According to Intel, the Russians booby-trapped all access to their boomers. Disturbing them while they were trying to crack the hangar controls would be what Colonel Klaus would call "inadvisable."

He glanced up through the top port as much as the helmet would let him. The hull of the Russian boomer curved far overhead, the point of one huge star visible to his left, a handful of Cyrillic letters to his right.

Rokossovsky, they spelled out. Marshal of the Soviet Union Konstantin Konstantinovich. Hero of the Great Patriotic War. Order of Lenin, Order of the Red Banner, Order of Victory. Effective viceroy of Poland for nearly a decade after the war . . .

. . . and throughout it all, under suspended sentence of death, courtesy of Uncle Joe Stalin. Jesus, what a system.

"Got it," Cruz said.

Strode lowered his eyes. Outside, the two suited figures were still huddled against the boomer's hull, tools and parts floating beside them. "Got what?"

Cruz raised his arm slightly. Within the gauntlet, Strode could make out a small white cube.

"About five or six ounces of what looks like Semtex. Blow both your fuckin' hands right off."

Strode fought down an impulse to demand why they hadn't told him they'd found it in the first place. "Good."

"Brace me," Cruz told Kieran. He tossed the explosive in the direction of Cygnus and swung himself clumsily back toward the hull. "Gimme some light here."

"No more cavities," he said after a moment.

Strode smiled. A dental mirror was a crucial part of their equipment.

"Okay . . . we'll crack this sucker in just a minute."

"Excellent." Strode could see Morris standing behind him, reflected in the plexi. He'd been so quiet that Strode had forgotten he was there.

There was a buzz in his earphones. He glanced at the board. A call from the *LeMay*. He carefully reached over and switched to the laser antenna. "Strode here."

"*LeMay* CIC here, Major."

Strode rolled his eyes. Who else would it be?

"Ah, how's it going?"

"We just disarmed their welcoming present, Colonel. About ready for insertion."

"Very good. Ah, still no sign of the crew?"

"No sir, not a peep."

"Very well, then. Watch your step, son. There's no trusting those bastards."

"Understood, sir. Out."

He switched off. Klaus was straightedge USAF—buzz cut, starched khakis, heavy horn-rims. He believed that anybody with more than an inch of sideburn was a hippie, and that all hippies were commies, and as for commies . . .

Well, Strode had been something of a hippie himself not all that long ago, and he was no commie . . .

He became aware that Kieran and Cruz were half-twisted around and gazing at the EV. He hurriedly switched over to cable.

". . . set to go here, Chief. What's the . . ."

"Sorry. I was on with the Big L."

"Ah."

"Understood."

"Awright," Strode said. "Gogol? You ready?"

"That's an affirmative," the assault team leader told him.

"Okay. Questions . . . No? Let's go for it, Micky."

Cruz bent over a small black box and manipulated it. Strode shifted his gaze toward the vast, closed hatch to their left. For a moment, nothing happened, then it started to slide open, moving upward like a garage door. He bit his lip when the lights inside remained off. But then they started glowing, softly at first, then brighter as the hatch slid up out of sight.

Strode shifted against his seat belt. Nothing. The hangar was completely empty, as far as he could see. Oh, there was equipment strapped against the bulkheads. But EVs, vehicles of any sort—not a sign.

There was one section not visible from the EV. "Gog— is there anything in that right-hand corner?"

"Nothing. Bupkus."

"God, this is so weird."

"You ain't shittin'."

Strode nodded as much as the suit would let him. "Well, it's not like we were expecting it to turn normal at this point."

"Okay—we're going in," Gogol said.

"Do it." The team entered the hangar. Splitting up and drifting slowly across the thirty yards to the rear bulkhead, shotgun barrels high and rotating slowly as they went. They reached the bulkhead and Strode shifted the EV about twenty feet to the left, facing the open hatch.

Cruz and Kieran were clambering around the hangar examining niches and equipment for any more surprises. "Clear," Cruz called at last.

Strode eyed the hangar, the assault team covering the airlock in the rear. He'd had a mild argument with Klaus about this—the colonel didn't like the idea of the EV actually entering the ship. But Strode just couldn't shake his mind of the image of the *Rokossovsky* taking off and leaving him with no way out. The colonel had at last told him to use his judgment.

"Bringing her in." He slowly slid into the hangar, coming to a halt about halfway to the bulkhead. Morris and Hinche climbed out to secure the EV. Strode unstrapped himself and grabbed for the case of claymores. At the hatch, he paused to glance at the bulkheads, the lock, the signs in Cyrillic, wondering if they'd find any answer to the question as to why a Soviet nuclear impulse vessel would head halfway across the solar system instead of parking itself at L5 as it had been ordered to do.

It took them a quarter hour to clear the hangar level. At six hundred feet long, the *Rokossovsky* had a lot of nooks, crannies, and corners that had to be looked at. Much of it on that level was parts storerooms, work spaces, and the like, large and packed with all sorts of stuff. Atmosphere was nominal, so they raised their helmet visors. This had the added advantage of allowing them to hear their surroundings unimpeded by the thermos-glass.

Another problem lay in the fact that Russian boomers got a lot of modifications after they were constructed. *Rokossovsky* had been modified quite a bit. He could see a lot of differences on this level alone. It was a relatively old ship, as far as boomers went, launched in 1977, just three years after the *Zhukov* went up. It was likely that Strode had seen this very ship back when he'd been in college, maneuvering around cislunar space leaving a trail of white-hot nuclear fireballs behind it.

He got the team back together and they headed for the next level, moving "up" toward the nose. The CIC ought to be located in that direction.

There was no lack of doors on the next level. They stretched off a hundred, hundred twenty feet in each direction.

"Personnel quarters," Strode muttered.

"Yep." Morris slipped past him and drifted over to a slot beside the closest door. Morris was G2, and could actually read the god-awful Cyrillic alphabet. "These are names."

"Okay." Strode gestured up and down the hall. "Let's clear 'em."

The first one he checked was the standard bunkie, larger than the ones on the *LeMay* but otherwise pretty similar. There were two bunks, unlike the singles on their ship, a couple of closets, shelves for books and whatnot. A battered map of Mother Russia on one wall, some personal photos, and that was it. As he was swinging around to leave, it occurred to him that they were doubled up, despite the size of the ship, so that they could keep an eye on each other.

He glanced up and down the corridor as he swung himself out and gripped the rail. The boys were darting in and out, none with anything much to report, as far as he could see.

Morris waved to him from the other side of the corridor. "You'll like this one. Take a look."

Strode kicked off and halted himself at the doorway before swinging inside. It was the same setup as the other room, bunks, closets, and so forth, but on one side . . .

For a moment, he was cast back to his own room on the *LeMay*. No maps of Russia here—the wall above the bunk to his left was covered with photos taken around the system. Valles Marineris on Mars, Pluto's Plain of Dis, the ice fountains of Europa. And there, the exact shot he had on his own wall, one of the most famous photos of the late seventies: the rings of Saturn, taken by Dyson himself.

A sense of something like kinship touched him as he regarded the photos. He thought he understood this guy, whoever he might be. Ah, "thought" nothing; he *knew* he did. It was the same impulse that had caused him to join up in the first place. To drop his potential career as a Deadhead for the USAF, with the intention of riding the boomers to the edges of the system, to see for himself the sights preserved in these photos . . .

Not that he'd actually seen any of them, spending much of the past four years on station in long, leisurely trajectories around the Earth-Moon system, on the front line of defense in the Cold War. "Somebody's got some soul on this wagon."

"I thought so."

"What's his name, anyway?"

Morris swung over to a shelf and deftly slipped a book out from under the restraining strap. "Ahh . . . Krilov. Anton Lazarovich."

Strode nodded silently. Bending closer, in that clumsy way you did in a suit, Morris glanced over the book spines. "Wow, this guy's studying everything. Propulsion, guidance, avionics . . ."

"Lotta books," Strode agreed as he swung himself out into the corridor.

By the time they cleared a dozen rooms, it was apparent they were going to find nothing. There were just too many rooms to search—not surprising on a vessel with a crew that could number anything from a hundred twenty to three hundred plus. They could easily waste the next two hours searching the rooms on this level and the next, which was also a personnel level.

There was a mixed-use level above that one. Strode decided to check that out next.

Emerging from the access tube, the first thing they saw was a cloud of what appeared to be standard 8x11 sheets drifting around the corridor.

"Paper," Morris muttered.

"Thank God for Intel," Cruz said.

Biting back an impulse to laugh along with everybody else, Strode said. "Okay, enough."

The men fanned out down the corridor while Morris

grabbed for a sheet, looked at it, and tossed it aside. Plucking another one out of the air, he frowned at it and clumsily reached out for another.

"Got the computer room here," Cruz called out.

Strode headed over to him. The room was filled with even more paper. He batted a clump aside to look at the hardware.

"Looks like a fuckin' museum," somebody said.

That it did. A collection of big mainframes with tape drives and readouts, all of them dark now. Strode shook his head. The PC he had on his desk back in the *LeMay* probably had more processing power than this entire system.

"I'm surprised they're not using abacuses," Cruz said.

Strode waved at the mainframes. "This is all IBM equipment."

"Really?"

"Yeah. Bought in false-flag operations. They don't know dick about—"

Morris had drifted in through the doorway, sheets clutched in his gloved hands. "How many nukes you think they've got aboard?"

"Well, it better be twenty-five," Strode said. That was the limit set by the Reykjavik Treaty.

"No." He raised the sheets. "They're talking one eighty-five on this sheet and . . . two oh five on this one."

"Pills?"

"Nope. Not kiloton yield. Fifteen, twenty megatons. They're warheads."

"Holy shit."

Twenty megatons . . . those were city-busters. With two

hundred of those, this single boomer could knock the US back into the stone age and go on to wipe out every Western installation in the solar system. Strode was beginning to get a vague picture as to just what the *Rokossovsky* had been up to. But it still didn't explain why this bird was bobbing around just within the orbit of Jupiter.

Morris gestured at the papers floating around the room. "Look through all these, find me the ones that got this emblem on top. See it—the sword and shield?"

Strode grabbed one himself, then another, wishing he'd taken the time at some point to learn Russian. There it was—a sword within a shield, star and hammer and sickle centered over all. The emblem of the KGB, the little friends of all things living.

"Okay," Morris was saying. "A lot these are duplicates . . ."

"We can sort those out. We don't have to read them for that . . ."

"Uh-oh . . ."

Cohn was floating above a big block of machinery in the corner, gazing at something just past it. Strode hoisted himself to a spot where he could see what it was. There was a fan of dark stains against the rear bulkhead. Blood spatter, and nothing else.

"Jesus H. Christ—they had three warheads allotted for *Moscow*—"

That actually made sense, if the theory Strode was turning over in his head was anywhere close to the truth. Kicking off, he headed over to join Cohn. The machinery he was floating above, half the size of a Volkswagen van, was apparently their printer. A block of paper remained in a hopper at one end, the top sheet fluttering in the air currents. There was a padlock hanging from a hasp on the cover for the controls. Somebody had sawed it open.

"They were printing these out here," Strode said.

"For what? To hand them out to who?"

"To the crew. Somebody wanted them to know about all this."

Cohn nodded at the printer. "Okay. And this guy . . ." He gestured at the bloodstains. "Got shot doing it."

"Looks like it."

"It's called *podsolnechnik*—Sunflower," Morris called out. "Operation Sunflower. That's the name."

Cruz was looking over his shoulder. "Well at least they got a sense of humor about it . . ."

A fusillade of shots rang out from the corridor. The men outside starting shouting and then returned fire. Strode heard the roar of shotguns as he headed for the door, struggling to grip his pistol with the oversized suit gloves.

They were still firing when he reached the door, two shotguns and one light MG. A suited man was pinwheeling slowly down the corridor in the direction they had come from.

Ardlino lowered his shotgun. "I got one. I swear I hit one of 'em."

"Awright," Strode said. He eyed the tube entrance where the attack had evidently come from. "Gog—you and Denny go up there and make sure that access tube is clear. Cohn, you go with them. We need a med . . ."

he began, but Naylor had already started after the tumbling suit.

He waited for the all-clear from Gogol and then got everybody in defensive positions. Morris was still going through the papers as if nothing at all had happened. Naylor joined Strode, letting out a long sigh. "He's dead, sir. Three rounds to the chest."

"Kieran?"

"Yes, sir."

Strode nodded to himself. "You did good, Omar," he said at last.

Naylor bobbed his head and moved off. After a moment, Strode glanced around him. "Page? Where's Page? Bring me the relay box, willya?"

He was reaching for it when all the lights went out.

"We've taken a casualty, sir. Keiran is KIA. This ship is definitely under control by hostiles." Strode squeezed his eyes shut. In the USAF, you didn't call boomers "ships." They were "spacecraft."

But the colonel had missed it. "Lieutenant Keiran? That poor boy. How did it . . . ? Well, that will wait. Ahh . . . I think you'd better return to the *LeMay*, Major. We need to confer on our next move . . ."

Strode made a disgusted face. He couldn't say he was surprised. Klaus had started out flying EB-47 electronics warfare aircraft out of Japan during the sixties. He'd later been transferred to tankers. A decade as a 135 pilot had given him a truck driver's mentality: stolid, cautious, and slow moving. "I disagree, sir."

"Ah . . . what's that, Major?"

Strode gave him a quick rundown on what Morris had discovered.

"They're not individual propulsion units?"

"No, sir, they're not . . ." Strode bit off his words before he could say "pills," another term Klaus didn't care for. "The yield is in the megaton range."

"I see. So the *Rokossovsky* was in fact some kind of backup for the Moscow plotters."

"So it seems."

It was as they'd suspected in the first place. It was simply too much of a coincidence that a nuclear-armed boomer had broken its assigned orbit and started heading for Earth at the same time that Boris Pugo and the KGB moved against the Soviet government. The Committee of National Renewal under arrest, Yeltsin shot for treason, people being executed in the streets . . .

But they'd missed Gorbachev, who reached a friendly Army base and rallied the people to resist the coup plotters. At which point the *Rokossovsky*, halfway between Earth and Luna, had lit off an entire string of pills and headed off in what seemed a perfectly random direction. It had taken the *LeMay* a week and half to catch up, at nearly unbroken acceleration, in the process using up most of its pill supply. They'd have to be refueled one way or another before they headed for home.

". . . we'll need to locate and secure that warhead cache." Or destroy it, if it came down to that.

"Agreed. You understand that we'll have to arm a warhead, Major."

"I wouldn't have it any other way, sir. I'd also advise that the *LeMay* move away twenty or thirty kilometers.

Their electronics seem to be degraded, but whether they can fire a weapon, I have no idea."

"And your next move, Major?"

"I'm gonna track 'em down and clean 'em out." A moment passed before he remembered to add, "Sir."

"Ah, all right, Major. Best of luck. And keep us in the loop."

Strode signed off. That last was going to be quite a trick. The hull of this bird was too thick for a headset radio to penetrate, so they'd been dragging along a relay box with a cable connected to the EV. Unfortunately, they'd about reached the end of the cable.

He turned things over in his mind for a moment, well aware of the team's eyes on him. Boarding tactics for spacecraft were still largely theoretical. In point of fact, this was the first time they'd ever actually been carried out. So this operation was going to be one for the books— either how it was supposed to be done, or how you never ever do it unless you're some kind of brain-damaged halfwit like Frankie Strode. "Awright—so we're not fighting the entire crew."

Gogol shook his head. "Nahhh—if there was a couple hundred of them, they'd be up our asses."

The others nodded and grunted agreement.

"I think we can take it for granted that they're KGB. Not combat troops."

"Used to beating up widows and orphans."

"More or less. So that's good. Now, they're going to be defending critical points . . ."

"CIC."

"Right. So we've gotta hit 'em there, and they know

we're coming." He ran his eyes over their faces, shadowed and distorted in the helmet lights. "Here's what we're gonna do . . ."

Strode studied the blank circle of the CIC entrance up ahead. The lights were still off, so he was using the lowlight slide-down goggles built into the suit helmets. They could lower over the wearer's eyes even with the faceplate in the up position.

It had puzzled him for a moment that there wasn't a hatch they could close, but after a little thought had realized that the ship's KGB unit would want open access to the CIC at all times.

He hoisted the pistol. It was a piece of shit called a Gyrojet, basically a handheld rocket launcher. It had the heft of a water pistol and he didn't trust it at all. But a recoilless pistol was still in the works, unlike the shotguns and grenade launchers the other troops were armed with.

He still had his visor up and was listening closely. He'd sent Heske into one of the air ducts. He had a spare conformal oxy tank and was supposed to toss it up the duct after ten minutes had passed. He was about thirty seconds late now.

On the opposite side of the ship, Kruger and Page were headed up a secondary access tube. They ought to be . . .

He heard a rattle that seemed to be coming from somewhere to his right. Immediately, there were muffled sounds from the CIC. He nudged Cruz, who has gripping the cover from the computer room printer. Cruz let it sail toward the entrance, assorted parts and objects attached with bungee cords banging against the metal bulkhead as it went.

Shouts rang out, followed by gunfire as the cover sailed into the CIC. Strode squeezed his eyes shut and lowered his head as the team fired four high-intensity flares into the space. The shouts got louder, the gunfire intensified.

"Let's go . . ."

Cruz and Gogol were already at the entrance. They slipped inside, shotguns blazing, just before Strode reached them. Strode swung over the edge and down to get out of the way of the rest of the team. He collided with a wall console with a *thud* and glanced around the space.

Four of his team—he couldn't tell one from the other—were blasting away at several dark figures silhouetted by the glare of the tumbling flares. They seemed to be well at home in mike, using the cover of the consoles as they fired back. As Strode watched, one of them was hit and slammed into the far bulkhead. He raised his pistol but couldn't find a clear shot.

The gunfire died down, both sides emptying their magazines more or less at the same time. As it started back up, one of Strode's boys was hit and went tumbling backward. Strode shot at a Russian, the round leaving a trail of fire across the space.

"They're cutting out," somebody yelled.

"I see 'em . . ."

Strode spotted the Russians slipping into the tube entrance at the far side, firing as they went. He fired again and missed, as he might have expected. Within seconds no further Russians were in sight.

"Cease firing," he shouted.

"Cease fire . . ."

The CIC went quiet.

To his right, somebody shouted the password: "White Rabbit!" Page and Kruger emerged from the secondary entrance.

Gogol sent two of the men to the tube that Russians had disappeared into. As they reached it, shots rang out. They sent a few shells down the tube and all went quiet.

Strode ducked as one of the Russians, clearly dead, sailed overhead. He glanced around. Two more Russian dead. Alongside the entrance, Naylor was working on their wounded man. In the flicker of the flares, Strode couldn't tell who it was.

Several spacesuits were hanging from what looked to be a portable rack to his far right. On the other side, Gogol was gazing down at something on the other side of a console.

"We got a wounded here, Chief," he called out.

Gesturing to Morris, Strode headed over to join him. He slowed down as he reached the console. At the other side, strapped into an acceleration couch, lay a Russian, his square Slavic face now covered with sweat, slicked-back hair strangely unmussed, high-necked dark coverall stained with two large patches of blood at the chest. Strode could see clearly that he wasn't going to make it. It was surprising he was still alive as it was.

The man raised a shaking hand. "*Krest, radi lyubvi k Bogu, krest.*"

"A cross . . . for the love of God, a cross . . ."

Strode bit his lip. "Anybody here got a . . . y'know, crucifix?"

"I've got one," Cruz said. "But I'm wearing it."

"Right."

Morris was bent over the Russian, whispering something in a soothing voice.

"*Krest, tovarishch, pozhaluysta . . .*"

Dolan suddenly slid up against the other side of the console. "Here . . ."

It was a cross, something Dolan had evidently thrown together just now, what looked like a couple of straightedges fastened with tape. Morris handed it to the Russian, who accepted it with visible relief and clutched it against his chest.

Strode eyed him in silence a moment. Grown up in some backwoods village, or an urban blockhouse no better than a slum, scooped up by the military and finding himself dying out here on the edge of creation. He'd want a cross, too.

He bent closer. "Can he talk?"

"*Chto sluchilos?*"

The man's eyes remained closed. "*Gebisti.*"

"KGB did this," Morris said.

"*Plekhov. U cheloveka d'yavol.*"

"Plekhov. A human devil."

"He's the chief political officer," Morris went on. "CO of the KGB unit on this bird . . . Part of a camarilla . . . that's a conspiracy . . . To destroy the perestroika infection, wipe out the main enemy . . . and create a new Russian imperium . . . a new Rome."

"Nice," Strode said. "What happened to the crew?"

"Mostly dead . . . Plekhov killed them. Some tried to escape in the EVs—he dropped a pill and vaporized them."

"Oh my God . . ." That was Cohn. He shook his head as well as he could in the suit and turned away.

"There was a gun battle . . . KGB having most of the guns . . . They captured the rest of the crew . . ."

"Where are they?"

The crewman's face contorted. He seemed to be laughing. "*Shestnadtsat'-V.*"

"Sixteen-B. Room number."

Someone brushed against him. It was Naylor, holding a syringe in one glove. "I've got some morphine for this guy."

"Good—one minute. What about . . . Krilov?"

"*Krilov . . .*" the man's eyes opened wide. "*Velikiy chelovek, Krilov.*"

"A great man, Krilov . . . he defied Plekhov, brought the ship out here, he . . ."

The Russian groaned and his head fell back.

"Major," Naylor said. "I've got to get back to Fenton."

"Give it to me."

He accepted the syringe and bent toward the Russian. It was obvious they'd get nothing further from him. As he gripped his arm, the Russian muttered something else.

"You'll find him with his bombs," Morris said.

He emptied the syringe into the man's vein. With his bombs? What did that mean?

The man's face went slack and his grip on the cross loosened. Strode patted his arm. "Sorry it ended up this way."

The crewman's eyes shot open. "*Vy ne zastrelit' menya.*"

He relaxed once again. Strode looked quizzically at Morris.

"You didn't shoot me," he said.

Strode swung away. A few consoles over, Cruz was examining something. He raised it and shook it at Strode. "Booby traps. They were working on a dozen of 'em here."

Strode nodded. He felt exhausted, far more tired than he had any right to be. He pulled himself past another console. There was a kind of board at the top for notes and messages. This one featured a number of pictures: Titan, Mercury, Earth from Phobos.

He smiled. He could guess whose station this was.

There was something on Mars that seemed to change and adapt as long as nobody was looking at it. The minute anybody tried to analyze it, it froze up solid as a piece of crystal. There was some kind of material floating around Jupiter apparently created deep inside the planet and then flung out into orbit, that couldn't be categorized as a metal or anything else. It was light as foam, harder than diamond, and superconducting. There was an ocean several miles under the ice sheets of Europa that was apparently the source of all those organic chemicals scattered across the surface. There was a brown dwarf, a companion star only a few diameters larger than Jupiter, less than a thousand AUs from the sun. Wonders piled atop wonders.

But all that had to wait. No hurry—they'd all still be out there. They'd keep.

We have to do some killing first, Strode thought. *Once that was done, maybe then we'll have time to look. If we don't have any more massacres to carry out.*

Fenton was arguing with Naylor. "Don't you go shooting me up with that stuff. I ain't staying back here."

"Mose, your shoulder's all fucked up, you can't use that arm . . ."

"I'll use the other one . . ."

Strode went over to them. "Mose . . . look at me. Tell me straight: Can you keep up?"

Fenton glared at him as if they'd been having this argument all too often lately. "Yeah, I can keep up."

"Awright."

"Gimme a couple codeine," Fenton told Naylor.

Strode raised an arm. "Gentlemen . . . assemble."

The team crept up the tube leading to the next level above the CIC, as spread out as they could manage. Cruz was in the lead, pushing an empty Russian suit ahead of them. It seemed that the suit rack was full of badly damaged suits (sabotaged, Strode suspected) that the Russians had been trying to patch up. They'd taken one of them, stripped some metal bars off the consoles and taped twenty feet of them together with duct tape (the material that would conquer the solar system), and fastened it on the end. Strode was betting that the Russians wouldn't recognize it as one of theirs before they opened fire.

The next level lay right ahead. Cruz slipped the suit out, then quickly pulled it back. There no response from up above.

Three of the team headed up the tube. Strode and the rest followed after they signaled all clear. They waited while the men made a quick examination of the corridor.

"They're demoralized," Morrow was saying to Naylor. "That's what I think."

Strode shifted toward them. "What about the rest of the crew? What if they cut 'em loose from wherever they're locked up?"

"Nahh . . ." Morrow shook his head.

"You don't think they'll fight for, y'know, Holy Mother Russia?"

"Rodina. That's what they call it. Mother Russia."

"Okay, the Rodina."

"Yeah—they'd do that. But they ain't gonna fight for the fuckin' KGB. I think this Plekhov is caught between a rock and a hard place."

"Well, I hope—"

Cohn appeared at his elbow. "We've got a large door up there with 16V on it. Is that the one the kid was talking about downstairs?"

"Could be." Strode reached for the rail and gave himself a push. "Let's take a look."

Dolan and Cruz were waiting by the door. Strode got everybody arranged, Dolan with his ZG SAW aimed at the door, the rest at either side.

It took Cruz a couple of minutes to wrestle with the handle. Somebody had strapped it down tight.

The door slid open. Dolan stood staring for a moment then let the barrel of his weapon drop. "Oh, Jesus, Mary, and Joseph."

Strode shifted to where he could see inside. All he could make out at first was shapes drifting in darkness. He impatiently flicked on his helmet light.

He gasped without will, without a thought in his head. Before them floated a shoal of dead men, most wearing the same coverall as the Russian down in the CIC, a few in officers' uniforms. Many of their faces were covered with blood, sticking to the skin the way it did in mike. There seemed to be dozens of them.

"What the fuck . . ."

"They decompressed these guys," Morris whispered. "They opened this room to vacuum."

"What *are* these fuckers?"

"I dunno, Micky," Strode said. "I dunno."

He gestured Cruz to close the door. It took him several tries.

A moment passed before Strode remembered to shut his light off.

"Let's finish this."

It wasn't clear where the KGB quarters would be—they were never marked as such on the blueprints. All they knew was that the Gebisti, as the Russian called them, were quartered apart from the crew, and that they held complete control of the ship's nukes.

All the same, it happened exactly the way that Strode thought it would. So certain was he, he had the claymores strapped to his belt free and armed even as the gunshots on the level above them started tearing into the Russian suit emerging from the tube.

Strode tossed the claymores ahead of him and then hugged the side of the tube. There was a flash, a concussion, and a *thud* against his Kevlar vest that left him breathless for a moment. Someone up above started screaming. Then the team burst out of the tube, guns ablaze as they raked the area where the flashes had been coming from.

Strode pulled his way up, favoring his right side. The claymore shot had cracked a rib or two, at the very least. At the top he saw three dead Russians turning in the corridor.

"Three others," Cruz said. "They went through that door."

The team was already after them. Pausing to one side, Gogol tossed a concussion grenade through the door. As it exploded he stepped inside, followed by Heske and Page. Strode moved after them.

Gunfire erupted almost immediately. Strode squinted against the flashes. A Russian flew backward, gun slipping from his hand. Gogol moved past him, kicking him aside. The place was something of a warren, a lot of doors and doglegs.

Just beyond one of them, a Russian crouched with one hand gripping his side, the other raised in front of his face. Strode had a single glimpse of terrified blue eyes as Gogol raised his shotgun and without a word opened fire. He kept pulling the trigger until the gun was empty.

Morris stepped past him and examined the dead man's coverall. It took a moment amid all the blood. "This isn't Plekhov either," he said.

"Okay," Strode said. "Let's watch our steps."

They moved on into an open space. Morris pointed at the door on the far side. "That's KGB quarters."

Strode eyed the Cyrillic lettering on the door. "Is that what it says?"

"No—it says '*zapreshchennyy.*' 'Forbidden.' That can only mean one thing."

The door was locked. Strode sent a couple men back

to search the corpses for keys. They returned with two sets.

The third key opened the door . "Careful," Strode said, hoisting the Gyrojet. "He may well be in here."

He wasn't. The quarters, slightly more impressive than the ones below, were empty. They went from room to room until they spotted the international radiation trefoil.

"Here it is," Morris whispered. He examined the door. "It's got two locks."

"They're using the double-key system."

"Right."

Strode handed him one set. Once they found the keys that fit, Strode counted off and they turned them simultaneously. The door slid open.

Glancing inside, Strode spotted a small package floating in midair accompanied by a couple of tools. Others were strapped on the bulkhead near the door at the far end. He saw a coded lock with a keypad on the door but it was dark—somebody had disabled it.

He and Morris moved toward the door. Strode batted aside the package, a pack of Russian cigarettes. Morris reached for a box strapped to the wall. "Geiger counter." He switched it on.

He jerked his hand back as the counter started chattering wildly, with almost no space between the clicks. He gazed wild-eyed at Strode. "Something's wrong."

Strode stared at the closed door. He licked his lips. With a single jerk on the railing, he pulled himself toward it.

The door swung wide. In the glow of his helmet light, he spotted open bomb casings, the wiring and parts scattered around the space. And beyond them . . .

He stepped farther inside. A man lay strapped on a makeshift couch. His skin was dead white, his lips red with blood, his scalp nearly hairless. Strode thought he was dead until the eyes opened wide and one hand rose gripping a mechanism with wires trailing to an intact bomb lying behind him.

Strode's voice came as a shout. "I am Major Francis Strode, USAF . . . I am here at the request of Mikhail Gorbachev . . ."

Krilov died two hours later. They spoke to him over the intercom—anybody who spent any time at all in that room would be as sick as he was.

After that they were busy—stripping the ship of its pills, getting it aligned, at last wrecking what remained of its control system.

Before they left, he made one last effort to contact Plekhov—for the record, if nothing else.

"You'll be alone," Morris called out over the intercom, as Strode told him what to say. "Everybody else is dead. You'll have no chance.

"This ship is aimed at Jupiter. In a few weeks, it will dive into the atmosphere, and there is nothing you can do to stop it."

That had been decided back in Washington, to calm any potential Russian paranoia. They had never caught up with the *Rokossovsky*. It had lit off for Jupiter as they approached, leaving them behind. That's how the record would read, anyway.

"You've got five minutes, Plekhov. Then we're gone."

That five minutes passed slowly, and in dead

silence. They left Plekhov behind and headed back to the ship.

Strode sat in the observation deck, his ribs bandaged, dead with exhaustion, unable to think very straight at all. The only thing he knew was that he'd had a brush with something that he'd long thought existed nowhere in this world. He thought of endings, and how they were sometimes transformed into beginnings. He thought about the ship he was watching plunging past the rings and into the great frozen cloud that was Jupiter. He thought of Titan, and Mars, and places as yet without names. He thought of the promise he had made to Anton Lazarovich.

A light-off warning sounded, and Strode closed his eyes. Five seconds later his eyelids flashed red. When he opened them once more, the *Rokossovsky* was gone.

I will see it all for both of us, he promised one more time, and went to get some sleep.

❈　　❈　　❈

J.R. Dunn is the author of the novels *This Side of Judgment*, *Days of Cain*—widely hailed as one of the most powerful time-travel novels to deal with the Holocaust—and *Full Tide of Night*. He was the long-time associate editor of *The International Military Encyclopedia* and is now an editor at *The American Thinker*. His nonfiction appears regularly on Baen.com.

HATE IN THE DARKNESS

Michael Z. Williamson

The perfectly executed move in art, sport, or war often seems effortless, an act of Napoleonic genius or Alexander-like daring and guile. But as most artists know, grace comes from planning, practice, and cunningly concentrated resources. Ships may be massively powerful, and insults, anger, and tenacity may abound. But sometimes the real resource is the ability to weigh the odds and calculate the best moves. At those times, no resource is more important to marshal than a calm and collected mind. Battles and, oftentimes, the fates of civilizations themselves, can turn on one man thinking clearly.

❀

Space is deeper than most people can grasp, even those who work and live in it. Star systems are islands. One can hop between those islands in days, with enough power and a jump point or phase drive. Doing it the long way requires even more power, and literal decades to centuries of time.

Which means those vast gulfs of scattered dust,

subspace matter, and scarce chunks of rock or frozen gas are devoid of anything of interest to anyone not a specific class of scientist.

Except a fleet of military ships hiding for their lives.

Freehold Military Ship *Malahayati* departed the remotest berth in human history, isolated in interstellar space at a location provided only to two of her officers, with instructions to scramble and destroy the data if the ship were captured. The idea of capturing a ship was ridiculous, except it had happened twice, both times to the enemy from Earth. One had been threatened into submitting, the other boarded through subterfuge by an elite team, and turned back on its former owners, until being claimed by yet a third party.

Malahayati was a destroyer, equipped with her own star drive, not dependent on a tow from a fleet carrier. She could operate independently, but would be woefully outnumbered and outgunned anywhere in UN space. She wasn't going to fight head-to-head.

Instead, she was going to live up to her nickname of *Hate*, and strike hard and fast in enemy territory.

Earth's fleet was numerous and well-supplied, though limited to and bottlenecked by the jump points between systems. The Freehold ships were few, with little backup, no major resupply and no defensible bases. The war wasn't being fought head-to-head.

Until now, *Malahayati* had ferried stealth intel boats around using her phase drive. She could go virtually anywhere, though there were few places worth going that weren't covered by jump points. It did mean she was less predictable, however.

Then the astro engineers had built a clandestine base, in deep space, where no jump points reached and which only a phase-drive ship with the proper astrogation could locate. It was nowhere, near nothing, with cold, distant stars the only scenery, and four warships the only company. Fewer than ten officers present knew where they were.

Astrogator Lieutenant Malin Metzger was one of them.

He was on this mission because of his mathematical skill. The proposed mission involved rapidly evolving four-dimensional geometric zones. After the strike, whatever Earth forces were available would try to hunt and kill the Freehold ship. The Freeholders had to fight, but they dare not lose any ships if it could be avoided. On the fly, he'd have to calculate zones of threat, velocity, evasion. He would be de facto commander during the operation.

Once clear of the station, *Malahayati* boosted long and hard at 1.5 G, building up velocity to use later. Crews cycled through watches as she accelerated endlessly, her power plant humming near full power. A supplemental fueling craft, precious and necessary, ensured she had full capacity once at speed. It detached and braked for reuse.

Captain Commander Hirsch was half-visible through the display tank in the pie-shaped C-deck. The command crew all had the battle display to share, and their own overhead displays for task-specific matters. Technical staff were a half deck below.

Hirsch said, "Proceed with mission." He wrote his departure order into the log, and it appeared on Metzger's display.

Warrant Leader Jaqui Tung on the helm said, "Sir, I am ready."

The captain flashed his maneuvers to her display, and she took it from there.

"All hands prepare for transition . . . phase entry imminent . . . Maneuver commencing."

There was really little to see or say. She had her sticks and display, and she made the warship move. He felt a momentary odd sensation, very déjà vu-like, only over his whole body, as they entered phase drive. That was it.

All the drama would be at the terminal end, and most of it merely mathematical figures.

Metzger reviewed his op-plan. It was content-heavy, and filled his screens, the hologramatic space in front of him, and the chart display. There would hopefully be minor updates in-system, but what they had was what the assault was based on.

More important than the assault was the evasion-and-escape phase afterward. He'd instruct Tung if he could. He might have to take instantaneous control or engage the AI to avoid eating all the missiles he was sure any Earth ships would throw at them.

He then closed and darkened his station, and reclined in his G couch. He'd spend most of the mission lying in it.

With medical help he slept. It was productive sleep, but not enjoyable. It was a military necessity and felt like it. Three divs, just under eight Earth hours later, his system woke him.

Captain Hirsch said, "Welcome back, Metzger. Are you ready to commence?"

"Sir, I am. I have the deck and the conn."

"They are yours."

They precipitated far out of Earth's normal routes, deep in the Kuiper Belt. They'd planned their original acceleration to give them the velocity they needed here. They were near five percent of c, devoid of most emissions, plunging in-system fast enough to wipe life off a planet if they didn't mind sacrificing themselves in the process.

They'd prefer not to do that. Nor would Earth, any inhabited planet, or major habitat let anything in such a trajectory impact. But that depended on detecting an approach, which was based on the assumption such an object would be reflective or under power, not a mostly black body against a mostly black background. Only planets had enough sensor area for that kind of defense. Habitats were vulnerable.

They fell in-system, taking only Earth hours to transit what would normally take days.

As they shot in, ship systems were reduced in power. The engines were shut down, reactors at standby, generating only enough for life support and basic operation, thermal leakage radiating aft. They needed to conserve energy for later, and minimize any outputs at all now.

Hate wasn't invisible. Her outer hull was going to radiate at some temperature warmer than 3 K. Part of the mission profile, while they weren't under thrust, was to put miniscule puffs of liquid helium out on the hull to cool that spectrum.

Playing the odds on someone else's sensor skill was part

of the operational planning. It didn't make Metzger any happier . . . even if the inverse-square law worked in their favor.

For now.

Metzger rested again under mild tranqs to maximize his function time later.

He woke on schedule, went below and refreshed himself and ate, and dragged back through the passage to C-Deck.

Once ensconced, he donned headset, visor, and touch gloves, brought up his screens, then waited. He attempted to appear casual, but was tense inside. This was it. And there was the time tick. It pinged all the command crew, and the ship came alive, even if not under power.

"Battle stations, battle stations. All hands as assigned and stand by for low emission protocols."

Metzger settled farther into his G couch. Even at their current insane velocity, he expected to lie here most of a day, with a very quick head break or two, and have food delivered.

If they'd miscalculated, he might very well die here.

The first part was intellectually easy, morally tough. It was a declared war. The target was a military terminal. It was unquestionably a legitimate attack.

It was also, practically speaking, a rear-echelon facility that never expected anything beyond sabotage. A major combat strike wasn't something they were prepared for.

The trajectory was clean, their ship all but invisible. The captain's orders gave Metzger final approval over launch, because it used his figures. The attack had been planned by himself, Hirsch, and the Strategic Office aboard the station. Everything that followed, though, was done with his calculations and his input. The execution was his.

He was about to kill a lot of people.

Their people had killed a lot of his people in his system, even if these individuals hadn't personally done it.

But they hadn't personally done it, and they were the ones taking the punishment.

It was time. He stomped on the quandary, secondarily unlocked everything the captain had already unlocked, and brought up his imaging displays.

He sipped water. He was thirsty now. He had no idea how he'd feel later.

"Separation," he announced. He thought he could detect a fractional change in the ship's balance as the drone, munitions, and impactor mass detached, but it was probably just a psychological effect.

Then it was back to waiting.

The station's active search functions should detect the Freehold weapons at a given radius, and not before. They were optimized for the standard range of orbital debris. Any runaway or sabotage ship was expected to show boost phase and be readily identifiable. *Malahayati* was a fuzzy nothing with near no emissions in the primary search band, as far as sensors went. They should not be detected. The infalling mass, however, would be, eventually.

Metzger turned command back over to the second officer, lay back to tranq out for a couple of more divs.

It was near midnight ship time when he woke, examined the image display, and checked status.

A dot showed their position, other dots showed the

station, two known patrol ships, several in-system cargo haulers, and the Freehold weapons' assumed positions. Slowly, as he watched patiently, the positions changed.

It was another long div of him staring and doing little before anything significant happened.

Next to him, but separated by a divider, Sensor "officer" Doug Werner said, "They just went hot. Their threat warnings are live. Subjectively." Werner was in fact a contractor who'd been conducting training aboard ship when the war started. Their regular sensor officer was somewhere unknown.

It was important to remember that what they saw had happened long seconds, entire Earth-minutes previously. The decision cycle would get shorter as they got closer. Though even distant exchanges might be unavoidably lethal, giving them only more time for regret.

The station's first response was fast and reasonable. An energy battery fired, and seconds of travel time later, a massive energy flux vaporized the incoming threat.

Which flashed into chaff that curlicued across space.

The second projectile was masked by the cloud, and didn't become visible to them at once. When it did, the battery fired again.

Then there was activity and re-set as one of the drone-launched missiles arrived on a completely different trajectory. Another battery fired, and another plasma flare lit the space. It was an expensive decoy, almost a ship itself, but the growing background clutter was degrading the station's ability to respond.

It was obvious to the station command that this was a deliberate assault. They sent out an open broadcast.

"Station Control to all vessels, we appear to be under attack. Remain clear of the Docking Control Zone and stand by to provide support. Gather any intel available and forward."

Watching their defense collapse was fascinating but tragic. Their tactics assumed rogue space debris or a critically damaged ship on collision course. There were plans in place to deal with a sabotage or suicide mission. There was no way they could yet have prepared for a non-jump-point entry by a warship that evaded all interception options.

The entire strategy of system defense was being rewritten right now.

Then the third frontal warhead arrived, too close for them to do much. They tried to destroy it, but it was designed to and did detonate close enough for a wave front that lit their shields with overload and scattered more metal dust. It was probably beautiful and terrifying up close. Here, it was numbers and icons in the airspace of Metzger's display.

The decoy's trailing booster stage detonated, a pure dummy, but close enough to require more reaction. Then a mass of lithic warheads, rocks, hammered down from behind the chaff screening, followed by one last warhead.

This one was a killer. It was an antimatter-triggered fusion device visible all the way out here, with a detectable radiation front. It flashed in the entire spectrum, even in visual range. It detonated close enough to melt some of the superstructure, and drive that vaporized material through the rest of the station.

What had been a UN spacedock was melted vapor and

shattered debris. Thousands of people and three ships still docked no longer existed. Hundreds died within the next several seconds, some few having just enough time to cry "Mayday!" into the void. Then silence reigned. The debris disappeared from sensors as it cooled into slag and ash, dispersing into the Kuiper Belt.

At least it was a clean death, he reassured himself. They might have had time to be scared. They probably wouldn't have felt a thing when it actually happened. Boiled, crushed or overloaded by enough radiation to cook every neuron instantly. Anyone else suffocated within seconds.

Captain Hirsch said, "Well done."

"Thank you, sir," he agreed. For warfare, it was well done. It was also something they could probably do again. Until the UN had phase drives installed, they couldn't use the tactic, as they'd found out disastrously when they tried to "clandestinely" enter the Grainne system proper through the jump point.

He'd just killed several thousand people who had no idea they were combatants.

The next few Earth-minutes were mass confusion as two patrolling ships lit their drives hot, started trajectory for the station, then powered down as pointless. If anyone had survived, they'd be dead before any rescue could reach them.

Probably, no one had survived.

Then the ships turned power onto active sensor sweeps and detailed analysis of all space around them. They would attempt to backtrack trajectories on the impactors and reduce their search cones.

The problem with space was that there was nowhere to actually hide. The second problem was the power outputs of a major ship's plant were significantly more detectable than distant stars, or local planetoids.

Captain Hirsch asked, "Sensors, can you get any commo?"

Werner replied, "Minimal. It's tight beam, little bleed, and encrypted. Senior Ustan is doing traffic analysis and looking for indicators."

Hirsch said, "So we wait."

Their current trajectory would have them safely out of system, well into deep space, and in prime phase drive options in ten days.

"I need a break," Metzger said. "Helm, please resume control."

Tung said, "Sir, I have control."

"Thank you. Captain, I need to walk a bit. May I have your leave? I'll be in the gym."

"You may. Thanks for your plotting so far. Please be ready for any notice."

"Yes, sir."

Metzger pushed and pulled his way aft, into the gym, and into the centrifuge. He could walk in endless loops, but it would work his muscles and burn off some stress. Being cooped in a G couch for most of a day was exhausting.

He wasn't the only one walking, but he took a brisk stride that had him slowly lapping two others. He recognized one of the engineers, and one of the weapons maintenance techs. They all politely ignored each other.

He'd just vaporized thousands of people, most of them not direct combatants, but support.

The UN was going to try to kill him and everyone he served with in response.

Hell, they were already trying to do that.

Was it worthwhile? Or would it just escalate to more nukes and kinetic weapons back home? Was it worth winning if there was nothing left?

Fatigue hit hard. How long had he been at it? Eight divs, almost an entire day cycle. Yeah. Rest and calculate, that was his life at present.

He was about to ping the captain for permission when an incoming message ordered him to rest. "If unable, report to the medical officer."

Moral quandaries aside, sleeping wasn't a problem. He made it to his cabin and collapsed onto his bunk with just enough consciousness left to fasten in against maneuvers.

Captain Virgil Ashton, UNPF, aboard the frigate *Laconia* twitched at the alarm. His first glance at the display showed nothing untoward in the vicinity. Helm was steady. Nothing looked out of line.

Then he saw the transmitted report.

Station *Roeder* was being hit hard. In the display, warheads and mass piled in bright flashes, overloaded its screens and smashed it to vapor.

Distress calls and beacons disappeared in cries and screams, then lonely silence.

Twelve thousand people had just died.

He tried not to twitch as adrenaline shot up his spine and he broke into a feverish sweat.

"Where the hell did that come from?"

Ahead and right of him, Reconnaissance Operator Alxi

said, "Sir, everyone is searching now. All ships, all stations."

It had to be the Grainne Colony, and it was a violent, mass attack far inside Earth space. And why hadn't Space Force acquired phase drive as soon as it was proven? It allowed things like this. Whichever ship had done that had avoided the jump point entirely.

Where was it?

The tactical display showed a trajectory that intersected the station at one end, and dissipated into space at the other. Somewhere along that arc, that attack had been launched.

Another image lit, the potential cone the hostile had taken after launch.

Fleet commed in. The admiral came on personally. Ashton straightened.

"Ashton, are you ready for pursuit?"

Ashton replied, "At once, sir. We have the track and can boost at once."

"Go. Frag order will follow."

"Yes, sir. We are in pursuit." He turned. "Navigation, Helm, maximum safe boost."

"We're on it."

Warnings sounded and *Laconia* accelerated.

Helm Operator Rao asked, "Are there any survivors, sir?"

He scrolled through the messages piling on his display.

He said, "There may be a handful in a tumbling section, and some in rescue balls if they can be reached fast enough. They were in the dock section."

"Does this count as a terror attack?"

Twisting his neck, he said, "Technically it is within the Law of Armed Conflict. They hit a military target during declared hostilities."

Rao snapped, "That's a BS technicality. Maintenance and support aren't combatants."

It had been inevitable, really, as soon as the UN had dropped KE and nuke weapons on Grainne. Sending second-rate troops for occupation hadn't been smart, either.

Ashton said, "Either way, we pursue."

"And then vaporize them." The man sounded enraged, his teeth clenched.

Ashton nodded. "Once we have that order, yes."

The Grainne ship was somewhere in that cone in the display. For now, their best pursuit trajectory was a shot down the middle.

Intel came in bit by bit.

Alxi summarized the Fleet Intel report verbally for everyone, even though it was in the display. There were a lot of things in the display, and they could be easy to miss.

"There was a lot of mass in that attack. The conclusion is it's one of their destroyers. Big enough for phase drive, but not one of their fleet carriers. Those are too valuable and too fragile. A compact, phase drive—equipped ship with mass load. One of their *Admiral* class. We've previously destroyed one, that leaves three."

Ashton said, "Good. I know their capabilities. Got them for review?"

"Yes, sir. Best known are on the display."

Malahayati was a destroyer, phase-drive conversion, twenty-five years old. Their frames were smaller and more compact than UN ships, mainly built around jump-point defense. It was still a bigger ship than his frigate. It theoretically packed missiles and beams, but wouldn't have been able to resupply easily. Two previous known engagements. It hadn't been seen in months. It was likely low on everything.

Ashton said, "Now we have to figure how much fuel they used, still have, and can spare."

This had to be punished, and *Laconia* was in a good position for it.

Rao reported, "*Quito* is astern, but can boost more. They're joining."

"Excellent, put me through. Shema, Ashton."

Captain Grade 2 Shema said, "Hell of a thing, eh?" She looked wide-eyed in shock, not fear. It looked odd on her North Asian face.

Ashton replied, "Yes. Are we going to try to bracket?"

Shema said, "First I want to parallax all our sensor info. There might be something that will show them to us. I've got your trajectory. I'm going to deviate slightly outward, just on a hunch they'd rather be on the outermost track to space they can use."

He said, "That makes good sense. Should I launch drones or waste a platform for intel?"

She shook her head. "I advise against it. We'll throw that at them when we find them. There are other ships that may be able to cross our scans and find something."

"Understood. I just hate to chase without knowing what I'm chasing."

She said, "For now that's all we have, but it puts us in a better position when we do find them."

"It does. Yes, ma'am. We'll funnel everything to you as we get it. *Laconia* out and listening."

"*Quito* out and listening."

Alxi said, "Sir, I may have something. An occultation of a star, and a rough trajectory, but it's barely outside the estimated envelope."

"Can you reconstruct a track?"

"I can." It appeared in the display. It didn't match either the estimated launch point or the current search cone, but it was too fast to be any kind of debris.

Alxi was good. She'd known where to look and found something.

It was his call to make. He made it.

"It's close enough to assign it as Unknown One. See what *Quito* can find."

"Yes, Captain."

Metzger felt he'd barely closed his eyes when an alarm woke him.

"Report to C-Deck."

He staggered to his feet and stumbled up the passage.

He was going to need a head break soon, but what did they have?

"They have us IDed," Werner said as Metzger walked around the catwalk to his station.

Second Astrogator Yukat was on duty, and she cleared the couch as he approached.

This was his mission, his plan, and he had to furnish the options to the captain.

He settled in to the still-warm couch and squinted until his gritty eyes focused and his muddled brain tracked. The trajectories showed as equations, charts, and graphical loops in the system 3D sim. The tracks were beautiful ballistic curves against gravity and real motion.

They all had potential intercepts.

Metzger addressed the captain.

"Sir, our options are decoy and evasion now, or continue ballistically until any pursuit closes, then conduct decoy and evasion. I had planned for a momentary diversion in trajectory toward jump point."

Hirsch said, "I recall. Do the latter. Any energy they expend now we won't have to fight against later."

"Understood, sir. Helm, my console has command."

"Understood, sir," Tung agreed.

He wanted to appear discreet, while being just noticeable enough for them to respond. This was why space warfare took segs or even days.

The correction for the jump point was simple. A huge solution set would accomplish that. This part of the set would actually get them there with enough fuel for a jump. This second choice would do so discreetly enough not to be seen. This one would just let them be seen, and give him the option of more visibility while still meeting the proper terminus. He mathematically shaved down a geometric shape until he had maneuvering options, minimum loss of fuel, and plenty of open space for evasion.

"All hands stand by for thrust," he warned, and pinged the message through text, audio, and klaxon. Thirty seconds later, his correction started. The ship boosted softly, .2154 G according to his figures, and held it for exactly 436 seconds. It cut to micro G.

Then it was back to waiting.

"Sir, request permission for induced sleep."

Hirsch said, "Absolutely. I'll need your brain at its best. Helm, take control."

Helm responded with, "Aye, sir. Helm has control."

Metzger shuttered his couch, pulled a darkened visor over his eyes and ears, and watched hypnotic red waveforms drift across his vision. His brain tried to calculate their shapes, while he felt warm and ensconced in his couch. He'd just figured out the saw-sine expression of one when it changed to another, and . . .

Aboard *Laconia*, sorted data piled up.

Rao reported, "*Mirabelle* just came through jump. They're on an almost-crossing vector, actually a very good position for an intercept, though tougher to get a good shot."

Mirabelle was a destroyer. She was almost as fast, closer to the hostile, and had better weaponry.

"Got him!" Alxi said. "Sir, cross-referencing ours and *Quito*'s scans with those from *Mirabelle* has him marked. Also, we apparently had a stealth boat behind orbit?"

Ashton replied, "We did? I wouldn't know. They don't talk to anyone."

"Well, they're talking to me now. Or rather, they're sending a very tight, burst-encrypted message to *Mirabelle*, who then tight-beamed us. So we're hopeful the enemy can't crack it."

The "enemy." That term hadn't been used much. They were the "opposition," the "resistant colony." After this, they were finally the "enemy."

"Is it in the display?" he prompted.

Alxi said, "It is now."

The enemy ship was moving fast, but unpowered, and that was a very well-designed trajectory. It took them far enough from the jump point or habitat to minimize visibility, but not so far in system to increase their flight time or expose them to in-system sensors or weapons.

Ashton called down to Engineering Deck. "Power plant, how much over max can we handle for a few hours?"

Commander Basco paused a moment, then said, "I can support ten percent over. Fifteen is probably safe but you'll need to sign for it."

"Fifteen it is. We're chasing this asshole down."

Another shape came on the display.

Navigator Mafinga said, "Assuming full fuel bunker, that's his possible trajectories to deep space. Once he hits the edge of that, he's clear."

"How much overlap do we have on intercept?"

Mafinga ran a cursor through the image.

"Currently over two hours."

Ashton twisted his lip. "Not a lot, but enough. Will higher boost help?"

"Sir, it will not. We'll eat through our own fuel."

"If we plan to wait for a recovery vessel, how much can we close?"

Mafinga swiped and tapped for calculations, and said, "That opens up options, but sir, I'd rather save that fuel for any course changes. We don't know how accurate these initial findings are, or what weapons they'll throw."

Ashton nodded. "Valid. They'll throw missiles, the

same as we will. He can't risk being seen and can hide missile drops easier than a beam. We can't pour enough energy into a beam for potshots. When are we in range for a firing solution?"

Tactical Officer Shin said, "Only about ten minutes to max range. But we'll have a much better shot in thirty-four."

"We'll wait if we can," Ashton decided.

Shin added, "I have an ongoing solution updating, sir."

"Closer means a larger warhead, correct?"

"Yes. It doesn't make a lot of difference normally, but in this case, the weapon mass is an issue."

He asked Shin, "Can we overboost the warheads?"

Shin said, "We can fake it with some additional jacketing. There will be more emission, and higher velocity fragments, but we'll lose some to the blast."

"Any hit will be a good hit. A few minor delays and he's stuck in system until we slag him. Do it."

Shin tapped info and swiped his display. "They're on it," he said.

Ashton signaled for his orderly.

He said, "Please have food brought to the bridge crew. Have our reliefs on mandatory rest waiting. This may drag out." He turned back to the command crew and said, "Rest breaks will be one person every fifteen minutes, with a junior officer filling in. We want to keep our information flowing smoothly.

"Let's fry this clown."

"I'm awake," Metzger said at once, before he realized there was an alert sounding in his ears.

He glanced at the displays surrounding him as the captain brought him up to date.

"They're in pursuit. I need your expertise."

"It looks like they corrected to match my anticipated course, and have deduced the shift since then. I'm determining any discreet evasion will be impossible. They've got us dialed in fine based on energy signature."

Captain Hirsch said, "That was my conclusion. We'd hoped to be farther out before detection."

Metzger said, "We might have been better taking a burn as soon as they IDed us, but we'd then be juggling fuel, too."

"Do you have a scenario to cover this?"

"Sort of. That one I discussed with you. Alpha three alpha."

The nature of forceline propulsion meant the ship had zones of speed, much like surface vehicles would reach speeds where energy to overcome friction increased dramatically to another plateau.

For now, Metzger made a course adjustment and applied a steady, low thrust to get them to deep space as quickly as possible. The math was simple. If they reached interstellar space before pursuit reached them, they were free. If pursuit reached them, they had to fight. If they had to fight, they had limited maneuver delta before they'd have to go ballistic and drift into position for phase drive. If they ate too much into their safety margin, they wouldn't have any star drive capability.

To fight, they had a modern electronic-warfare suite, but once within range of mass or beams, they had six and only six configurable warheads against their two pursuers.

"Okay, I assume I'm going to have to lead on this since it was my calculations. I'll need food, induced sleep between activity, and the medical officer to keep an eye on me. If that meets your approval, sir, it should be a half seg before they manage to do anything relevant. I'd like to drop under again. If they close within those parameters or seem to detach anything that might be a weapon, wake me at once. With your permission, sir?"

"Do so. I'll have a cook on call for whatever you'd like when you wake up."

"Right. Thanks. And first, head break."

He took care of business, returned and snuggled back into his couch, and waveformed back into unconsciousness.

He knew he'd been asleep, but all he saw was increasing waveform complexity and modulated tones. The machine was pulling him back awake.

Then he was conscious and removed the mask.

A glance at the displays showed a third ship, a picket destroyer, closing, though not yet in range to be combatant.

"Captain, I'm aware of the display. Are there any other updates?"

"You have all the data available."

"Understood. Helm, maintain your control for the present."

"Helm retains control, understood, sir."

It was embarrassing to be surrounded by what were effectively servants. Still, it was for his benefit as he drove this beast alone.

He stretched in place and probed at an itch under his shoulder where a fold of uniform had irritated him.

He recognized the Third Chef in one of the couches for support staff and observers, and said, "Chief Lalonde, I'd like a cocoa, please. Double dark, regular cream, splash of butter and half-sweet. A dark smoke ham roll with smoked gouda and peppered-egg filling."

"At once, sir," Lalonde agreed, and hoisted himself aft.

He turned to the surgeon, Lieutenant Doctor Morgan.

"I feel okay, a bit groggy. Is there anything you can give me for focus and attention without affecting my ability to sleep, ma'am?"

She took his thumb, pressed it against a metabolic probe, then checked the data.

"I will formulate something," she agreed.

"Thank you. Captain, I'm ready to resume."

He checked the plots and trajectories, looked at the astro sims for possible corrections. Those were based on the available energy-consumption figures for those ship classes, and *Malahayati*'s exact figures.

"Sir, I recommend we continue. I expect they'll shortly get a firing solution. I want to launch in return, wait for that incoming weapon to get to a precise point, then use that as maneuvering screen. If I time it right, ours will detonate after theirs, and that will be a second screen. Two maneuvers well-hidden in fuzz should dramatically increase our chances with little waste of available bunker."

"You're not going to hit them with it?"

"I think a near miss is achievable. I expect they'll simply evade if it gets too close, and we lose any effect. If I can judge when they'll maximize their evasion, I can detonate just before that."

"You're playing chicken with fusion warheads."

"Exactly, sir."

"Proceed. Mister Metzger?"

"Yes, sir?"

The captain spoke very carefully. "If you believe you have failed and we are pending destruction, please do not make any announcement. It won't make any difference. We fly until we win or die."

Metzger said, "Yes, sir. Though I'm quite sure I have the odds on this one."

"Excellent."

He'd better stay awake for now. He'd likely need more drugs before this was over.

Had it been most of a day cycle already?

Right then, the assigned surgeon returned.

"Here is your cocktail," she said.

"Thank you." He took it, she gestured, he chugged it.

It tasted like slightly bitter grape juice. Not bad.

"I may need to drug heavily in a div or so. To stay conscious."

"If you do, I have that standing by."

"Thank you."

Werner reported, "I believe the new arrival at the jump point is another destroyer. *Warren* class."

"Correction time?" he asked.

"We are roughly six light-seconds from the point."

"Understood."

The data showed on his display, as did the lag time. Whatever he saw had happened 5.94 seconds previously. That also would change as vectors closed.

Well, that limited his maneuver options. He didn't dare get closer to that ship. That was probably part of their plan. He blacked out an entire chord of possible trajectories.

Now he had to think about decoying that one, at approximately the same time.

It wasn't just the three craft in play. It was the light-speed delay in sensor response, then the much slower craft response. If any of them saw his maneuver, it would be a wasted effort.

Both trailing craft could be screened if his warhead detonated there, relative. He set that to remain a "fixed" variable, maintaining optimum position.

He could screen the other one in that fuzzy locus there. He might only achieve a partial obscuration. Damn.

"Surgeon, I need you to consult with the senior engineer. Specifically, I need to know how many frames aft we need to clear, and what shielding we'll have, regarding how close I let their incoming warhead approach before I evade. Captain, do I have your permission?"

She asked, "You are trying to avoid casualties by the narrowest margin?"

"That is correct. Microseconds and meters may help."

Hirsch said, "Please proceed."

Morgan nodded to them. "I will find out."

"Please hurry, ma'am," he added as she clattered around the catwalk. "They just launched. Subjective. It's on the way. Appears to be less than six hundred seconds to impact. Captain, please tell the engineer I need to know our maximum safe energy level on a single maneuver, and our maximum power output. Stress the comparative urgency."

Boy, did that sound calm.

At least it would be over quickly.

The captain barked, "Engineer Major Hazey, I need you in this discussion now."

Metzger returned to his task. If they'd launched, and he was getting a refinement on the missile because it was under full boost, he needed to drop his . . . then. Unpowered. By not boosting, his would be harder to detect, even if they expected it. That increased his probability. They needed a hit, he only needed a screen.

Really, at the far end, if he maintained sufficient delta V, or reached clean space seconds ahead of any pursuit, they won. The enemy only won if they hit him.

A blinking notice showed in his panorama, yellow and coded as Engineering. He opened it.

It looked as if everyone could move to Frame 70, and he had a shield-rating factor for the best field they could cast astern, plus internal ballast blocking. That allowed him to create a variable depending on the size of the warhead inbound. For output, the note said, "Emergency rating is one hundred thirty percent, but I'm willing to support one hundred thirty-five percent under the conditions, if it's under a ten-second burn."

He had to assume pursuit would want to send the most powerful warhead they could for area effect. They also needed it fast, however. Judging from that motion, he wanted to say it was on the high end of the spectrum. If it was less, he'd be more detectable if it failed to destroy them. If it was more, they were all dead.

I'm basing it on assumed flight characteristics of a missile we've never seen in combat, he thought.

That was all he had. He should drop the device . . .
now. Then a VDAM—Volume Denial Dispersed Mass
Weapon. It was only tungsten jacks, but the relative
velocity would make those into potentially deadly
projectiles. Most likely, the UN shields would block the
debris, but the particles might score hits, and they might
deny chunks of space to support craft.

Both were blown out by hyperpressurized nitrogen,
and had a gas "jet" for movement. It was little delta V, but
it meant they would be harder to trace to source, and
slightly closer to pursuit. They'd engage thrust
momentarily before impact.

Captain Hirsch asked, "May I assist in any way?"

"Not at this moment, sir, though the tube crews should
keep the warheads live and be ready to change delivery."

"They will."

He needed to actively fire at that third picket. It
needed to be the dirtiest warhead they had.

"Can they sheath the next warhead with something to
increase the fuzz?" he asked.

"Stand by," the captain said and turned to query.

He said, "Standing by. I will be maneuvering on
momentary notice. All crew should be restrained."

A few moments later, the captain said, "Munitions says
it's as dirty as it can get. Characteristics on screen."

He wasn't a munitions specialist, and he wasn't really
a sensor expert. He tapped both officers into the display.

"Advise me, please," he said, and flashed figures.

Werner said, "You want to keep them behind the sixty-
two percent mark of the radius. Assuming their gear is
what it was last time we did an exchange."

Munitions Officer Hadfield lit into the display and said, "This isn't dirty in the radiation sense. It's remarkably clean. The sheathing will create all kinds of high-energy fragments that will be a temporary cloud. You'll have perhaps point two seconds. After that, we'll be brighter than it, at that boost."

"Thank you. That really doesn't help my calculations. I'll be playing by ear."

He regretted saying that, especially that way.

He added, "Your advice is valuable. I'll do my best with it."

He launched the second missile and let it burn for the target. They knew where he was and would expect him to shoot.

The tumbled warhead astern was still functional, and pursuit seemed to be willing to risk it, or unaware of it. They were at full thrust, possibly six G.

"Our maneuver is going to be hard, violent, multiaxis, and hot. I'm momentarily going to use all power for thrust and kill everything else."

Captain said, "The crew are informed."

In the sim, vectors closed. That explosion would hopefully shield *that* cone, and overlap with that explosion and the other cone.

He set the system to implement his maneuver on that exact time tick, and stood by to override.

No, it was going to be right now.

Astern was a danger-close explosion. *Malahayati* creaked and popped as the reactor drove at 140 percent. Everything went black as power surged undiminished to the engines. They shifted, heaved, and rolled, G pulling him in three directions at once. The straps cut into him and he bumped his shoulder on the couch frame. Then everything went still as thrust stopped. Lights and enviro came back on.

They hadn't blown up, and the enemy hadn't blown them up.

"Stand by for round two," he announced.

Two more ticks crossed each other, the warheads he'd launched hopefully blinded pursuit, and as the debris clouds cooled, the engines hummed again, at 136 percent of rated capacity. It felt even rougher, with the vectors combining to make it very uncomfortable.

They were in a slightly longer, but much faster arc for clear space, and down a measurable percentage of their available delta V.

"Well done, Lieutenant," the captain said.

"That's only the first, sir," he replied. "My options were limited. Slower or longer trajectories would expose us to more fire, so I had to choose faster and or flatter, and they know it. We've gained seconds, possibly Earth-minutes. All three are still in the chase."

Ashton watched the displays. A creeping caret represented their missile, seeming to crawl toward the enemy's probable mark. Only when one realized how many thousands of kilometers each centimeter represented did the speed become apparent.

Alxi said, "There was possibly a very faint change in motion. It could be jettison of mass for moment gain. Or it might be a launch."

"A loiter missile, I assume?"

She nodded. "It would have to be. There's nothing showing yet, and an immediate launch would paint them."

"Understood," he said.

The other ships would have firing solutions, soon. One of them was bound to score a damaging shot eventually.

It was a pointless war, with the numbers the way they were. Grainne couldn't win. As brave as this attack was, it was worthless, suicidal, and only serving to piss more people off.

"Sir, our missile has positive lock."

"Good! Let's see what we're about to kill."

Data came back. Yes, *Admiral* class. *Malahayati*. The fact it was named after a famous Earth commander just made their claims of being independent even more ridiculous. Trajectory, thrust, likely fuel load available. Now the track matched very closely to what they had from the attack. And damn, she was burning. How did they get to .049 c and still have maneuvering margin?

The missile finished and detonated. There was a ripple of approval among the crew.

Shortly, the combined sensors should tell them what, if any, damage had been done.

Alxi said, "Sir, we have vector on incoming threat. I think—"

A massive explosion showed in the display, on the view screen and on sensors. *Laconia* trembled from the wave front against her shields, and several loud bangs echoed and clattered.

Someone said, "Son of a bitch, the fuckers hit us."

Chief Engineer Basco said, "Damage report: shield containment needs flushed. Minor rad damage in forward sections, including Control. Outer hull breaches, count three, contained. Minor damage to drive antenna two. We've lost about point two G of boost capability."

That was an amazing shot. On the other hand, the UN ships weren't playing hard to see so were easy targets. The damage, though, would slow *Laconia*. *Quito* would have to take lead.

"Status on the enemy?"

"Unknown, sir. We've lost them. They apparently maneuvered after either or both detonations."

That bastard.

"Someone else should have data," he demanded.

"Sir, *Quito* was in our thrust shadow, and *Mirabelle* also took fire, though only close enough to act as a screen."

"That devious bastard," Ashton said in respect.

He addressed his staff. "Make your best guess on cones of potential and I'll do the same. We'll compare. Start scanning immediately. They may be damaged, too."

"Yes, sir."

Metzger studied the available sensor information. Light-seconds mattered.

"Bogey One is down slightly but measurably in acceleration. I think we hurt them with something."

Engineering reported by audio and display to him and the captain.

"C-Deck, I cannot authorize any more boosts over one hundred thirty percent. I was serious on my limits, and we've strained containment. You'll have to expect that to drop on future high-energy burns, too. I'd say I'm not happy, except I want us to win. We have to be alive to do that, though."

"Understood, thank you, sir," he replied. Yes, it had been a risk. They'd needed everything they could get.

Gods, he was tired. His eyes were getting gritty, and his guts sour.

"I need something mild to eat."

"Banana?"

"Yeah, thanks."

He took a moment to color code all his envelopes to make it easier to grasp them at a glance. If . . . once . . . they got to green zones in those fascinating shapes, they'd be safe from intercept. They had the velocity advantage. Earth had three ships and less need to save power. They could call for refuel. Though much farther and they couldn't. They were reaching their own recovery envelope.

Worst case, we might take three more ships with us, the hard way.

They were incrementing toward green on Bogey One. It was going to get passed by Two shortly. If the UNPF was smart, it would stay in the race as recon, and he'd still have to deal with it.

He had three warheads, and three pursuers. He could drop five more VDAMs, and it was possible that had been what damaged Bogey One, though it could have been the warhead or even internal overload from the pursuit.

Someone handed him a banana. He ate it in three bites, then sipped cold tea.

Captain Hirsch said, "I would like to suggest you consider if further damage to Bogey One will cause Two to stop to rescue, and take both of them out of the running. Do you have anything against that?"

The captain was politely saying he was about to give an order.

Think. Think.

"Sir, unless we are able to damage life support or structural integrity, they can batten down on minimum and wait for rescue. I don't think we can reliably plan to effect that."

"You are correct. If that becomes a viable option, do take it."

He said, "Sir, I intend to cause as much damage as possible as we depart."

Hirsch replied, "And if we don't, I will cause them even more."

"I understand, sir."

Really, capture would probably be worse than death. Out here, very few civilian craft would detect anything. The UN could claim destruction for both PR purposes and cover, then do whatever it took to get intel out of every member of the crew, probably starting at the bottom. After that, space was an unfillable graveyard.

He asked, "Munitions, what effect would a VDAM have if detonated fractionally before and next to a warhead?"

Lieutenant Hadfield asked, "Are you trying for more ionization fuzz?"

"I am."

"It's not efficient, but it will work. You will get some congealed particles afterward, as well, but they will only be fractionally efficient for impact kills."

"Please configure the remaining warheads for that.

That leaves us two more VDAMs I can use to jack off."
The tungsten pellets were tetrahedrons, not quite jack
shaped, but the joke was obvious and common.

"Now I am hungry," he suddenly realized.

Lalonde asked, "What do you need, sir?"

"I know it's off schedule, but any chance of that pot
roast soup from last week?"

"I think I can have something in a few segs."

"Please."

At least he'd eat well as a condemned man.

Bogey One was going to drop out and be only a recon
source. There was no reason for them to play a game, and
they were farther back in the engagement envelope.
Bogey Two was continuing to advance, and would
eventually move out of envelope, if they didn't detect
Malahayati. So far, so good.

Bogey Three's course was going to bring them a lot
closer before receding. It was unlikely they'd avoid
detection, even with the oblique, almost skew trajectories.

He ran sims on when that detection might happen, and
what Two could do in response. Would it be best to
maneuver again the moment they were seen? Or use
incoming fire as another distraction?

He realized Lalonde had a bag of stew at his shoulder,
and mumbled "Thanks." He squeezed out a mouthful and
resumed figuring.

Calculations showed that given their own fuel margin
and established trajectories, any further maneuver would
slow their escape. The obvious fast curves would be
attacked preemptively. If he waited for incoming, his
available volume and options would shrink a lot.

"As soon as they detect us, we have to maneuver again. Realistically, that will be our last maneuver."

Hirsch demanded, "Elaborate, please."

Metzger ran through his reasoning and figures. "An immediate maneuver gives us the broadest envelope and them the widest search volume. If we wait, we have fewer options, and they will be slightly but relevantly closer."

"Understood. Maneuver as you see fit. After that, what is your call?"

"If they detect us after that, we're on a very tight fuel margin. We need enough to get us into phase, and to somewhere we can precipitate and expect help." If they dropped into normal space light-years from anywhere, it would take years for any message to get out.

"Please keep me advised on that margin," Captain said.

"Yes, sir."

If they couldn't do it, the captain was going to try to take at least one pursuer with them.

Really, there weren't any other options.

Metzger was the only one aboard who could prevent that.

"Sir, I think I can drop a loiter mine onto Bogey Two. The problem is, the residue of the detonation, microseconds as it is, will be enough for them to track this trajectory. Even with onboard maneuvering."

"Save it until you believe we're exposed."

"Understood. That increases the probability of a miss, however."

Hirsch acknowledged, "Yes."

"Confirmed."

Engineer Hazey reported, "Astro, we're losing

efficiency. Adjustments require shutdown, so you need to assume loss of delta V. I've got a chart for you."

Metzger looked at the chart and clenched his jaw. He added the figures and reassigned everything. The envelopes changed and narrowed.

Werner said, "Incoming fire."

Metzger scanned the tank. There it was . . . "From where?"

Werner said, "Unknown. Bogey Four assigned, not identified."

"Stealth boat," he said. "There's no reason they don't have them the way we do."

That meant another set of sensors they had to evade.

"So the good news is, I can not bother evading behind their detonation fuzz. We can boost freely, then go silent after our screen."

Captain said, "I'm going to work with you on this. We need as much boost as we can get without shorting ourselves on the phase entry, but we also need to appear to not be concerned about energy consumption. That keeps their search envelopes larger."

"I agree and thank you, sir."

Captain asked, "The next question is why they revealed that boat by firing."

Good question.

"I expect it's a loiter missile. They want us to think the stealth is there and waste resources. But it doesn't matter where it is. Just that it can ID us."

Werner said, "That may be, but I'm doing everything I can to find emanations or occultations that might show their maneuvering . . . and I think I have."

Bogey Four showed in the tank. It would have come from forward of the jump point, even forward of the UN base there.

"So they have a secondary base we didn't know about, and most of them don't, either."

Werner continued, "They also have really good missiles. It seems to have IDed us and locked."

Hirsch said, "And that's why they revealed the asset."

Werner replied, "Has to be expensive."

Metzger asked, "Do I need to waste a warhead?"

Werner wrinkled his brow. "I think you can stop it just with jacks. Add in flash and reflection chaff."

"Agreed, and done."

The charges were dropped in soft, deep vacgel that would make their signature even less visible than everything already was. All combatants were looking as much for dark holes in space where none should be as they were for emissions.

Captain said, "I have a boost solution for you."

Metzger looked at it.

"That only allows us two more evasion burns."

Hirsch said, "Yes. I'm trying to draw them into wasting power in pursuit, and minimize our exposure time. If they think we're in more of a hurry, I'm hoping they get careless."

His eyes were beyond gritty, stung with sweat. He could barely visualize the equations. Everyone here had stayed on with him. The entire combat crew had to be wired. Third Chef Lalonde kept bringing food and beverages, Morgan brought stims. In between, some of them got combat naps. No one was going to rest at this end.

"I have no reason to dispute it, sir. Just noting we're limited on future evasion."

He brought thrust online and the frame hummed.

Twelve seconds of light lag time later, Werner said, "They're boosting in pursuit."

"Good. Now we see if it works."

The burns had been carefully selected to this point to align them with Jump Point Two. This was to encourage the UNPF to concentrate forces on each side of the point. The four pursuers were hoping to chase them into a blockade.

It was likely, though, that someone had assumed the possibility of phase drive, since several Freehold warships had it, which freed them from the fixed points.

Now was when they'd find out. If the enemy all planned to converge near the point, it would increase the safety envelope when *Malahayati* deviated farther from that course.

Captain Ashton saw the emission blip. "We have them. Thank *Gemdi* for the assist. Cut to minimum shipboard expenditures and chase those bastards down."

Rao asked, "Why would they head for the jump point?"

He shrugged. "Maybe they were towed in-system. Or damaged."

"Would they still have jump drive after a refit to phase drive?"

He shrugged again. "We don't know. I think that's more likely than them not being converted."

Engineer Basco asked, "Could they have ripped the

phase drive out to reuse it, and plan to either lose this ship or slam the jump?"

That was a good speculation.

"Also possible. *Mirabelle* is going to cover the route to the point and prevent transition."

Alxi said, "Well they're visible now, and we're getting a lot more data. They can't win."

"No," Ashton agreed. "But they can't surrender, either. They're probably convinced we'd torture them to death or something, and they have to know we can't trust their intentions and will shoot to kill. So they may try to take someone with them. Between our ships, we have enough missiles. Fire when you have a solution."

"Will do, sir."

"Sir? They're firing."

Metzger was brought into a discussion between the captain and the engineer.

"Commander Hazey, is there any way at all to recover some of our drive power?"

Hazey said, "The only way to improve efficiency is to send an engineer aft to the reactor, under power, to make adjustments. They will die. And I guess if you're going to give that order, I'll do it, because I can't morally order anyone else to."

Metzger said, "I understand. We will try hard to avoid that." No, he could not request the captain give that order, not if there was any other choice at all.

"Thank you."

He said, "Then I guess it's time to make our last screen and burn, drop a loiter mine through the fuzz, jack off

with everything we have left, and hope we power enough
to clear system."

Hirsch said, "I see your envelopes. I have nothing
productive to add. It's your mission, Astrogator."

"Understood, sir. We will initiate this maneuver on my
mark. Countdown on screen."

Klaxons alerted the crew. Reactor power. Acceleration
and boost. Danger-close detonation. Stand by.

The weapons rolled out, improving the ship's mass
ratio fractionally. The screening warhead detonated, and
boost cut in.

Engineer Hazey was going to be furious. Metzger had
entered a command code to bypass the locks Hazey had
set in place. The program pushed the reactor to 141
percent of max, well over emergency max of 115 percent,
and his warning of 125 percent. It was all or nothing.

That boost tapered down to 125 percent, then 120
percent, then stopped. They were still inside the debris
sheath from their own detonation. Metzger itched. It was
psychosomatic, but he was inside a fusion explosion, or at
least the edges of it.

"They'll track us out of that, eventually," he said.
"Hopefully, they first think we scuttled, then draw some
wrong assumptions."

Engineer Hazey came into the net.

"I want command to understand I am very, very
unhappy with my recommendations being ignored. It
should be noted at this point, if another vector change is
needed, I will have to sacrifice a member of this crew to
effect reactor repairs. I hope it was worth it."

Hirsch intercepted the call.

"I authorized it as an emergency measure, and felt it best not to alarm anyone with the status, in case of failure."

Damn, he was a good commander. All he'd said was for Metzger to proceed and Metzger hadn't said how far he was pushing it.

Hazey said, "Understood, and I comprehend the circumstances. Now please log my objection for the record, because this poor beast is going to need an overhaul if we survive."

But Bogey One was now out of reach, and Bogey Two was losing vector. Unless they had boost they hadn't exploited, they were probably out of it. Bogey Three could still potentially intercept, though they'd strain any known limit and need recovery afterward.

Bogey Four was still unknown, but a stealth boat likely didn't have the fuel ratio for any kind of chase like this.

Werner said, "Our loiter missile just went live. Intel on Bogey Four and Bogey Three. Not a lot, but it improves the estimates. Bogey Two is now evading."

And with that, Bogey Two dropped completely out of the race. No matter what they boosted, nothing known would let them pull enough G to intercept.

"Well done, Metzger," Captain said.

"Thank you, sir, but we still have Number Three."

Ashton clenched his jaw against very negative feelings. Anger, frustration, fear, all boiling over.

They'd evaded the contact envelope of the enemy missile, and in doing so, lost any hope of catching that ship. *Quito* had maneuvered around it, being that much closer, but between fuel margin and the vector changes, she was unlikely to catch them, either.

He muttered, "Damn whoever is flying that bucket. He's in league with gods, or devils."

He saw the updated data in the display and said, "It's bad, but *Mirabelle* has them. Exact current trajectory plotted. She'll chase them down and slag them."

Helm Operator Rao asked, "Sir? How deep have you ever gone? Because we're going a lot deeper before this is over."

He looked at the plot.

No ship he knew of had been this far out. They were well beyond the heliopause.

"It's been an impressive chase."

Rao said, "Are we going to offer them terms?"

"Those terms would be war-crimes tribunals. They might win on a technicality. I doubt they want to risk it. They're going to run until we kill them. If they run low on power, they'll probably scuttle. I expect that ship is stripped to nothing."

Rao gritted his teeth. "Makes sense. We can't let them get away or they'll do this again."

"Exactly that. We'll keep scanning. Every bit of intel we get helps stop them now."

Bogey Three was moving farther into the green.

Metzger said, "We have a single warhead, sir. And a minimal amount of energy margin. We're already likely to need a tow and refuel on arrival home."

Captain said, "I see the figures." The two of them were the only ones with the coordinates of their base.

Hirsch continued, "Strip out any gram of mass we can spare. Dump oxy, water, anything. We'll use that missile as we leave."

The operations officer, Commander Cortes, said, "Yes, sir, though we already stripped almost everything."

Across the deck, Metzger could see the captain's gaze. "Then strip more. Uniforms. Underwear. Crew can manage in a single coverall. If we have to, we'll dump that. Shlippers only. Unclamp any backup equipment and have that standing by. We might need that more, but if it'll save us, it goes. If it can serve as reactor mass, get it in there. If not, queue it to jettison."

"Sir."

The order was given, and below, crew feverishly abandoned personal clothing and items, ripped out spare equipment, dumped containers. Reaction mass crept up slightly from a handful of material that was usable as fuel without reconfiguring the process. The rest showed on a graph, which corresponded to increase in delta V and thrust.

I've spent the last two day cycles staring at a screen full of math and coded graphs, Metzger thought. Most people would have no idea what they were looking at. To him, it was their life or death.

A short time later, Werner said, "Incoming. Can't ID the type, but it's got hellacious delta V."

Captain asked, "Can you call impact time?"

"Estimate only. The thrust is shifting continuously and apparently randomly within a range, more as it closes. We can't run."

"Can we evade?"

"If we do so just before detonation, we might spoof it."

Hirsch said, "Then configure that last VDAM and whatever chaff and decoys we have. Metzger, you and Werner make the call. Blow, jettison and boost."

"Yes, sir. Werner, what's our call?"

Werner said, "We'll have milliseconds in the danger-close envelope, and we need to call that conservatively."

"Can we evade now?"

"I expect it has enough range to track and follow. It's very active. We're zeroed . . . and now there's two more launches."

This was it. Either they reached that safe plateau in space, risked entry this close to the primary, or tried to evade high-yield warheads at fractional c.

Forcing steely calm into his response, he asked, "Can you give me a range on its expected detonation?"

Werner said, "It's on your feed. Updating as we go."

The missile showed as a dot with a glowing marker over it, fading from yellow to purple.

"Well, I think we can take a full second on the window. How fast can we get out of the envelope, allowing for response time?"

Lieutenant Hadfield said, "I think point five is pushing it. You didn't want to max boost again, did you?"

"Do we need to?"

Hirsch said, "Given your figures, one two five percent will suffice. One three five is better."

"One three zero. Split it." *And hope we don't blow up our reactor, or just render it incapable of powering the drive.*

Werner said, "Well, we're about to find out. It's on you."

"Alert, jettison and boost."

Metzger clenched up. G kicked, the ship's frame creaked, something thrummed as a too-close detonation caught them from the aft port lower. The dot in the display flashed bright, and figures scrolled. It was forty percent more than assumed, far beyond what they'd anticipated, and inverse-square law was their friend as they fled.

Aboard *Laconia*, Alxi shouted, "Detonation. I think *Mirabelle* got them!"

He then added, "Damn. *Gemdi* reports boost."

Ashton asked, "They got out of that?" The enemy crew were demons.

"Sir, we believe they were damaged, possibly severely. That missile got close enough they were in the plasma sheath."

"But not a hit."

Alxi said, "No, sir. That class of missile has been having frequent problems. A factory defect."

"So the contractors screwed us over again. The enemy is still maneuvering."

Alxi said, "Yes."

"So they got away."

Through clenched teeth, the recon officer said, "I admire and hate them at the same time."

Ashton asked, "What's the word on the rest of the salvo?"

Alxi looked at his display and carefully said, "Captain . . . nothing can reach them on their new track. All five will burn out and abort detonate."

"At least we haven't made it less safe with debris."

Oh, he was furious. They'd fired eight missiles and possibly caused some damage. Four ships were scattered across the Kuiper Belt and would need support craft to recover, taking weeks in which they were known to be unable to protect assets. His ship was damaged. *Roeder* had been lost with all hands, three ships in repair, nine boats in dock, over thirteen thousand casualties.

And the enemy was now at an insane .06 *c*, too far out for anyone to reach with anything. By the time any updated sensor info reached the in-system defenses, even those powerful beams would be too late. The request was sent anyway.

Then, as they watched, the ship contorted inside a phase field and disappeared.

"Command is demanding a report."

Ashton felt a ripple of cold adrenaline.

"I'll take that in my cabin."

Command would probably understand. The media and the public would not. Captain Virgil Ashton and his peers were going to be crucified in the press.

Captain Hirsch said, "You're keyed in on damage report."

The report tumbled in and Metzger caught the important parts.

"Eight dead . . ."

"Fifteen critical injuries . . ."

"Reactor feed damage, containment shaping defect, max power down to eighty-nine percent . . ."

"Frame damage, hull damage, contained . . ."

"Life support holding . . ."

Completely out of context, he asked, "Captain, what's the fastest you ever traveled?"

"I'm guessing you're about to tell me."

"We're at almost point oh six c."

Even with a modern, well-tuned forceline drive, that took enough energy to power one of Earth's continents for a year only a couple of centuries before.

Werner said, "Three more launches. Tracking five. On your display."

Metzger looked. The five all showed as colored marks, vectored toward their own tag.

None of them had carets in the green zone. None of them could reach *Malahayati*.

"We're clear," he said. "Barring something our intel didn't find, farther out than anything else they have, we're clear. Sir, I request permission to secure and sleep until phase entry."

"Granted. Well done, Astrogator. You are relieved. Don't worry about phase entry. Second Astrogator Yukat and I can handle it."

"Thank you, sir. And all of you."

He rolled painfully out of his G couch and staggered aft. The surgeon assisted him to his cabin and onto his bunk.

With battle damage, short power, and massive velocity to counter, they barely made it. *Malahayati* precipitated rather farther from the base than Metzger intended. They were four light-hours out. It would be ten days on minimal power and half rations before anyone would reach them.

Four hours was 1.5 divs. It was that long again before a response came to their report and request.

"Fuel and drinks on the way. Welcome home, *Hate*. Congratulations on your mission."

That nickname seemed to fit perfectly.

Captain said, "Mister Metzger, I saved one bottle of sake for such an eventuality. Will you do me the honor of serving the command crew and yourself?"

"Yes, sir!"

❖　❖　❖

Michael Z. Williamson is variously an immigrant from the UK and Canada; a retired veteran of the US Army and USAF; a best-selling and award-winning writer of SF and fantasy; a consultant on disaster preparedness and military matters for TV, movies, government agencies, and occasional private clients; and a bladesmith. He's best known for the "Freehold" universe.

THE STARS ARE SILENT

Gray Rinehart

With its shifting waterscapes, terrifying weather, and utter exposure to the elements, the sea has been known to drive some sailors—we won't say most—a little batty. How much more might faster-than-light travel warp the human mind? And if, to push a big ship through the gulfs between the stars, an astrogator has to simultaneously be aware of multiple realities that exclude one another and yet must exist in the same moment, who could blame that sailor if he senses a psychotic breakdown around every corner. He had better pray to the space gods, however, that the break doesn't come in the midst of battle. In that case, there might be no pulling back from the brink of insanity itself. In fact, when you have no choice, it might even help to go a little wacko.

We spun—spinned? span? spen?—no, spun. Words, grammar, symbolic thought were, are, hard to come by in

the tank, where all is, was, has been, will be, sensation . . .
inside-outside-beyond-before-during, always during. We
strode across our corner of the galaxy and we spun—
twirled? revolved?—and knew we spun, know we spin,
because the screaming stars move around us.

The stars roar out their colors, shout their X-rays and
radio, proclaim their presence in the universe, and we
march between them in time to their music . . .

Changeover was nominal, logs and operations in order as
expected—Khalid *was* an excellent deck officer—but the
lack of any replies from Fleet twisted Biermann's colon
almost as much as the slow progress repairing the drives.

Damn the **C**-drives, anyway.

If they got them retuned they could make for
Tristemon with all haste and report in person. From
there, the word would get to Hefner and Conmarra and
the whole fleet.

Likely their distress calls and reports hadn't been
received yet. The depths of **C**-space were sometimes hard
to reconcile with the passage of normal space-time. A
mind could guide a ship through its secret portals and
down its narrow alleys, but messages and data and other
ephemera often evaporated or arrived all out of time or
place. He'd spent the worst nine months of his career on
a stint in Comm/Intel, trying to make sense of jumbled,
jangled message fragments that floated up from the
condensate.

Of course, it could be as simple as that the regional
headquarters at Conmarra was collating theirs with other
reports. Whatever the case, he was glad Khalid was on his

way to break the news to Captain Norris that, in addition to C-transit still being down, engineering had fabbed only sixteen missiles from the asteroid they'd commandeered upon entering the Grendel system—a fraction of the number they'd spent at Descartes. The old man was already cranky enough, being trapped in sickbay while the grafts took on what were left of his legs.

Biermann switched on a confident attitude as he climbed the ladder down to the CIC. He would have found the expression easier to manifest had he been going up to the main bridge, but with the bridge blown all to hell . . .

Biermann knew he shouldn't fret—at least not publicly. Drives and weapons rated a lot higher than starting to grow a new bridge. At least it smelled a bit less like hot metal and melted plastic in the CIC than it did in the rest of the ship.

"Good morning, Tac," he said.

"Good morning, XO," said Sullivan.

That would be the limit of formalities for both of them.

"All clear in our sky?" he asked.

Sully spoke without turning around; after the Descartes incident she preferred to be heard and not seen. "An in-system ripple, toward Pyrite, just as we rounded Grendel. Earlier ones were outbound, and all at system's edge."

"Who's in the tank?" he asked. He knew it was Giordano, but wanted to see what Sully said.

"The Italian."

Sully was a fine officer, but not known for her subtlety. Doc had done a great job on her face, but the burn scars called for more regen capacity than *Tigris* had to offer

right now. What burned the XO was that the captain had
denied his request for a brevet promotion for her—

But that had to wait. Biermann played a quick-sim of
all the C-space ripples Giordano had reported. They were
hard to see in the display, the multiple dimensions
flattened so—observed rather than experienced the way
they were in the tank. If only that experience could truly
be articulated.

Sully was right: Most of the ripples were tangential to
the Grendel system, following the vector from Tristemon
toward Descartes—probably traders who hadn't gotten
word of the Kellador attack and wouldn't have the push
to change their headings before they emerged in normal
space and found themselves facing the squids.

But the last one, right before their orbit took them
behind the red dwarf Grendel, was directly in-system. It
was so new, it had come in while Khalid was briefing him.

Biermann breathed out slow as he noted the trace.
Tigris's orbit was tight around Grendel, and out of sight
of its planet for now, but the chance was small that the
new arrival was a human ship. Pyrite, the flare star's only
companion, was aptly named: It was a little larger than
Earth but of dubious value. The ripple *might* be a
smuggler or pirate, but the only easy systems from here
were Tristemon, Descartes, and KX-31, which was more-
or-less off-limits since it was a Kellador system. And this
track came from the general direction of Descartes . . . it
might be another ship that escaped the attack, but it
planted, watered, and tended a seed of paranoia in him.
Had one of the squids' ships trailed them?

Pyrite might actually interest the Kellador. As

amphibians they had a preference for watery planets, and Pyrite was a little over eleven percent water by mass. But it was several parsecs inward from the convex "edge" of the Kellador Lens, the volume of space that marked the intersection between the human and Kellador spheres of influence. The squids had never encroached that far into human space before. Then again, they had never attacked human settlements like they did around Descartes, either.

The *Tigris*'s orbit around Grendel was so close and fast that the star would eclipse them for only a little over six hours; he set up a holographic countdown timer and hung it above the main display. The watch had just become much more interesting.

"Who's next in the tank?" Biermann asked. Everyone reacted a little differently in the sensorium, and some were more coherent than others.

"The spic."

"Ensign Sullivan, is that a term of endearment?"

Sully snorted. Her close-cropped red hair waved an impolite salute and settled down. "Not a chance."

He chided himself briefly for not enforcing a higher standard of discipline on his watches, but he needed to have done so four months ago when he first came aboard at Conmarra. Still, he was content as long as everyone did their duty: Loyalty and competence were more important than decorum.

Biermann turned the display to a more convenient angle. He worked his tongue at a piece of dehydrated apple skin stuck between his molars while he swept through various options. They should be fairly well hidden from whoever had just entered the system; they rode less than five radii from the star, and even this dim star's output would mask some of the power their singularity set produced. Engineering was holding its output at thirty percent, enough to run fabricators and regular systems but not engines, and was supplementing with solar power even though their arrays were optimized for different wavelengths than Grendel produced.

He was glad to know that Ramirez was next in the tank; they needed a clear head synched in if ships were starting to vector in to their position. But at the moment Biermann and Sullivan were the only two souls in a CIC that usually held a half dozen, since Giordano in the port tank didn't really count. Descartes had left holes in every duty roster, controls were slaved together in sometimes awkward ways, and the only upside was that the steely sphere seemed more spacious than usual.

"Where *is* Chief Ramirez?" he asked.

Giordano's time in the tank was . . . Biermann pulled up the spacer's cumulative tank time to see how far she was from the limit. Her total was low enough—unlike Biermann's own, which officially precluded him from diving in for another month—but her shift time was already deep in the amber zone. Biermann frowned. *Tigris* ops were short staffed enough after Descartes; they didn't need to risk losing someone to tank psychosis. And it wasn't like the chief to be late. By now he should be stripped, masked, and getting in the starboard tank, ready to take the next rotation.

Sully said, "No idea, Lieutenant. I don't have a tracker on him."

The ship did. Biermann swept the display clean and

brought up personnel traces. He imagined his own chip vibrating as *Tigris* queried it and verified he was in the CIC. He chose alphabet, it was just as quick as sorting by duty section: R . . .

"What's he doing still in the rack?"

No answer; Sully knew the question was rhetorical. She was astute like that.

An incoming intercom icon flashed in the air above the screen. He touched the pip before the caller spoke. "CIC, Biermann."

"Ricky, this is Doc."

Brief panic surged in him, but Doc wouldn't sound so calm if he were calling about the captain. "Beacon" Lyles had been making progress, though; had she . . .

"I need to report a loss."

Biermann caught himself in time to sigh rather than moan; another condolence message to draft.

"Can you pipe the details up here in writing, Doc? Right now I need to find someone to roust Ramirez. It's his turn in the tank."

"No, Ricky, it *is* the chief."

Time seemed to stop for Biermann, the way it did when he was in the tank. He physically shook himself, from his shoulders down through his hips like a wet dog, to snap back to realtime/realworld.

"Sully, find me a duty officer for the starboard tank, now. Doc, what the hell are you playing at?"

"No games, Ricky. Chief Ramirez was found unresponsive in his bunk, oh, call it twenty minutes ago, and pronounced by me right before I called. Rough estimate, he's been dead two hours or more. Maybe heart, but I won't be sure until I take a closer look."

Biermann wiped his forehead and his fingers came away wet. "Do you have what you need for that?"

Doc coughed out a quick, sharp laugh. "Everything but time and space, with patients everywhere. But I'll make time and find space, at least for a quick assessment, then we'll wrap him up and put him in the freezer." He left unsaid what Biermann already knew: *with the others*. A lot of provisions had had to be thawed, and *Tigris* had many fewer mouths to eat them.

"Does the skipper know?"

Doc paused—long enough for Biermann to grasp that Doc had called the CIC because he, Biermann, effectively *was* the skipper while Captain Norris was incapacitated. Before Biermann could say anything to correct that impression, Doc said, "I haven't told him yet, but he probably knows. He knows I got called down to crew quarters. I'll give him the rundown when I bring Ramirez into sickbay."

"Good. You need me to get a detail to make room in the freezer?"

"No, I'll take care of that. I'll send you a report as soon as I have it. Doc out." The intercom icon flashed once, went gray, then shrank to nothingness.

Biermann vaguely registered that Mbali had come into the CIC and was talking to Sully, when another ripple entered the system. This one came in high in reference to Grendel's ecliptic plane, roughly from where KX-31 should be, and angled down toward Pyrite's orbital position.

"Shit," Sully said from the tactical station.

Two incursions in the span of . . . less than an hour? Both headed toward the only planet in the system? It smelled like a rendezvous to Biermann. And a rendezvous smelled like trouble.

He dialed in to Giordano's perception as best he could with the shallow-depth screen. He considered overlaying the automated C-space detection grid, but it never captured the same nuances that a person did—the programmers built it to relay the sensorium's output, but the multiphasic layers always blended together in odd ways. No one fully trusted the machine to make sense of the signal compared to the noise.

Biermann's interface plate, on the back of his neck right over the fourth cervical vertebra, itched. The liquid trail running down his back from it was imaginary, but Biermann shivered nonetheless as he glanced toward the starboard tank.

Mbali stood above the tank's open mouth like a child at the end of a high dive: He hadn't raised the privacy screen, and sweat glistened on his naked back and legs as he looked down, tentative, into the iridescence. The crystals glowed pale green from Biermann's tangential viewpoint, like the shallow water of some tropical lagoon, but looking straight down they would drink in light and fade to deepest black. Mbali stepped gingerly over the hatch rim, retreated from the initial shocking cold, then climbed down the ladder with slow, measured steps.

"Get in there, M-B!" Biermann snapped.

Mbali glanced behind him, the clear mask over his nose and mouth fogged slightly with his exhalations, then faced forward again and lowered into the crystals with more dispatch.

"Get him dialed in, Sully, we need him online—"

Another ripple vectored in, reported from Giordano's perception. Like the last one, this came from KX-31.

God, this is Descartes all over again.

At Descartes, of course, they had been in a powered synchronous orbit around the largest moon of Homeawayfrom, the system's innermost gas giant, not in a tight freefall orbit only a few radii away from the star.

They had come in clean, received welcome messages from the capital and from the *Uljas*, and slipped into an assigned slot. The skipper had sent the standard courtesies and invitations for delegations to join him aboard *Tigris* to toast Captain Gustafsen and *Uljas* before they dropped into C-space en route to Salem, their next port in the "Conmarra Circuit" rotation pattern. Captain Gustafsen wanted to delay the *Uljas*'s departure, because Descartes was a better port of call than Salem. As a joint human-Kellador world, nine parsecs inside the lens-shaped zone of contention, Salem was less a symbol of peace as the name was meant to imply and more a source of friction.

Captain Gustafsen's launch had barely moored back at *Uljas* when the ripples of Kellador ships started coming in.

Now *Uljas* was lost, Descartes was lost—presumably Salem had been lost some time before—and *Tigris* had barely made it out, crippled, on a run back to warn the rest of the Fleet. Who knew what *Uljas* might have found at Salem, but their delay and the fight they put up were probably all that allowed *Tigris* to escape.

The display convulsed in front of Biermann. Was Mbali locked in yet? Giordano should be emerging, but . . .

"That's not a ripple," Biermann said, "that's a wave." The traces were so numerous that the system now positively identified them as Kellador.

Sullivan whistled, as if she admired what they were seeing. She crossed to the port tank, waiting for the green light to activate the extractor. "What is that, a flotilla?" she asked.

"No," Biermann said. "It's an armada."

He verified that the tracks were converging on Pyrite, and double-checked *Tigris*'s position against the planet's. The ship would come out from behind the star in less than five hours now. He pulled up an intercom icon and activated it as several traces broke away, high and low. He held his breath for a moment, wondering if they would come in toward Grendel.

"Engineering, CIC," he said through the tightness in his chest.

"Engineering, Chief Ollecki."

Biermann spilled the situation as concisely as he could. "Any chance of getting C-drive back before we come around Grendel?"

The pause might have been diplomatic, or dramatic, but was probably just checking status. "Not completely, sir. We verified good alignment through most of the lattice, but we haven't applied anything other than token power yet. We have to spin up the singularity set for that. Lieutenant Gaines estimates we'll have the C-drives at fifty percent in about six hours, and eighty percent in twelve. Ninety percent will take the better part of a day."

"I don't like the sound of that, Chief, and I'm damn sure the old man won't. Pull everyone you have off everything else—and I mean *everything* else—and push that curve to the left. We're too exposed here."

It would be particularly true when they spun up the singularity set and it began radiating into C-space. Otherwise, a ship that doesn't want to be found can avoid it pretty easily. Normal space is enormous; ships are tiny. A disabled ship that *wants* to be found is a difficult target, even if they can make themselves look like a bright spot against the backdrop of space. Most beacons are directional, and if they set a beacon on a slow scan they have to hope that another ship's fast-scanning antenna is looking in their direction at the right time. The odds are against it, unless that other ship knows just where to look.

Biermann continued, "We'll have to hold off spinning the baubles much faster until we're ready to move, or else we'll shine brighter than Grendel to their detectors. That means sticking with our deployed arrays for now. Hopefully the only thing they have looking this way are coarse star sensors—but since Grendel's a flare star you *know* they have some other sort of observations going on. We'll yaw a few degrees to port before we clear the star, to try to minimize any reflection off the arrays." He pictured their orbital transit in his mind: They were much smaller than a star spot, but would cross the surface slowly enough that any observer would know they were in orbit and not on the star's surface. He said, "If we can't get the drives going in, say, four hours, is there any way you can task a couple of riggers to distribute some of that asteroidal material around, so we look like something natural? It's okay that we're three-axis stabilized, it just looks like we're tidally locked, but we don't need to show too many sharp edges if we can help it."

"Only if we stop extractions, sir, which means we won't be growing any more missiles."

"That's okay, Chief," Biermann said. "We'll never have enough missiles to take on more than a couple of ships. Just make sure the ones we have are rigged fast and hot."

"Aye, sir, will do."

"CIC out," he said and killed the icon.

That's when Giordano screamed.

Biermann couldn't see the port Sensory Enhancement Neural Interface Chamber, or S-E-N-I-C—officially "scenic," unofficially "cynic," but shorthand throughout the fleet as just "tank"—because the privacy screen was up. He always appreciated that, because the tank had the same effect on him that particularly good REM sleep had: He came out of it with a rampant erection.

That wouldn't be what Giordano was screaming about.

She sounded as if she were being doused repeatedly with scalding water: short bursts of pain followed by sharp intakes of breath, over and over. A quick glance at the display confirmed that she'd gone seventeen minutes into the red.

Biermann pulled the privacy screen off its supports and threw it down; expediency trumped modesty. Giordano had her back to him: she was on her knees, hunched over the hatch, and her screams had moderated into full-forced yelling into the tank.

"My legs are in there! My legs!"

"Sully, get—"

She interrupted. "Corpsman's on the way, Rick!"

Every case of tank psychosis was unique—even the same person had different reactions if they went through it more than once. Back when he was newly assigned to the *Vindicator*, patrolling the inner edge of quadrant IV of the Kellador Lens, Biermann had come out of the tank with symptoms of steroid-fueled Tourette's combined with the sure conviction that he had been poisoned and the only antidote was anhydrous ammonia. He didn't remember any of it, precisely, but he'd seen the log recordings. Not his finest hour.

After a moment or two of sobbing, Giordano straightened up and looked around. She stared at Biermann, and made a mournful tone like a motor straining to turn against a brake. Her eyes filled with tears.

"I forgot to bring the snacks," she said. "Someone else had brought Merinda berries but no one ate them and I picked them up to keep them away from the ants but while I was watching the ants the birds flew down and got them, got the berries."

Biermann wasn't sure how to interact with Giordano, if the spacer even knew where she was or who she was talking to. He held up his empty hands, in hopes that Giordano would know he wasn't a threat.

"Those birds don't even like Merinda berries, no one likes them, they're too sour but they make good pies if you add enough sugar."

Where's that corpsman?

Giordano sat down and scooted back, but was blocked by the tank's mouth. "Nana made the best pies, I liked the apple and cheese, but while she was picking the apples the birds came down, the birds came down, I hate those damn birds . . ." She brushed her hands through the air, slapping at imaginary birds.

Biermann wondered if the birds Giordano was talking about were really the ships that had vectored in. He hoped Sully was watching the screens and Mbali's outputs.

Giordano turned to her right, to the port bulkhead. "Nana! Bring my gun, bring my gun." She looked again at Biermann, and seemed puzzled by the corpsman who had just stepped up to Biermann's side. "A human amoeba," she muttered, then sighed like a pneumatic tire losing pressure. She looked down and brushed her thigh. "My poor legs," she said. "My poor legs."

The corpsman—Malinowski, Biermann saw—snuck up to Giordano's side. She stuck a dermal patch on her neck and said, almost too soft for Biermann to hear, "Let's see if we can fix your legs for you."

Giordano's head turned in an exaggerated arc, as if she were moving it around some obstacle. "Do you know where they are?"

Malinowski smiled. "Sure I do. Now, up we go," she said as Giordano collapsed against her. The corpsman was as broad-shouldered as Biermann, and hoisted the spacer with little effort.

Biermann nodded to her and turned away. She had her job to do, and he needed to get back to his.

※　※　※

Sully briefed him while Biermann pored over the status. Mbali was online, and the total traces into the Grendel system now stood at forty-three. Twenty-five had converged on Pyrite, which was bad enough, but eighteen had arrayed themselves into half-AU orbits around Grendel on three different orbital planes—and then gone quiescent.

They had to be doing overwatch of the system, so if *Tigris* so much as swished her figurative tail in terms of spinning up her singularity set, enough detectors would see her C-space emissions that they would pinpoint her orbit in a flash. Sully had already alerted the engineers to damp their systems down to twenty percent, which left Biermann to assess the strategic situation and their tactical options.

He was not surprised at the next call that came in.

"Well, Lieutenant?" Captain Norris said. "How do you propose to get my ship out of this jam?"

"Run like hell, Skipper, quick as we can," he said, and scrolled through icons until he found the captain's favorite book. "I'm pulling up the page while we speak: 'If unequal in all respects, be capable of eluding the enemy, for a small force is a prize for a more powerful one.' I don't have any intention of us becoming a Kellador prize, and we still need to deliver a report to Tristemon. If we can leap before they see us, we have a chance to make it this time."

Captain Norris's voice, usually smooth and profound, seemed almost manic over the intercom. "Doc won't let me come up and play, since I don't have two feet to stand on, but there's more you can be thinking about. First, if we'd made it all the way to Tristemon from Descartes we wouldn't be here and able to observe this buildup—so maybe getting the C-drives knocked out of alignment wasn't all bad. Second, go back to the Nine Grounds and think about them: The squids are in frontier ground, and if they press on they'll be in serious ground. Or you might think of Descartes as being the frontier ground, since it's closer to the Lens, so here in our sphere they'd already be in serious ground. Either way, they're extending themselves . . . and they'll eventually reach too far.

"But the fact that we're here may make this death ground, for us. And if so, remember: 'Invincibility lies in defense; the possibility of victory is in attack.' Now, get to it."

The idea of the Nine Grounds went all the way back to Earth, several hundred parsecs and many more hundreds of years away. Biermann found the chapter and skimmed the text, wishing his memory was as good as the captain's so he wouldn't have to look up the references.

Frontier ground was a sally into enemy territory, and serious ground was a deeper run at the enemy: One was advised not to stop in the frontier, and once in deep had to resort to plunder to keep supplied. It was a problem that had plagued invaders from the earliest wars, and the logistics of space had only made the situation worse. Sure, with fabrication equipment a ship like *Tigris* could catch an asteroid and mine it to make spare parts and components, or skim a gas giant for volatiles, but that was good only up to a point; the piece of apple still in his teeth reminded him they couldn't plant and grow fresh fruit as quickly, for instance. It meant long supply lines, vulnerable to accident and interdiction, which was why outposts and colonies, and even spacefaring vessels themselves, had to be as self-sufficient as possible and to exploit resources as they came available.

Biermann thought about Salem and Descartes being exploited by the Kellador, about what that meant to the settlers and their families. And if the squids pressed on from here at Grendel they would hit Tristemon, Hefner, even Conmarra itself.

He checked his countdown clock: two hours, fifteen minutes before they emerged from behind Grendel and had line-of-sight with Pyrite.

Biermann knew what death ground was, but he paged over to the entry anyway. In death ground a ship or an army, down to each individual spacer or soldier, could survive only by fighting. No alternative, and no chance of survival short of being the only force alive at the end.

Forty-three to one, and *Tigris* with fewer than a score of missiles, dropped that chance—of survival through victory—to nothing.

Biermann sighed. He had been proud to tell his family he was joining the Fleet, since his father had served under the Leonine banner for a decade himself. His father had been quiet, almost pensive, at the news, and at one point had pulled Ricardo aside. His father's words might well have been the captain's.

"It's old advice, but you shouldn't fight a battle you don't believe in. And you'll find that battles are only fought when someone believes in them strongly enough.

"What I mean is, every battle has people on both sides who care deeply enough to fight it. Otherwise, they wouldn't bother—and the side that doesn't bother will find itself at the mercy of the side that believes in their cause. There must be some minimum level of belief to sustain any war very long.

"But sometimes the only option is to fight. In that case you better develop the requisite amount of belief, and quickly. Otherwise all that's left is to surrender."

The intercom icon flashed a moment before Doc's voice came through. "CIC, Sickbay."

Biermann checked the timer: a shade over an hour until they came out from behind Grendel. "Who died this time, Doc?"

"Ha, not funny. I did a quick scan on Ramirez, and the captain thought you needed to know the results."

He glanced toward the starboard tank, where Mbali was standing in for the chief. "Was it his heart, like you thought?"

"Not exactly."

Biermann rubbed his eyes. "I don't have time for mysteries, Doc."

"His heart's not damaged like it would be if he'd been in cardiac arrest. But he does show a lot of synaptic degradation. Looks like tank saturation."

"That doesn't make sense," Biermann said. "Ramirez was under the line on everything, never showed any effects after a turn in the tank."

Doc said, "He had a couple of episodes before you signed on here."

"Severe?"

From the tactical station, Sullivan said, "Negative. The spic was a pro."

"Sullivan's right, Ricky—Chief Ramirez's reactions were always within normal limits, even the brief episodes he manifested."

"Holy hell, Doc, what are you saying?" He didn't want to hear the answer, but the obligation came with the billet.

"There's a good chance our SENIC equipment is corrupt."

Thirty minutes left before they cleared Grendel and, like the old saying, "no way out but through."

The projected tracks of the squids' observation ships formed a virtual cage around the star, but a loose one. Biermann knew the ships were still out there even though they weren't emitting anything detectable. It was only a matter of time before the Kellador noticed *Tigris*, no matter how low they spun the singularity set.

He called engineering, and Lieutenant Gaines answered. Biermann asked, "What's our drive status, JT?"

"We've brought the drive alignment a little closer to spec. If we fired up now, we'd be at sixty-two percent."

"That'll have to do—and good work. Sully has a juke-and-jive planned and programmed for Mbali to execute, and sixty-two ought to get us to Tristemon even though we're not in position for the best exit route." He had made up his mind before he called, but he hesitated for a moment before he said, "We're going, just as we are, quick like a rabbit. Pull in the arrays now, then spin up on my mark, and not before, copy?"

"Aye, Skip, spin up on your mark."

Biermann didn't bother correcting JT, but he wondered if Captain Norris was listening and how much shit they would both catch later—if they made it to later. "Once we're at minimum drive power, Mbali will fly us the hell out of here. The window's going to be pretty narrow, and if we miss it . . ." He wasn't sure what to say.

"Understood."

Biermann took a deep breath. "Stand by, then."

He turned his head back and forth across his display. It took only a couple of minutes for the arrays to be stowed and the light to go green, but it felt like a couple of lifetimes.

Biermann turned from his display to Sullivan's. She must have felt his eyes, because she turned to face him. Her half-melted nose and the burned patch on her right cheek glistened with sweat, so much that under the tactical lighting they looked freshly bloody. She nodded to him and turned back to the tactical station.

"Engineering, CIC. Power up . . . *now*."

The singularity set at the center of the ship was shielded and shunted enough that the only sensation was a slight increase in gravity and lighting. Biermann turned his attention to the reports coming from Mbali in the tank.

As expected, within two seconds the Kellador lookout ships above, below and on the system's ecliptic fired up their own power sources and became, through the higher-dimensional perceptions funneled into the tank and its occupant, beacons as bright as when they entered the system. Almost as quickly they exchanged their languorous orbits for powered flight and began converging on Grendel, because the *Tigris* itself was so close to the red dwarf. Biermann sounded the klaxon for transition into C-space. The power output ramped up, crossed the activation point, and Biermann readied himself for their convergence—

A clang like a gong erupted from the starboard tank and all the feeds from Mbali went chaotic.

"Brain break!" Sullivan yelled, and hurdled her console to check the tank.

Biermann had never seen anyone have a psychotic episode *in* the tank. His display quivered as if it were filled with indigo-tinted water frozen instantly solid. With the sure knowledge that the Kellador ships weren't frozen as the display showed, but were still approaching, he swept the display clear and signaled a medical emergency in CIC.

The tank hatch opened and Mbali breached. His long dark form came up and out in a fountain of scintillating crystals, and he grabbed Sullivan by the shoulders. She twisted free and lunged at him; her forehead smashed his mask and his nose behind it. He flopped backward, arms flailing, and ended up halfway out of the hatch with Sullivan atop him.

Biermann moved the only direction he could think to move, with an equal mixture of determination and terror. *In death ground, fight.* He shed his utilities and everything else before he crossed the broken privacy screen, grabbed the facemask and fitted it, and jumped into the portside tank, slapping the activation plate on his way into the dark, freezing depths.

The crystals bit, bite, tore, tear, eat, burrow, nest, hatch, grow . . .

Cool hot flanking warmth, olive pathway, mirror gate, push-pull-spin-reach . . .

Converge.

—The interface phased in and out, and in those instants Biermann's conscious mind was vomited back into the real world instead of being swallowed in the flood of sensation—

Time-aqua-space-flower, contract-condense, walnut-motion within marble-motion around musk-motion, spin-parallax-inertia . . .

Musk? Proximity-fright-cold.

—A squid ship, boosting in-system barely to port and down—

Anger-plunder-march.

Vector. Emerge. Strike. Strike.

Pain!

—Hull breach around bulkhead fourteen like a sock to the jaw, two compartments bleeding out souls and volatiles like teeth knocked out—

Converge.

Condensed cool clanging molasses waves, distant despairing stars, adjacent rancid not-stars—

—Targets, missiles, trajectories, projections, predictions—

Emerge. Strikestrikestrike. Converge.

Emerge. Strikestrikestrike. Converge.

Emerge. Painpainpain.

—Body blow, broken ribs, bulkheads forty-nine through fifty-six, internal bleeding, last missiles, make them count, run like hell—

Strike . . . strike . . . converge.

Garlic spin. Azure gate. Pestilence march. Starry trumpet harmony, buzzing sewage not-star cacophony—

Many countless innumerable immeasurable incalculable—

Chime spin, loyalty spin, kerosene burning, ammonia spin, khaki gasping, vanilla spin . . .

Jasmine march. Doublequicktriplequickrunrunrun. Ginger spin . . .

The face before him had once been human. Maybe it still was. Part of it was, bruised purple above one eye, opposite a melted mass. The bruised part was crying, noiselessly.

The universe was quiet.

He shivered. His mouth was full of frozen spinach that filmed his teeth as it dissolved into bits like crushed apple seeds. Teeth? It seemed odd to have teeth. He tried to fold his wings over his body, but they weren't where he had left them.

Where was his father? His mother? Was this ruined woman his human? Why was she sad? Why was he so, so cold?

The sky was steel, and very close, and crisscrossed with lines and lights. Not star lights.

Another woman, big but without a bruised and bloodied face, touched his neck. She moved her lips, but no sound came out.

He could not remember how to sing.

He felt suddenly tired, as if he had flown the breadth of a continent without anything to eat. But warmer . . . warm enough that soon he didn't mind that he'd lost his wings . . .

"Ricky?"

He could hear, but words were no substitute for starsong. What he heard sounded . . . clinical.

"We need you up and about, spacer."

He could speak, he thought, but it seemed . . . mundane. He could move his head. *No*.

"Come on, now. You've got the next watch."

He felt . . . something. Hungry?

"Lieutenant Biermann?"

Different voice, more melodic. Still not the stars. Sounded . . . official.

"Sully?" His voice was a rough croak. He did not sing. He knew not how.

"Sir, we'll come up on Tristemon in about thirty minutes, ship's time."

That was . . . important. "Okay. Good."

"It would be best if you could join the watch."

He seemed to be missing something, but he could not decide what it was.

"Does he know about the captain?"

The captain?

"Not yet."

What—

"Lieutenant Biermann, I'll tell Lieutenant Darzi that you're not available. He'll handle the system entry and make our reports."

What?

He could . . . open his eyes. Dim, yellowish light. Not stars, not a star. Ship lights. Hair that shade of red should be Ensign Sullivan . . . but her face was different. Burned? "Sully?"

"Yes, sir?"

He had . . . questions. "Where's . . . Captain . . . Norris?"

Ensign Sullivan stepped back, and Doc put his hand on her shoulder. Doc leaned over, thin . . . with fatigue? Worry?

"The second hit we took breached sickbay, Ricky. I was responding to injuries in the fore quarter from the first hit, but everybody—" He covered his mouth for a second. "We lost everybody who was in there. Including the captain."

Second hit? First hit? Why had the captain been in sickbay? Ricky—his name was Ricky . . . Biermann. He remembered that much. And if the captain was gone . . .

"Doc?"

"Yeah, Ricky?"

He wasn't sure he could stand. "Give me some go juice, then Sully can help me to the bridge."

Sullivan and Doc looked at one another, then Doc said, "The bridge is gone, Ricky. Ever since we got hit at Descartes."

An avalanche of memory buried him.

Seven hours later, Biermann and Brevet Lieutenant Sullivan sat together in Captain Alcor's quarters aboard the *Interceptor*. Just a little over two weeks before, Biermann had dined on this very ship with Captain Norris, and shortly thereafter *Tigris* left *Interceptor* to watch over Tristemon and headed on its way to Descartes.

Sully had done most of the reporting. Biermann was content to let her and the log recordings tell the story, especially since part of it involved him sitting naked and largely unresponsive on the CIC deck after they had pulled him out of the tank.

Captain Alcor praised his honor and integrity and action. She lauded *Tigris* and marveled at how they had sailed into Tristemon like a comet, spent of missiles and nearly of crew as well. Her compliments washed over Biermann like a zephyr and left him cold. He tried to listen between the words, to pick out the stars singing in the background, but he was deaf to them now.

"The alert's going out," Captain Alcor said. "I've assigned two couriers as scouts until we get more ships here, and one has already sailed to Grendel to verify whether that task force is still there. No one's reported any contact from the Kellador government, so we don't know if this is just expanding and shoring up their sphere, so to speak, or actually trying to invade ours.

"I don't know about you, but I worry about what the politicians will do. You can't placate a truly determined enemy. Try to appease them and they take it as weakness and attack again, harder. Counterattack without destroying them, and they'll store up their anger and resentment until they're strong enough to strike again." She drank some of her coffee. "If we're fortunate, the Kellador will turn out to be a casual enemy. I just hope we're not too casual about responding to them."

Biermann nodded, mostly out of politeness. His coffee was untouched, surely cold. If the Kellador came to Tristemon as quickly as they had massed at Grendel, there was little the Fleet could do. Lieutenant Garzi was out piloting *Tigris* to find a good asteroid for Gaines to use as refit material, but it would take months to undo what the squids had done. In the whole of Tristemon's gravitational influence, only *Interceptor* and *Del Vecchio* were in fighting trim; but at least they were on the alert now.

He let Sullivan lead him to the cutter they had been assigned. He presumed they would go to the LaGrange outpost—he wondered if Captain Norris would have considered that to be "key" ground, equally advantageous to friend and enemy alike—until *Tigris* returned. While the pilot ran the preflight checks, Biermann gazed out the window, wondering where the Kellador were going, where their advance would end, what the Fleet would do with him, and whether he was as broken as he seemed to be.

He listened, and listened, but could not hear the stars.

We stride across the galaxy and we spin, we whirl, we pirouette beneath the wailing stars . . .

But on all the frequencies that matter, the stars are silent.

❈   ❈   ❈

Gray Rinehart is the only person to have commanded an Air Force satellite tracking station, written speeches for presidential appointees, and had music on *The Dr. Demento Show*. He fought rocket-propellant fires, refurbished space launch facilities, "flew" satellites, drove trucks, processed nuclear command and control orders, and did other unusual things in his rather odd USAF career, and now he is a contributing editor for Baen

Books, a singer/songwriter, and an author. His first novel, *Walking on the Sea of Clouds*, was published by WordFire Press, and his short fiction has appeared in *Analog Science Fiction & Fact*, *Asimov's Science Fiction*, Orson Scott Card's *Intergalactic Medicine Show*, and several anthologies. His alter ego is the "Gray Man," one of several famed ghosts of South Carolina's Grand Strand, and his website is graymanwrites.com.

EXCERPTS FROM TWO LIVES

Sharon Lee & Steve Miller

In the heyday of sail, a ship of the line, properly oriented toward the enemy and with cannons unlimbered, was the most awesome weapon of her day—if she were captained by a capable commander fighting under the right circumstances. A starship with equivalently scaled power might protect a world as it is being born. Or destroy it. Yet in the wrong circumstances, such awesome power may find itself yielding to a mere scratch. For Time and Change are the universe's ultimate ships of the line.

Averil 21, 407 Confederation Standard Year

"Beam Banks One and Two, go live as leads. We have identified and targeted a threat. Prepare to fire on my command, on radar's central target. This is not a drill, you will go to full combat power. Saturate the disc at all wavelengths."

Proper quiet, proper response. The ship's routine went on but the air circulators changed speed and life-support panels grew angry red as combat-power overrides initiated. Small bells echoed the necessities of combat: hatches, airlocks, and pressure doors sealed.

"Combat power up." Nerves in that voice, but it didn't squeak.

"Lead banks, we'll need three consecutive full-power bursts from each—lock that in! Bank Three, slave to Bank One, two point seven five second delay, wide angle. Bank Four, slave to Bank Three, ultrawide angle. Banks Five through Twelve, go to high alert. Missilery Section, watch for bulk breakaway going in-system, target at will. Section leaders, you will particularly react to bulk breakaway coming our way."

The crew shared glances. They'd deviated, on captain's orders, from what was to be a calm and peaceful direct rendezvous with the RosaRing.

Meteor shields went live automatically. The target was a little over a tenth of a light-second away, so energetic debris wasn't an immediate threat.

The captain said nothing, watching this crew's first live-fire action. The sub-captain was sweating: His experience on this system was simulations. His battle experience had been on ships whose entire beam output was negligible compared to any single projector in any of the battleship's twenty multibeam projector banks. There was a reason these beams were called planet busters, as they were about to prove.

Radar showed the target, distance and rotation. Like many planets, there was ice at the poles. Like many planets there was atmosphere. Like many planets, one might target the broadside equator, where rotational stress assisted the destructive effects of incoming beams.

The captain and the sub-captain had spent several sessions in the captain's cabin perfecting this plan. The crew thought it merely the third drill, but the target *was* a danger to Trikandle; the sub-captain had done the math the captain required.

The sub-captain's orders from the captain: develop an attack sequence, prepare the crew through drills, and then give the deck commands required for the kill, on the captain's signal. The captain required excellence from those who served under him.

In return, in those sessions, he displayed excellence. He'd shared the words and codes of exigency—the ship's self-destruct sequence, the code of relinquishing command, the codes for . . . all of them. Smit had taught him, and he passed the ship's necessities on.

The captain listened to the deck, the radar, the hum of power that underlay the deck, the stars beyond, just as he'd seen Admiral Smit listen. The form was Admiral Smit's axiom: Effective command radiates power; those under command bask in the rays of their orders.

Watching the screens, feeling the universe flow around him, the captain radiated command, looking firmly at the sub-captain and saying *"Ni faris,"* into the mic that reached only the sub-captain's headset.

A startle there, a so-brief pause. The sub-captain's glance fled from the captain's face to his command screen, and he echoed the captain to his crew. "We commit! Fire!"

The deck thrummed and the power was an audible rasp ending in a noise that was . . .

"Zap!"

The sotto voce comment by a crewman unseen barely beat the squeal of discharge that thrummed the entire fabric of the battleship. On screens crew throughout the ship saw what happens when a bank of planet-buster projectors hurls the forces of chaos.

The captain blinked. Some teaching moments have more impact than others. When he'd accepted this mission on that Day of Changes, when he'd last held Verita in their own bed, he hadn't expected to train a crew so raw, nor to have orders on file permitting such a mission. Things were going well, seventeen days in system.

Change Year Day, Sumtap 01, 404 CSY

They'd begun that Day of Changes knowing there'd *be* changes.

This was not their first Day of Changes; they'd learned the meaning of it together as child scholars, learned the joy of festive food and guessing games, learned later of the small pains that might come from the day, then, the larger ones as schoolmates and first crushes were pared away by the necessities of more adult pursuits.

Eventually they'd pled their cases one to another for more than stolen kisses and learned to trust in each other's hard-driving ambition. They turned to each other rather than others, asking "How do we solve this?" or, admitting being at wit's end: "Solve this!" They wore matching bands of custom Triluxian in honor of their plans.

His ambition led him to the fleet, in search of opportunity as it recovered from the debacle of the Battle of Azren Clouds. He'd risen quickly, leading several raiding missions and rescues before being attached to Admiral Smit and *Implacable.*

She, drawn to research, joined the efforts to extract the most dangerous secrets of the Ligonier Library, where her skills at academic infighting were as recognized as her scientific insights. Nor had Verita shared all her solvings with the academic community, reserving for herself and Kiland the news that she'd moved from theory to actual practice several strains of those life-constructions thought lost in the collapsed universe their foremothers had fled.

While the old guard flailed at the changes wrought by dusty carbon clouds invading their trade lanes, Kiland and Verita shone as beacons for the future. Let the failures retire or suicide—they dealt only in power and success.

On that memorable Day of Changes, they played before the clock buzzed them officially into the dawn. Verita began by nipping his ear and spooning him, her hands busy, mouth full of kisses and words; promises, teases—and *more,* her potent arms pulling his shoulder, aiming his willing mouth and . . .

After they'd sat in their atrium, cheered by their nakedness as ocean breeze brought them spring's promise of more than mere renewal. What sprang from this year would crown their lives.

By tradition, they arrived at dusk, he from the south, she from the north, at their own front door. Flowers and gifts they each carried in profusion, the promise of change strong in their hands while their faces were a little secret, the mouths a little sad under the smiles.

"I will be your slave tonight, my love," said Verita, as they exchanged delicate fragrant bouquets on their threshold. "And you will solve my passion.

"Unless," she added, as she followed him into their home, "unless you demand I solve for you, in which case I will take tomorrow."

"Slave or solve." He laughed. "I'll savor either."

He trembled with lust, though they were still dressed, and his eyes darkened his smile. But her smile, too, was near fled, dancing on the tip of her tongue.

"Is it well, *Katido Volupto*?" he whispered, and shed his burdens as she shed hers, the hall table not large enough for the wealth of gifts they had brought.

"It is," she said. "It is so well it is nearly perfect. The project goes forward . . . yes. But until it is announced, I can hardly tell you more. And for you?"

"Yes, it is nearly perfect. Next week, I return to space!"

She laughed, and was relieved, nearly knocking him down as she wrapped herself about him, filling his eyes with her kisses and his ears with her demand, "Tell me, tell me that you will not be lonely. Next week I go to space, as well!"

Averil 04, 407 CSY

Implacable in a hurry was a sight to be seen, which was good, since there was no way of hiding the fearsome output of its antique power units. The mighty timonium plasma sets spewed neutrons and neutrinos alike while powering the last ship of the line from any of the Cloudgate armed forces. She left behind an elemental thermal signature that might cloud an astronomer's view of the cosmos for centuries, but the chance of there being such, here, was negligible.

Ship of the line was a misnomer when applied to *Implacable*, for most ships of its type fielded two centuries ago were gone. Of that generation of *batalsipo grandas*—a dozen dozen ships more powerful than entire modern star fleets—only *Implacable* held air. The others were victims of their wars or, as often, dismantled for resources.

Verita watched the secret news of *Implacable*'s arrival. Station Ops was slow in this; her own equipment better tuned—she'd had budget for new installs while Ops was stuck with original equipment. So much of the mission was on scant budget, including using the mighty *Implacable* as a towboat! However, the calculations had worked well for the incoming trip, with the transit from Jump point to Trikandle's one-hundred-day orbit a mere twelve days. This time *Implacable* was too awkwardly placed for such a quick run, she knew.

Kiland's Change Day news had placed him back aboard the vessel that had made him one of the most powerful men in the reformed Confederation. The same Change Day saw Verita leap to her lifelong goal—science leader of an expedition that could return the Confederation to greatness.

As principal investigator she was technically second-in-command of the RosaRing, an agricultural lab repurposed into a self-sufficient xenoplanet research laboratory. The administrator's position was higher in the flow charts, but Prenla Verita was the reason the RosaRing had been dispatched.

Among the last messages from *Implacable* as it departed system had been several for her, under admiral's seal—sent by Kiland, with Admiral Smit's approval. Each was more full of promise than the last, and the final promising what they'd suspected: Smit was retiring, and he favored as commander of *Implacable* none but Kiland.

Now orbiting the fecund planet Trikandle, the real mission of the RosaRing was daunting: hurry Trikandle through an evolution toward the oxygenated photosynthetic atmosphere required to add it as a populated Confederation world. This was hands-on work—with satellites, imaging systems, drones, rovers, and observer craft.

The Confederation's directors had risked much in mounting the expedition at all, and they'd cast for glory over stability, rushing their claim on the Trikandle system by making the station a permanent fixture.

The atmosphere on Trikandle was an unbreathable amalgam: storms of methane mixing with unstable compounds, leaving odd pools of multilayered liquids . . . including water. Measurable pockets of oxygen enriched the atmosphere in deep valleys and craters. It was now oxygen rich for a world where free oxygen had hitherto been bound to rocks or was a trace gas high in the atmosphere.

On Trikandle life roiled, it flittered, it rolled; it

gathered itself into mats of color and motion, it launched itself against barriers of other life with potent chemistry of acid and base. It grew through ceaseless life cycles of solution and dissolution. As it writhed into toxic tentacles, grew sniffer stalks and eye puddles, it fed a future Verita was struggling to direct.

Verita was supported by the work she'd done since graduate school, fed by secrets pilfered in the great war more than a century gone by, when *Implacable*'s weapons led the attack on Quadraterra's defenses and stood guard over the looting of the Ligonier Library.

Some of that looted knowledge had been useless; the physics of a closed and finite universe did not translate perfectly to this one. But in the end times of the old universe, there'd been clones and all manner of living abominations shaped by the unknowable minds of the Great Enemy, *Sherikas*. That there were detailed instructions of the building of such pseudolife was a secret Verita held close.

Scientists at Ligonier Library had plotted their control of the new universe, using the tools that had won the old. They'd been pushed to unleash at-will terraforming, wild cellular advances—and much of their knowledge had come to Verita's hands.

Verita's ambition supported Kiland's. They were a good team politically and would carry their bloodlines to the top of the Confederation's hierarchy. Well-placed by birth and education, they would easily live two centuries or more. Their Confederation would sweep aside the remnants of the old Terran Empire, the Liadens, and even the Yxtrang.

In Verita's display screens *Implacable*'s thrust sparkled across many bands, infernos created by in-system engines that were no longer welcome in most habited systems.

The Confederation's pride and joy . . . well, once there was a new source of accessible wealth under their control, a whole new planet to be used, followed by many more to be farmed at will—then, *Implacable* could be a regal exemplar of their might!

Kiland's parting message going out she knew by heart, and believed it still:

"I live to serve your needs and solve your problems, my Verita. Our next Change Day together we shall reprise and surmount all our dreams and fantasies."

And now—*Implacable* was back, and all of their future beckoned.

It was the sixth hundredth day since the special pair of rovers was unleashed.

Today Verita studied the area called Quozmo. The implication of the new, bolder streaking on ground and air was clear to her, though she really wished to be sure it was not yet clear to Admin Desler. Admin was only a few days returned from her course of enforced rest. In other days her episode might have been called "nervous exhaustion." Admin's work had become more difficult with the several suicides among the staff overworked with aging equipment and shredded schedules. Desler, a tenured academic appointed to the post to remove her from a politically sensitive position, was unequal to the increased stress.

It had taken time for the crew psychologist to

understand the situation and by then, Admin Desler had been in a precarious state. She was taken under care, some of her work redistributed to Verita and to Desler's assistant.

The right corner of the screen showed a notification—ground-side ops. She gestured and took the voice call.

"Investigator, I've a message from Quozmo Ob2. They've lost relay from the Debae and Dabbie rover pair again and they're down to four drones, three of them lightweights. Do we want the drones all back now?"

Verita pushed back at her hair—if Kiland didn't prefer it long enough to brush and caress she'd have cut it short.

"Condense the last of the valley images and send them to me. Begin reacquisition interrogation on the rovers. Work on that, priority!"

The rover teams . . . the rover teams acted like they were sentient. They weren't, of course, Verita never quite dared bringing both parts of the legacy together. Though for this, she had considered it.

The rovers *were* semiautonomous. They could go for years without input—collecting, analyzing, reporting when queried. The pair's self-selected braided trail method was working so well she'd asked the next units be programmed to emulate it. The lead rovers were encountering pods and accumulations of . . . things. Life. New life. Life chosen and sown by her will, growing in a wilderness of chaos.

The valley the rovers roamed was a tectonic artifact, more a long gash than a crater. The upthrust of plateau at the far end looked to be impact residue, but her studies confirmed the heights as cooling volcanic plumes, recent.

Those plumes generated thermal activity in the valley, a rich source of energy and minerals. Minerals including timonium, platinum, gold.

The valley was geologically active, with three rivers rushing into it. The hydrocarbons were interesting, but one of those rivers ran seasonally as water, as it did now, sometimes sharing the riverbeds, sometimes competing. Within the last year, spongy mats of winter vegetation had begun catching against the cliffsides, and the oxygen levels were notably higher.

"Yes," Verita said to ground ops, "recover the drones, as long as they haven't been below the pressure threshold."

"Altitude threshold, right, not height threshold? We've been pushing, as you requested. There's been wind and updrafts around the mount—we've been using that to keep the glidefoils active beyond normal duration."

Verita closed her eyes, considering. Yes, she'd approved that. There shouldn't have been any problem there, surely . . .

"Show me the flight paths. Show me recent weather, too."

As those screens came up, simultaneously there was a shout from somewhere down the hall and a chime.

The admin's voice rang out throughout the RosaRing.

"Attention, all staff. We have a distant Jump arrival confirmed and are awaiting ID. Scan Security, please man your stations. Timing is appropriate for our Year Three Rendezvous."

Verita grinned, even though she'd known. She had so much to share with Kiland, doubtless he for her.

In the meantime, she had a decision to make.

She leaned back, sniffing at the flight paths now on screen as if she could scent a hint of ammonia, or of the crystalline precipitate which sometimes wafted to the gravel beds left behind after the flush of spring floods.

The pressure gradients were in flux. The stronger of the atmospheric currents had tunneled through the flat current they called the mesostream, which sometimes held considerable water vapor. The visualization showed a convective dance then, as if ramped high into the sky by the volcanic uplands, high into the stratopause.

Technically, the drones were not to fly as low as the stratopause, where the temperatures neared the freezing point of water. In such conditions microbes might be found on normal worlds.

Verita made her decision.

"Call them home."

Averil 04, 407 CSY

"What's the measure on that? Are we even at the right star? Where's the gassers?"

Kiland's sarcasm was inappropriate if nearly inaudible.

Automatics admitted that yes, *Implacable* had come to the right place despite her recalcitrant Struven units and the haste of their departure. The gas giants rolled in their orbits, the companion brown dwarf continued its distant, lonely journey three-quarters of a light-year away among rocky clouds of debris. *He* read them that quickly, but his crew . . .

His crew checked their instruments, followed protocol, eventually they nodded at him.

He signaled the traditional arrival announcement. It went out without the usual time-to-dock, though, and he . . . did the math himself, signaling the sub-captain to do the same.

"Shield at basic," he said, but the automatics were seeing to that, the junior officers chasing behind, just in case.

"Weapons checks, threats?"

There were no threats.

At full in-system power it would take them days just to overcome the fractional errors; right now they were moving at significant velocity *away* from their target. The revamped crew was still learning the ship—Admiral Smit's veteran crew would never have arrived so far off the mark, or so unsure of the recover.

"Attention, *Implacable*, we are arrived and making our way to the RosaRing. This will not be a twelve-day jaunt; expect full maintenance routines. Deck officers set duty cycles. Acceleration alerts within the hour."

Kiland looked to the sub-captain.

"Three channels, in the clear, Captain. The time signals are there, but no space weather roundups. The orbital elements are automatic, but the star observation reports ought to be continuous."

"Record what's there, get us synced, ask for what's missing. Send captain's regards to the RosaRing's Trikandle Expedition. Tell them we're bringing treasures from home. Once comm schedules are established, send and request the archives. In the meanwhile, let us compare projected courses, shall we? We have work to do."

Averil 05, 407 CSY

From Principal Investigator via RosaRing Secure COMM 7 for Captain's Eyes Only

Point A: My joy and strength, the investigation has moved rapidly beyond experiment and is well into proof. The rover pair are the perfect delivery system—I utilize testing systems on board to recreate the binary delivery methods outlined in the records we inherited. These are superior organisms, they continue to multiply not only in the track of the vehicles, as I'd intended, but well beyond. I expect great things, and find myself limited by materials and conditions on station. I expect you may solve many of my minor problems.

Point B: I remain your devoted slave at all times.

PI Verita

Averil 7, 407 CSY

From Captain, Implacable, to RosaRing Secure COMM 7 for Principal Investigator Only

My Beauty Beyond All, you astound me with your progress, which is prodigious and worthy. You exceed our original goals for so early a date. My progress is less pleasing, our dreams delayed by both orbital mechanics and politics.

Admiral Smit's retirement was received with much division. His ascension to council head was contested and defeated; he demurred taking vice chair. My position is at risk; the opposition demanded the immediate dismantling of *Implacable* as a threat to border peace. This failed, but our military mission has been de-emphasized, and my term on the Fleet Council, which is statutory as *Implacable*'s commander, may end after this voyage.

My crew is far less than full strength. Many retirements and cost-balancings have gone into effect. Review the appended, please. Many experienced officers and crew were replaced by fresh graduates, as if I head a training squad!

Implacable's whole mission is a bargaining point between the parties, as a support ship for the RosaRing. We shall move forward. Your success is paramount to our success.

I am, as always, willing to command such an eager supplicant. Remember that in restriction is liberation.

Captain Kiland

They had in the course of their bed-talk discussed much that was secret and that stood her in good stead now. The charts, spreadsheets, and projections revealed Kiland as an optimist. Ship's provisioning had suffered. Even a five-year mission was perilous. Weaponry updates were off the budget, savings were achieved by replacing seasoned staff with new graduates, positions left empty, and militia called up for training. Ship's company included too few experienced pilots, and too many untested crew.

Alone in her suite, Verita suffered for Kiland. His setback made her success ever more important. Re-energized by his necessity, she applied herself more fully to duties at hand.

Averil 14, 407 CSY

From Principal Investigator via RosaRing Secure COMM 7 for Captain's Eyes Only

My Strength and Direction, one is desolate to be less than perfect in all things for you. I must request technical aid as well as spiritual solving. So often your lessons bring me clarity.

In the face of Station Admin's orders to conserve fuel can *Implacable* offer assistance until the fuel and drones you carry are delivered? Might a more militant drone-recovery protocol be employed? Can you read signals and plot better courses? Assure me—assure the station!—with your guidance.

I suggest and cannot demand; my Strength reflects yours at all times.

Your latest lesson assists my considerations and will be recalled as often as possible until we are joined again in the harmony of a Perfected Evening.

PI Verita

Kiland's tactical officers enjoyed the challenge of the long-distance scan and solve; they caught the orders as a frolic, as if they were back at school. He had them look for ways to improve the drone's routes, to search for threats in the system, and all threats to the RosaRing. They daily requested more information from the ring. They worked with energy, concentration, amusement.

He was less amused than concerned. The ship's skills depended far more on the practicing of things his staff recalled only from school than they ought.

As captain he deserved a crew capable of supporting his—and the ship's—necessities. Therefore he would push the boundaries of these youngsters. They would become the crew *Implacable* deserved. Each order would be carried out with dedication and devotion. Each solution would be born of submission to the necessity of mission. They would learn. The sub-captain in particular needed growth if he were to serve as a proper second.

Averil 17, 407 CSY

From Captain, Implacable, to RosaRing Secure COMM 7 for Principal Investigator Only

Sweet Touch of A Giving Noon, the crew relishes drone tracking. We thank you for the opportunity. The more experienced appear reticent to enjoy our adoption of a Joint Mission. The brightest see that dedication to Mission is all they want.

Your administrator professes surprise at *Implacable*'s ability to compute simple math and solve minor problems in interception. Yes, we can access the telemetry channels of your drones; we pick up signals from your rovers as well. Confederation leaders at many levels lack understanding of what this ship is and what it can do, as they lack an understanding of the RosaRing's potential. We will show them all; we will demonstrate that, together, we can transform planets.

Your administrator embraces details? Perhaps you may offer her more to deal with, so that she may be fully involved in details. She need not be overly concerned with flight planning now that the RosaRing is again in *Implacable*'s shadow.

The tender's copilot is a former naval officer; he ought have none of the finicky training the head pilot admires. I append a flight plan for the tender—discussed at mess among the more forward of my sub-officers—which may permit the tender to better retrieve your drones as well as utilize the gravity well to regain lost energy.

I have engaged the copilot in a radio correspondence; we discuss a campaign long past in which a ship not unlike the tender was able to overperform simple guidelines designed for ordinary pilots. I, of course, have no orders to give about what must be pilot's choice, nor you; we may simply discuss, suggest, and request.

I remain devoted to the Delicate Delights and such arts you perfect through me, I admonish you to please yourself and please me in all you do.

Captain Kiland

Averil 18, 407 CSY

The pilot's message was not quoted in full; it was apparent

that Kiland's suggestions had been acted upon. Alas, the pilot and copilot were barely on speaking terms. She? She was unnerved by information that there were now stains on the skin of the tender, where it had driven deeper into the atmosphere than ever before, bringing with it all of the drones. It was a daring mission, no doubt. The pilot had been on sleep shift when the dive sequence began and went to the administrator straight away after they'd returned to the RosaRing. The tender pilot . . .

The tender pilot was not a biologist.

The tender pilot was not a chemist.

The pilot was a pilot. Stains on her ship offended her; and she found them a clear sign that pilot and copilot needed a break, each from the each.

There were also stains on the drones, which the pilot cared about not one whit. That was someone else's job. Drones were tended by their own staff, their samples double-checked in the lab.

Verita grimaced. She'd been enjoying a crew amused by the understanding that the *Implacable*'s captain and their own prime investigator were a link-couple. Now she needed to become again the firm scientist and see the entirety of the crew reminded of the necessity for proper isolation technique and contamination control sequences.

Cha-bling went the annunciator. The administrator's direct line shattered the usual screen image, followed by an image of the administrator herself, chewing her lips, staring at the screen still blank on her end.

Verita composed herself with a deep breath and a straightening of her lab coat; she moved three empty stim cups from screen range. Another centering breath and she was ready to be distantly polite . . . .

"Your comm fails to display, Verita. If you are present, reply so I don't have to send a messenger. This is rather important!"

She composed her expression to what she hoped was a look of general, unalarmed interest, then finished her reach to activate the visual display on her end.

"Important, Administrator?"

"Yes, important! There's an outer-belt asteroid on a collision course with Trikandle. The captain has sent me a secure message! A strike on the planet is within the margin of error, he tells me."

Verita felt her pleasant expression vanish—

"Our mission!"

The administrator offered a grim little smile, apparently pleased with this reaction.

"Yes, our mission, indeed, yes. Also, our station. I gather this 'pass' as he calls it is not immediate but needs be dealt with. There is some factor of resonances and such still being determined. I am not informing the crew, wishing not to spread alarm."

The administrator pursed her lips, her visage taking on the near rictus she assumed when issuing commands not to be denied.

"You shall not tell the crew, do you understand? I *will* direct the captain to inform you of the technical details, and *I* shall decide what needs be done. I have promised a reply within two shifts, so hold yourself ready for consultation."

With that the screen went back to ordinary.

⌘　⌘　⌘

The crew took direction well; they'd even taken to the maintenance-plus-pursuit staffing. Given that they were technically shorthanded, with entire Fleet Operations sections of dozens reduced to shifts of pairs, this was a fine way to return the ship to the spit-and-polish days of Smit.

The sub-captain in particular seemed to relish his extra duties. While he'd commanded a small vessel in recent peacetime, his service had not been properly recognized. Passed over several times for political reasons, he, like Kiland, was a volunteer to the *Implacable*. A man with ambition made a good ally.

The sub-captain's shifts responded for him as well as they did for the captain, and he had enough camaraderie with the crew to have a mathematician come forward with the threat the asteroid posed several orbits out—which was to say, eleven hundred and seventy-two Standard Years, away. They would chase that asteroid down now. It was the duty of a captain to remove known space hazards.

Reward? The crew would see and taste their own power. For the moment they worked harder and fell into the proper crew-spirit.

Averil 22, 407 CSY

From Principal Investigator via RosaRing
Secure COMM 7 for Captain's Eyes Only

My full heart, my hot blood, surely you have outdone yourself! The destruction of that menace delights. It was good that the event could be shared, though some, like the administrator, were shaken by it. In fact, the administrator, speaking confidentiality, considers she might order passage on *Implacable* rather than attempt another three years. She asks that I hold updates on my work for the moment.

I have agreed that I could share burden of a Joint Command with her second, and on the other side I have spoken with the Second, who is willing to have promotion sooner. She has been consulting with the physicians to that end.

Admin's oversight of operations has been recently uneven; meals have been late due to minor problems with the energy systems, the air circulators are changed to manual on some shifts as they are affected by a glitch in the attitude controls as we maintain our synchronous orbit above the prime research zone. It is vexing, but to be expected with the staff waiting for decisions easily made. It will be solved soon, I am certain.

On the practical side, the chief tender pilot placed herself on sick leave. The tender's new pilot has been dropping off-the-record radiosondes along with the regular drones. These drop parallel to the rovers; they are wonderfully useful. I see exponential expansion to the limits of the habitat boundaries. We should see blossoming that will change Trikandle sooner rather than later.

My work consumes me nearly as much as my desire to offer myself up to you.

PI Verita

The captain was pleased. The crew was brazen in their newfound self-esteem. They'd done something violent and powerful, they'd destroyed—down to gas, plasma, gravel, and powder—a worldlet. The ship might have landed there, the crew might have walked suited in the ravines, collected water from the ice packs. It had been *a place*, and by their action it was gone. They were ready, eager, proven. They searched for more threats, they honed their skills at drills to battle station.

The captain let them strut for themselves; he was willing to admire them, their newfound ambition. They were no longer in awe of the ship—now they were in awe of themselves! Someone had even slipped him a recording of a new song sung on the ship. Made by the same mischievous mathematician who discovered it, the song celebrated *Implacable* and her captain and described the obliteration of the asteroid. The old Fleet might be gone but the urge of youth to bathe in the glory of power had not died!

Averil 24, 407 CSY

From Captain, Implacable, to RosaRing
Secure COMM 7 for Principal Investigator Only

My Second Heart, I do so desire to share your tremble. Your work engages my crew; we study Trikandle with our sensors and shall share our findings with you. Particularly involved are crew in meteorology and mathematics. I am informed that some regions we'd imaged last trip have changed drastically in these three years. There are streaks of new color evident on the continent you concentrate upon. Also dots of that new color are seen where the rivers flow, around shore lines, ridges, elsewhere. Are the currents and winds so strong? Do the tender flights and the drones work so hard? I shall return to the High Command with evidence of your success.

As always, thoughts of your touch and tone beguile me to sleep; I seek your ministrations.

Captain Kiland

Averil 26, 407 CSY

From Principal Investigator via RosaRing
Secure COMM 7 for Captain's Eyes Only

My Partner in Sense and Sensation, I quiver at your approach. The administrator may now opt for very early transfer to *Implacable,* as she is finding sleep and concentration difficult. Several of the lab crew are reporting such issues as well—I ascribe it to general excitement over the approach of your ship.

The changes you report outside the river valleys we've studied amaze. I am not so much sleepless as vibrating with energy and anticipation. I hope the cargo shifts will allow the new drones among the first items available; the old ones have become unreliable. We lost one to weather, an upper current overwhelmed it. A second drone found it crash-landed outside of our prime valley with a large burden of unexpended biotic canisters.

Do tell me you have new challenges and rewards for me, I seek to please you soonest.

PI Verita

Averil 27, 407 CSY

From Captain, Implacable, to RosaRing Secure COMM 7 for Principal Investigator Only

Your burden is mine; you will find my requirements a pleasure.

I have requests from your station administrator asking of arrangements for a ceremony of arrival; I hesitate to authorize an on-docking event out of hand. She mentions the possibility of a transfer; paradoxically she requests it and can order it and seems overmatched by her position, indeed. My staff must prompt hers for ordinary transmissions and data sharing, she runs an unprofessional operation, I am afraid.

Can it be that there is a weather wave spreading your new biotics? Is it a chemical reaction catalyzed by the increase in oxygen? Our observers report a surge of color changes on planet; the spectra show unusual mixtures, the temperature sensors show wild variations. Have you science you can share on this?

Supplies will be offloaded by pod and bin, we have become a cargo vessel and are not suited to it! The sub-captain reports basic supplies in the first rounds, and then laboratory items, by necessity of the pod mounts. The pattern is preset.

Do not doubt that I will be firm with you, very soon. I long to hear you whispering.

Captain Kiland

Averil 29, 407 CSY

Glaring at the screen in front of her, Verita rotated the troth ring on her third finger without looking at it. The weight and the repetition were comforting. As much as she twisted it, she couldn't change the fact that docking with *Implacable* was just sixteen hours away, and things were getting worse instead of better.

This latest news from the lab sections was not good. Four of seven biology technicians in the drone research area were on sick call and both of the service mechanics.

She clicked off the message; the staff knew their work. She'd get to them later with a pep talk about yesterday's results. Now, she needed to concentrate . . .

This was not how she'd intended to display a well-controlled station! The mechanics complained of different maladies—one of skin rashes leaving behind a kind of scar, the other of dizziness with headache. All complained of strange odors and odd tastes; she'd not visited the hangar for days to avoid the sneezes that had become common there. Her own tests . . . well, she was not a medical doctor. It just seemed wise to be cautious and remain in her offices and suite.

It was unfortunate that replacement drones could not be brought to bear sooner. He should have known that chasing the asteroid would add delay . . . but no, nothing about this was *his* fault. Nothing.

Verita opened her eyes realizing that she'd been

swimming in the half-sleep she'd become prone to. A chime in the halls had woken her, one of the administrator's many notes to maintenance.

She was in her own chair, office door locked, so no one saw her start to wakefulness. She was sleeping short shift as she tried to keep up. The returned rovers reported astounding amounts of local free oxygen in the long midafternoon of the planet's forty-hour day. Not an atmosphere breathable by humans, by any means, but one promising explorers might walk the world, extracting the oxygen they needed directly, within a century, perhaps even a decade. She wanted to see it sooner, she wanted to make it happen in a rush of . . .

A chime woke her; the screen was filled by the administrator, her face blotchy and busy with tension.

"Investigator? The tender is under my direct control. Understand me? Until I leave! The pilot's under doctor's care for exhaustion. The backup pilot is nearing the same point. People are ill all around you because you push too hard. You push everyone too hard, Verita."

Kiland suppressed the yawn by force of will as he went over routine schedules on the bridge. Smit had always done his paperwork on the bridge, too—it was good for the crew to see the leader at work. Lunch was only moments away . . .

"Captain?" The sub-captain's voice was firm. "I don't have any incident reports from the station on this—would you like to take a look on the main screen? I was having some of the crew practice long-range visual ID and we were getting mismatches—"

At high magnification the RosaRing spun in space, filling the screen. The station silhouette was clear but the alternating angled white and blue stripes, clear on large parts of the hull, were smudged and blotchy, as if overlain by a layer of greenish rust around the protruding docking bay on the lower reaches.

"I don't think I've ever seen anything like this, sir."

Kiland's boredom fell away, memory jostling his concentration, trying to come to the front of the mind.

He pointed at a second screen.

"Put some samples from our outbound recorded images there, Sub-Captain, close as you can to a match. Ask Station Operations if they've suffered any gas leakage or maintenance issues they haven't passed on? Get as good an image as you can for them. . . . And ask Ops . . . no, ask the administrator's office to share results of the routine tests they've run on our docking ports and loading locks. Also, request current readings on the inner docks."

"Sir!"

The sub-captain issued commands, brought the bridge to alert, used the keypad to search images and bring them live on screen, ran a match, adjusted sizes.

The ordinary sounds on the bridge fell away; watch partners messaged quick notes or whispered.

The captain hand-signaled the sub-captain, who approached, bowing slightly to hear the captain's order.

Instead, the captain asked, "Were you on academy on the mount, or on the islands?"

The sub-captain, caught by what seemed a non sequitur, hesitated and said "Why, like you, the islands, sir."

The captain nodded, then nodded toward the images on the main screen.

"So you are familiar with the Citadel's wind walls? Perhaps along Chespick Beach, or the tidal falls at Injridge?"

The sub-captain's features showed remembrance, a touch of a smile for some assignation late night at oceanside, where the waves and wind conspired to produce a lovely romantic place overseen by ancient star-bleached walls smudged at base and higher with the greens, browns, and even reds of algal scums.

Recognition blossomed and . . .

"There's nothing to grow, there's nothing to grow on if there was . . ."

The sub-captain quieted, perplexity wrinkling his youthful visage in much the way passion might.

Kiland nodded and sighed. "Not an oxy world yet, is it? Who knows what's a balmy seaside for what's already growing down there?"

"Station Ops—sir, I'm afraid we woke them up. Our contact is somewhat unfamiliar with standard comm protocols and has 'gone off to find someone' in charge—"

The air quotes were audible.

"—who's apparently dealing with an engineering issue. There seems to be some confusion . . . the administrator hasn't answered a direct call, sir. The automatic transmissions have become sporadic."

"Is anyone talking to us at lower levels?"

The sub-captain queried his consoles.

"Engineering reports they had a contact yesterday, asking for suggestions on dealing with a sluggish stability ring. . . . We sent them updates and a testing program."

Kiland stared at the images, pristine and stained. This could go wrong . . .

"Try again for the administrator and send lunch to my office. If the administrator's office does not respond within five minutes, connect me with the principal investigator. I'm declaring a System Alert; chief pilots should sim-up on irregular rendezvous and docking."

Averil 30, 407 CSY

"Prime Investigator, sir."

Verita heard the connection go through, and looked up. He was handsome, stern. It was good to see him, her own . . .

"Captain Kiland," she said, "I'm informed that the administrator's second is escorting her to the tender, as she is planning to transfer before *Implacable* docks. If both leave this station at the same time, I will be in charge."

There was no privacy, of course—the sub-captain was monitoring the line—so she said no more than the immediate information, waiting for his voice, his support . . .

"We've no flight plan filing on that, Investigator; I'll alert my staff to the potential, though if the stability of the ring is in question they ought not plan on launching."

"There have been some irregularities in the spin,

Captain, I think as a result of preparation for docking. There is some issue . . ."

"Are you aware, Investigator, of the buildup on the ring's external surfaces?"

Kiland's face was calm, his voice too neutral to be glad of. Beside his face were video images of the RosaRing looking disreputable, like an out-of-use parts dump.

"I am not—"

"We must have clarity about these stains, Investigator. If they are involved with your stability issues they must surely be solved before we can begin docking. We must have the test results for our docking pilots."

Verita floundered. Her expertise was in living things, not in mundane issues of habitat upkeep. She . . .

"My staff is stretched thin, Captain," she told him, reaching for time to think. . . . "And I am not yet in charge. I will have to study this to . . ."

His expression went bland and she saw him sigh. Then his face went gentle, and she became frightened.

"We cannot enter into final docking procedures until we're sure of the docking mechanisms. Have you access to the records? Surely the dock integrity tests have been done! We cannot query your computer directly without permissions and I cannot risk docking until we have updated information. You must act so that we may properly arrive!"

The sub-captain took the orders without blinking. If the crew blinked, they did so with face bent over screens, following their orders. In a few hours they would be well away from the RosaRing, orbiting the planet and pacing the station at a distance, any docking approach awaiting developments.

The captain did what a captain does: he let his crew work. It was possible that he could have stepped into any one of the work streams, but they were becoming teams and he would have unbalanced them. The sub-captain directs the crew, the captain directs the sub-captain, and has the big picture.

The tactical crew studied the images; some savant had their computers going over accidental information drawn from the drone reports they'd intercepted. There were more images to be studied for change over time, and possible insight into the stability issues, if engineering could be roused to take a look . . .

Engineering—only a few of the current crew had been on the mission which had brought the station here! Engineering was studying the feasibility of a cold-latch using the very pod mounts they'd used to ferry it here in the first place.

The pod transfer systems. . . . If the standard docking system was compromised, the cargo transshipment would be a logistical terror.

"Captain, Station Ops has someone with experience holding down the deck now, sir. We've got one clear line, and they're asking if we can get some medical advice for them in a hurry. They have a lot of sick people, sir, and she says the administrator's locked in the tender bay, refusing to come out. There's unrest."

Kiland stared into the reflection of deck lights in his troth ring for a half a second.

To the sub-captain: "Add me to the listen list, get a

medic online, take any information you can about the physical plant situation. Try to patch through to the line I was on with the principal investigator last shift, open to the command chairs only."

"Sir," was the response, and then he listened.

"And this is?"

The image came from RosaRing's medics; he shared it back across space and waited.

Verita winced when she saw it, her indrawn breath loud between them.

"There is this as well, and this, all isolated within the last hours. Tell me about them!"

Captain to subordinate, the last demand. Verita nodded and began.

"The last image is a fairly common nanopump; it is available for use on restricted crops on many worlds. It biodegrades over time; that one is close to the end of utility. I use them in my work.

"The second image appears to be a blood platelet from an oxygen breather. I'm assuming it is human, and it is malformed—perhaps it has been paired with a nanopump and become separated.

"The first image is an anomaly. We see two of these cell structures, intertwined, one with a cell nucleus being—let us say examined or read—and one with a variant cell in, let us say, production. It uses an alternate chirality to induce evolutionary opportunity."

He said nothing for a moment, shared a list of symptoms . . .

"And this . . ."

"Is not surprising."

"This is native to Trikandle, and it is infecting humans through some strange happenstance?"

Verita glanced at the screen, which made it look to Kiland that she'd been avoiding looking at him.

"No, it is not natural to the world. It is not natural anywhere. We brought it. I introduced it. It is of the *Sherikas*."

She looked at him as if he were in the room with her.

"It ought not to have been able to do this, I swear."

"The entire mission is in grave danger, sub-captain; nothing medical personnel on board the station have tried have been more than palliative; the filtration approach has failed entirely. We must act quickly and responsibly . . ."

Captain Kiland piloted the captain's gig alone; he'd done so as a young officer and had had the ceremonial honor of piloting Admiral Smit's farewell flight from the *Implacable*. Going over the log books he'd long ago discovered that he had more hours on board than any other and now . . . and now he was the best able to bring the tiny vessel to the scene of the crisis.

They'd jury-rigged infection monitors once it was apparent that the kitchens had been infested, or the air filters or . . . and so maybe it *was* true that the only person on board the RosaRing free of the mutagenic was the principal investigator. He carried two of the touch-free monitors and eight of the *Implacable*'s biohazard suits, while he wore a standard spacesuit he could shed in an outer lock. The gig could use the smaller connects and emergency ports, and he had a target, a hatch well away from the crew quarters where the sick were lying where they fell, or hiding in the darkness as systems went offline.

The sub-captain was overseeing refitting a wing of half-empty crew quarters into an isolation ward, though by now there was word of deaths among the ill, and odd behaviors among the living. They'd gotten some hope, though, from a few stalwarts who switched to backup air supplies early . . .

It was a largely silent voyage. Several hours for the gig, a considered lifetime for Kiland. They'd mapped out as best they could the ports where the stains were, and clearly the hub ends were both affected. The tender's failed launch made that port inaccessible as well.

His targets were the several ports in the area of the labs, ports largely unused since the station was first provisioned by massive temporary dry docks long before the mission to Trikandle. The station was visible to the naked eye against space, strobes pointing to the parts he didn't want to visit—he was avoiding the central hubs in favor of the outer ring, the lower quarter of the outer ring once he'd got oriented. The thing was huge—of course it was, that's why it had taken the *Implacable* to move it!

"Kiland? They gave me this as a direct channel."

He froze. There was too much to say now, and most of it said or shared before. He needed to concentrate. And . . .

"Verita. Yes, I am here. Approaching. Be calm. I'm cruising along the hull, watching section numbers go by. Yours will be soon, Verita."

The contact was voice alone, so he watched the

structure go by as he corrected for spin. He doubted that he wobbled, and he waited, glad that she could not see his face.

"Kiland, we have always been honest, so I will be honest. I am not well. It is not mere tension—you know that I know tension. I—I fell and bloodied my nose, Kiland, and it stopped instantly. But, I have tools. I am good at my work.

"My blood shows changes, too, Kiland. Please, fly on by, Kiland. Fly on by!"

She was away from the microphone some moments but he heard and said: "It is too late for me to fly by, Verita. We are committed. I must see and report for myself.

"Tell me your exact location. I will find the port closest to you. I will . . ."

He was under the bulk of the thing, with white and blue and white and blue and white and blue blurring before his eyes to white. . . . Then blue. He matched velocity until the surface below him barely crawled and then, numbers and letters.

"Forty-four AGAAGF/FE," he said out loud as the gig answered his touch sweetly, approaching hatches auxiliary collars could link to. A hatch outlined, as if sketched over from within, by a collar of red and green crystals around the more prosaic ceramics meant to guard the ship close, even in the no-space that was Jump. His cameras surely transmitted that to the *Implacable*, surely the sub-captain saw the signs . . .

"Yes," Verita said, "that will be several doors down. I can go there, Kiland."

"There is a wobble," he said, which was true of the ring's motion and not his own.

"The next hatch will provide a better attachment angle. I will check that."

The little vessel let the ring slide on by, and in a moment he heard a sound that might have been a cry or a cough and . . .

"Kiland, I am not well. It will take me some minutes to get to the next airlock."

"No matter, the time," he said, "*Implacable* awaits my order."

"Yes, but I should move while I can, you see . . ."

"I have seen what I need to see, Verita. I shall return to the port where you are now. We shall be together very soon."

The gig bumped very slightly against the stain edging the port. "*Implacable*, I am docking. We have blue, blue, blue. Without doubt, we have blue, blue, blue."

"Kiland, tell me where to move?"

"Stay there, Verita. I will come to you. I am solving this."

"Beam Banks One and Two, go live as leads. The captain has declared a lethal threat situation. We have identified and targeted a threat.

"Prepare to fire on my command, on radar's current target T02. This is not a drill, you will now go to full combat power. Your target should be oversaturated at all wavelengths until plasma. Repeat, until plasma. Await my command."

"Beam Banks Three and Four. Your targets are any

rapidly vectoring objects showing planetary escape velocity. Your targets should be oversaturated at all wavelengths until plasma. Repeat, until plasma. Await my command."

"Beam Banks Five through Twenty, your planetary grids are pretargeted and programmed. You will fire until plasma. Repeat, you will fire until plasma. Await my command."

A decisive moment, the image from the gig, showing an empty pilot's seat and board. The forward cams show a fringe of strange color around the docking collar, growing.

"All fire," says the man. "All fire, all fire."

Somewhere, a singer is sobbing quietly at her terminal. The ship trembles. And trembles again, the ship's rotation bringing all the beam projectors to bear, one after another, a rotational broadside searing the ether.

There is silence, and then, loud in the silence of tense breathlessness there is the news of solving:

"Zap."

❧   ❧   ❧

SF convention favorites **Sharon Lee** & **Steve Miller** have been writing SF and fantasy together since the 1980s, with dozens of stories and several dozen novels to their joint credit. Steve was Founding Curator of Science Fiction at the University of Maryland's SF Research Collection while Sharon is the only person to consecutively hold office as the Executive Director, Vice President, and President of the Science Fiction and

Fantasy Writers of America. Their newest Liaden Universe® novel, *The Gathering Edge*, is their twenty-sixth collaborative novel. Their awards include the Skylark, the Prism, and the Hal Clement Award.

ICEBREAKER

Dave Bara

How do you react when you're the small-fry sub in the vast ocean of Europa and you're faced with the boomer of your nightmares: a Chinese battlecruiser determined to jump the claim that will make your fortune? Captain Dizzy Ramos knows what she's going to do: redeem her honor as a warrior after a lifetime of bad luck. Damn the Chinese. Damn the crew. Damn the heavens above. For she knows full well that to turn around as much bad juju as her career has acquired might very well require the ultimate sacrifice.

The icebreaker USNS *Morant* spun through near-Jupiter space, firing her retro-rockets and slowing her spin rate as she fell inward through Europa's light .134 Earth-gravity well. Europa's molecule-thin oxygen atmosphere created a microburn of scars on *Morant*'s skin. Unsightly, but nothing that would cause her captain the slightest concern.

The chemical rockets fired again, slowing her descent to less than five kilometers per second as her accompanying rotation also slowed. The large nuclear engine, nicknamed Berta by the crew, took over then, firing up at the base of the cylindrical spacecraft. Berta glowed red-orange in the dim light of the icy moon, slowing the *Morant*'s vertical drop even more. Her speed now halved, and then halved again, she slammed into the ice, cracking the surface of the Galilean moon for a good kilometer around the impact crater she formed. Automatically, metal impact shielding peeled back from the spacecraft, revealing a crisscrossing scaffold of framework holding Berta in her place.

Slowly Berta descended to the glaciated surface. She contacted the ice sheet and set off steam plumes venting away from her touch. Then she began rotating, spinning ever faster as she cut through Europa's ice, seeking the relative warmth of her inner ocean.

Captain Dizzy Ramos of the *Morant* watched all this on her allscope, a combination of high-definition camera, periscope (for ocean use), and telemetry monitor. She turned from side to side as she'd been trained to do. Captain Ramos did everything by the book, and that was a big reason why her crew hated her.

"Ice is two point two kilometers thick, well within the range the prospectors gave. Should take Berta thirty-nine minutes to burn through. Plan for release into the ocean at forty-five minutes from my mark," said Ramos. She waited a few seconds, then said, "Mark!"

"Acknowledged," said the first mate, Aleks Kolorov, in his thick Serbian accent. "Forty-five minutes to ocean birth." That's what he always called it, equating the *Morant*'s insertion into the well-traveled Europan oceans to a baby's birth from her mother's womb. Dizzy Ramos hated that analogy, almost as much as she hated Kolorov. She rolled the allscope back up into its holding position to clear more room on the tiny bridge, then turned to Kolorov.

"Have the navigation charts loaded into the scope by the time we drop," she said, trying hard to ignore the smell of him. Shipboard protocol called for two showers a week. Kolorov rarely took advantage of both his turns, and it disgusted Ramos.

"Aye, Captain," said Kolorov. "As soon we've docked with Berta again I'll let you know when we're ready to get underway."

"I want to be up here when we do the docking with Berta, not after," snapped Ramos. "I'm captain of this ship, Mister Kolorov."

"Yes, ma'am," said Kolorov. Ramos strode off the bridge with as much authority as her five-foot-three-inch frame would allow. As she passed Kolorov's station, he flipped her off behind her back. Once she was gone down the stairs, Kolorov turned to Ivan Massif, the navigator, a tall dark-haired lad from Ukraine.

"She stinks," said Kolorov, crinkling his nose.

Massif laughed.

Berta was done with her drilling work two minutes early. Despite Ramos's orders, Kolorov started the re-docking procedure, using the metal framework to slide the *Morant* down through the external scaffolding and into Europa's salty ocean. Then he called down to Ramos.

She was seething when she came back to the bridge, quickly using the allscope to watch the reconnection of the *Morant* with Berta, her main engine drive. Once attached again and fired up, Ramos ordered the *Morant* to get underway.

"Mister Kolorov," she said to her first mate as the *Morant* started moving, "was there something unclear about my instructions?"

"No, ma'am," said Kolorov. "But there are certain things not worth bothering the captain about."

"In your opinion. If this were a military ship—"

"Ah, yes, ma'am, but it is not. The *Morant* is a merchant ship, so orders have more of a feel of guidelines to them, no?" he said.

"I'm going to bring you up on charges when we get back to Ceres," she said.

"You already tried that twice, without success. Perhaps it's time you just gave it up and left the running of the ship to me. I've served on the *Morant* for a dozen years. You've been captain for less than two. You should leave running the ship to those of us who know her and concentrate on achieving mission objectives for the company instead," he said.

That infuriated her. In the military every order was followed, down to the letter. If Captain Ramos was being honest with herself, though, she'd acknowledge that after twenty years in military service, adjusting to being a merchant had been a difficult transition.

"I'm writing you up, Kolorov. I may not be able to

discipline you but I can sure as fuck fine your ass off my ship. Two thousand this time. Next time twenty-five hundred, and so on, until you're gone from here, so get used to that," Ramos said. Kolorov shrugged her off.

"That won't even dent my bonuses for exploiting this find. Do what you want, Captain. I doubt the company will complain when we come in early and under budget." And with that he turned back to his board.

Ramos went to her comm and called down to engineering. "Kish, what's the situation with our pipeline?" she said.

Daniel Kish, one of seven crewmen aboard, responded quickly. "Pipeline extrusion is ready to go, Captain. We have more than a hundred klicks worth of folded pipe in storage ready to unfurl. Shouldn't be any problem getting to the target area."

"Good," she said. "Carry on."

The target area was a recent find of a large natural-gas field by company surveyors that could be pumped out, cooled to -62° C, liquefied, then transported via the *Morant*'s flexible piping to massive tankers that would haul it back to Earth. There was enough just in this single find to fill one-eighth of the Earth's needs for most of a decade. And with a population of thirty-three billion, Earth had a lot of needs. There were the colonies too, about a million on Luna, two hundred thousand on Mars, and about fifty thousand on Ceres, but those were small potatoes and mostly taken care of by the smaller companies. Earth Resources Tech was one of the big ones, the biggest, unless you counted the state-run agencies in China and Russia. Dizzy could have signed with any of them after the Fourth War, but she chose ERT, and despite her crew of assholes, she still believed she'd made the right choice.

After setting up the pipeline extrusion equipment, Ramos ordered the *Morant* to be on her way.

"Mister Massif, set course for the Cambridge Shelf, as fast as Berta can get us there."

"Yes, Captain," said Massif, and laid in the course to the navigation screen so everyone could observe it. Six hours running full out.

An hour later and everything was running smoothly when the trio heard footsteps on the open metal staircase leading up to the bridge. To Kolorov and Massif's pleasant surprise it was Mischa Carr, the main nuclear tech that monitored Berta's functions and radiation levels aboard *Morant*. She was the only other female aboard and the only one either man would consider sleeping with. Massif had had that pleasure more than once, but so far Kolorov had been locked out of her bedroom, to his frustration.

She came up to Ramos. "Captain, I have something to report," she said.

"Go ahead," said Ramos.

"I've been tracking Berta's radiation levels since we started her up, and I've been picking up some anomalies in the readings," said Carr. Her obtuseness made Ramos impatient.

"Just spit it out, technician. What anomalies? I haven't got all day."

"Well, ma'am, I detected what I thought was leakage. But when I ran the diagnostics again I determined that the residual radiation was not coming from Berta. It's coming from outside the ship, and it gets stronger as we approach the gas field."

"How far away is it?"

"I'd say about sixty klicks, ma'am."

"Any idea what it is?"

"No ma'am. But I can say with certainty it wasn't here when the survey team came through."

"That was two months ago," said Ramos. Then she turned to Kolorov.

"Radiation protocol, first mate. That's an order."

"She just said it's sixty klicks out. You want us in those sweat suits the whole run in?" protested Kolorov.

"Those are my orders, first mate," she said. *Or I'll shoot you where you stand*, she thought. Then she left the bridge for the quiet of her cabin and away from the stench of Kolorov, which was sure to get worse.

When they got within a couple of klicks of the anomaly, Kolorov called Ramos back to the bridge. Absently he wondered what she did in her cabin all day. Maybe she slept with Kish. *Maybe she just runs a goddamned sex toy all day long*, he thought.

The radiation suits were hellish. So much padding that they made you sweat like a pig on what was already an overheated and cramped bridge. Kolorov smelled bad, even to himself. He contemplated using one of his shower credits when this ride was over.

Ramos came on the bridge in her full radiation suit and faced her first mate. "Status?" she demanded.

"Radiation levels are within acceptable levels, Captain," said Kolorov. "Can we take these damn sweat suits off now?" Ramos said nothing but responded by calling Mischa Carr to the bridge. When Carr arrived Ramos conferred with her, then allowed everyone to take off the radiation suits.

"Thank Christ," said Kolorov. He and Massif exchanged glances of disgust as they quickly peeled out of the silver suits and Kolorov lit up the bridge cooling fans. Ramos gave him an irritated look but said nothing, then motioned the two men over to her station. She turned to Carr.

"So in your opinion, technician, what are we dealing with here?" Ramos asked.

"Based on the recorded levels of radiation I'd say this was some sort of marker, designed to attract our attention. It's higher than background radiation but not high enough to be considered a weapon," Carr said.

"So we wore those damn suits for nothing," said Kolorov.

"I'm letting you run the cooling fans off company power, first mate. Just be thankful for that, and hydrate. You should be fine. Unless you need a break in your bunk to recover?" said Ramos. Kolorov raised up in defiance of his captain.

"Not needed, ma'am," he said.

"Good. Ivan," she said, turning to Massif, "take us in at one-quarter speed, then hold our position at five hundred meters. I want to know what this thing is."

"Yes, ma'am," replied Massif, then he smiled at Mischa and went toward his station. She smiled back.

A few minutes later and Massif reported in. "Positioned at five hundred meters, ma'am," he said.

"Good," said Ramos, then turned to her allscope. "First

mate, please monitor from your station." Kolorov switched on his plasma monitor and Mischa Carr came to join him. Kolorov allowed her to sit at his station while he stood behind her. He winked at Massif, who flipped him off in return.

Ramos looked through her allscope, pushing in the view repeatedly until she spotted the object, floating in the brine and projecting a glowing yellow light into the darkness. She kept refining the view until she got a clear view of the object.

"Those look like Chinese characters on the side," said Carr.

"Anyone read Chinese?" asked Ramos.

"Not if I can help it. It's all gook to me," cut in Kolorov. Ramos ignored him. Then a monitor alarm started to beep.

"What's that?" asked Ramos, concern in her voice.

"A telemetry packet," said Massif. "The thing is broadcasting in over seventy languages. I'll try and isolate English." He shuffled around for a few seconds, then brought up the message on the monitors. It was in all-block letters.

"TO ALL PASSING SHIPS AND SURVEYORS. THIS AREA AND ITS RESOURCES ARE CLAIMED IN TOTALITY BY THE FREE REPUBLIC OF CHINA. ANY INCURSION INTO THE AREA DEFINED IN THIS PACKET WILL BE CONSIDERED AN ACT OF WAR AND WILL BE MET WITH TOTAL AND COMPLETE ANNIHILATION OF ANY SHIP IN VIOLATION OF THIS CLAIM."

"Well, they talk tough," said Kolorov.

"What's the extent of the area they're claiming?" asked Ramos.

"It's about three hundred thousand kilometers square, centered on this claim marker," said Massif.

"That engulfs our entire claim," said Ramos.

"But we were here first," said Carr.

"It doesn't matter if they have more muscle in these waters than we do," said Ramos. She turned to Kolorov. "How much armament are we carrying?"

"Standard composition. Six eleven-kiloton torpedoes. Just enough for blasting out rock, not enough for fighting anything big," he said. Ramos turned to Massif.

"What's the ID of the ship that left this marker?"

"Just a second," said Massif as he scrambled through the data. "It says 'FRCN-9960'."

"Jesus Christ," said Kolorov, turning to Ramos, "that's the fucking *Mao Zedong!*"

Ramos contemplated that. The *Mao* was the most powerful interplanetary warship the FRCN had. She was loaded with enough tactical nukes and conventional torpedoes that she could shred the *Morant* in seconds. There was no way they could survive an encounter with that monster.

"What's the *Mao Zedong*?" asked Carr.

"The fucking devil in the dark," said Kolorov. "A boomer."

"What's a boomer?"

"A nuclear-powered and -equipped submersible warship. We're just an icebreaker. Absolutely no match for her. She destroyed half of the ERT fleet on Ganymede," said Ramos, "and now she's here on Europa."

"So do we give up our claim and turn back?" asked Massif.

"That would be the sane thing to do," said Kolorov.

Ramos turned to her bridge crew. "We go on," she said. "Our claim takes precedence."

"That doesn't do us any good if we're dead at the bottom of the ocean," said Kolorov.

"I'm not going to lose my job over what could be nothing more than an intimidation tactic. We go on. Those are my orders," Ramos said, then she started to walk away. Kolorov cut off her path, towering over her.

"You're fucking nuts if you think we can challenge the *Mao*," he said.

"I hope it won't come to that," she said, then brushed past him roughly, followed by Carr. Kolorov went to his station, then opened a drawer. He pulled out his sidearm in full view of Massif, loaded in a cartridge, then primed a round before putting it in his holster. He looked right at Massif.

"For her sake, I hope it doesn't," he said.

Captain Ramos lay on her bed, staring at the blank ceiling. The thoughts going through her head were old ones. It had taken her seven years to get a field command in the North American Navy during the Fourth War. She captained a guided-missile sub-destroyer named the *Agamemnon*, a real bitch of a boat with caterpillar drives, surface-to-air missiles, nuclear armed, no less, and both air- and sea-based cruise missile/torpedoes. And she was so damned fast. But that was over twelve years ago.

She'd been a rising star in the Navy then. In line for a full battlecruiser command. But the fortunes of war could often be unkind. The *Agamemnon* had detected a Chinese supercruiser hunting in the South China Sea east of Palawan Island. She'd tracked her, undetected, she thought, into a tight pass through an undersea mountain range eighteen hundred meters down. The supercruiser made it into the pass and Ramos ordered *Agamemnon* to follow. There was a turn in the pass, and for forty-five seconds she'd be running blind, unable to keep a photo-sonar lock on the supercruiser. When *Agamemnon* made the turn, instead of having a direct shot at the supercruiser's stern, she was facing her torpedoes instead. The torpedoes hit an outcropping on the undersea mountain range, and the rocks fell on her boat, just as they fell on her command. *Agamemnon* spent eight days under those rocks. She lost forty percent of her crew before she was rescued, then had to be scuttled. Dizzy Ramos's rising star fell faster than a meteor. She spent the rest of the war commanding a variety of auxiliary ships: repair scows, minesweepers, even a sonar detector sub. But she never got to see the bridge of a battlecruiser, and after twenty years she retired from the Navy and signed up for the merchant marine.

She got up from her bunk, restless, and pulled up the topographic maps of the gas field. There was precious little cover on the shelf, and very few places to hide. But the *Mao* didn't need to hide, she was bigger, faster, and stronger than anything on Europa, even if technically it was a combat-free world. She had no doubt the *Mao* would take out the *Morant* at the drop of a hat. She had to have a different strategy than traditional submarine warfare. She had to find a way to make the *Mao* chase her, all the way back to her landing hole.

She hit the comm. "Mister Kish, how much more speed can you give me?"

"We're at full now, Captain," said Kish.

"That's not what I asked you. How much more?" There was a pause, then:

"Fifteen knots, sir. But it will put a terrible strain on Berta, and she's already due for an overhaul when we get back to Ceres," he said.

"Do it," she demanded, and cut the comm. Then she opened up her desk drawer and pulled out her sidearm, loaded it, slipped it under her tunic, and lay back down on her bunk.

Fuck Ceres, she thought. *And fuck the* Mao.

Before returning to the bridge, Captain Ramos stopped by Mischa Carr's station on deck three. "Mischa," she said, surprising the young tech.

"Ma'am," said Carr.

"I need you to do some calculations for me."

"That's part of my job, ma'am."

"I want you to keep these calculations to yourself for now. It involves the *Mao*," said Ramos.

"Understood, ma'am. What do you want from me?"

"First, I need the atomic yield that would result if Berta were to go critical. And second, what would be the yield if we attached one of the torpedo warheads to her."

"As a detonator?"

"Yes." A look of concern crossed Carr's face.

"I can probably have that for you in an hour, ma'am," said Carr.

"Faster, if you can, technician. We may have trouble sooner than that."

"Understood, ma'am."

"Carry on, technician." And with that Ramos was off to the bridge.

The run into the gas field was tense on the bridge. Kolorov was being even more of an asshole than usual. Massif stayed quiet and out of the conflict, while Ramos was simply firm and to the point. Engineer Kish came through with the extra speed he had promised, and within the hour they were poised over the field at the prime mark the surveyors had identified for starting the drilling. On Ramos's orders, Kolorov dropped the automated drill on a tethered line and the device started doing its magic, grinding through meters of rock on the shelf to reach the gas. A plume of vapor shot up out of the drill vent when they hit the gas field, confirming the find. Kolorov hit the cut-off valve and meticulously extended the extruded tubing the *Morant* had been trailing from the drop hole down to the drill, then used robotic arms to secure and seal the tubing.

"We have a positive connection, Captain," said Kolorov.

"Good. Open the valves," replied Ramos.

"That will start the liquefaction process and fill the tubing with the gas, Captain. What's the point if we don't have tankers coming for four days?"

"I have my reasons, first mate. Now do as you're ordered."

"Aye, ma'am," Kolorov said as he hit a sequence of relays. The gas started flowing into the drill processor, where it was compressed and liquefied, then started pumping through the tubing and toward *Morant*'s drop hole, where it would be secured by the valve on the other end.

"Gas is compressed and pumping," reported Kolorov.

"Good," said Ramos. "Mister Massif, take us back the way we came." Massif looked to Kolorov.

"Same course, ma'am? Don't we want to avoid the *Mao*'s marker?"

"Exactly the same course, Mister Massif. Those are my orders." Then Ramos was off the bridge again. Massif looked to Kolorov, who shook his head.

"Crazy bitch."

As the *Morant* approached the *Mao*'s warning marker, Ramos demanded Mischa Carr's calculations on the nuclear yield of Berta.

"What have you got for me, technician?" asked Ramos over her room comm.

"Well, the U-235 that Berta runs off of is too diffuse to ignite on its own. But my calculations indicate that if we added two of the torpedo warheads to Berta as detonators, we could generate a point five megaton blast wave, with an approximate kill range of four kilometers. But obviously, if we did so, we would lose our main means of propulsion and be stranded here until we could be rescued," said Carr. Ramos thought about that for a moment.

"Take five of the warheads and link them to Berta. Leave one torpedo armed. And don't tell anyone about this," ordered Ramos.

"Y-yes, ma'am," said Carr.

"Do you have a problem with my orders, technician?" asked Ramos after noting the slight hesitation in her voice.

"That's a lot of yield, ma'am."

"It is," agreed Ramos. "And we may need all of it to get out of this alive," she said. With that she shut off the comm. The big fish wasn't going to elude Dizzy Ramos again.

Not this time, she thought.

Ramos was on the bridge with Kolorov and Massif as they approached the *Mao*'s claim marker.

"Three kilometers to the claim marker," reported Kolorov.

"Distance to the gas line?"

"Ten kilometers," said Kolorov.

"Any sign of the *Mao*, Mister Massif?"

"Negative, Captain," said Massif. Ramos got on the comm.

"Engineer Kish, please load torpedo six into the launch tube," she said. Kish acknowledged her order through the comm.

"Mister Kolorov, target the claim marker and prepare to launch on my signal," said Ramos.

"Are you insane?" said Kolorov, angry. "You want to bring the *Mao* down on us? Send them an invite to fight us? They'll crush us!"

"I don't think so, Mister Kolorov. Now follow my orders," Ramos said, icy cold. Kolorov stood to attention but refused to move an inch. Ramos flinched, almost pulling out her hidden sidearm, but deciding against it at the last moment. She got on the comm again.

"Mister Kish, load firing control into my console," she

said, all the while staring down Kolorov, who was wearing his sidearm openly. Kish acknowledged, and presently she had targeting and firing control on the nuclear-tipped torpedo on her overhead console. She calibrated the targeting on the claim marker, then released the launch control.

"Captain," said Kolorov. "Don't make me stop you." She looked at him. He had his sidearm drawn on her. She didn't hesitate. She fired the torpedo.

Kolorov held his fire.

The torpedo launched out of the firing tube and quickly closed the distance to the *Mao*'s claim marker. The explosion set off alarms throughout the *Morant*, and she shook considerably as the shock wave swept past her. The crew held on to any support they could find. A few seconds later, all was calm again.

"Resume course, Mister Massif," ordered Ramos. Then she once again brushed past Kolorov on her way to her cabin. This time she stopped at the top of the stairs and turned back.

"And Mister Kolorov, if you draw your weapon on my bridge again, I expect you to use it, because it will be the last chance you'll ever get." And then she was gone. Behind her, the bridge was deathly quiet.

The *Mao Zedong* was on the *Morant*'s trail an hour later.

"How long to the drop hole, Mister Massif?" asked Ramos.

"One hour, nineteen minutes," replied Massif. Ramos turned to Kolorov.

"Closing rate of the *Mao*?"

"She'll catch us nine minutes before we reach the hole, but we'll be vulnerable to her torpedoes fourteen minutes out," said Kolorov.

"Steady as she goes, Mister Massif," said Ramos.

"Aye, Captain," said Massif, giving Kolorov a concerned look across the cramped bridge. Kolorov stepped out of his station to approach Ramos.

"Captain, if we get Mister Kish to push the engines to overdrive we can probably escape before the *Mao* can catch us," said Kolorov evenly. Ramos looked at him.

"I want the *Mao* to catch us, first mate," she said. Kolorov frowned.

"Captain, that doesn't make any sense. The *Mao* is a battlecruiser. We have no chance against her. If you persist on this course, I can relieve you under maritime law for endangering your own crew," Kolorov said.

"Return to your station, first mate," said Ramos. Kolorov didn't back down, didn't move.

"This is my last warning, Captain. If you don't change tactics, I will relieve you under maritime law." His hand went to his sidearm. Ramos eyed him directly, with barely contained fury on her face. She reached up and hit her comm. "Technician Carr, to the bridge please," she said, then changed the channel. "Mister Kish, to your bridge station please." At that Kolorov turned and started back to his station.

Ramos pulled her gun and shot him twice in the back.

Massif froze at his station. The sound of Kish and Carr

running up the gangplank to the bridge filled the now deathly quiet room.

"What the fuck!" Kish said as he saw Kolorov's fallen body. Carr stayed behind him, scared. Ramos still held her gun, arm extended in a threatening manner.

"Mister Kish, you and technician Carr will remove the body, then return to the bridge immediately," Ramos said. Kish stared her down, but said nothing. Then he and Carr started moving Kolorov's body.

"Mister Massif," said Ramos. "Steady as she goes." Massif swallowed hard.

"Understood, Captain," he said in a shaky voice, "steady as she goes."

The first sign that the *Mao* had arrived was a conventional torpedo fired across the *Morant*'s bow. They were fourteen minutes out from the drop hole. Kish had replaced Kolorov at the first mate's station and Mischa Carr was at engineering. Ramos was determined this was the crew she would achieve her greatest victory with, but she wouldn't hesitate to take out anyone who disobeyed her orders.

"Distance to the *Mao*," she demanded from Ivan Massif.

"Six kilometers and closing fast," said Massif with just a slight quaver of fear in his voice. Whether the fear was caused by the approaching behemoth or by his own captain, even he wasn't sure.

"Captain," said Carr, "they're sending a comm."

"Let's hear it," said Ramos. The comm spit out a long string of angry Chinese gibberish.

"They sound pissed off," said Kish.

"I would be too if I was them," said Ramos. "Ivan, how close are they tracking to our pipeline?"

"They're right on top of it, ma'am. Closing fast. Four klicks now," said Massif.

"Perfect," said Ramos. Massif gave Carr a worried look while Kish remained focused on his board. "They're going to want that pipe, it saves them a bunch of development time. They'll hug it all the way up to the drop hole. If we get there first and hook it up to our release valve they won't be able to take us out. They can't fire on us with a live nuke or they risk igniting the whole pipeline, hell, maybe all the way back to the shelf. So they'll have to back off. How close to the hole now?"

"Just three minutes out, Captain," said Massif. Ramos smiled.

"We're too close. They can't nuke us now. Take us up that drop hole, Mister Massif," said Ramos with a smile. That made everyone on the bridge relax a bit.

Massif guided the *Morant* to the hole and inside, where the grappling hooks started pulling her up the hole. The *Mao* continued to send out threatening comms, but she had stopped her ascent four klicks below the *Morant*.

"Sir, the *Mao* is now starting to drop away from us. She's heading for the pipeline!" said Massif.

"She'd rather risk cutting the pipe than losing it to us," said Ramos.

"Won't that set off the gas?" asked Carr.

"It won't if she's able to clamp off the pipe with her forward claws and seal the line. Then she could take it

anywhere she wants and just attach a new valve pump,"
said Kish.

"We won't let that happen. Let me know when they
start to cut the line, Mister Kish," said Ramos. She turned
to Mischa Carr.

"Technician Carr, prepare to release Berta."

"What?" said Kish. "Are you mad? Without Berta we
can't get spaceborne again!"

"I'm well aware of that, Mister Kish," said Ramos with
an icy stare. "There will be a tanker here to rescue us in
four days. We will survive."

"Just on batteries? Without Berta we'll freeze well
before they get here!" said Kish. "Is this why you killed
Aleks?"

Ramos responded by pulling her sidearm again and
leveling it at Kish.

"I *can* do this myself, Mister Kish. Now do you plan on
following my orders or not?" she said. Everyone was
frozen with fear. Kish said nothing more. "Technician
Carr, you will follow my last order."

"Yes, Captain," she said. Ramos checked her board.
The emergency release for Berta was glowing red on her
command panel.

"Thank you, Mischa. Now step away from your console.
Mister Kish, activate the long-range comm." Kish did as
ordered, then also stepped away from his console. "Mister
Massif, status of the *Mao*."

"Steady at ten klicks distance now. She's clipping
the line, Captain. Preparing to clamp the line," said
Massif.

"How long will that take?"

"Approximately four minutes," said Massif. Ramos waved him away from his station. The three remaining crew of the *Morant* stood together in the center of the bridge. Massif put his arm around Carr while Ramos leveled her gun at the three of them.

She checked the comm uplink. They were locked with the relay satellite. Everything was ready.

"What I do now, I do for all of us. Our names will live in history," she said, then she hit the release button.

Berta disconnected from the *Morant* and dropped down the hole and back into the Europan ocean, heading straight for the *Mao*.

Ramos watched as Berta did her intended work, falling ever closer to the *Mao*. Ramos looked one last time at the detonator button on her display. Then she pressed it.

Ten kilometers below the *Morant*, Berta exploded in a nuclear fireball that quickly engulfed the *Mao* and ignited the gas line. Red-gold flame seethed through the gas line off into the distance, heading for the gas field in a chain reaction of burning liquid fuel. Upward the blast wave came, striking the *Morant* and melting the ice shelf around her. The crew were thrown around the bridge like toys. Ramos held onto a support pole with all her might. Once the initial blast wave was over, she was the only one conscious on her burning bridge. She struggled to her feet and hit the comm uplink, getting a green light on her panel. The comm was linked to the relay satellite. She opened the comm channel.

"This is Captain Diane Ramos of the Icebreaker USNS *Morant*," she said in a halting voice. "We sunk the *Mao Zedong*. Repeat, the *Morant* sunk the *Mao*!"

Then she slumped over the railing and dropped to the floor of her bridge.

Outside, the scaffolding holding the *Morant* melted and fell inward through the drop hole, the *Morant* following in quick succession.

Back into the briny depths of the Europan ocean.

❋　　❋　　❋

Dave Bara is the author of The Lightship Chronicles series (*Impulse*, *Starbound*, and *Defiant*) published by DAW Books in the US and Del Rey in the UK and Europe. He was born at the dawn of the space age and grew up watching the Gemini and Apollo space programs on television, dreaming of becoming an astronaut one day. This soon led him to an interest in science fiction on TV, in film, and in books. Dave's writing is influenced by the many classic SF novels he has read over the years from authors like Isaac Asimov, Arthur C. Clarke, Joe Haldeman, and Frank Herbert, among many others. He lives in the Pacific Northwest.

TRY NOT TO KILL US ALL

Joelle Presby

Sometimes, you have to scavenge to get by. That's always been true, and it's not likely to change just because the technology improves. Only what you're scavenging gets a little shinier. When the survival and well-being of the planet means stealing a priceless energy source from alien-controlled space . . . you do what needs doing. Joelle Presby brings her experience with real-life submarines to this game of cat and mouse.

Senior Chief Luther Albro intended to save the world today. With a slender build and a balding head, he was the best hope humanity of A.D. 2318 had, at least in his own opinion. The officers always had other perspectives.

Amusement sparkled in Captain Michael Knupp's blue eyes when Albro finished his operations brief. Even Petty Officer Rodgers noticed, and of the three junior shinerrite technicians, the young man seemed least observant. Li and Morales wore those careful blank faces most spacers learned in boot camp.

"Thanks for the brief, Senior Chief," Commander Jules said. She was the ship's executive officer, and had been a shinerrite tech herself once before going officer. The respect on her warm brown face, at least, was calming. She understood how challenging his job was. Shinerrite retrieval missions could easily get them all killed. Or even see Earth annihilated, if the screwup were big enough.

The aliens, annoying, egotistical super beings that they were, mostly viewed humanity as mildly cute wilderness animals. But the aliens left behind the shiniest bits of space trash, and humanity had come to love the stuff. God only knew what the material did for the aliens, but for humanity shinerrite was better than gold, hydrocarbons, and reprogrammable nanofiber all rolled into one.

The spaceship, which Senior Chief Albro would be running tactical control for during the retrieval mission, had a power system running on just one cubic meter of the stuff. The rest of the mass of their enormous spaceship existed to shield that power system. And of course they needed vast tanks of rocket fuel for puttering around on stealth.

Albro imagined spacecraft engineers of ages past sneering at the idea of rockets serving any sort of stealth role. Those futurists of a few centuries ago would have been right if the ship were hiding from other humans or even from intelligent aliens. But—Petty Officer Morales jogged his elbow. The polite tap pulled his attention back to the present.

"And that's all we've got from engineering."

Commander Jules finished her part of the report. "And all divisions reported in reconfirming secured for rocket operations. We're ready."

"Two planets, one sun, and a bunch of masses that might be shinerrite and might be alien killer bots." Captain Knupp grinned as he summarized Albro's situation report. He turned to Albro and winked. "Try not to kill us all."

"Will do, sir." Albro refrained from adding anything caustic about it being officers who got ships killed and not the shinerrite techs.

Too much outspokenness in his past might be why squadron had elected to have him cross-decked to this ship when Captain Knupp's last senior shinerrite tech suffered a mental breakdown at the beginning of their outbound deployment. Nobody seemed to care that Albro had just been about to return home to Earth after eight months and three days outside Sol System. The master chief from squadron who'd been sent out on the little parts-and-repairs ship to retrieve Knupp's prior senior shinerrite technician and drop Albro off in his place had even had the nerve to suggest this extra deployment was exactly what Albro needed to brush up his record for the master chief boards—as if Albro needed any help when he already had one of the best shinerrite retrieval records in the fleet!

Still, it was nice to have a captain willing to take a course directly through a new system only recently abandoned by the aliens. Albro hadn't expected to have his recommendation accepted. Most ship captains were too cautious to enter a system like this one.

In a few moments, their powerful shinerrite drive would reverse to slow the ship and then turn off. Orbital physics would continue their ballistic momentum straight through the system where their sensors could figure out in detail what was out there and where the deadly bots could also counterdetect the ship if he did something stupid like turn on the shinerrite drive or allow flecks of shinerrite from a passing mass to smear across the ship's hull.

There would be more shinerrite available here, but there'd also be more of the aliens' automated trash clean-up devices.

Commander Jules sent everyone off to their stations before Albro could decide if this new ship's captain was an improvement over the one on his last ship or not. It seemed a solid enough crew, but something about Captain Knupp made the back of Albro's neck twitch.

The captain of his last ship had been terrified of everything, always second-guessing, always delaying the mission when a few quick tactical decisions could have had their cargo bay full of shinerrite and ready to head on home after only weeks away instead of dodging around system after system always looking for an easier collection.

"Captain Knupp is descended from one of the Centauri System survivors," Petty Officer Morales said as she strapped in.

"So am I," Albro admitted. There weren't a lot of them. Humanity had started collecting shinerrite before fully understanding the dangers of the aliens' cleaner bots.

The things were stupid, so it wasn't completely unreasonable for the early explorers to have misjudged the situation. And back then ships had not returned for a lot of reasons, so understanding hadn't made its way back to the populated stations in Sol System until a truly massive disaster had hit humanity's first long-term outposts in the Centauri System.

Even now the recruiting posters made fun of the aliens' cleaner bots as Space Roombas from Hell, but the things the aliens left orbiting their playground systems were nearly indestructible and would track a bit of stolen shinerrite across the galaxy if they were ever allowed to catch a sniff of a spaceship carrying it.

The things were dumb but tough. The bots' programming sought out the alien trash which degraded into shinerrite. The massive machines compacted and vaporized the stuff, breaking apart any other matter that might be splattered with trace amounts of shinerrite, be it a spaceship, a station, or, in humanity's nightmares, a planet. A single bot had followed a ship home to the once-thriving human space stations in the Centauri System. It had destroyed them all. Only the oldest ships without shinerrite drive tech had been able to escape. The Sol System Navy could not allow that to happen to Earth.

Too much shinerrite had been used and spread around the old homeworld to be gathered up and jettisoned out into the beyond now. Besides, it was so extremely useful that not even the cultists who worshiped the unresponsive aliens as gods seriously wanted to stop exploiting it.

Thankfully the aliens had made the bots only as hellish space Roombas. They looked for shinerrite and only shinerrite. Sufficient thicknesses of matter shielded the signals the bots used to find the next blob of shinerrite.

The cleaner bots didn't attempt to smash through planets or fly into suns only because the large celestial bodies blocked signal transmission.

The bots didn't reason, didn't extrapolate, and didn't plan. They were dumb and deadly.

"Prepare for system entry," Captain Knupp's voice sounded over the shipwide announcing system.

Albro double-checked his straps and noted that Morales, Li, and Rodgers had all secured themselves properly as well. On the shinerrite drive, they had no need of the careful padding and belts, but on a ballistic course with only rockets available to readjust, things could get bumpy.

"I hope we find some shinerrite this time," Rodgers said. "Last deployment we coasted through a system three times and only tracked bots."

"The first pass is for intel. The second for collection." Li parroted the manual.

Why would a ship captain make a second, let alone a third pass through a system with more bots than collectable shinerrite? Albro frowned. "We'll see what we see."

Their sensors rewarded him soon enough.

They entered as planned on a course to pass near the large gas giant where a few masses too small to be bots would be in rocket range for a pickup if they proved to be shinerrite and not ordinary space debris. The system's sun hid the smaller planet from them, but it had a fast orbit and would swing around the sun's horizon early enough in their course to give them a good long look at anything around it.

The one object Albro had been certain was a bot—based on size and trajectory changes seen from their telescopic view outside the system—had merged with another large mass before they began their ballistic insertion. That would be a bot busy consuming a shinerrite mass, and it would soon pass out of the range of their sensors as it orbited, with the mass it worked to consume, around the far side of the gas giant from them.

Everything worked out as Albro expected—except for Captain Knupp.

Commander Jules was responding to Albro's small course corrections from engineering like a good textbook executive officer. But Captain Knupp wasn't hanging over his shoulder like any reasonable nail-biting ship's captain would.

Albro took a deep breath, cleared his mind, and focused on the tactical plot. The precision radar and navigation had a corner in the far side of the central control room and repeater screens on the bridge. His team—Morales, Li, and Rodgers—were the sensor operators who would identify all the shinerrite and all the bots, and he'd be the one adjusting the ship's course to keep them all hidden and alive.

Navigation plots were limited to celestial bodies like the two planets orbiting this distant star and the various comets passing through the system. The aliens and all things related to them were best tracked with shinerrite sensors. Regular orbital bodies obeyed the laws of astrophysics just fine.

Things that were made from shinerrite—especially things like bots and the alien debris that hadn't quite finished decaying all the way into raw shinerrite—didn't. Or at least didn't always. The bots followed their programming. The masses decaying into shinerrite deposits were unpredictable: sometimes acting like a space rock of any other material and sometimes sluggishly moving under power. Shinerrite required special sensors. The bots could send out active pings, but that would get a ship detected and destroyed. So shinerrite technicians used passive detectors. They recorded the bearings to the shinerrite masses and moved their own ship to get more bearings and calculate ranges. Precision, caution, and training kept them alive. "Hide with pride" was the shinerrite tech motto for a reason.

Albro's own master plot of the shinerrite and all identified or suspected bots in the system could be mirrored on the captain's and executive officer's consoles at whatever stations they wanted to use. The empty commanding officer's seat just over Albro's shoulder gave him unpleasant images of Captain Knupp storming into central control battered and bleeding from being slammed into bulkheads during one of the many rocket accelerations they'd be making during the pass through the system.

"Bridge, Central," Albro called over the ship's comm system. "Anyone seen the captain?"

"Right here, strapped in and ready to go," Captain Knupp answered.

Albro paused. Captain Knupp was on the bridge and not coming to central control at all. Surely not. He'd make a polite recommendation. "We have a little time before we need to thrust, if you were going to come down to central, sir."

"I like the bridge," Knupp replied. "Better view of the stars on the big repeater screen. Don't worry, I've got your shinerrite overlay pulled up too, so I'll be following along just fine."

But what about the poor crew on the bridge? Most captains started to sweat pretty badly when the bigger shinerrite deposits got close, and Albro didn't see a reason to waste rocket fuel on evasions when the sensors showed only a near pass and no actual threat of hull residue. Captains shouldn't cry in front of non-shinerrite techs. The other crew didn't expect it and wouldn't know how to deal. But even senior chiefs don't tell captains that over an open circuit. So Albro settled for: "Aye, sir."

The petty officers were giving Albro nervous glances, so he did what his own senior chief used to do.

"Officers." He shrugged. "Not our problem. Let's see about getting some shinerrite." He gave them a grin. There were advantages to not having to phrase all the directions to his techs in calm soothing tones. Sure, if they made a mistake, the ship would be lost. But there were four bright minds here working together, and they had plenty of historical data backing up their tactics.

Attempts to communicate with the aliens had so far failed, but with shinerrite, humanity had learned to locate them. The aliens chose solar systems and played in them or did whatever it was that aliens cared to do for decades, sometimes more, and then moved on.

His team understood what was out there. Missing ship's captain or not, they started to track and tag contacts immediately. The ordinary diffuse plasma swirling through the interior of solar systems carried long signal waves sent out by the cleaner bots. The waves were swallowed up soundlessly by most matter, but when they hit shinerrite, the signals bounced back in a clear alien echo almost louder than the initial wave signal.

The cleaner bot's pitch would rise in a closing Doppler scream, roar lower after it passed, and be cut off abruptly at the target. Optical sensors would fill in the silent details later at mere light speed to show the bot crashing through everything in its way. The bot would clean and clean until all the target shinerrite was gone, and once more soft deadly pings would announce a resumed search.

The transducers human engineers had originally built in the Centauri panic to detect cleaner bots could also pick up signals from the shinerrite itself. A few meters of lead proved to be effective shielding against those human-built detectors, so the Sol System Navy used ten meters around the cargo bay and twenty around the main drive's power generator. Just to be sure.

Of course Albro's ship couldn't actually use that drive with all the shielding in place, but every spaceship had secondary systems and they'd have to get well away undetected before they could re-engage the main drive and return to full-power operations.

Planets and suns were good shielding too. Gas might not be the most effective shielding material, but in the amounts present in a gas giant—well, quantity had a quality all of its own. Their ship coasted into a position near the center of the system. The small inner planet of the rocky telluric type not usually favored by the aliens circled on the far side of the sun, and the gas giant loomed ever larger in their viewscreens. The hints of shinerrite they'd begun to detect from the edge of the system separated out now in three distinct masses in the gas giant's orbit.

Albro's team had bearing lines plotted for two tumbling blobs of shinerrite and a confirmed datum on a third currently being consumed by a cleaner. That was the one he'd expected to be around the horizon of the gas giant by now. He'd had the speed of the combined masses orbit off by half. It would still pass around the gas giant's horizon soon, but it would not reemerge for hours.

A smile began to tug at the side of Albro's face. They were on a first pass through a system with several shinerrite masses in range and no bots nearby. That other planet would almost certainly have bots on or around it, but maybe he'd get one of those rare first-pass collection opportunities. He let himself grin because there was no captain around to get nervous.

That third deposit spun away from them in orbit around the system's large gas giant and its bot went with it.

"Crying shame," Petty Officer Morales said. She had scratched notes with a light pen on the side of her trace screen, estimating the size of the deposit being consumed.

"Not for us." Albro corrected. "That's too big to fit in our cargo hold." He paused for a moment to bring up an overlay of the system bodies pulled from navigation's computers. "Morales, how long before that deposit's orbit puts the gas giant fully between us and the cleaner's sensors?"

"One minute, thirty-eight seconds," Morales responded

immediately. "And over twelve hours before it emerges on the other side. I can calculate exactly—"

"Belay that." Albro turned to Rogers and Li. "After that thing slips behind the gas giant's horizon, I'm going to have the bridge change our course to head toward it. But slowly. Work bearing solutions for me on your possible contacts after the course change. I don't want to be headed toward it any more than fifteen minutes. Morales, keep up your dead-reckon trace on the cleaner as it goes behind the planet." He repeated himself in more formal phrasing to update the bridge.

"Got it," Captain Knupp acknowledged.

Albro twitched. He preferred a crisp "Very well, Senior Chief," but the screen tore his attention away.

Morales added a small dot on their display to show where, invisible behind the gas giant, the third deposit and the dangerous bot orbiting with it would be.

"As I maneuver us around," Albro continued, "you need to remind me anytime my course changes move us outside the sensor shadow of that gas giant."

She nodded and made adjustments to the display to show a slightly shrunken horizon line circling around the gas giant to account for the point where the gas thickness of the planet edge would stop providing sufficient shinerrite shielding. Albro nodded, pleased to not have had to remind her to do so. The captain would see it too, along with the draft courses his other two petty officers were working on.

Albro called the bridge with the first set of accelerations, and the commanding officer executed his course change. Albro gave Rodgers and Li a full six minutes of bearing plotting time before changing to the third course. They'd need it to triangulate estimated locations for their shinerrite deposits.

Something in the nature of shinerrite made their sensors great at line of bearing but not so accurate for range detection. When they needed extreme precision to scoop a bit of it into the cargo bay without scraping anything against the hull, using multiple precision bearing lines to calculate and recalculate their target's location became common sense. With a fourth course change, his petty officers should be able to give him orbits and plot a retrieval course.

The last system his previous ship had visited had been too crawling with cleaner bots for even Albro to recommend an entry. The ship's lead shielding around their shinerrite power system only made them near invisible while coasting or on rocket power. Stealth and safety were not the same thing. The crew of a safely unlocated spaceship could starve to death waiting for an opportunity to engage shinerrite drives and leave a system with too many cleaner bots. They needed planets and suns to hide behind before engaging their drives and beginning the hopscotch home through empty systems.

So while he checked the petty officers' calculations and saved them in the corner of his screen, Albro also started looking for a way to get the ship out.

And he kept an eye on that second planet. It would be having a planet rise over the sun's horizon real soon now.

Albro keyed his microphone to speak to the bridge and engineering. In the most bored voice he could manage he said, "Change to next course now. Expect a second bot to clear the sun's horizon. Possibly in five minutes."

Rodgers, Li, and Morales gave him uniform pale-faced expressions of horror. They had some work to do before they'd be ready to run their own tactical plot teams. If Captain Knupp had been in central, he might have freaked just from their expressions. Shinerrite technicians couldn't afford to show fear like that.

"It's fine," he explained. Since there weren't any officers around to be panicked by the details, he told them his reasoning. "Our intel says the aliens left this system only a decade ago. It's too cleaned up to have had only one bot working on it. Behind the sun is the only place another bot could be or we would've been picking up its signals."

"But why five minutes?" Li said.

Albro rewarded them with a broad grin. "I have no idea if there'll be one there at all. But five minutes is a little while from now. This'll keep engineering ready if I need a quick maneuver without getting them too keyed up to react. If there's a bot out there, it'll probably be on or near the system's other planet. If it's working on a shinerrite deposit, it'll stay there until it finishes. If it isn't, it'll charge toward one of our two right here as soon as it gets a clear signal."

"But what if there isn't a bot at all?" Rodgers asked.

"I did say 'possibly.' Remember to always say possibly." Albro gave them a wink.

"It might not slow down very much before it starts consuming one of these deposits if it is there," Morales said. She had draft courses on her screen from the rising planet's surface and math multiplying a typical bot's mass by the max speed of one on full shinerrite drive power. Not quite correct, but close.

"They always slow just before impact," Albro reminded her. "The lab tests show shinerrite will splatter if impacted like that, so that may be why their programming doesn't allow it."

"Are we sure?" Li asked. "There could be another bot just in the sun's orbit, not near the planets at all."

"Could be," Albro acknowledged. "But not in this system. Our outer scans were thorough enough that we would have picked any of those up as shadows far too large to be sunspots."

He had expected at least small shinerrite debris in heliocentric orbit in this system, but their in-system scan had yet to pick up even trace amounts of shinerrite near the sun. It was an anomaly and those always worried him. Stuff too close to a sun wasn't recoverable by humans, but usually there was one near-melted hulk of a cleaner bot powering from one sunward bound shinerrite deposit to the next. What if there were not just one unlocated cleaner bot in this system but two?

"Contact solution!" Li reported—finally finishing the calculations for his assigned deposit near them in the gas giant's orbit—and he rattled off his shinerrite deposit's details. This one would fit in the cargo hold.

Albro held off planning to collect it until he got a good view of the other planet.

Rodgers cursed under his breath at being second to finish his calculations, but, Albro noted with approval, he still ran his numbers three times to check them before making his own report.

"Very well," Albro acknowledged them both and had them plot collection courses, which he checked against his own. No errors this time, and he always appreciated extra checks.

He didn't usually have a choice in which deposit pickup to attempt while staying undetected; so far, either of the two petty officers' collection courses would work if no bots waited on that inner planet. But neither collection could be accomplished before the planet came into view. The two deposits were caught by the gas giant's gravity well but in a tumbling unstable orbit where they spun around each other.

Some parts of the alien trash weren't quite decomposed all the way down to shinerrite yet. That matter transition created some interesting orbital mechanics. Albro rechecked the numbers both petty officers had sent him to account for the continued wobble. The plots still worked. A little messy, maybe, but he could pull it off using the precision radar for the final approach. On a tactical scale the masses would be a challenge to collect, but not impossible. Their spins around each other had a consistent cycle and their joint decaying orbit around the gas giant spun them toward his ship.

He tried to estimate if he could fit both deposits in the hold. From the faintness of the signal, Li's deposit was significantly smaller, maybe only a few meters in diameter.

"Planet rise," Morales reported, pointing at the system's sun on their plot and the small planet about to come out of eclipse, "in three, two—" She drew in her breath sharply and skipped straight to the more important report. "Multiple cleaner bot signals detected. Three, no, two . . ." She paused trying to figure out her screen.

"They're on the planet," Albro said. "It's got an erratic spin. It should be tidally locked, but isn't. Maybe the aliens did something to it or maybe the decaying relics malfunctioned to cause it. Once the bots have it all cleaned up, solar gravity will eventually stop that spin, but not while we're around to care." He added throbbing red markers to his screen's overlay—just in case Captain Knupp on the bridge didn't recognize what the icons for bots in detection range of the ship looked like.

"Surface craters." Li bit his lip and stayed focused on his own screen. He had copied Albro and used the ship's optics to supplement his shinerrite view to see what Morales hadn't. "Hopefully that means they're too broke to escape the gravity well."

Hope is not a plan of action. "Possible," Albro acknowledged and looked to Morales for the rest of her report. She glanced at Li's screen and immediately recognized the cause of the shinerrite signals blinking in and out.

"The bots are deep in surface craters which are shielding their signals sometimes. I think there's four of them on it," she finished. It wasn't standard reporting, but Albro would take it. She was giving him the information he needed and most importantly, staying calm.

This is why a normal commanding officer would be here with them in central. Five bots in a single system with only two planets for cover far exceeded recommended safety margins, and they hadn't known how many to expect from the outer system scans.

He called Captain Knupp.

"Recommend abort recovery mission and abandon this system, sir. We can reverse course and use a combination of the gas giant and system primary to cover our exit under full power."

"Senior Chief!" Morales interrupted.

Two cleaner bots finished their work on the planetary surface at nearly the same time and shrieked locator pings across the system. Li and Rogers hit red-alert warning buttons in unison as both their deposits were detected.

"Wait." Albro held his breath. The cleaners' signals also hit a moon-sized deposit in orbit around their inner planet. The bots launched together, with no synchronization, and nearly clipped each other as they slammed into the moon. With a smaller target, they would have collided.

Morales sent him the sensor analysis on that deposit. Lots of rock in it and very little shinerrite. It probably was a moon strewn liberally with alien trash rather than what it had initially appeared, and it wouldn't hold one cleaner bot long, let alone two.

His last commanding officer would have been screaming by now for allowing them to enter a system with five active bots. But without anyone screaming in his ear, Albro could think. He blinked at his screen. He liked that moon. And he could still see collection options. He keyed in updates to his plot.

"Captain." Albro double-checked the ship's orientation and started to talk fast. "Resuming recovery mission and preparing for system exit within the hour.

"Cargo, open recovery bay to vacuum. Prepare

retrieval arms for operation. Engineering, standby for system exit at max speed."

Slightly too much tension showed in his voice because Albro could hear the fear in the cargo bay operator's acknowledgement. Commander Jules answered for engineering, though, and she sounded perfectly bored. The former shinerrite technician was ready to back him up.

Lines appeared on his screen marking the future course of the two bots on the inner planet's moon. He hadn't drawn them, and his petty officers didn't have the authority to push data to his master plot. Albro smiled; the executive officer still remembered her stuff. He gave the commanding officer the beginning of an update, only to be cut off.

"Got it, Senior. Do your thing," Captain Knupp said.

"Recovery bay doors open," cargo reported.

The bot-infested planet continued to rise as its orbit brought it farther around the sun. The planet's own spin turned the two on-surface bots away from them, but they'd be turned back again before too long.

The gas giant's solar orbit ran in the same ecliptic, but not as fast, and while the spin of the deposits Li and Rodgers tracked were bringing them closer to the ship, the timing was going to be tight. He sent his planned courses to the team. Morales checked them against her track for the gas giant's hidden bot and gave him a silent thumbs-up.

He told the bridge the next course and they complied. Their ship, never the sleekest thing to grace the starways, scooted backward on reverse thrusters to scoop Li's deposit into the open hold, slam shut the cargo bay doors, and jettison the now contaminated recovery arms into the back of Rodgers's deposit.

"Clean capture," Albro reported to the bridge as soon as his scans showed the hull had escaped any particulate smearing.

"Syzygy!" Rodgers breathed in admiration seeing his untouched larger deposit align with Li's and the bot-infested planet just as they executed the recovery. If any of the bots on that planet had had a lock on it, that particular piece of shinerrite had not spontaneously vanished from their sensors. It had merely passed behind a larger chunk of shinerrite and not reemerged. The cleaner bots' processor systems would not know it was missing until they cleaned up Rodgers's deposit and found it hadn't incorporated the shinerrite from Li's deposit into its slightly increased mass.

Albro pointed at Rodgers. "Feed the bridge continual course corrections to stay in alignment. I want your deposit between us and that inner planet. Don't close to more than half our current distance. I don't want any back-splattered shiny from our jettisoned arms painting the ship's hull or any of our rocket plumes getting close enough to turn bits of shiny into vapor."

"Got it, Senior Chief." The delight in Rodgers's eyes shone.

"Engineering, Bridge, prepare for exit course," Albro said, reading off the route waypoints twice, "and hold for my mark, repeat hold for my mark." Both stations acknowledged the planned course and waited.

At the touch of a finger, Albro added Commander Jules to his private comm line with Captain Knupp.

"We're about to witness an impact," he said. "I'm getting us out of here while we still can, but I think the scientists back home are going to want all the sensor data we can get."

"Engineering is ready," Commander Jules replied immediately.

"Override," Captain Knupp said, and even Albro flinched.

"What—" He snapped his mouth shut, thankful that he hadn't keyed the mic to transmit the partial question.

He turned to his petty officers. The officers knew what was going on from the plot lines, but he'd forgotten to update his own team. "The two bots from the moon are going to collide and at least partially disable each other, maybe explode." He pushed his predicted tracks to their screens. "We could have used the collision flare to get out of the system on full-power drives without being detected."

"Could have?" Rodgers repeated.

"Prepare for heavy maneuvering," Commander Jules announced. Echoes of her words sounded down the passageways from the shipwide announcement. That was right, but nothing else was.

The captain was up to something.

The ship did hold steady in the mass shadow between the uncollected shinerrite and the planet, but the thrum of the rockets weren't cycling down for a transition to shinerrite drive and a smooth high-speed transit out.

"We're going to miss it," Morales muttered.

Albro shook his head even though the petty officer was right. He had delivered the report. Sometimes officers chose extreme caution, but this made no sense.

Instead the flurry of reports from engineering to Captain Knupp announced all drives were ready for max power on his order.

"Mark," Albro whispered half to himself, but all three petty officers froze in sudden focus on their screens.

A doubled Doppler scream worse than any training audio file shook central control. The two bots streaked down the plot lines at their target. Their own fragile ship hid just beyond. If he'd been wrong and the bots didn't slow, would the combined mass of bots, ship, and shinerrite crash into the gas giant's surface? He was certain, or almost so, that the collision wouldn't leave one of the bots functional enough to attack and tear their ship apart.

"Mark," repeated Morales in wonderment.

The blindingly fast acceleration only shinerrite drives could manage had hurled the two bots off the moon and across the inner system. Before the end of petty officer's word, the bots were a roiling mass of collided debris.

Physics had its sweet revenge, but the programming in the things fought back. Drives reformed and fought to continue their core programming. Even while shattering against each other, the two-bot mass slowed to avoid a similar collision with the deposit they'd never reach intact to clean.

Albro breathed relief.

A familiar grating noise accompanied the executive officer's voice saying, "Cargo doors full open. Main drive's shielding removed as ordered, Captain."

"Now!" the captain shouted.

Albro and his team floated in their restraints as the ship powered on shinerrite drives not to flee out of the system, but to zip around the remaining deposit to hurl their entire cargo bay load of shinerrite at the two-bot mass. And just as quickly, Captain Knupp scooted them back into the deposit's sheltering shadow.

Warnings flashed everywhere. Hull surface coverings around the cargo doors alarmed for high shinerrite levels. Inability-to-stealth warnings blared. Automatic counter clocks for the two bots on the inner planet and the one on the far side of the gas giant flashed new urgent countdowns alarming about how soon they'd be able to detect and tear apart the ship.

And Senior Chief Albro stared at the master plot instead. The masses that had been bots were gone.

A mere blob of shinerrite hurled at speed without any programming to slow it down had cracked the indestructible. His sensors showed a fine mist of shinerrite expanding outward in a hemisphere wave shape flaring out away from the impact. Mass pulls from the sun and two planets began to deform it immediately with no evidence of any bot programming remaining.

"He did it." Albro blinked. Then he looked at the clocks. "Shit. We're still screwed." He slammed down the button for emergency sweepers and ripped his straps off.

"Come on," he yelled at his blinking petty officers, "we've got to get the skin cleaned now!"

They were already running behind him when the executive officer's announcement caught up with reality.

"Secured from shinerrite drive. Shielding restored. Shinerrite spill in cargo bay aft! Hull splatter warning." Commander Jules announced, "Red alert—sweepers, sweepers, all hands report to cleaning stations."

Albro had no time for niceties. The engineering repair team was on the hull when he arrived. They flung the contaminated surface panels off the ship as fast as they could be identified. Albro scrambled out onto the hull himself with a handheld sensor and spacewalked his inspection with all three petty officers trailing behind.

"All surfaces clean," Albro reported, "I say again all ship surfaces clean."

"Very well, Senior Chief," Captain Knupp replied. "Our fine engineers will have replacement retrieval arms installed in an hour or so. When the inner planet's spin puts those other bots back out of detection range for a bit, let's get that last deposit collected and get out of here. We've got some things to report to squadron."

Albro and his team did as ordered. They collected the second deposit during the next inner planet rotation. Captain Knupp again used shinerrite drive in-system to kick up their speed while hidden by the gas giant's mass on one side and the inner planet on the other. Then with shields locked tight into place, they flew out of range into the outer system with a full cargo bay and a smug ship's captain.

Albro tracked down the ship's captain for a chat during the out-system wait. Doctrine required coasting along on exit velocity after leaving a system. A ship had to ensure they'd escaped undetected with no bots following along behind.

Nothing was coming but they had to be sure.

He found Captain Knupp outside the chief's mess looking for him.

"Good job, Senior Chief." The captain's eyes still

sparkled. He poured Senior Chief Albro a cup of coffee. "Very well done," he said, "And try not to kill us tomorrow either."

"Same to you, sir." Albro accepted the coffee. "Same to you."

❖   ❖   ❖

Joelle Presby's latest novel, co-written with David Weber, is *The Road To Hell*, which continues the Multiverse series.

Joelle graduated from the Naval Postgraduate School where she studied how to find and kill submarines and also met a charming submarine officer. During her military career, nations with significant submarine fleets stubbornly refused to go to war with the United States. But even though she was neither a war hero nor cannon fodder, she did still get the guy.

Joelle's book collection has survived fifteen household moves and three hurricane-induced floods. She's lived in France, Cameroon, the United States, and Japan. She and her husband, the submarine officer, live in Virginia and prefer living with hurricanes to moving again.

In addition to loving science fiction and fantasy, she is an avid fan of storm-surge prediction models, evacuation routes, and keeping personal libraries in easily portable ebook form.

SKIPJACK

Susan R. Matthews

Battleships are loaded with weapons by definition. But to take the battle to the enemy, sometimes the ship itself may be used as a weapon—or even the crew. Yet no matter how far we venture into the galaxy, there will always be a place for honor, at least for the thoughtful among us. And even though the democratic ignominy of death lies at the end of the star road for every man, some ways to die are definitely more elegant than others.

Tension in the top ops room of the central command bridge had been growing watch by watch, so when Flaxon on monitor station alpha invoked an inset image on one of her screens, Hoppo—station XO, and duty officer on deck—was at her side even before she spoke. "Now, where did *that* come from?"

Everybody was newly alert at once, a keen edge of focused curiosity to the military standard of watch awareness. Nobody knew why they were all feeling it. In the closely confined station community, body language as much as anything broadcast its own signal, even when the person transmitting had no clue that a secret—that there was a secret—had been revealed.

"Track trace?" Hoppo asked, leaning one shoulder up against the hard outer curve of the monitor station's clamshell. Flaxon was seated, but the station itself was raised; he and Flaxon were eye to eye, as well as side by side. She shook her head, her frustration clear from her expression. "First time we've scanned that slice this shift. Between the moons, and the cloud. Low-traffic area."

Enemy ships inbound for their base slips at Parnel Station generally snuck around the edges of Mohund's disk, using the fierce ion storms in its upper atmosphere to fuddle the sensors of remote observer stations and cloak their presence. That was hazardous enough, but Skanda Republic forces and Hamstead Vrees alike had refined their tactics over the years of this war—raiding into unfriendly territory, hunting each other's supply convoys—and risks had to be taken. As far as Hoppo knew, though, Skanda was the first to stage a ship trap this close to a Vrees base of operations.

"I haven't seen one of those old hulks since—" Mull on stats had called up shipcode, was watching screen images pop up on his display. Hoppo could see his point. It was a heritage-model ship raider, a relic of the early days of the war when everything had been going Vrees' way and the sinister smile of the ship's projectile nests had grinned into the nightmares of honest ship-service crews large and small. He'd recognized the type right away, but he wasn't about to admit it.

Years ago. "Any teeth left?" Hoppo asked. This was getting interesting. "Can we catch traffic?" Vrees not only wasn't making old-model class-nine commerce raiders any more, they weren't even making the armament. The manufactories had been starved out for lack of material. No sense dedicating any of Hamstead Vrees' increasingly scarce war materials resources to arming obsolete raiders: it was all Skanda's war, now.

Lacquin on comms was working his whisperers, scanning for information hidden in the noise. Flaxon had dropped a peeper, state-of-the-art, undetectable to all but the newest and best of the Vreeslanders—which were beautiful war machines, nobody grudged them that. Skanda ship service's research and development branch could hardly wait to get their hands on any that survived to the end of the war, when they'd be duly handed over under the terms of the unconditional surrender that Skanda demanded.

"All tubes but one empty so far as I can see, DO." That was him, Hoppo; duty officer. XO, too. "One stuffed with scrap rock." The peeper generated a three-dimensional report, in miniature. Hoppo reached out his hand to flick one of the projectile nests with an experimental forefinger: empty, all right. And somebody—to judge from what Lacquin was kludging together on comms— was having a party.

"So what's on, do you think?" Hoppo asked, looking over to Mull's station. Mull pushed away from his boards; Hoppo thought he was within a hair of actually clasping his hands behind his neck and leaning back in satisfaction to put his feet up on the rim of the plot shield. "Old-old,

DO," he said. "In pieces and patches, core like a rat's nest. Propulsion's got to be soaked. Index sit for happy-gas poisoning, and the ship's scrap. Hardly worth the trouble of pulling it in."

So the crew would be dead anyway, before too much longer. Happy gas meant that ship's propulsion had started to self-cannibalize. It would keep pumping its toxic mix of atmospheric contaminants into ship's atmosphere until there was no breathable oxygen left. People with happy gas were already too far gone to climb into their environmentals, or they wouldn't still have the happy gas.

And yet he had his orders. The civilian spooky crew that was hiding out deep within this ship-trap station had issued clear instructions, if by word of mouth: something was expected. Captain Wircale, the station commander, hadn't been told what it was; only that they were to pull in everything they could reach, effective yesterday, duration of protocol to be communicated at a future date.

"We can at least try to save some crew." The orders were ears only, so Hoppo reached for a good cover. "Bring them in." By the looks of the scarred old scow heading blithely toward them, nobody in Vrees' headquarters would think twice if it fell silent. "Smell for self-destructs and scuttle protocols. Hope it can still dock, without taking too much of a new technician's trim."

That was a standard joke, the inexperienced pilot driving a ship too far to one side and colliding with the bumper wings of a docking slip. In this case it was serious. That crew was clearly impaired: but if ship's autos were still on line, Hoppo's watch could braid signals together and guide the ship safely in. "Yes, sir," Mull said. No relaxing now, square to his plot shield, pulling in data.

Lacquin on comms hit a muter, cutting out any background noise. They'd done this so many times now that any one of them could have recited the script in their sleep.

"Ship on approach, this is Lorent Havens," Lacquin said. The home base the ship would be seeking, sanctuary, safety. "Identify yourself, and transmit your ident codes. So we can welcome you back."

Hoppo waited. Time passed. Had they heard? Were they too deep into the happy gas? Lacquin tried again. "This is Lorent Havens. Identify yourself."

Still nothing. Just as Hoppo turned his head to call for a boarding party to be put on immediate alert, something came back. "Shifflack!" the ship said, and giggled. "Vreeslander Shifflack. Aren't we a little close to Perdition still? Moved the borders? We've got a story to tell."

"Perdition," the dangerous route through Mohund's asteroid belt and its moons, constantly changing, constantly evolving. Lacquin put some juice into the signal; and it clarified. *Skipjack*. Vreeslander *Skipjack*.

"Had to shift, attack destroyed base, limited capacity." That was their story. A ship trap was a false haven, luring Vreeslanders into Skanda hands for the diminishing of Vrees' fighting strength and the salvage of goods, and human intelligence, from ship and crew. "Can you dock on ship's power? Clear to come in, but we'd better hurry. Before Skanda gets a fix and sends unfriendlies."

"Confirmation codes," *Skipjack* said; and Hoppo grinned. "Coming at you. And good news. Oops! Didn't say anything. No news. No news at all." *Skipjack* might be all but dead of the happy gas, but they were still the crew of a ship of war.

"Transmitting." Could they match codes in time? Yes, Vrees had finally realized that Skanda had captured its encrypt programs and the newest keys. Vrees changed their secure sequences on a random generator: did *Skipjack* know that? Or was *Skipjack* still operating on a generation encrypt prior? "I get clear pingback, *Skipjack*, can we initiate acquisition? We can have a party meet you, you're leaking happy gas, all due deliberate speed advised."

Silence. Hoppo knew he wasn't the only one here holding their breath. When *Skipjack* spoke he let his breath out gratefully. "Oh. Yeah. Right. Codes confirmed, Lorent. Open-ing-ning-ning pull lines for passive transit." In the background Hoppo could hear the giggling, and confused chatter. *What. Happy gas? Where are we? Lorent. Made it. Heroes.*

"Me down to the dock slip," Hoppo said. "Medical teams on full alert, there's what, twenty people on board? If I remember my briefings?" If he remembered from his childhood passion for the Vreeslander commerce raiders, that was to say. He'd had to turn his romantic passion into a more socially acceptable pursuit of a career with Skanda ship service, as he'd grown older. "Tarleton. You have the watch."

"Very good, DO," Tarleton said. With a nod and a wave Hoppo left top ops to hurry down and meet the Vreeslander commerce raider *Skipjack*.

He picked up a Security escort on his way down to the

ship's bunkers. He found Infirmary staff assembling for
mass casualty, in light of the number of crew probably
aboard; Mull's data indicated eighteen souls. Within the
corridor leading on to the ship's bunker, Hoppo and his
Security changed into clothes that mimicked Vrees'
uniforms in design and color, though without any rank
markers or station identification. The lie direct in person,
face-to-face, was one step further than Hoppo was willing
to go.

The loading ramp that led up into the ship's cargo vault
was deployed, and an environmental team was already
there, working on flushing *Skipjack*'s contaminated
atmosphere. It would take time to do properly, but in the
meantime a limited exposure to happy gas was no threat
to a healthy soul.

Skipjack was a short, squat, massive monster with its
weapons carried like lane domes on a landing field across
the manta-ray sweep of its flattened outer flanges. It was
too unbalanced of aspect to be graceful; but Hoppo
remembered the Vreeslanders of the previous generations
fondly for all their lack of elegance. He'd studied the specs
for hours, when he'd been a child.

"Stand by for station management and medical teams."
Lacquin's voice echoed within the ship's bunker. "Please
prepare to evacuate the ship, quarters are open to
accommodate."

A woman came stumbling to the head of the loading
ramp from the interior of the ship; her speech was slurred,
her uniform undone, one trouser leg bloused and the cuff
of the other flapping around an unaccountably bare ankle.
"Come on," she called, steadying herself against the

leftmost flange of the ramp. "Made it. C-come on. Hurry, think the banks have been leaking, but it worked. We won, we won."

Hoppo tapped the piplink at his collar. "Party proceeding by invitation," Hoppo told top ops. A double meaning, there, though he hadn't intended it. "We're going in. Wish us luck."

The corridors were claustrophobically narrow, cramped, low ceilinged; Hoppo was a tallish man, himself, and his head almost brushed the top tiling. It was the trade-off for the armament carrying capacity; once the propulsion systems had been adjusted for the mass required for a stable firing platform, there wasn't much room left for crew amenities.

It was going to be a tight fit getting the medical litters through here, but they'd make it work. Handing the woman off to medical as he passed, Hoppo moved into the cargo vault with his team, transit glims coming up along the perimeter walls as they went. The woman must have been camped out in the cargo vault, waiting for them; for how long?

"Got you on track, XO." Hoppo kept an ear cocked to his piplink, listening to Mull almost absentmindedly. "Proceed forward from your location, there'll be a fairly large access secured with a roll shutter. Take the lift up, probably level five, if *Skipjack* follows its specs." Past that, crew laundry, and shift rooms. But he wasn't going to say so.

"Through," Hoppo said, so that Mull could match their progress to his scans and follow along. "This must be a main access corridor? I hear singing." Right. Sleeping quarters for the crew assigned to each of the ship's watches. He could see open doorways, and as they passed—he wanted to find the command center—he could see people, ship's crew.

In one room, three people at the common table, drinking, laughing, toasting Hoppo's party as they passed without any apparent interest in their sudden appearance. In another, two crew seated opposite each other over soup bowls or cereal bowls, one of them with her face flat to the table, asleep.

Mull came back to him. "Continuing on. There'll be kitchen facilities, common mess. Forward by another half a ship length, command bridge, five people, we think." Hoppo glanced back over his shoulder, quickly; there was a line of litters and people to steer them, turning into the crew rooms as they came to them. Efficiency. They'd wait until the corridors were clear of litters to start taking people out, to Infirmary.

The sound of Mull's voice had caught someone's attention, because someone called out from a room up ahead. "Hey!" Someone sitting on the floor at the open door, leaning out into the corridor; Hoppo hoped he wouldn't fall over. "Glad we made it. We did it. It worked. Can hardly believe it." The crewman hadn't fallen over yet, but it was a near thing, as the man waved drunkenly. "Come in. Have a drink. There's—ah—something to drink."

"Maybe later," Hoppo said, nodding. "Welcome. We've got to get on." People with happy-gas poisoning weren't expected to make sense, and he was anxious to identify himself to *Skipjack*'s captain. Eighteen people, Mull had said. Hoppo had counted eleven, so far; but when they found the command center and Hoppo did a quick survey he came up one soul short. There were only six people there, and none of them appeared to be paying attention.

He stopped on the threshold, taking it all in. Bridge littered with snack packets, meal trays stacked on the floor by the entrance. Crew members on station, but nobody in proper uniform, and several of the stations had gone silent. That could easily be because *Skipjack* was safe in bunker and operating on station systems, of course.

"Excuse me." He had to raise his voice, because there was someone's music playing rather loudly. Somebody should at least take an interest in his appearance, shouldn't they? This was the command center, not crew quarters. "Excuse me," he repeated, more loudly yet. "Which one of you is the captain, please?"

Lacquin had found someone to talk to not long ago, a woman; there were two here, one of them at a comm station. Hoppo wondered if they'd lost their last remaining voice of reason to the happy gas, but surely it wouldn't have gone from half-here to gone in so short a time?

The man sitting at the observation station didn't turn around; he just sat there, giggling. The one at the weapons station at the left appeared to be unconscious. There was no one on ship's onboard systems. One of Hoppo's party sat down and made a few experimental gestures to see whether the board would respond. Mull's analyses had verified that the ship was cold and quiet—no active weapons systems primed to blow up, no self-destruct sequence on countdown—but cross-checks were always nice.

"The captain?" The woman at the comm station had no boots on at all, and only one sock. Her jacket was open, her cuffs were undone, and her shirt was unbuttoned down to her waistband, but her undershirt was clean enough. "Oh, him. We had a little trouble." He didn't think she was the person Lacquin had been talking to; for one, she sounded a little more coherent. "So we locked him up. Maintenance space, somewhere. Should probably get him out, whoever you are, he'll be annoyed."

She was maybe more coherent, yes, but she didn't make any better sense, not really. What she seemed to be saying was ugly: it sounded like mutiny, and there'd never been a mutiny on board a Vreeslander commerce raider, not that Hoppo had ever heard. They'd been known for their esprit and their close-knit unit cohesion. Mutiny would be startling enough in any crew, but on a ship like *Skipjack*? "Tell me what happened, Executive Officer," Hoppo suggested, hoping he'd guessed right about her position on board.

"Little trouble with vents, yeah," she said. Over his piplink Hoppo could hear medical reporting to Tarleton, whom he'd left in charge in top ops: *Pretty far gone. Some of these crew in very serious condition. Don't understand it, not usual happy gas, but we'll update soonest.* "Don't know what got into our Finnie. Couldn't handle the *Skipjack*. Went a little spare, but he should be all right, he was okay when he went in."

"And where is the captain now?" By-name identification would clearly have to wait. The woman laughed.

"We forgot to write it down. Should have painted the

wall. He's around here somewhere." She'd gone off into a singsong sort of a clearly improvised tune, and the phrases were breaking up in the middle. "Okay now. No hard feelings. War's over. Surprise, Skanda Republic. Shoes. Other foot."

Hoppo touched his piplink. "XO here. Need a biometric trace for single person, possibly isolated situation, all we have to go on is quote 'maintenance area somewhere' end quote. Hurry." One of the other crew had taken her feet off the middle of the status boards to spin back and forth slowly in the workstation's chair, her arms windmilling at full length as though she were doing her dyechee warm-ups.

The possible executive officer was chanting, now, like a schoolchild doing count outs at a pash game. "Here in an instant! There yesterday! *Skipjack*! *Skipjack*! Saved the day!"

Hoppo's piplink bipped at him. "Tarleton, XO. Carstairs hears someone pounding on the wall, from the inside. Halfway between mess area and command center. Extraction in process." And the litter teams had caught up with Hoppo, moving onto the bridge to evaluate and evacuate the crew.

"Good," Hoppo confirmed. "On our way." He was glad of an excuse to get away from the singing executive officer of a crew that might have mutinied against its captain; and eager to hear what its captain—if that's who they found in the wall—was going have to say about it all.

The wall panel had been fastened on the outside, a detail that was expressive of horror. When Hoppo and

Carstairs wrenched it open, the imprisoned man within tumbled out in an ungraceful heap, saved from colliding headfirst with the decking only by quick action on Carstairs's part. For a moment Hoppo wondered if they were too late; but then the man twitched feebly, his movements strengthening as he got his arms and legs straightened out. Hoppo didn't envy him the muscle cramps he'd be having.

The rescue air mask that Carstairs held to the man's face did its usual magic. When Carstairs propped the man up against the corridor wall, he didn't fall over. "Who," the man said, and coughed. "Who are you, and what are you doing on my ship?"

He didn't sound like he had happy gas. He didn't sound happy at all. Shining a light into the cramped dead space behind the rivet plate in the corridor wall, Hoppo pulled out a canned-atmosphere bottle with its stopcock open, nearly depleted; he could see others there, too, some still full. That would explain why the man wasn't incoherent from happy-gas poisoning.

He could see an open emergency survival package, as well, which also explained why the man wasn't half-dead from dehydration. On the other hand, Hoppo didn't know how long the man had been in the wall.

"My name is Jens Hoppo," he said. This man was *Skipjack*'s captain, according to what the admittedly mildly incoherent XO had told them. Circumstantial evidence, howsoever preliminary, confirmed; that made Hoppo the commander of a boarding party, and *Skipjack* the spoils of war. Lying to *Skipjack*'s captain about the truth of the situation was not on the books. "XO, Skanda

Republic base Aika Lynn. You and your crew are my prisoners, sir. May I have your name?"

Leaning up against the wall, the man received this news in silence till the last, when he made a very convincing attempt to take Hoppo by the throat. It was a surprise: an impressive one. "My name, hell, what about my crew? Status, Hoppo."

Said crew had apparently tossed their captain around a bit before they'd put him away. He was a little bruised and doughy around the face, and parts of his jacket were torn and smeared with a brown stain that certainly looked like dried blood to Hoppo. *Could have done that part himself, though, maybe,* Hoppo thought, *trying to get out.*

"We've taken seventeen crew into custody, Captain, all suffering from happy gas. Fairly well advanced. One or two may be past help. Under care in Infirmary, where we'll be taking you next, sir."

"Infirmary big enough?" the captain asked. He spoke a clear strong dialect of Skansa, with just a hint of a Vrees accent. "*Skipjack* docked?—False colors." Yes. That was exactly it. Aika Lynn's mission was to lure enemy ships into captivity for weapons research and resource harvesting. If the mysterious people in need-to-know residence had a mission redirect they had yet to share that, or any other, information. "Help me up, Hoppo. My name is Fenroth, Captain, Vreeslander *Skipjack*. Is the war over?"

"Sorry, sir." Captain Fenroth would know how to take that. Hoppo had questions of his own, lots of them, but they were going to have to wait because a man couldn't answer fully and frankly in the condition Fenroth was in. "We're sending you to Infirmary for clinical evaluation, Captain. We'll talk again later."

He could guess that Fenroth had a nasty headache, with the knock on the head he'd clearly sustained. Blood dried and bruising gone sick yellow, so he'd been in the wall for a few days. Hoppo nodded at Carstairs, making a sweeping gesture of his hand that went all the way up his arm. "Transport."

Then he clicked his tongue against his upper palate to get his piplink's attention. "Hoppo back to top ops," he said. He didn't wait for a response; he had too much to think about. There was a consistent theme to the crew's babbling: the war being over. There had to be a reason for that to be in the forefront of peoples' minds.

Was there enough happy gas in the world to make them think this old hulk was some sort of a secret weapon? Why had they locked their captain up in the wall? He'd had plenty of superior officers he'd have liked to jettison in a small box, but nobody went for mutiny. Nobody at all.

Head lowered, brain full of thoughts, Hoppo came barreling through the curtain slats into top ops at full speed. "Flaxon, forensic trace, I want to know exactly where that came from. Mull, status of atmosphere? And can we match any weapons signatures to archive—" Then he stopped, because two of his own Security were suddenly standing right in front of him with uncomfortable expressions on their faces.

"Good man." That was Captain Wircale, Aika Lynn, commanding. Hoppo knew the voice immediately, even before he saw her. This was a problem, because CO and XO were almost never supposed to be in the same place at the same time, and especially not on the operational bridge where a mishap could take out the ship's entire command structure in one go. "These are all good questions. Needing answers."

Security stepped aside. They still looked unhappy to Hoppo. Maybe it was the civilian on the bridge; tallish officer, research and development weapons branch. She looked calm and matter-of-fact, but her eyes had a snap to them that looked like excitement to Hoppo. "This person?" she asked Captain Wircale, who nodded. Well, Hoppo thought. R&D. So that was what those secretive people in "infrastructure analysis" were doing.

Now that Hoppo had had a moment to consider it, he thought Wircale looked a little uncomfortable herself, and Wircale, for all her professional competence and well-earned reputation as an effective leader, was a woman who generally preferred her comforts over the alternative. As who wouldn't? "My XO, Director. Hoppo, this is—"

"Nobody of importance." Director Nobody cut the captain off smoothly, and without hesitation. "Less said the better. Why am I here, XO? Curiosity, nothing more. I'll wait for those chromos in your office, Captain. Hoppo, there's nothing here requires your attention, I believe? I need a tactical analysis, all new reports, past six days, and cross-check it against the archive. Thank you."

Of all the things he could say about civilians showing up in top ops, interrupting the captain, issuing orders, one was safest. "Very well." The captain wasn't objecting, so it wasn't up to *him* to object. Captain Wircale was as capable of objecting as any officer Hoppo had served under. "Target of inquiry, Director?"

She frowned. Maybe he wasn't supposed to call her "Director." Maybe he should stick with plain unadorned Nobody. "You'll know it when you see it, Hoppo, or your reputation overstates your intelligence. I'll leave you to it." *Get on with your work.* She wasn't being rude, Hoppo decided. She was just used to saying what she wanted and getting it soonest.

So long as that was the way it was going to be—

Hoppo knew Beeler's station was empty this shift, because stores and logistics only updated four or five times a day and they didn't have a current metrology mission. Spinning the vacant clamshell toward him Hoppo sat down and got to work.

It had been a day since Hoppo and his people had captured the Vreeslander *Skipjack*. Now he stood in the captain's office, Director Nobody in Captain Wircale's seat and everybody else standing—the better to admire all the chart plots on the wall, Hoppo supposed. Captain Fenroth was here as well: patched up, cleaned up, beard and moustache neatly trimmed and you couldn't find him by smell in the dark anymore. Hoppo envied him. Fenroth had probably even had a refreshing night's sleep, and a good breakfast. What Hoppo wouldn't do for a change of socks.

"Thank you for coming, Captain Fenroth," Director Nobody said. "Or for bringing your ship here, at least." She beckoned to one of the Security to come forward with a comfortably padded chair, and set it down at Fenroth's side. "Please. Sit down."

Wircale didn't have a Security post in her office; Hoppo knew that, because he chopped off on the duty rosters periodically. So the Security was here on Nobody's account. Captain Fenroth looked at the chair, then back at Nobody, saying nothing. Hoppo wouldn't have minded sitting down himself, if Fenroth wasn't going to be using the chair; but it was a nice point of military courtesy, one Hoppo appreciated. Captain Wircale was station commander, who outranked Fenroth by definition. As long as Wircale was on her feet, Fenroth would stand, never mind who Nobody might be.

"I'd like to see my crew, please," Fenroth said. "A medical report, at least." Seemed reasonable enough to Hoppo, but Nobody shook her head.

"A few things to discuss first, Captain Fenroth. Your ship. Don't tell me. I'll tell you." She stood up, brushing by Captain Wircale on her way to a chart on the wall. Hoppo knew that one. He'd built the data. "Now first. Vrees ambush of a civilian refugee convoy. Tarris, eight days' transit time ago, of course the report came in two or three days ago."

Fenroth nodded his head, once. "Munitions transport, as I heard it," he said. Director Nobody brushed off the correction.

"Our intel says there was a particular ship of interest there, that's you, Fenroth. Old, clumsy, slow moving, but managed to destroy a food transport anyway, months ago at Nurrs. We've been watching."

"Weapons-critical raw materials, actually," Fenroth

corrected politely. Hoppo could see Captain Wircale not-smiling, just a little.

"Semantics," Nobody said, dismissively. "We had identity match between the C9 ship at Nurrs and the one at Tarris, same subclass, and there were only twenty-one of them in service at the commencement of hostilities." Or of declared hostilities. War, Hoppo thought, for Fenroth; Fenroth didn't say it. "And twenty ships of that class have been destroyed during the course of the present conflict. Yours is the twenty-first."

Skipjack was number twelve in the production run, actually; Hoppo had looked it up, when he was running the forensics, because there was the obvious confusion. Somewhere. Also the part about—

Director Nobody nodded at one of the charts on the wall. "Chemical trace on the impact weapons that destroyed our humanitarian refugee transport. It matches your empty · projectile tubes, Captain. Interesting. Wouldn't you say." She didn't wait, which was perceptive of her, because Hoppo didn't think Fenroth was going to answer that one. Fenroth was still watching her patiently: as though he was waiting for her to get to the point.

"And then there's you, of course. Captain Belknap Fenroth. Finnie," Nobody said.

"To my friends," Fenroth noted, but Nobody ignored the interruption. She was good at that because she'd had so much practice, Hoppo supposed, and clearly knew the importance of keeping her edge. She just kept talking.

"Egret Plume, Gowire raid, good one that, I'm told. Wheat-Ear Clasp after Cotton. Twenty-nine kills, eighteen of them our fighters, Captain, but that bit about you rescuing passengers after Natalise—propaganda, and clod-handed propaganda, at that. You people made it up."

Her analysis, maybe. Now that the director mentioned it, Hoppo finally connected the man with the mission. If that was "Finnie" Fenroth—and his XO had called him "Finnie," hadn't she?—he was one of the more successful of Hamstead Vrees' raiders, if a bit of a romantic, by reputation. What he'd done at Natalise had been failure to close with the enemy, perhaps, but it was a great story. Several of Skanda's line officers had been disciplined for failures of their own, failure to intervene.

"And there's more. Your ship's presence at Tarris. Your armament. You." She nodded emphatically in the face of Fenroth's polite disbelief. "Voice analysis confirms your presence. What's the saying? Of all explanations once the impossible are excluded the remainder howsoever improbable, and so forth?"

But that wasn't improbable. It was impossible. The only way a ship could be at Tarris eight days ago and here yesterday was to travel at the speed of communications, and the speed of communications was the speed of light.

There was no such thing as a ship that traveled at the speed of light. If there was, it would certainly look sexier than Captain Fenroth's old heap. That was an irrational argument at best, Hoppo knew it was, but the whole thing was fantastic from start to finish—wasn't it?

Except nobody had mentioned the habharite, yet.

The door behind Hoppo had opened, somebody had come in; the same not-really-uniform as Nobody, but strangely enough Fenroth seemed to recognize him: and a look of profound contempt flashed across his face, almost too quickly to be identified.

"The director knows all about *Skipjack*, Captain Fenroth," New Nobody said. "And I'm sorry, but it's simply too important to leave in the hands of the ship service. All you people ever think about is war."

That was unfair, in Hoppo's opinion. Or maybe not. The ship service did think a lot about war, almost exclusively about war, because they happened to be right in the middle of the ugliest one in recorded history. Though maybe not in the middle anymore; nearing the end for Hamstead Vrees. That was what "unconditional surrender" meant. So Hoppo knew who New Nobody was, now, if only in a general sense: a traitor.

"*Skipjack*'s a ship," Hoppo said, because otherwise he was going to say something like "schmuck this flip," which would compound the breach of protocol by a factor of two or three. "He's the captain. He'd know."

Yes, he remembered what *Skipjack*'s XO had said to him: *Here in an instant, there yesterday,* Skipjack. But he was already guilty of one unauthorized interruption, so it was probably better to save that one for later. No, he wasn't going to keep it to himself, of course not, but he'd just decided that he liked Fenroth better than he did either of the two Nobodys. Judging by appearances. He was just that shallow.

"Your ship is contaminated with habharite," Nobody said. Now that was something Hoppo *did* know about. Mull had slipped him the stats. Habharite when it married up with gregor particles as they decayed was a precursor to the jhilin elements, almost supernatural quantum identities whose creation and decay was held to be much more than merely planet destroying. Gregor particles were so arcane as to be practically mythical, however.

That was the sum of Hoppo's knowledge, so he listened carefully to what Nobody said next, hoping for enlightenment. "It is in fact the most concentrated reservoir of habharite we've ever seen, and we've been looking, because we have our own research programs. The conclusion is inescapable. We know, Fenroth. We have all of the research."

New Nobody fixed his eye on Hoppo's face, accusing, affronted. "No, *Skipjack*'s *not* a ship," he said. "It's a research program. Light speed." He shifted his gaze. "And somebody's cracked the code, and it wasn't us, Fenroth. We knew the ship service was up to something, but we never dreamed you'd actually get somewhere. So how does it work?"

Captain Fenroth chose this moment to sit down, absentmindedly pulling on his captain's cap, which, as Hoppo was happy to see, had been cleaned up and brushed neatly. Interesting choice, Hoppo thought: military code. Director Nobody didn't seem to realize she'd just been insulted. Of course Fenroth could just be tired. It hadn't been more than a day since they'd pulled him out of the wall.

"How about this," Fenroth said. "There were actually twenty-two ships in *Skipjack*'s class and configuration. We used prerecorded dialog for transmissions at Tarris. The chemical signature is faked. We were tasked to transport habharite, and somebody screwed up in the containment-and-shielding department. One way or another my crew are rapidly dying of habharite exposure masked by happy gas and there's nothing to be done about it, so I'd like to see my people now, please."

Nobody nodded. "And we'd like to see your secret log. Oh, we're sure your cruise log is in order—" Holding up her hand in a placating, patronizing manner, she waited while Fenroth bit off an instinctively angry rejoinder before continuing. "Just as we're sure there's another, more interesting one. We could tear your ship apart looking for it, or you could surrender your log, and your journals, to us here and now. After all, they'd be going to my esteemed colleague anyway, wouldn't they?" New Nobody, that would be, who nodded as Fenroth looked back over his shoulder with a near-voiceless snarl. "So give them to us now. And then you can rejoin your crew."

Hoppo waited while the gates clicked in Fenroth's mind. New Nobody and Nobody clearly in intimate cahoots, so there was a certain degree of logic to Nobody's argument. Whether or not Fenroth decided to surrender his log in the absence of an authorized military authority—whether or not Fenroth would admit to there being a private, secret log—he was a true enough captain to want to see his people, even when his people had roughed him up and locked him up in the wall of his own ship.

That was either wonderful or idiotic. For himself, Hoppo had tried to learn the new, more corporate, model of duties and responsibilities from the new breed of officers coming up in ship service, but he'd consistently failed so far. There were traditions in ship service. They died hard.

"I'll need a guide," Captain Fenroth said, standing up at last. "Captain Wircale. Please note that I submit to this irregularity under protest as contrary to the Prize Conventions for treatment of enemy combatants taken prisoners of war."

"Someone discreet," Nobody said to Captain Wircale, talking over the tail end of Fenroth's statement. Wircale nodded.

"So noted, Captain Fenroth," Captain Wircale said, leaving it up to Nobody to decide whether Wircale had just ignored her. "XO Hoppo, if you would accompany Captain Fenroth, please."

That was rank acknowledging rank. Also minimizing exposure, Hoppo supposed; he was a senior officer, he'd already been on board *Skipjack*, and Nobody seemed satisfied. He wished the captain hadn't tagged him for the errand, because it felt a little dirty; but Captain Wircale was already having a bad day, and Hoppo didn't like the idea of giving Nobody anything to smile about.

"Very good, sir." And right away. Captain Fenroth didn't know how quickly people were dying, because Infirmary had been cautioned against telling him. Hoppo knew, though. Fenroth probably did, too, because he hadn't been surprised to hear about habharite contamination. All the more reason to hurry, so that Fenroth could say good-bye, maybe good riddance.

Hoppo stood to one side politely to allow Captain Fenroth to precede him out of the room. There was a Security posting standing ready to escort them, of course; Fenroth was a prisoner of war. Not to be allowed off on his own to seek out the secret, and constantly moving, cabaret they ran on Aika Lynn with all-volunteer talent and whatever they could come up with to drink.

Hoppo himself had been awarded the prestigious Three Half-Empties on one memorable occasion for his medley of mostly remembered nursery rhymes, but there was nothing in his life to compare to the Vreeslander Egret Plume, with or without the Wheat-Ear Clasp.

"Parole," he said to Fenroth, who had his eyes fixed on Hoppo's face, with a clearly communicated "what are we waiting for" message in his expression. Now that Hoppo could stand nose to nose, he couldn't help but notice that Fenroth wasn't as old as Hoppo had at first taken him to be; and that he was tall, for a Vreeslander commerce raider's captain. Vreeslander crews ran shortish, because of the narrow corridors and low ceilings.

"Specifications?" Fenroth asked, because a prudent man considered carefully what his parameters were before he agreed to them. Security didn't twitch. It was part of standard prisoner in-processing to pair each crew member up with a sympathetic listener of equal or just subordinate rank; being taken prisoner was stressful, people talked, out of nerves or relief at being alive or disgust at the same fact. Fenroth would know that. They knew each other's tricks, at least in general outline.

"To remain in custody, and execute all reasonable undertakings required of you. Saving only your duty and your honor, under code." To surrender his secret logs to Director Nobody, which didn't quite fall under things consistent with a captain's honor. Still, Nobody had presented it to Fenroth clearly, and Fenroth had apparently accepted the quid pro quo. Turn over your secret logs; see your people.

If Fenroth gave his word the logs were as good as in Director Nobody's hands already. She'd get them just a little bit later than immediately, that was all, Hoppo decided. A few minutes. An hour. It was already all but finished, the war, and Hoppo had got through it all without a single black mark on his record, which he considered to be a failure of a sort. He was going to have to hurry if he wanted to get that checked off his list before it was too late to acquire a shadow on his wartime career.

Fenroth nodded. "Word of honor." And Security knew the drill. Hoppo gave them the nod, *go wait in the canteen for a while*; and started down the hall. "It will be this way, sir."

The route he took was a little circuitous, maybe. A sudden dodge into a janitor's closet, and then out the other side. A shortish stroll through a maintenance aisle in silence. Director Nobody's people had locked off service access to the ventilation systems when they'd moved into the floor above, so there was no danger of meeting anybody in particular until Hoppo opened the door that would let them back out into some of the more well-traveled administrative areas. Infirmary, in this instance. Fenroth might even recognize it. He'd spent the night under observation, after all, in his own cell and everything, not like his people.

"Hope to be excused a small detour, sir," Hoppo said. Fenroth's people were on the open ward, because Aika Lynn didn't have enough by way of individual quarantine for that many people, and happy-gas poisoning—

habharite poisoning, for that matter—wasn't contagious.
The ward was as secure as it needed to be, with Security
posts on site. "Handing you off to my squad leader for a
few, Captain. Sorry, but I've got to get some stims or I'll
fall over."

Sergeant Turapa stepped up and saluted a point
halfway between Hoppo and Fenroth. Maybe she knew
who Finnie Fenroth was. Maybe she was just being polite;
Hoppo couldn't tell, and he didn't care. He wasn't making
it up about needing the stims.

Fenroth pushed his cap up off his forehead to the back
of his head, stone faced, moving slowly into the open bay.
The first patient he came to raised herself up in bed as
well as she could, in her clearly weakened state, and
Fenroth put his arms around her for a fervent embrace,
his eyes tightly shut.

Hoppo went off for a word with Carstairs, because it
wasn't his business what Fenroth had to say to his crew
and he knew he could trust Turapa's good judgment. He
took his time, because he wanted to make sure to check
all Carstairs's usual haunts in Infirmary, stores, equipment
locker, the friendly technician on duty for sick call. He
didn't find Carstairs, in the end, but it was Carstairs's rest
shift—he suddenly remembered—so he swallowed the
tabs the friendly technician gave him and came out at the
far end of the open bay to retrieve Fenroth from Turapa.

Fenroth was just finishing his rounds. His cap had
gotten knocked a little sideways, in the process. He was
leaning down low over one last crewman, a fistful of
bedcovers in his hand; kissing the man's forehead, oddly
enough, pulling the bedcovers forward to cover the man's

face as he straightened up. Another one gone, then. That made at least eight by now. Not quite half of them. Deterioration was accelerating.

"Thanks, Sergeant," Hoppo said to Turapa. "I'll take it from here." Fenroth looked as though he wouldn't have minded some stims himself right about now. Hoppo wondered what he'd had to say to the crew that had roughed him up and shoved him into a crawl space; hadn't that been his XO, the woman he'd hugged?

Fenroth was clearly feeling the strain, stopping under the ventilation grate in the ceiling, tilting his head back to let the cool air blow in his face. Quarantined air, in Infirmary; filtered on the way in, filtered on the way out, no cross-contamination for communicable diseases. There were important people upstairs, after all. Spooky crew. High-level researchers with a sideline in treason, so Hoppo didn't like them now that he knew, even if it was to Skanda's benefit.

"Well, hurry on," Fenroth said, turning his back on the now-closed doors into the open bay. "Time to be made up." Fortunately Fenroth had turned left at the junction, so they were going in the right direction. "I hope you're feeling better, by the way."

As thanks it was very indirect, and so understated as to be practically undetectable. Hoppo didn't mind. This man was Captain Belknap Fenroth. His people were dying. "Much improved, thank you, sir. Yes, this way."

Still there was something wrong.

He just couldn't get it all laid out and organized, but the medication was powerful stuff, and he had hope.

❄   ❄   ❄

There were Security posts at every access point to Fenroth's *Skipjack*, but they didn't give their own XO any trouble. The cargo vault ramp still stood open, flushing atmosphere; near the end of the cycle, Hoppo expected.

At the head of the ramp Captain Fenroth stopped just short of the threshold and took off his cap, bowing his head. He stood there for a long meditative moment; then he put his cap back on with a decided tug and saluted the empty air. He turned to Hoppo. "Well, then," Fenroth said. "With me."

Hoppo knew the way. He'd studied *Skipjack*'s plans on Mull's analysis report, and maybe just a little bit longer than absolutely necessary. He remembered *Skipjack*'s predecessor ships from the days of his childhood fascination, and the basic layout hadn't changed much between the end of the last war and the start of this one.

The captain's cabin was between the mess area and the command center, not far from where Fenroth had been shut up in the wall: close to the bridge, and accessible. "This is it," Captain Fenroth said. "Me first?" He held up his left hand, flattened, to palm the biometric admit control beside the door, but paused politely for Hoppo's go-ahead.

For a moment Hoppo wondered whether *Skipjack* would explode when the captain's door was opened. But his tech people had scanned the ship and reported it clean, no detonation circuits standing by for a closed loop to blow up the ship, no stores of explosive materials cunningly secreted here and there just waiting for their chance.

"After you, sir," he agreed. Fenroth put hand to read pad at the wall plate, and went in. It smelled a little stale, as though ship's ventilators didn't quite penetrate; other than that it was little different from a junior officer's cabin on a Skanda corvette: small, tidy, and only a commissioning picture on the wall—with a few medals tacked up beneath it—to show who was living here.

Hoppo wanted to go examine Fenroth's honors, breathe on them, touch them perhaps. The Hamstead Vrees Egret Plume was an actual bit of an egret's plume, and Fenroth's bore not only the banner but the Wheat-Ear Clasp in brilliants; Vrees' rarest battle honor, only thirty awarded. There was the service badge every crew member received at the completion of seven successful engagements, and one Hoppo didn't recognize. He restrained himself. He hadn't been invited.

Fenroth laid his cap down on the worktable in the middle of the room and crouched down to open a little cabinet set into the wall at the foot of the neatly made bed. There was something a little odd about that, though Hoppo couldn't put his finger on it; but Fenroth was just standing up, now, turning back to the table.

"Here's the necessaries," Fenroth said, putting glassware—two tumblers, a tall flask—down on the table before letting himself fall heavily into the chair, its wear pattern apparently fit to his rump by long usage. "Sit down, XO, there's the bed. Join me in a drink. We should have time to get through the bottle, and I've been holding on to this one, it'd be a shame to let it go to waste."

As a stash of secret documentation, this wasn't one. Had Fenroth changed his mind, now that he'd seen his crew? That wasn't possible. He'd given his word. "Ah, the director will be waiting for your secret logs, Captain."

"Aren't any." Fenroth filled both glasses full to the brim. "So no breach of honor, as I see it. I couldn't give her what she wants either sooner *or* later. Nothing to turn over." When Hoppo didn't move to take the second glass, Fenroth clinked the base of his against the lip of the one still on the table, draining half his pour in one swallow before he set it back down again and coughed. "What I told that sludge Ratine and your director was the truth. Just not all of it. And too late now either way anyway, so. Cheers."

Hoppo ran through some calculations in his mind, but none of them worked out. "Why do you say that?" he asked. "There's no bomb on this ship." He sounded more confident than he felt. "Including this ship itself. So what's going on?"

Fenroth nodded. "What do we need for a bomb, though, XO?" he asked. "Explosive material, and something to set it off. Well. It's already set off. Nothing any of us can do, or I'd be telling you to abandon base, in—ah—" There was a chrono on the wall, right across from where Fenroth sat. "Uh, starting four or five hours ago, if your evac sequences are anything like ours, and we're counting on it. There'll be no outrunning it now. Have a drink. Really."

Slowly Hoppo sat down. "Where's your detonator?" Fenroth wouldn't have mentioned "something to set it off" if Fenroth wasn't sure it couldn't be disarmed. Whatever it was. "I have crew here. I deserve to know."

Fenroth said nothing, waiting patiently. Reaching out

for the full glass of untouched liquor Hoppo waved it in Fenroth's direction before he drank. He wasn't ready to clink on it. Common bran-mash brownie, in the bottle. Hoppo had been drinking it all his life.

"We planted the 'Skipjack' scheme in ship-service R&D to flush out traitors like Ratine," Fenroth said. "Then we found out about Aika Lynn, and realized we could do better. All we had to do was get our traitors here, in one place with your R&D, and we could wipe everything clean. I don't know if you've noticed. But Vrees isn't winning the war."

Defeatist talk. Punishable by death. No worries, then, because Fenroth clearly expected to die. Hoppo didn't want to, though he was increasingly—almost serenely—certain that he was going to, soon. "Surrender's unconditional," he reminded Fenroth. "Your research program will just be taken over."

Just like last time. That hadn't worked out so well, really. There'd been a ferocious appetite to make Hamstead Vrees pay for the suffering that Skanda's citizens had endured, but the punitive sanctions Skanda had imposed had only made Vrees the more determined to express their reinforced resentments in material form.

"There will be no such program found, XO, not with people like Ratine holding it so close to their chests. All the actual documentation is in his people's custody, under personal supervision at all times, at an undisclosed location. Here. This station." Fenroth drained his glass and refilled it. Hoppo declined a refill with a polite shake of his head, and Fenroth leaned back in his chair, still talking.

"Aika Lynn will be gone." There was too much quiet certainty in Fenroth's voice for Hoppo to doubt his sincerity. And when a man like Fenroth was certain, and sincere, the odds on his being mistaken were not encouraging. "Any knowledge remaining will be within our ship service, and mostly in people's heads, and nobody needs to know how conceptual the whole thing is. We gain leverage. It won't be much, but it will be a start."

It was quiet in the room. Fenroth drank; Hoppo drank. Fenroth spoke again. "And if nothing else, death to all traitors," Fenroth said.

Hoppo wasn't satisfied. "You sound sure of yourself." Altogether too sure. "But you haven't explained how it's supposed to happen."

Fenroth squared himself to the table, holding his glass in both hands. "Like this. You heard your research director say they knew about the habharite? Our research suggests your people have gone one better. They've got hold of some actual gregor particles. They're using it in their research, here, at Aika Lynn."

Suddenly Hoppo could see it, and it was beautiful in the abstract, the inexorability of it all, the power of the explosion, the inevitability of detonation. "It'll be shielded." He was thinking hard, trying to remember everything he'd been instructed not to notice about selected traffic from undisclosed points of origin carrying undisclosed cargo. "If there's anybody who knows what could happen, wouldn't it be scientists?"

"Shielded, yes." Fenroth's glass was empty again. Maybe he was a little nervous, after all. Strangely enough that didn't make Hoppo feel any better. "From cross-contamination in the laboratory. Not from habharite decaying through the walls. Existing facilities, right on top of your sickbay, not quite top of the line. And habharite travels fast."

Fenroth standing in the corridor outside the sickbay, his head raised to feel the breeze from the ventilation shaft. Starting off in the correct direction to return to *Skipjack*, as if by pure chance. Slowly, reluctantly, Hoppo nodded his head.

"Your crew. They're the detonator." Habharite exposure masked by happy-gas poisoning, Fenroth had said. In the infirmary, which was shielded for biological contaminants but not arcane and transient subatomic particles, and beneath the quarantined spooky-crew floor. "Nobody pushed you into the wall without your leave. Setup from first rough."

No. This was too careful a plan. Fenroth nodded; sadly, it seemed. "So long as there was somebody to talk to, you'd wait to talk to them. We needed the time for your infirmary to be adequately contaminated, to give the habharite its chance. And it needed to look good enough for you to believe it."

Bed neatly made. That was why it had caught Hoppo's attention, he realized. Fenroth had known he wouldn't be sleeping there again. He'd left it shipshape, in the best sense of the term. He'd known the assault was coming. They'd all been working to plan; and it was a beauty.

That didn't mean he'd toast Fenroth, "Finnie" Fenroth with the Egret Plume and Wheat-Ear Clasp, or his crew, or his mission, or his ship. There was something they could probably agree on, however. Hoppo lifted his glass.

"Winning the peace," he said. "That much I'll give you, Captain Fenroth."

He could reach Captain Wircale, he could reach top ops, his piplink was active. But there was nothing anybody would be able to do. What had Fenroth said? It was too late to outrun the explosion. He'd only be contaminating the last minutes, however many there were, with terror and panic, rather than the sudden and immediate annihilation that would come.

There was plenty left in the bottle. After a moment's silence, Hoppo refilled both glasses; it was Fenroth's bottle, but Fenroth didn't seem to mind. "Well," Hoppo said. "While we're waiting, then. Tell me about it. Natalise, with the refugees and the intercepts and the Skanda delaying action. Tell me everything. Take your time."

"Finnie" Fenroth. Decorated commerce raider captain. Here, sharing a bottle with Hoppo, knowing he was about to die, and everybody on this base with him. Nobody else needed to know; that was a decision, a responsibility, that Hoppo took on himself.

He wasn't going to live to be another day older. But from this moment until the end of his life he could be happy, listening with a child's heart to a true story of duty—honor—adventure from the man who'd lived it, and given it to the world.

※　　※　　※

Susan R. Matthews has run out of interesting things to say about herself, but one basic fact remains: she's been living with protagonist Andrej Koscuisko of her Under Jurisdiction series for a very long time (in a manner of speaking). Her wife is getting pretty tired of it, too, but he was there first. Maggie and Susan have only been married for thirty-seven years.

Although her own branch of service during her two-year stint on active duty was Medical Administration (where being constantly mistaken for a nurse just because she was a female officer was a constant irritation—tells you how long ago *that* was), she has recently immersed herself in the history of German U-boats in World Wars I and II. In the absence of new English-language books on the subject she considers that her next logical step is to learn to read German.

HOMECOMING

Robert Buettner

It's a given that capital warships of their day become technological scrap as time passes and systems advance. If the spirit of a ship can be said to live on, perhaps it is in the hearts and souls of its officers and ratings. And where there is a spark, there is the will to defend what remains— as well as the will to protect the bright future that such old, great ships were built to secure.

Patricia Reisfeld floated forward, along the cruiser's half-mile-long centerline passageway, as she left behind the engineering space that comprised the rest of the mile-long ship's length. She propelled herself by self-taught, gentle pulls on the handholds that lined a steel tunnel five times wider than she was tall.

Her heart pounded, but not from exertion. A short-for-her-age eleven-year-old already weighed zero in the centerline passageway. Her heart pounded because each handhold grasp dislodged still-wet blood from her fingertips. In zero G the blood coalesced into crimson spheres that drifted forward beside her, in formation with her teardrops.

The *Bastogne* forward of the engineering space was a cylinder of layer-caked decks that rotated around the ship's centerline, and were presently packed with six thousand civilians like her, who sought refuge from the rebellion that had destroyed their homes on Weichsel.

When they had all been upshuttled to the great ship nine weeks earlier, Captain Hicks had stood before them, his hands on his hips, atop a platform erected in one of the cruiser's echoing, empty cargo bays. Blond, young, and with the know-it-all confidence that annoyed Outworlders about Trueborn Earthmen, he had announced that the deck rotation rates had been adjusted to Weichsel normal. So everybody's weight would remind them of home until they returned.

But a weeping, malodorous old woman dressed in rags, crowded in alongside Patricia, had shaken her fist and shouted that he knew as well as they did that for them there would never be a homecoming.

Now, seven hundred yards forward from that cargo bay, and from the no-go line that separated the engineering space from the rest of the ship, Patricia arrived at the Airtite door that led away from the centerline passageway and eventually to the ship's bridge. She stopped herself there by clinging to the door's handhold.

Like most of the ship's doors, it was usually open but now was sealed. It didn't have a palm-print ID plate like the engineering space's armored door did, just a round, glowing red PRESS TO OPEN plate that anyone could use. But when she pressed her free hand's palm to the plate the door stayed sealed, just like every other door she had tried as she moved forward.

She pounded the plate with her fist, so violently that her body drifted away from the door into the passageway's center. But the door didn't budge. "Farts!"

Patricia tugged herself back to the panel labelled INTERCOM above the DOOR OPEN plate, and depressed the press-to-talk switch. "Hello? Is anybody there?" She repeated it three times, but again nothing. "Farts!" This time she screamed it so loud that it echoed up and down the empty passageway.

The echo died and she glanced over her shoulder toward the engineering space. She couldn't go back there. So she propelled herself forward again.

In the rest of the ship as it rotated around her, beyond the steel tube that confined her, she assumed that the grown-ups, whether passengers or crew, hadn't missed her. They were still ignoring a kid who, despite a 136 IQ, both asked too many questions and thought she knew too many answers. Being ignored annoyed her. But the possibility that no one else remained alive to ignore her terrified her.

By the time she reached the cruiser's nose, where the centerline passageway dead-ended, her blood and tears had dried. The passageway widened out, forming the forward observation dome. When she saw that the circular door that separated the dome from the centerline passageway was wide open, she sobbed and pumped her fist. "Yes!"

The transparent dome beyond the door was, as described by the ship's library channel, a flawlessly transparent hemisphere seventy-five feet in inside diameter and sixteen inches thick, machined from a single Weichselan quartz boulder. Once the *Bastogne* had deorbited Weichsel there was no view for grown-ups to gawk at, just blackness sprinkled with a few stars that didn't even twinkle. So for weeks the dome had been her empty play space.

For hours she had relieved boredom teaching herself to somersault in zero G and watching the red numbers change on the big time-to-destination and current-speed display.

But as she pushed off into the dim-lit dome today she sucked in a breath and widened her eyes. "Wow!"

A week earlier the *Bastogne* had emerged from its last jump, popped out into the Mousetrap, and begun decelerating from one-third light speed. The Mousetrap wasn't really a trap, just as the ship's bridge wasn't a bridge. "The Mousetrap" was just the name applied to a volume of empty space into which emptied dozens of Temporal Fabric Insertion Points, through which C-Drive ships like the *Bastogne* jumped, and thereby shortcut physical space. The Mousetrap was the Human Union's principal interstellar hub, even though only one star within the Mousetrap's emptiness possessed a planetary system, and that "system" consisted of a single, uninhabitable gas-giant planet, Leonidas.

So today, instead of star-pricked blackness, she saw Leonidas's vast disk, glowing orange and striped with ochre and lavender storms that eddied across its surface.

Two tiny shadows dotted Leonidas's animated glow.

The first, distant beyond the dome, had to be Leonidas's sole satellite, the forty-mile-long black spindle that was the hollowed-out moonlet named Mousetrap. As the only habitable space within *The* Mousetrap, the library described the moonlet as "the universe's costliest real estate." Because the shipyards and port facilities inside Mousetrap had been purchased and repurchased with human blood throughout the Pseudocephalopod War's decades-long surges and ebbs.

The second shadow was inside the observation dome, a lone person anchored by one hand to the grab rail that ringed a person-sized transparent tube that protruded from the great dome, and formed the ship's forward-most point.

The library said the observation dome and its protruding tube, called the navigation blister, were vestiges carried forward from the earliest ship designs. She thought they looked like a giant boob with a giant nipple. Not that she had anything to compare them with yet.

As Patricia floated toward the person her heart leapt. She was not alone. Better, the man wore a ship's officer's gray coverall.

She drifted up behind him in the silent dimness, touched his sleeve. "Sir?"

He grunted and stiffened, but stared ahead, ignoring her like all grown-ups did. His hair was gray, his eyelids drooped as though he was very tired, and his cheeks were as gray stubbled as her grandfather's.

He said, "I'm not a sir. Not anymore."

She squinted at the epaulet on his shoulder. Where

ship's officers had a gold insignia of rank sewn there was just a rectangle of snipped white threads. "Oh. You got demoted?"

He nodded. "Busted so far I resigned my commission."

She pointed at his bare epaulet. "What did people call you before you resigned?"

"Chief engineering officer."

"What do they call you now?"

"John. But you can call me Mr. Dahlquist. I came up here to avoid people calling me *anything*. So do you mind?"

"*Listen* to me! I—" She paused, furrowed her brow. "Did you get demoted for drunkenness?"

He snorted. "What?"

"You stink of whisky. My grandfather—"

"Don't tell me. Drinks because of you?"

She said, "He's not even here. He and my mother stayed on Weichsel and sent me to live with my aunt."

"Lucky them." He tossed his head at the blackness beyond the dome. "Why don't you go play outside?"

Patricia narrowed her eyes. "That's a stupid joke."

"Who said it was a joke?" He puffed out a breath, turned to look at her, and his jaw dropped as his body stiffened. "What the *hell*?"

She peered down at her blood-soaked coverall as she spread her arms, bloody palms up. "I'm all right." She blinked as the tears returned. "It's not my blood. It's the Marine's."

He frowned. "Marine?" Then his eyes widened and he reached out and grabbed her shoulders. "One of the Marines who guard the engineering space door? Or the bridge door?"

She nodded as the tears burned her eyes. "The engineering space. I went back there today like I usually do. That painted line that if you cross it they shoot you? I stand behind it and try to make the guards laugh while they stand at attention. Most of them pretend I'm not even there. But he shushed me once, then smiled, and gave me a fist bump."

The old man called Dahlquist squeezed her shoulders tighter, his fingers trembling. "What happened to him?"

"It was a Tribal. A Sep. He wasn't wearing a Tribal shawl, just a Colonial singlet. But under his singlet he was carrying one of those curved bone Tribal knives. He—" She choked on the words and instead drew a finger across her throat.

Dahlquist's brow wrinkled. "Sep? You're saying a Tribal, a Weichselan separatist, was embedded among the refugees?" He turned his face away from her and muttered something that she suspected was a very bad word, because her grandfather had said it only once, when he stuck himself with a hypodermic by accident.

Dahlquist turned his face back to her. "The Marine's dead?"

She nodded as she wiped tears. "No respiration. No pulse. Not that I needed to take one."

"How the hell do you—?"

"My mother's a surgeon. I tried to stop the bleeding. But both carotid arteries were severed."

"Why did his buddies let a pipsqueak like *you*—?"

She shook her head again. "The Seps already killed them all."

"Seps? Not just one?"

"Twenty. But you let a lot more than twenty Seps board this ship, you know."

"*I* didn't let anybody board this ship. The chair commandos at CentCom diverted us to Weichsel."

"I've heard them talking to each other ever since we all came aboard. The Seps speak Standard now, just like everybody else on Weichsel. Just like you and Captain Hicks do. Only somebody like me, who was raised outside the Iceline, would recognize their accents. I told crew members. I told other passengers. But grown-ups just tell a kid to go play in vacuum. You being a case in point."

Dahlquist cocked his head. "They let you get away?"

She shook her head. "They ignored me because I'm a kid. They held the Marine commander's palm to the door's ID plate, so the door opened, before they killed him. Then they all ran into the engineering space and locked the door behind them."

Dahlquist turned and squinted at the big digital display on the information panel alongside the navigation blister. It advertised the ship's casino, but also showed in red numbers the ship's speed and its distance to destination. The speed number stayed constant at 96,000 miles per hour, but the distance-to-destination number was decreasing so fast that it blurred.

Dahlquist ran his fingers across the sealed hatch that led ahead into the navigation blister, then rubbed the wrinkled skin on his forehead.

He asked her, "Why'd you come all the way forward? Anybody would've helped a kid in your shape."

"Every other door off the centerline passageway was sealed. The emergency intercoms are all dead, too."

He muttered the bad word again, this time through clenched teeth. He peered out again at Leonidas and Mousetrap, both of which already looked bigger. Then he turned away, pushed off, and drifted toward the wide door through which she had entered. The old man moved so fast in zero G that she barely kept up. But then he probably had more practice.

Dahlquist stopped a hundred yards back along the centerline passageway, at the sealed door she had tried earlier that led to the bridge companionway. He tugged a folding knife from a coverall pocket, then used one of its blunt blades to remove screws from a plate below the HATCH OPEN and intercom controls. He reached inside, tinkered, and a moment later the circular door whispered open like a camera lens iris.

Her eyes widened, too. "You fix this ship with *that*?"

They kicked, feetfirst, into the companionway, a narrow staircase that spiraled away from the ship's centerline like a spoke away from a wheel's hub.

Dahlquist shook his head. "Not by choice. New ships come with specialized tools for every task. Old ships come with empty places where the tools used to be. And in *Bastogne*'s case it's worse. The reason she was chosen to pick you all up was that she had enough room. The reason she had enough room was that she was empty. The reason she was empty was that she was deadheading back to Mousetrap to be scrapped."

"She's superannuated? Like you."

"She's a lot more superannuated than I am. But before a ship gets scrapped she gets stripped of every ounce worth saving, from galley spoons to screwdrivers. All of which makes our problem worse." He wrinkled his forehead. "'Superannuated?'"

"It means—"

"I *know* what it means. I'm a drunk, not an illiterate. What I don't know is why a pip-squeak like you uses words like superannuated."

Within yards rotational gravity pulled them to the floor treads, and they followed the staircase down as it wound toward the deck's outermost rim.

At a sealed, hinged intermediate door Dahlquist knelt at its latch and worked his screwdriver magic again.

She said, "A pip-squeak is a person too small or insignificant to deserve respect. Please don't call me that."

Dahlquist grunted as he twisted a stubborn screw. "How about 'annoying small person'? Unless you've got a name."

"Patricia Wynant Reisfeld. My mother, the surgeon, is the Wynant."

"Ah."

"My grandfather was a professor of English—what you call Standard—back on Earth."

"Trueborns? Well, that explains the annoying."

"Actually, it doesn't. I unnerve adults because I'm extraordinarily gifted."

"Modest, too. Why'd your parents bring a kid to an ice ball like Weichsel?"

"Parent. My father was the Reisfeld. He died before I was born. Mom's therapist suggested a change of scene to facilitate her acceptance of his death. Treating Tribals outside the Iceline on Weichsel was the biggest scene change available. My grandfather came along with her to help raise me."

"Brave man."

"But mostly to establish a planetwide program to teach Standard to the Tribals. So they could assimilate."

"Well, that's working out great."

The intermediate door swung inward on its hinges. An acrid haze, tinted red by the companionway's emergency lights and stinking of burned metal, drifted out across them.

Dahlquist nudged her behind him, then crept down the spiraling stair tread. He clutched his pocket knife, blade extended, in his right hand, while his left groped through the haze.

At the staircase's next landing he stumbled over something and she fell too.

It was a body, another Marine, faceup, and Patricia had fallen across its boots, which seemed small.

She stifled her scream with her own palm, as Dahlquist hugged Patricia's face against his side so she wouldn't see.

They stood, and she pushed away from Dahlquist.

The Marine's boots were small because she was female, and her throat had been slit just as surgically as had the throat of the Marine who had smiled. The door behind this Marine, which she had defended to her death, lay on the landing alongside her, its hinges scorched where they had been severed.

Patricia shuddered, then whispered, "It's okay. The first one scared me so much I couldn't think. This one just makes me so mad I don't *want* to think."

Dahlquist knelt alongside the female Marine and drew his fingers across her dead eyes, so the lids closed and she was no longer staring. Then he turned to Patricia and stabbed a finger at her chest. "Scared and mad are what you can't be now. Thinking straight under pressure wins unwinnable battles." He pointed at the door opening, and at the scorch marks at the jagged hinges. "And thinking straight seems to be something our Sep buddies are good at."

"What do you mean?"

"They realized that the only weapons they could smuggle past the gangway sensors onto this ship would be made of organic material compatible with the scanned individual. A Weichselan Tribal's knife is carved from one of his ancestor's ribs, isn't it?"

"You're smart."

"They're smarter. Bone knives won't defeat modern arms after the first couple sucker punches." He pointed at the empty holster at the Marine's waist. "So they foraged her sidearm, and probably her rifle." He flicked two of three empty cloth loops on the Marine's left pack strap. "The only way they burned the hinges off the door she was guarding was with two of her own FEDs they had to kill her to get."

"FED?"

"Focused Explosive Device. Detonating a conventional hand grenade in a starship's like hitting a golf ball in a shower stall. A FED blows a hole in what you want and not in what you don't." He tapped a metal cylinder the size and shape of a Coke plasti that was clipped in to the third cloth loop. "I suspect the only reason they left this one is they were in a hurry to reach the next line of defense. A bone knife's quiet, but it can't cut steel. A FED cuts steel, but the bang spoils the surprise."

"Does all this smoke mean the Seps won up ahead, or lost?"

"Maybe both. Come on."

The next line of defense turned out to be another blown-off door and another murdered Marine. But this doorway was now guarded by a live Marine.

"Halt!" Helmeted head cocked sideways, he shuffled toward them, sighting down his rifle's barrel as he aimed it at them.

Dahlquist shoved her farther behind him. "Where's Captain Hicks, Tom?"

The Marine squinted through the haze. "Dahlquist? Why are you out of the brig?"

Dahlquist sighed. "Read your dailies, Tom. Since you transferred to bridge watch, the captain converted the brig into quarters to accommodate all our guests. Now I sleep in a booth in the steerage cocktail lounge, on my own recognizance."

Patricia peeked around Dahlquist at the Marine.

He slid his finger off the trigger, but kept the rifle pointed at Dahlquist. "Guests my ass. They're Separatist hijackers, Dahlquist. Weichselan Tribals. At least some of 'em. Took down eight Marines aft. And five of my squad here." He saw her peeking out from behind Dahlquist and shifted his aim. "What's with the brat?"

"She's a *kid*, Tom."

The Marine slid his finger back to the rifle's trigger. "A kid covered in blood!" He jerked his head at the dead Marine at his feet. "Before Walker died he told me the Tribals used a weaponized kid to get close to him."

"She's no Tribal. One of those Marines aft bled out all over her while she was trying to save his life."

The Marine snorted. "Who told you that? Her?"

Patricia stepped out from behind Dahlquist, stared past the rifle muzzle into the Marine's eyes and spread her bloodstained hands. "It's true. He was my friend. If you think I'm lying, shoot me."

"Friend?" The Marine narrowed his eyes. "What was your friend's name?"

"Martinez."

The Marine kept his eyes locked with hers and the rifle's muzzle pointed at her face while with one hand he patted the name tape above his breast pocket, which read BROWNING. "Nice try."

He tightened his finger on the trigger and her heart skipped.

"Hector. He told me his first name was Hector. He said he has a sister my age named Rosa who looks just like me."

The Marine kept staring. Then he blinked, lowered his rifle, and stared past her up the stairway into the dark. "Hector was my friend too. And Rosa's taller than you."

He took a deep breath, then asked Dahlquist, "How'd you make it this far? When the Tribals locked themselves inside the bridge, they locked down all the mains at the same time."

Dahlquist swore again. "I was hoping it was Hicks who locked them down. So the bastards *do* have control of the bridge *and* the engineering space." He coughed and swatted at the smoke. "But Hicks obviously survived and is in charge."

"The XO was in command on the bridge, not Hicks, when they stormed it. So yeah, the captain's still in command. How'd you know?"

"The bridge capsule's armored with nine inches of reinforced plasteel and so are all the control conduits that lead away from it, and so is the engineering space's forward bulkhead and door. An experienced officer would know that by the time the plasma cutter they're using up there at the bridge, that's making all this smoke, burns through it'll be too late."

The Marine stared. "Too late for what?"

"Tom, don't be such a jarhead. I was this ship's chief engineer for fifteen years. Hicks didn't even graduate Command Basic Course 'til fifteen *months* ago. I knew enough to get us this close to the bridge. Maybe I know enough to unscrew this pooch. At least let us pass so I can try."

The Marine paused, then stepped through the door and said over his shoulder, "I'll see what they say up there. You stay put, Dahlquist, or I'll blow your squid head off. Yours too, ma'am."

Patricia peered up at Dahlquist and puffed out a chest she wouldn't have for a while. "He called me 'ma'am.' Do I look older?"

Dahlquist smiled down at her and shook his head. "Military courtesy. A display of respect. The best way a civilian can earn a jarhead's respect is to befriend another jarhead in trouble, Ms. Wynant Reisfeld." He paused. "Don't you have a nickname?"

She pouted. "No."

Dahlquist consulted his wrister then sighed. "Might as

well share our secrets. Tom's a good man, but if he moves as slow as he thinks we'll be here awhile."

She crossed her arms. "You first. Why were you alone in the observation dome staring at Mousetrap?"

"I was born there. Hadn't seen the place in forty-two years."

"For you this is a homecoming."

He shrugged and swallowed. "Not the kind I wanted. Not for me, not for this ship."

"Why?"

"The *Bastogne* was built in Mousetrap. Before you or I were born. As a battle cruiser during the Pseudocephalopod War. Her name commemorates some Trueborn-on-Trueborn violence that most of the Outworlders who built her, and died in her, never heard of."

"Battle cruisers don't have casinos and cocktail lounges."

He nodded. "True. After the war she was refitted for mercantile service. Then she got so old that not even a chief engineer who loved her could keep her healthy. She was coming home to Mousetrap to be broken up for scrap, stripped naked, with a novice captain, and a skeleton crew. She deserved better."

"Ships are machines. But you talk like you married this one."

Dahlquist shrugged. "Machines don't lie. They don't leave the cap off the toothpaste even though you asked them not to. Or throw the tube at you if you forget their birthdays. All machines ask is maintenance. After fifteen years together a man and a machine can grow closer than some husbands and wives do. So I didn't take the old girl's end well. Three months before the *Bastogne* got diverted to pick you up, I got drunk at the wrong time. A rating serving under me almost lost her leg as a result. The *Bastogne* deserves better. But I deserved what I got."

"Oh."

"So now *Bastogne* and I are both coming home to die, disgraced and too old to matter." Dahlquist paused and stared at the smoky and still-empty companionway beyond the blown door. "I think that story's pathetic enough to earn a reciprocal one. Don't you?"

She stared at the floor plates. "Peewee."

"What?"

"My grandfather says good things come in small packages. So he calls me Peewee."

Dahlquist covered his mouth with his hand like he was rubbing his cheek, but his eyes smiled. "Hell, that's just like calling a machine 'she.' Just an old man's way of saying he loves you."

"The last thing he said to me before I boarded the upshuttle was 'Go forth and do great things, Peewee.'"

The Marine returned, his rifle now slung over his shoulder, and led them through the door toward the bridge.

The companionway tripled in width when they emerged from it into the space in front of the massive bulkhead door that isolated the bridge from the rest of the ship.

The space was dim, but crowded with unsmiling crew and armed Marines. All of them watched as two goggled men knelt alongside a wheeled machine, directing a pencil-thin white flame at the bulkhead's base. Crackling sparks and smoke fountained from the spot where the flame contacted the bulkhead, and the flame's flicker lit the others' faces.

The goggled men paused to inspect their progress, and found only a shallow, glowing furrow in the metal.

Peewee followed Dahlquist as he walked toward Captain Hicks, who stood, feet planted and arms crossed in the dimness, watching the plasma cutter's progress.

Dahlquist paused along the way and patted the shoulder of another officer, younger than Dahlquist but older than the captain, who wore old-fashioned eyeglasses that hooked around his ears and lay across his nose. His uniform nameplate read MACDOUGAL.

Dahlquist whispered, "The new brass looks good on you, Mac."

The man turned to Dahlquist and his eyes widened behind his glasses. "Johnny?" Then he whispered back, "Looked better on you."

"How you holding up as chief engineer?"

"*Acting* chief engineer." Macdougal shrugged. "I'm an astrogator, not a wrench."

Dahlquist tossed his head toward the captain. "How's Hicks holding up?"

Macdougal gave his head a shake so small only Dahlquist and Peewee saw it. "Drowning and he knows it, Johnny. He's too scared and too angry at the hand he's been dealt to play it. But there's no point pushing him."

"If somebody doesn't push him we *all* drown, Mac."

Dahlquist patted Macdougal's shoulder again, walked

past him and when he reached Hicks he stood straight and saluted. "Captain."

The younger man scowled, and didn't salute back. "Dahlquist? Come up from the bar to appeal your administrative punishment?"

"Sir, the captain will recall I affirmatively waived my rights and accepted your decision. I'm only here to offer advice on the current situation."

The captain nodded toward the sizzling sparks and spoke loudly enough that those around him heard. "We have the current situation under complete control. Once we penetrate the bridge capsule locking mechanism, we'll overpower the Tribals and regain control of the ship."

Several crewmen had cocked their heads to listen to the discussion.

Dahlquist leaned toward the captain and lowered his voice. "Sir, a word in private?"

The captain frowned, but stepped away from the others as Dahlquist followed. Peewee hunched over, tried to look ignorable, and followed the pair of them.

Dahlquist pointed at the sputtering plasma torch. "Captain, that torch won't penetrate the capsule for an hour. Meantime the ship's not slowing down. Without control of either the engineering space or the bridge the book says we can't slow her down or steer her."

"Dahlquist, I know what the book says."

"Sir, there's more to it than what the book says. On present course and at present velocity we will impact Mousetrap's North Portal in fifty-seven minutes."

The captain leaned closer and hissed. "Goddammit, Dahlquist. I know that! I also know that I was *ordered* to take these refugees aboard my ship with minimal vetting. So CentCom and the politicians would look good. But history won't say that. History will say that I failed to prevent assassins from infiltrating my ship. History will say my ship didn't have escape pods and even pressure suits, so it couldn't be abandoned. It won't say that every ship gets stripped before it's scrapped. Fifty-seven minutes from now it won't be my problem, though. It will be my wife's problem. Because she will have to explain to my son why his dead father was the first captain to lose a capital ship to hostile action in a century."

"Sir, you need to focus on solving the problem, not on what history will say."

"Exactly. The problem is bigger than you or me or even this ship. If history says all of us on this ship went down swinging, with courage and grace, maybe the Union will be inspired to win the next round. And the war."

Dahlquist pressed his lips together. "Captain, I don't question your courage. I do question your assumptions about the stakes and about available alternatives. With respect, losing with courage and grace is brave and noble. Losing when you could win is stupid. Especially when there's more to lose than you think."

The captain stiffened. "You said you were here to help. Insubordination helps no one."

"A civilian can't be guilty of insubordination. Dammit, Richard, I am trying to help, if you'd just listen!"

The captain blinked, stood silent.

Dahlquist said, "You're right that what you're doing here won't work. Mousetrap hasn't been equipped to interdict anything bigger than smugglers' fast movers for decades. The kinetic energy generated by a capital ship impacting Mousetrap at ninety-six thousand miles per hour, which is the velocity we're locked at, won't just vaporize this ship and everyone in it. It will reduce Mousetrap, and the eleven million people who live in it, and the dozen or so capital ships that are refitting there post-jump on any given day, to a debris field that in a few million years may coalesce into a ring around Leonidas."

The captain's eyes widened.

Dahlquist said, "Without Mousetrap's waypoint facilities for post-jump refits, commerce among the planets will shrink to a trickle. Without Mousetrap's shipyards it would take decades just to rebuild enough ships to build a new waypoint from scratch, so nobody will bother. The Union will devolve back to the five hundred isolated planets it was before the war. The separatists won't just have won this battle. They will have won the war. With a single shot that murdered eleven million people. History won't be kind."

The captain stood still as stone, eyes wide and staring.

Dahlquist said, "But we can stop this."

The captain whispered, "I'm listening."

"The observation dome and navigation blister are carry-forwards from the first capital ships. They were a redundant system that allowed a single officer to helm the ship by eyeball and hands-on controls in case of emergency."

The captain shook his head. "They were vanity boondoggles. The contractors built them in to appease admirals and generals who had been seat-of-the-pants pilots. The navigation blister's been used exactly once in history."

Dahlquist nodded. "But it worked. So every ship still has a dome and a blister."

Captain Hicks snorted. "Every ship still has them because the passengers like to look out the big window. So what are you proposing?"

Dahlquist pointed at the plasma cutter. "All I need is that. And two ratings to operate it."

"We only have one plasma cutter. And there's no point. The controls don't activate just because the blister hatch is breached."

"I don't propose to cut the blister hatch open. The hatch unlocks automatically *when* the controls in the blister activate. Just as important, once they activate they lock out the bridge controls. One pilot in the blister can slow the ship to drift approach velocity in seconds. And once the bridge controls are locked out, all the Seps will have done is confine themselves in the bridge and the engineering space 'til Mousetrap can send up reinforcements equipped to dig 'em out."

The captain crossed his arms and shook his head. "The controls only activate in the event of a defined emergency."

"Exactly. That plasma cutter can't cut through the bridge capsule in time. But the hull's thinnest point is where it joins the observation dome. The cutter can open a finger-width breach through an inch of plasteel in five minutes. The ship should react to the pressure-drop emergency within one minute."

"*If* the ship reacts to a slow leak. *If* a blister hatch that hasn't operated in years unseals. *If* an entire vestigial system that hasn't been tested or maintained for decades works." The captain stepped to one of the cutter operators and tapped the man's shoulder. "How long?"

The man shrugged. "It seems to be going faster now, sir."

The captain turned back to Dahlquist and shook his head. "I can't do both. Too many uncertainties your way, Dahlquist. We will continue with the plan currently in progress."

"Too many *certainties* your way, Captain. Seven inches of plasteel left. Forty-four minutes left. It's impossible!"

The captain turned away.

"Dammit, Richard!"

The captain called to the Marine named Tom. "Sergeant, please escort Mr. Dahlquist out of here."

"Aye aye, sir. To where?"

"As far as it takes to assure he doesn't further delay or disrupt this operation. If he tries to come back here, shoot him."

Peewee tugged Dahlquist's hand and whispered, "Hicks is being a jerk. You can't just leave!"

Dahlquist hissed, "Zip it, Peewee."

As Dahlquist, Peewee, and the Marine reached Macdougal, the younger man grabbed Dahlquist's arm and turned to the Marine. "Sergeant, I'll have a private word with Mr. Dahlquist if you please."

The Marine glanced back at the captain, who was peering over the shoulders of the men operating the plasma cutter, then at the rank badges on Macdougal's epaulets. "Aye aye, sir. Make it a short word."

Macdougal whispered, "See? He's irrational, Johnny. Look, whatever you're planning, I'm in. Better, you join the rest of us." Macdougal slid one hand into a coverall pocket, then drew it out so that a pistol's butt was visible.

"Mutiny, Mac?"

"Desperate situation. Desperate measures."

Dahlquist shook his head. "Not my style. Or yours. And certainly not the jarheads' style. They'll drop you all before you get your pistols out of your pants. And by the time the smoke cleared it would be too late anyway."

Macdougal said, "You have a better idea?"

"Maybe. I just need an extra pair of hands. Can you slip away from this zoo?"

Macdougal shook his head. "Like you said about the jarheads. Deserting my post in the face of the enemy will just earn me a summary bullet."

Peewee tugged Dahlquist's sleeve. "I don't have a post. And my hands are fine."

Macdougal looked down at her as though she had materialized from thin air and his eyes widened behind his glasses. "Huh?"

Dahlquist sighed, then said, "Long story, Mac." He stared down at her, then nodded. "You'll do."

The Marine sergeant escorted them as far as the post he had guarded when they first encountered him, then resumed his duty.

Dahlquist led her back the way they came, just the two of them, now climbing the staircase instead of descending.

When they reached the body of the female Marine, Dahlquist knelt over her and plucked the remaining FED from her pack strap.

Ten minutes later they arrived back at the observation

dome hatch and Dahlquist opened and closed it twice by pressing its control plates.

Peewee asked, "If the Seps closed all the doors, why was this one still open when I first got here?"

"The manual controls here work, but the circuitry that connects it to the bridge wore out years ago."

"Will your idea win the war?"

"If it works, it'll keep us from losing it for now. That's the best I got. Come on. I'll introduce you to hull plate five-six-six-eight."

She followed him as he pushed off, then drifted to the dome's edge, where its thick crystal and the hull's steel joined.

He pulled the dead Marine's FED from a pocket in his coverall, then held it in both hands and moved it slowly toward the hull.

Clank.

The FED clung to the steel like a big gray wart.

Dahlquist smiled. "Magnetism."

Peewee peered at the speed display, then out through the dome. In front of them Mousetrap now loomed huge, and behind it Leonidas filled her field of vision like an orange sky. "It's already too late!"

"Huh?"

She pointed forward. "Newton's first law of motion says if the ship stops from ninety-six thousand miles per hour now, you and I will keep moving forward. We'll squash onto the dome like bugs on a skimmer's windshield. So will everybody else."

Dahlquist shook his head and smiled. "The only good that came out of the Pseudocephalopod War is we stole

C-drive from the Slugs. Newton knew gravity, but he didn't know gravity could be manipulated. This ship moves within a self-generated envelope that insulates it and its contents. We can stop on a dime, astrophysically speaking, and we won't feel a thing."

"I doubt that."

He raised his eyebrows. "Really? Did you get squashed against an aft bulkhead when we deorbited Weichsel and accelerated to one-third light speed?"

"Oh. So you're going to shoot off this bomb and make the ship leak. Then you're going to Superman over to the boob nipple, climb inside, and put the brakes on."

"Not the way I would have described it. But yep."

"That sounds too easy."

"Yep." Dahlquist's eyes glistened. "Peewee, if Hicks had given us that plasma cutter we could have made a tiny leak. But what we have is this FED. An FED can't defeat nine inches of plasteel. But this one will blow a hole through one inch of steel so big that the air in this dome will evacuate down to practical vacuum in thirty seconds, give or take."

She frowned. "Explosive decompression. You won't be able to go over there and steer."

He nodded. "I'll need to be in place at the hatch at the moment it unlocks, and be holding on to the grab rail for dear life. Because anything inside this dome that isn't bolted down is going to get sucked out into vacuum when the hull blows." He pointed at a knob on the FED's end, from which a red button protruded. "The maximum delay time on this is fifteen seconds. After I rotate the knob to set it, you wait until I get hold of the grab rail. When I give you the thumbs-up, press this red button. Then kick off hard as hell and drift back out into the centerline passage. Close the door behind you. Should take you eight seconds, tops." He poked at her. "Be sure you close the hatch behind you. It won't close automatically in response to the decompression because it's busted. Got that?"

"Close the hatch. Got it." She kept frowning. "You can breathe in the navigation blister?"

Dahlquist bent down and twisted the FED's timer. "I'll hold my breath."

"Another stupid joke."

He whispered and his voice cracked. "The blister's designed to function during an emergency. In an emergency an operator is presumed to be wearing a self-sustaining pressure suit. But all of this ship's pressure suits are boxed up in a surplus equipment warehouse three jumps behind us."

"If I push the red button, you'll die."

"Not immediately. I'll be conscious and animate for a good thirty seconds. Plenty of time to hit the brakes."

She shook her head. "I won't do that."

"If you don't push the button, I'll still die. So will you. So will eleven million other people. You don't have to be Newton to do the math."

"The captain said the controls are so old they won't work."

"Some of us old things still work." He shrugged. "It's an unavoidable risk."

Peewee shook her head as her tears welled up again. "No. No. I can't."

Dahlquist turned and peered again at Mousetrap as it rushed toward them. "It's all right. There wasn't anything left for me to do there." When he turned back to her his old eyes were moist, and he reached out and brushed her cheek with bony fingers. "Go forth and do great things, Peewee."

He pushed hard, shot toward the navigation blister, grasped the grab rail then turned back to her and pumped a fist, thumb up.

She clutched her trembling right hand with her left to control its shaking, extended her arms, and pressed the button with her right index finger.

The bomb clicked, then spoke. "Fourteen."

She stared at it, paralyzed. She hadn't expected it to talk.

"Thirteen."

"Not fair!"

"Twelve."

She spun a somersault, kicked, and made it through the open door into the centerline passageway as the bomb said, "Five."

She turned, looked forward, and watched as John Dahlquist clung to the navigation blister's grab rail, his back to her. He appeared as serene as he had appeared in the moment when she first saw him, an hour earlier. But now it seemed like she had known him all her life.

His voice echoed in her memory. "Got it?"

Got what? Her heart skipped and she spun and stretched her fingers toward the DOOR CLOSE plate.

Boom.

The detonation, focused or not, stunned her, and within the confined space the concussion stabbed at her eardrums like knife blades.

Escaping air roared past her, and though she stretched her arm the inches between her fingertips and the plate grew. "Ahh!"

Debris sucked from the centerline passage stung her cheeks as it struck them, then caromed away. She paddled with decreasing effect against air that kept growing thinner. She grabbed at the door opening's lip as she was dragged across it, clutched it so hard that the metal edge cut her fingers. She grabbed the lip with both hands then thrust herself back, into the centerline passageway, and punched the DOOR CLOSE plate with a bleeding fist.

An instant later she rested, gasping, with her back against the closed door, the maelstrom of escaping air muffled by steel that now insulated her from vacuum.

When she turned toward the closed door, she pulled herself, hand over hand, to the quartz porthole set in one of the door's panels and peered through.

At first the view through the dome opening seemed as black as empty space. Then she realized that the ship had come to rest nose first against the black, pocked rock of Mousetrap's skin. Even what must have been a gentle tap against the Moonlet's surface had shattered the great quartz dome. The navigation blister had been driven back into the dome by the impact, crushed like a discarded cola plasti amid enormous, jumbled crystal shards.

"You okay?" Macdougal, the officer who wore glasses, drifted up alongside her.

She nodded. "Fine. We stopped?"

Macdougal nodded. "No thanks to our efforts at the bridge. But yes. Dead solid perfect. Almost. Thanks to Dahlquist. Nobody's sure yet whether the Seps will surrender, fight to the death, or fall on their knives. But it's over. Johnny?"

She pointed through the quartz port.

Beyond the ruined dome John Dahlquist, face and limbs frozen and frosted by the cold of space, lay upon the craggy ebony surface of the small world where he had been born, now still, spread-eagled, and staring back at them with dead eyes.

Macdougal stared through the port, then tugged off his glasses and wiped away tears. "Not the homecoming you deserved, was it Johnny?"

Dr. Patricia Wynant Reisfeld sat in a folding chair on a temporary stage erected in front of the immense cruiser moored in Mousetrap's berth nine.

Fourteen years earlier the ship had been snatched from the scrapper's jaws, already torn down to metallic skin and corroded bones, only after the pleas, and threats, and unkeepable promises sworn by a twelve-year-old girl who wouldn't take no for an answer.

The rescued *Bastogne*'s remains had then dangled for four years, a forgotten, frozen carcass moored above Mousetrap's stark crags while the wreck's sole champion raised awareness and money to resurrect it. The awareness had been difficult enough. The money, over the ensuing ten years, had always fallen ten percent short of the contractors' ever-increasing estimates.

She turned in her chair and peered back along the reborn cruiser's now-modern, bunting-draped mile-long flank. Only when a starship floated in its berth could a human being comprehend its majesty.

At the rostrum the Governor General of Mousetrap, to whom the Lord Mayor of the Free City of Shipyard had yielded, completed his remarks, turned, applauding, and introduced her.

She stepped to the rostrum, gripped its sides with both hands, and peered through the projected prepared text that hung in the air and separated her from her audience like a luminous wall. The crowd was bigger than most she had lectured, cajoled, and inspired; smaller than some.

On her left was the crew, in crisp and white uniforms as new as their ship, officers seated, ratings at ease in ranks behind them.

To the crew's right sat the bureaucrats and union presidents and captains of industry who she had jawboned, and coddled, and wheedled when money ran short or when progress took too long.

Front and center sat the Homecoming Foundation's principal donors. Some she recalled as self-important demagogues, others as compassionate geniuses who seemed too nice to have built empires. Among them fidgeted a half-dozen donors in off-the-rack suits, who had been selected to stand in for the tens of thousands of grassroots contributors who had given the price of a meal they really couldn't do without.

The bulk of the audience, on her right, were two thousand displaced Weichselans, some survivors fourteen years older than they had been when they left home, some descendants of Weichselans who hadn't survived until peace had been restored. These Weichselans would be the first refugees the foundation and its glistening ship would repatriate to their homes. But they wouldn't be the last, as long human cruelty created refugees.

She reached past the christening champagne bottle that awaited on the rostrum, switched off the prompting projector, and leaned in to the microphone. "I seem to have lost my extensive prepared remarks. I'm glad of that. And, trust me, so are you."

She paused until the laughter ebbed.

"Fourteen years ago, during the worst of times, two wise men challenged me to go forth and do great things. Today I hope marks a step toward meeting their challenge, toward the best of times."

She had carried the champagne bottle here specifically for this purpose all the way from Earth, a birthplace she had visited often over the past fourteen years, less because it was the green, warm antithesis of Weichsel than because it was where the money was.

The Lord Mayor and the Governor General flanked her as she stepped alongside the ship's observation dome, the bottle held inverted in both her hands.

As the bunting that covered the ship's new nameplate dropped away, she broke the bottle against it, and a constellation of bubbling droplets glistened beneath the berth's floodlights.

Patricia Wynant Reisfeld spoke into the microphone that the Lord Mayor held for her. "May you voyage far and keep safe all who travel within you, and forever honor the memory of the hero whose name you bear." She leaned toward the ship and pressed her fingers against its moist crystal dome. "Godspeed, *John Dahlquist.*"

❦   ❦   ❦

National best-selling author **Robert Buettner** was a Quill Award nominee for Best New Writer of 2005, and his debut novel, *Orphanage*, Quill-nominated as best SF/Fantasy/Horror novel of 2004, has been called a classic of modern military science fiction. His ninth novel, *The Golden Gate*, is set in the near present, but has a giant spaceship in it just like his first eight. Various critics have compared his writing favorably to the work of Robert Heinlein, which proves you can fool some of the people some of the time.

He was a National Science Foundation Fellow in paleontology, served as a US Army intelligence officer, prospected for minerals in Alaska and the Sonoran desert, and has been General Counsel of a unit of one of the United States' largest private multinational companies.

He lives in Georgia with his family and more bicycles than a grown-up needs. Visit him at www.RobertBuettner.com.

NOT MADE FOR US

Christopher Ruocchio

The boarding party: it may be the toughest military task force of them all. You are headed straight into the enemy's den, invading his innermost sanctum—all of which you try to accomplish while being all but surrounded by those who want to rip you apart limb from limb. Now imagine having barely opened your eyes from quiet interstellar slumber only to find yourself facing an enemy that looks and acts like a combination of all the nightmares you thought you'd missed while in suspended animation. Well, nobody ever said the plight of the space legionary was going to be easy!

"I think they thawed out the whole Chiliad," Larai said at mess. She hadn't touched her food. The printed beef had gone cold on her tray. That bothered me. Can't say why, only that Larai usually put away her rations faster than either Soren or me—faster than anyone on the decade—which were crazy, small as she is. Not today. She just sat there, hands on her bald head. Hadn't spoken the whole meal. Not even touched her coffee.

Soren don't usually talk much, so I said, "You sure?"

She nodded. "Heard one of the medtechs say H-Deck was emptied out. Ninth Century's out of the ice. Guessing the Tenth's not far behind."

"That mean a big campaign?" I said.

"That means a *fucking* big campaign," Soren put in, setting down his fork.

Took me half a second to realize he was eying me. "What?"

"You've not had a proper campaign, son." He had this weird look in his eyes, like he were my da back on Aramis. I was about to respond when a voice came from my right. Gave me such a start I dropped my knife.

"My money's on annexation, lads!" I didn't see the decurion sneak up on us, but there he was: Peter Thailles in his black fatigues. He looked a little older than he had when I'd gone into the ice, making me wonder if he'd run up his clock somehow while we slept. Soren says officers always time-out faster than us groundlings. He noticed I'd dropped my knife and—clapping me on the shoulder all friendly—added, "Sorry, Oh-Four! You frighten that easy? Scarier than me's coming, you mark my words."

I didn't say anything. I don't like the decurion much. Probably shouldn't write that, never know when an officer will root through my things. He's a decent enough officer. Just don't like the way he talks to Larai and the other ladies in the decade, but he's my commander . . . and I guess that's what I should expect from some black-barred patrician like him. All the ego of a nobile, none of the sting—gives him a real chip on his shoulder. "Reckon it's Normans," he said, leaning in over his dinner tray. "Reckon brass picked out another one of their freeholds. We'll see how long they hold free, eh?"

"Hopefully good and long," Soren said, jerking his head at me. "Last annexation I was on took seven *years*. Weren't even hard. Those Normans can't fight for shit."

Decurion Thailles narrowed his eyes. "Language, Oh-Six. This isn't that three-bit whorehouse they raised you in."

If Soren didn't like the decurion talking to him like that, I couldn't tell. Old bastard grinned lazily at the officer and said, "Were a four-bit whorehouse, sir. Might be they cut you a discount."

I had to wait until the others started laughing before I joined in. Even so, I kept my eyes down on my tray and didn't look the decurion in the face. His eyes freak me. Too blue they are, like a bird's egg. Ain't natural. Earth and evolution didn't mean for men to have eyes like them, but the pats and the nobiles do what they want. Chantry lets them. Ain't that kind of pride a sin?

"They told you something they've not told us?" Larai asked the officer.

The decurion, he turned to her—and I still don't like the look in those eyes of his—and he said, "They're always telling me things, Oh-Five, but they haven't said a thing." He were in the dark much as us, then. That makes sense, right? Captain Vohra's supposed to give us a talking-to over internal comms, but no one's heard from her or Commander Kolosov. Shuttles have been going back and forth from the *Sword of Malkuth* and the *Prince Raphael*, though. Business as usual. I know it's been only four days, but am I wrong to want some kind of clue from on high? I've heard everything from pirates to Extras to Thailles's Norman theory. One kid in the Third Century said something about Mericanii war machines like in the old stories, but his centurion gave him extra PT for saying that shit, so I doubt we're flying into the sort of hell they write operas about.

Going to sleep. Hope there's more answers tomorrow.

There's this moment, right after I seal the helmet on but before the cams come on, where it's completely dark and mostly quiet. You can hear everyone else kitting out: seals hissing in place, laughter, the grind of straps tightening, someone swearing at their tunic for not draping right; but you can't really hear straight. You're alone. Then the suit comes online, puts up a set of readouts in the peripheral: heart rate, blood pressure, charge levels on plasma burner and phase disruptor, communications channels with my triad, my decade, and up and up to Captain Vohra on the command line. Then the vision flips on, filling the inside of the helmet with a flattened-out version of the world. How they do it I don't know. Chantry swears there ain't no demons in the suit thinking for us, and they'd know, but the helmet's visor sifts out a lot of the crap: shadows, tricks of the light, that sort.

That moment—when I stop looking at the world with the eyes my mother gave me and start looking at the screen the Empire tells me to use—that's when it changes. I ain't me no more, or not just me. I'm *them*. I'm *Empire*.

※　※　※

The ten of us piled into our shuttle, pressed tight together, pauldrons grating as we get jostled by the thrusters firing. "Shields at full charge!" the decurion called from the back of the shuttle, behind his three triads. "Oh-One, you and yours start shooting the minute you're over the lip! You heard the captain, there are no friendlies on the other side of that door. Second and Third, fan left and right, secure a position near the shuttle—we may need to make egress fast." I wasn't looking at him—barely heard him through the blood hammering in my damn ears—but he must have turned to the pilot officer in back because he said, "You keep the engines warm, boy, and keep an eye out for anything coming at you down the hull. No idea what sort of hull defense they're fielding, but if you get jumpy, you scream."

Thailles kept talking, but I don't remember much of it. I was staring at the door. Perfect round, it was, and wide enough to fit three legionnaires shoulder to shoulder. When it opened, I had no idea what would be on the other side. Laser cutters on the outside could make a door just anywhere, cut through anything short of highmatter or the long-chain diamond they use on some warships. Our shuttle would clamp onto the outer hull like a burr don't come off, cut its way in without causing a leak. This was the sort of thing you think about when they scoop you up in the levies—or when they got you in the signing center like me. You think about seizing Mandari trade ships operating in Imperial space without papers, about putting down rebellious lords with as little loss of life as possible, about reclaiming stations captured by the Extras or bringing some colonists into the light of the Empire.

Something hit the ship then, or nearly did. Maybe it bucked our shields. I lurched sidelong into Larai, who shoved me straight again. Funny how little you hear things, just by the sounds pushed into the hull. Shrike shuttles are small, fast, ugly things not meant for the sky. Outside, they look like cigars, or like one of the sword handles the Imperial knights carry around—only bristling with little engines. They're fast. Damn fast. Suppression fields cut most of the inertial bucking, but someone out there was firing on us, and that changed things faster than the field could track, rattling us in our armor. Don't remember much else of the approach. Don't even know how long it was. I was watching the clock in the corner of my suit's visual field, but the numbers wouldn't stick. Only thing I remember's my breathing. I was sealed in my suit, sealed in that shuttle. It was all I could hear outside the groaning of the ship. I was breathing like I'd been at wind sprints, or sparring for a good hour. I looked back, past the three soldiers behind me and Thailles to where the pilot officer sat in his chair. Unlike the rest of us, I could see his face through his visor. He was gritting his teeth.

Then it went real quiet, and Soren said, "We close to the hull? Inside their line of fire?"

"Stow it, Oh-Six!"

"Wish we could get a look at the thing," I said.

"You wouldn't see shit anyhow," Larai said.

"I said stow it!"

We hammered into the side of the ship, and I had to hold to a loop on the ceiling to keep from falling on my face and knocking Oh-One into the door. Something high-pitched whirred like a metal demon in front, and I thought of little teeth chewing on whatever it was we'd clamped onto. I know that ain't right, but I can't shake it. *I* was shaking then, even though I didn't *know*. I was so scared. Like I said, that door could open on anything. Anything. I imagined Extrasolarian mutants all metal and slime, or Jaddian janissaries in bright silk and those mirrored masks of theirs. Maybe I was picturing monsters like the ones the lords keep for sport, or pirates like I used to play at as a kid on Aramis. And that were just the shit I'd heard of. I tried to tell myself I were ready for it, trained for it. It didn't matter. Back at camp on Orden they said you forget everything you learn the minute the shit hits.

I did.

The whirring stopped, the door opened. Just inside, the walls of the ship glowed like old coals where the Shrike had cut in, and all was dark beyond. Not that it mattered. Helmet cameras compensated for the low light inside, boosted visuals with infrared and sonic mapping. Everything looked gray, and there wasn't much to look at.

"Blackened Earth!" said Oh-One, leading the way in.

"The hell sort of ship is this?" Larai said.

Soren were praying, muttering under his breath just soft enough I couldn't make out the words. Someone told him to stop, and he did, turning left to look down along the hall. Everything looked green and granular. I kept my plasma burner down, arms straight, waiting.

The gravity felt off. Lighter. I didn't like that. Heavier's easier to deal with than light; suit's exoskeleton kicks in. Low grav means less control.

Thailles jumped down out of the Shrike. I could make

him out in the light of the shuttle door, taller than the rest of us and with the two red dashes on the blank white plane of his visor above the right cheek to mark his rank. The left side of his visor was painted in, black with a yellow bird on in profile—his house's seal. The way he hefted his burner rifle, he looked downright terrifying, red cloak drifting in the micrograv. He oversaw deployment of the mapping drones—which went spinning off into the dark—and said, "Oh-Six, take yours down and right, I want to know what we're dealing with."

Soren gestured understanding and we went off down the hall, if you could call it that. The walls were like cave walls, and the floor was uneven and rolling, like we'd come into an asteroid someone'd dug out. My foot splashed in something.

"What kind of ship is this?" Larai asked, repeating the question from earlier. She shined the light off her plasma burner up at the ceiling . . . highlighting where huge pipes were bracketed to the stone. "There're no lights."

"Mining rig, maybe?" Soren put in, turning back to look at us. "You seen any doors?"

"No, sir," I said.

"You don't have to *sir* me, boyo." I could hear the grin in his words. "Stay sha—!"

I remember seeing him standing there, lit by the backscatter off Larai's and my plasma burners and green in my suit's viewfinder. Then I blinked and he was gone, knocked flat on his ass by *something* that came flying unseen out of the dark. Whatever it was banged off his shield, making the energy curtain momentarily visible, casting faint lights up the stone walls. I flinched away.

Larai surged forward, weapon raised. Fumbling with the controls on my vambrace, waving my weapon 'round like an idiot, I dialed my suit lights all the way up to give her something to see by, ready with cover fire. Soren was a good two meters back from where we stood, struggling to his feet. For a second, I couldn't find whatever it was that had hit him, but Larai swore all kinds of fierce and moved off to his left.

"What the hell is going on?" Thailles's voice rattled in my ears. "Oh-Four? Oh-Four!"

"Something hit Oh-Six, sir!" I kept looking, weapon up, careful to keep Larai out of my line of fire. Spotted movement in the dark, turned toward it. I panicked, squeezed off a shot, plasma burner coughing violet light. "Contact! Contact!" The thing were small, and I must have missed, 'cause it came tearing into the light and straight at me, forgetting about Soren. It were a snake, a flying snake about as long as my forearm and just as big around. I saw its teeth flash in my face—and then I were flying, knocked off my feet just like Soren. Plasma light flashed and my head rang when I smashed into the wall. Larai stood above me, offering a hand. I took it.

"What in nuclear hell was that?" Soren asked, sounding a little worse for wear.

I followed Larai over to the smoking remains of what she'd shot, keeping my weapon—God and Emperor, I'd been useless—trained on the damn thing.

"It's a machine!" Larai said, nudging it with her boot, "Look!" She made a warding gesture with her free hand. Protection against evil.

Crouching, I looked. It weren't teeth at the business

end of the snake, but bits like on the end of a drill. I swore, and said, "Imagine what that'd do, if it got past your armor."

Thailles came in over the comms, and Soren explained. "Oh-Four and me got knocked the hell down, sir. Some kind of drone . . ."

"You ever seen something like this?" I asked Larai, looking up from where I was crouched over the thing.

She shook her head. "No."

"Think it's Extras? They use all sorts of crazy-ass machines, right? Evil shit? Shit Chantry burns you for?"

"Could be." She straightened, checking the safety on her burner. "Never been up against them." She took a second, keyed up her own suit lights to match mine. Up ahead, one of the pipes was venting steam into the hall. Somewhere behind, I heard a *thud* banging through the wall and knew another Shrike cutter had grappled the hull and that somewhere another decade was on their way in. I could see the map of the ship taking shape in my suit's display, threads linking up like spiderwebs as the other decades deployed their drones.

"Best get moving," Soren said, "want to find a door or something."

Something screamed.

Earth and Emperor preserve me. The sound of it . . . like metal tearing ice.

I didn't want to be a soldier. Didn't want to leave Aramis. I done it for Minah. For the boy. I didn't want to be there. I wanted to throw down my gun and run back for the ship, hide there with the pilot officer until it were over.

They came out of the fog, and I still don't quite believe it. The stars ain't had anything like them around when I gone under. The worlds changed while I been froze . . . got . . . monsters in them now. And we got sent in to fight them without a word of warning.

At first I thought they was men. They had arms and legs like men. Walked like them. But as they got closer and got into the light, I saw they wasn't like us at all. They were tall. Taller than Thailles. And the arms stretched to their knees. And their faces—if they were faces—were like our visors. Smooth. White. With eyes big as my fist, black as space. No nose, no ears, but a mess of horns like on some devil from up on the Chantry walls.

I staggered back, mind locked up like I was some kind of idiot. Didn't even see the knife in its damn fist until it was on me. I couldn't think. I just froze, figured I was dead already.

"Carax! Down!"

My name got through to me. Not sure if it were Soren or Larai what said it. I fell into the wall and a shot flew past me, going wide as the *thing* lurched toward me. It stopped, pulled something from its waist, and threw it. One of those drone things. I heard someone cry out, tried to make myself aim, tried to control my breathing. I raised my burner and fired, hit the thing in the shoulder, but that didn't hardly seem to slow it down.

There were more of the things then, three or four coming out of the fog down the hall. Loping, doglike, only on two legs. Another shot went past. In the shaking lights off our suits, I saw teeth like broken glass snarling. It didn't go down. *It didn't go down.*

A huge hand grabbed me by the neck and pushed me up the wall. It squeezed, but the suit underlayment hardened and wouldn't let it choke me. I could feel the fingers tighten. I panicked, dropped my gun and tried to pull its fingers off me. They were like steel. And the face . . . Earth and Emperor, the *face*. I seen statues of Death in Chantry, all skull with empty eyes. Up close it were like that, like someone forgot to finish it, but poured white wax over a skeleton and called it done. Horns snarled above those huge eyes, curved back in a crown. We was nearly eye to eye, only there weren't nothing in its face, no light like a man has, no fire like a woman. Just empty. Flat. Like my da's eyes had been when I seen him dead as a boy.

That made me think of my boy and Minah, and I remembered my knife. I pulled it from my belt and brought it up under the monster's arm. Must have found something, because it hissed and dropped me. I fell like a bunch of sticks, slipped down the wall. Damn ankle went out from under me, and I think I yelled. Don't know what happened to the creature. Soren came out of nowhere, holding his burner out, one-handed, the other pressed to his side. The old man fired, shouted, "On your feet!"

That were when another loomed up out of the darkness, a long, white blade in its hands. I tugged my phase disruptor free from its holster, raised my arm. The thing hummed silent in my fist, and the energy current struck it blue in the chest. It went down spasming, long arms twitching as the disruptor burned out nerve channels and fried the creature in its own meat. Soren looked down at me. "Thanks."

I nodded, trying to find my wits. My first real fight. I

wasn't ready. Not for this. I should have been back on
Aramis. Should have lived to death with Minah. I could
still run. Thailles would have me whipped, but whipped
ain't dead, and the Shrike weren't far.

Thailles's voice was filling my ears on comms, shouting
orders that didn't mean nothing anymore. Sounded like
they'd found *them* too. It weren't real. This were just some
nightmare I wasn't supposed to have. The hull around us
shuddered like we was inside a metal drum. More Shrikes
clamping on. More soldiers. Maybe that were the seals
popping on cryofreeze. Maybe I was waking up.

"Carax, stand the fuck up!" Soren screamed. In a lull,
he fiddled with his burner—swapping from shot to torch
mode—then turned and sprayed a great stream of plasma
fire over the things.

"Carax!" Larai added.

I was so gone I thought it were Minah for a moment,
and that got me standing. The disruptor had no kick to it
like the burner, so I pointed one-handed at another of the
monsters, leaning against the rough stone wall. The
energy bolt found its mark on the side of its head, and it
went down smoking. Think I shouted something, because
Soren glanced back over his shoulder. "Nice shot!" I could
hear the grin in his voice. He sounded normal. Maybe he
needed to sound normal.

Then it all went wrong. More wrong.

The wall blew apart in a flash of light and Soren were
. . . he were just gone. Him and the demons. One second
he was standing there, looking back at me, then nothing.
The wind blowing out howled louder than the explosion.
My ears rang. I couldn't think. I was ripped off the ground

and thrown out the new hole. The wind froze around me and I spiraled out into the Dark. Something grabbed my leg. One of the demons, it had to be. I kicked, figured I'd smash its skull-face in. Only then the words screaming over my suit's comm got through to me: "Carax! Carax, it's me!"

Larai.

You're not going back to the ship now, farm boy.

"It's not real," I kept saying. "It's not real. It's not real."

But it were. I tried to stop us tumbling, but as we got farther and farther away . . . I could see it. The ship—if it was a ship—was huge, so huge it vanished into the Dark, lit only by the running lights of a hundred Shrike cutter craft clamped on the outer hull. "Is that ice?" I remember it was the first coherent thought I'd had since the shuttle door opened.

"What?"

"Ice!" I tried to point. "It's covered in it." In the light of the shuttles, we could see pieces—just pieces—of a ship growing out of the Dark. Parts was metal, parts stone, all covered and glittering in a thick layer of ice. We was still getting signal fed in from the mapping drones on board, and I could see the full scale of the craft taking shape in the corner of my eye. It were huge. Bigger than the *Valorous,* bigger than any ship I'd ever heard of, so big it distracted me from the fact that Larai and I were careening out into naked space.

"Oh-Four, Oh-Five! Report!"

"Thailles?" I practically choked. "Soren's dead. Got hit by something from outside." Just then another explosion tore into the icy mass, and we saw flames spill out behind a blinding flash and fade to darkness. "Larai and I are . . . sir. We're dead."

I weren't scared. Maybe I didn't have no scared left in me.

"What?" Thailles said. "I'll have none of that. You two get the hell back here and help us hold until the whole Chiliad's on board this damn ship. I'm not losing anyone else. I—"

"We got blown outside, sir."

The Decurion swore. "How?"

"Something hit the outside," I said, "hull defense, maybe? Or one of ours? Didn't get a good look." The words was just spilling out.

Larai cut in, "You can't send the shuttle for us?"

Sounds of fighting over the line. The only sound in our world, except the breathing. I already knew what Thailles would say. Was thinking about Minah, about what it would be like to see her when the Earth comes again. And the boy. We'd be a family, right and proper. And there wouldn't be no demons.

"No."

Larai's hand tightened on my leg where she still held on. She swore. I had to shut my eyes, the spinning were making me sick, watching that impossible big ship get farther and farther away. I tried to guess the distance. We might have only been a thousand feet out, but that were good as light-years, unless . . .

Unless . . .

Unless I did something very stupid.

"You still got your burner?"

"What?"

"I lost mine when that . . . that *thing* grabbed me," I said. "Do you have yours?" I looked down at her where she held my ankle, and it were like I could see through her visor and feel her eyes watching me.

"What are you . . . ?"

"Just give it over!" I snapped, head going clear. Minah would wait. The Earth had not come back to us today, and even if the priests was wrong and the universe weren't made for us . . . I didn't think Soren would want me giving up. I'd already betrayed the old bastard's memory with my coward's thoughts, but I wasn't going to just let us die. We'd have to find our own way back to the ship.

It were harder than I thought getting the gun from Larai—without losing it or her in the Dark. Took longer, the stars all around, cold like eyes watching. I had both my hands free, and fed a cartridge into the side of the weapon.

I remembered that in orientation right before the freeze a couple of the others—I forget what decade they was—got busted racing in one of the null-G parts of the *Valorous* with fire suppressant tanks, using them to fly around one of them big storage bays. Got dressed down direct by the captain herself for that shit, rest of us had a laugh. This were the same thing, only the burner had a little more kick to it.

No air to pull out there, nothing around us but our suits. I switched the burner to torch mode and squeezed off a couple short bursts. The violet plasma streams slowed our roll enough that I could point the thing straight away from the ship. Larai got the idea and held on with both hands. I were not going to die out here, choking on my own fumes. I weren't going to let Larai go the same way. No.

Just had to get back to the ship. I tried to keep that in mind. *We just have to get back to the ship.* I tried not to think about the demons, about their white hands and those black eyes.

I fired, squeezed the trigger down for a good five seconds. "You all right?" I asked Larai, shouting despite the comms tying us. She nodded, but didn't answer. Maybe she thought she were going to be sick. I get that. We wouldn't be the only ones thrown out into the Dark. I tried not to think about that, about our brothers and sisters dying out there. Or about what else were dying with us.

The frozen ship got closer, flickering in the running lights off our shuttles clamped to its surface. I fired again. A good, long burn. The ship must have gotten closer, but it didn't seem to. A note blinked in my suit helmet, and I expelled the burner's plasma reservoir with a click that went all the way up my arm.

"Damn torch mode burns through the packs fast," I said, and slotted one of the replacement reservoirs into the gun. Fired.

Fired.

Fired.

"This the one we got blown out of?" Larai asked, pointing down into the hole. The ice around it was cracked, whiter than elsewhere in the light off our suits. The metal beneath tore inward, stone shattered. Debris drifted there, like it was floating underwater.

Peering over the edge of the hole, I shook my head. "No, don't think so. Don't recognize it." Not a hall inside. Looked like some sort of cargo hold. Red lights hung from what I guessed were the ceiling, faint as old coals. I wondered if these demons saw in the dark, or if they was blind. My da used to tell me things what live in space go pale over the years, living in the dark of their ships. Hadn't happened to me so I figured he was full of it, but I can't stop thinking about that white hand on my throat.

"Decurion?" I tried my comms. Nothing. "Decurion Thailles, this is Oh-Four. I have Oh-Five and we've made the ship again. Repeat, we've made the ship." I looked at Larai, tried to imagine her face through the visor of her helmet; those big eyes wide or narrowed. Were she scared? Or did she set her jaw that way she had? Seemed like she was taking this whole situation better than me.

She tried Thailles on her comms, then toggled over to the main channel.

Nothing.

"They jamming us?" I asked, not wanting to think about the other option.

"Must be, reckon we can only hear each other because we're right here. Give me my burner back, eh?"

I passed the gun to her. "Could try raising the *Valorous*."

"Done that," she said, swinging herself down through the hole. "We've got to find a unit. Any unit."

I followed on after her, stomach lurching as the gravity field inside the ship snagged us out of null G and dropped us to the floor. Storage containers and bits of trash and broken hull filled the hold—and more than a few bodies. None of them was ours, though. Just . . . them. I stopped a second, mindful again of the breathing in my own ears. "The hell'd they not tell us for? What we was getting into? Scaring the shit out of us don't make sense."

"Bet they didn't want us panicking aforehand," Larai shot back, checking the charge on her plasma burner. I wished I hadn't lost mine. "You imagine? Ship full of two thousand Legs learn they're walking into this? Captain don't want that."

That didn't sit with me, still don't. "You reckon they were afeared of mutiny?" Then another idea hit me, and I said, "You reckon this is *first contact*?"

I could see her shake her head. "I bet that happened while we were icicles, Carax. The world changed while we were getting our beauty sleep."

Tried raising Thailles on the comms again as we crossed the floor of the hold toward what looked like doors. Faint blue lights pulsed next to them, and I wondered if they was sealed up against the vacuum. They was, and Larai used her burner to cut through the black metal. Wind started whistling out—you could see it cooling the red edges of the hole she'd made. We forced our way through. I never heard such noise: the wind screaming out, weird alarm howling like a stuck pig, and us only still on our feet because of the rail inside the hall we pulled along.

". . . rendezvous at . . ."

"They're coming out of the walls!"

"—all back! Fall back!"

Snatches of comms chatter broke through as we pulled ourselves down the hall. Up ahead, I could see a massive bulkhead beginning to close. The blue lights flashed

ahead even as the ship rocked under what I guessed were
more collisions from Shrike fliers clamping on. I had to
turn down the audio relays in my helmet—the static kept
snapping in my ears. "Come on!" I shouted, doubling back
to haul Larai past me and up the rail. The door was closing
slow—way slower than they did on our ships during drills.
Maybe it were old, maybe it were broken, maybe all those
prayers I said in Chantry as a boy was worth something.
We made it to the other side.

The alarm were still going, all high and thin sounding.
Reminded me of the whistle Crazy Hector used to control
his dogs back on Aramis, like there were more sound we
wasn't hearing.

"The hell are we?" Larai asked, and I saw the problem.
The mapping drones had done a merry job sketching halls
and chambers in all kinds of details—but we wasn't on it.
Whatever were jamming the comms were jamming our
suits' telemetry, too.

"No idea," I said, more comms chatter crackling in my
ear. None of it made sense. I went a ways up the hall,
disruptor held straight-armed and ready. Couldn't hear
nothing, couldn't see a thing outside what my suit lit up.
Bits of cloth hung from the walls, black and blue, painted
with these round symbols in white and red and pale
yellow. They fluttered in the air—still not settled from the
venting. Passages opened behind some of them. That
scared me. Whatever these things was, they didn't seem
to need their eyes much as Larai and me.

"Looks like we have to find a way up—" I broke off,
the next thought hitting me like a tram. "I wish Soren
were here."

Don't know why that didn't settle in sooner. Maybe it were because we were only just then getting time to breathe. There hadn't been time to really think about it until then. The old bastard hadn't even seen it coming.

I didn't get time to keep thinking about it.

"You cage!" something screamed. Or something like that. "You cage! You cage!" Then a bunch of sounds that made no sense. Then Larai shouted. One of the . . . *things* had emerged from a side passage and grappled her. It happened so fast. She hit the ground and it stooped over her like a revenant in the stories they used to tell us as kids. I didn't see a weapon, but it had its hands on her face. Them long fingers found the hardware clasps there and worked them free. I heard Larai gasp as the seals vented, could hear the air hiss out as the pressures balanced. The faceplate of her helmet fell away, and the creature lowered its face to hers. She screamed.

I fired.

The disruptor burst caught the creature full in the back, and it slumped where it crouched over Larai. Thin gray coils of smoke rose out of my suit lights and away into darkness. I lowered the disruptor, stepping forward to look down at the beast. Only then did we see it were different, not dressed in the black armor the ones up top had been, but in simple gray clothes. There were a hole in the back of the shirt where the disruptor had taken it, smoking and black where the nerves had burned away.

"Are you all right?" I asked, crouching to hand Larai back her faceplate.

"It stinks in here," she said, taking the mask back. It took her a moment to shake herself free. Dead, the creature was all a tangle of limbs. Larai kicked it, ran a hand over her face. Took me a second to see she was shaking. "Its teeth . . ."

"I seen them," I said, checking behind one of the hangings.

"They go all the way back . . ."

"I said I seen them." Talking about it only made it worse. I couldn't listen anymore. All I could think on was getting back. Getting up. I decided I wasn't going to go out like Soren. It didn't matter if Minah was dead back home. Her and the boy. I were still fighting for them. For Aramis. For Earth and Empire—even if the Empire didn't give a shit about me. Even if all they do is tax me and ask me to die fighting their wars. Shit, they're better than these monsters. Anything was. And I weren't fighting for no Empress anyhow. I were fighting for home, for whatever family I had left—even if they didn't remember stupid old Carax who flew off to be a soldier. Wherever they were, whatever had become of them, I am still me. Still alive. I had signed up for them. I was still fighting *for* them. *That* hadn't gone anywhere, that hadn't changed— whatever else had.

Larai tried to get her mask back on.

"Black Earth! Bastard broke one of the seals." Still swearing, she tripped the catch at the base of her jaw and pulled the rest of the helmet off by the neck flange.

"Tiny gods, it's rank in here." She sniffed. "Smells like ass."

"I'll keep my helmet on, then," I said, forcing a laugh that failed to reach her. I was trying not to think about what her losing her helmet meant. About how vulnerable it made her. We hurried on, checking behind the hangings and around corners that branched off and wandered down into darkness. Off the hall, the rooms were more like little caves than real rooms. Here and there the natural stone would give way to a dead or blinking console, the screen so faint I couldn't see anything on them, even in the full light of my suit lamps. Once or twice we thought we heard something in the dark, but it were nothing. Larai stuck close.

After Earth knows how long like this, at last we found a passage leading up. It weren't no stair, but a sort of ramp spiraling up and out of sight.

"Smells like plasma burn in here . . . all cooked," Larai said. Without her suit, her voice sounded thick and muddy in the air. "Where is everyone?"

I spoke through my suit speakers. "Maybe they're higher up? Fighting the others."

We'd gone into a side room then, a series of small rooms behind a black hanging. Food—some kind of raw meat, looked like—lay on a table high as my chin. Storage cabinets in the walls made of some sort of flow-mold plastic. "I don't think this is a military ship, Larai." I'd found a tiny figure—bits of carved bone and metal pegs— shaped like one of the monsters. There were a faint blue flush in its hollow cheeks, and it had this sort of black robe. Dress. Thing. It were a toy, or I felt sure it must be. I put it in my sabretache with my extra air cells. It had a long knife in its hand, like the one I'd almost been stabbed with.

"Carax, come here."

I moved to stand by her. She'd climbed up onto a step

by the table to get a better view of the food there. I swore. Meat, a huge piece of it, bones pulled apart and yellow-brown from the oven. When she spoke, her voice went all kinds of distant. "I recognized the smell." She reached out, turning the food a little on its tray. It had been roasted in its skin, the flesh crackled and leaking juice. As she turned it, the lines of a tattoo—some Mandari symbols— came into the light. She said again, "I recognized the smell."

I swore, "Earth and Emperor." From the size of it, she had been a woman. Once. Pieces of her were set on smaller trays about the table, half-eaten. "We interrupted their meal." I thanked Earth I couldn't smell, not through the suit. I wanted to throw up. To cry. To kill something. I staggered back, vision blurring a little. "Where did they get the . . . the body?"

"I don't know," Larai said. "Captured a ship before? Maybe that's why we're here? Revenge?" She shook her head. "Justice."

"Reckon there are more prisoners?"

I didn't hear Larai answer. The comms channel chose that moment to spit out more noise.

"What?" I said.

"I said did you hear—" She whirled, fired. The plasma left a glowing pockmark in the wall. "Something ran past us!" Then she was gone, back toward the hall. I followed, cursing to myself, but glad to leave that place and its terrible meal. Suit systems relayed an amplified model of the tunnels around, ghost paths off suit sonar showing the way around corners. I heard Larai shoot, saw the flash of plasma fire backscatter off the walls. When I caught up with her, she was standing in the middle of the hall, in an arch opening onto a massive space. At least, it felt big, I couldn't see the roof in my suit lights, even with my vision enhanced.

"Where'd it go?" I asked.

"Where do you think?" she hissed, jabbing her burner at the room ahead.

"Shit." I didn't like the look of it. We'd climbed a fair way since reentering the ship—and seen almost nothing in all that time—but this spot were so exposed, and there was only us two.

There weren't nothing for it, but had I known what were out there, I'd have liked to stay in that arch another hour, or gone back down and out again. I don't expect to be quit of the memory until they put me back on ice. But I didn't know that, and I opened my damn mouth. "We got to make a break for it."

"What?"

"Well, we can't stay here."

"If there's anyone out there, they'll see us. We should turn out the lights."

"Then we won't see shit. These things live in the Dark, Larai," I said. She swore, but in that way she had where I knew she agreed with me. She was all pale looking in the scant light, like one of Them. "You ready? Your shield still good?"

"Took a bit of a hit on the way outside," she said. Then, "Yeah."

I checked my disruptor, keyed up the spotlight under its slit of a barrel, and hurried out into the Dark at a jog. Larai moved past me soon enough, but held pace just in front of me, which was good. I still had my helmet, so my vision were better. I could see ahead more clearly. Even so, I didn't see the others until we were on top of them.

Until they screamed.

There must have been half a hundred of them, all gathered around the foot of a huge, black stone, between the arms of some shrine or altar built in the grotto. The darkness stretched out forever around us, and even the door we'd come through were lost. Red lights burned remote as dying embers on the arms of the shrine, cast upon the carved surface of the black monolith. Were they praying to it? Or only sheltering themselves, hoping to ambush us as we went by?

These was no soldiers. These was others like the one I'd shot in the back, dressed in simple clothes and not armor at all. But they was still monsters, still with slitted noses and black eyes the size of my fist, like I'd walked into some goddamned tomb. Larai fired before I could think, taking down two, three, four. The beasts hissed and drew back. But they didn't draw up like I expected, using their height to scare the piss out of me. They shrank down, away. Some fell over the others to get *away*.

"Wait!" I shouted, and were surprised when I didn't sound scared. I sure felt scared. "Larai, wait."

"What is it?" She'd backed up so we stood almost shoulder to shoulder. I reached up and unsealed my helmet, letting the mask slot back properly. "What in Earth's Holy Name . . . ?"

"They ain't soldiers. Look."

Without the flattening of the helmet's vision, I saw what they was. Monsters, yes, with glass fangs and those

horrible, melted-skull faces. But with my own eyes I could
see the way their nostrils flared, eyes wider than seemed
possible. They was scared. Same as me. Or maybe their
scared is different. They ran, scattered toward exits I
could only guess at. The noise they made—high and
cold—I haven't stopped hearing it. I put my helmet down
on the floor, lowered my weapon. That's when I heard it.
Shots. Plasma fire. Yelling.

Soldiers. Legionnaires.

Humans.

We stood there stunned, watching them go—watching
still more huddle against the black monolith or against the
arms of the shrine. I must have turned my head for two
seconds, but it were enough. I heard Larai scream even
as something huge hit me full in the side, and I went down
with one on top of me. It shrieked like metal tearing, like
cold wind.

I thought about Soren, about the meal we had found . . .
about my Minah and the boy. The creature's arms were
like iron about me, fingers wedged between the plates of
my armor and the underlayment, tearing. I felt a clasp pop
somewhere about my ribs. For a moment, I'd forgotten
the disruptor was in my hands, forgotten the creature was
not armored. Its breath hissed in my ear, and I thought it
were going to bite me. I fired, insulated from collateral
nerve shock by my suit. The creature went limp as a sack
of wet oats, and I peeled it off me, staggering to my feet
again.

Another of the creatures had Larai pinned down. Her
burner'd been knocked away, and it had each of her wrists
in its huge, long-fingered hands. It stooped over her, its

face near to hers. I remembered their snarling, jagged teeth, and didn't hesitate. I were done hesitating. I squared my shoulders and fired. There were a flash of blue light and it fell on top of her.

Better to fight. Always better to fight.

I kept my disruptor raised, circling away from the shrine and the crowd of demons. Slowly. Sounds of fighting and gunfire came from up the hall. "Over here!" I cried. "Over here!" Then more quietly to Larai, "You all right?"

"Help me up!"

The beasts nearest me turned, unsure where to go. I could see the fear in them eyes, and knew it were fear like mine. One saw me and froze. Larai said something, but I couldn't hear her. I was watching the creature. Its huge eyes. Its horns. Its white hair tangled on its shoulders. It looked at me a good long time, flinching away. Not knowing why, I held out my free hand, above my head. I smiled. It cocked its head, took a step forward. Then I saw the stains about its mouth, on its chin. Red stains on the blue-white face.

"Carax, what are you doing?" Larai hissed.

"Quiet," I said, and moved slowly for my sabretache. I fished the strange doll out and held it out, keeping my disruptor primed, aimed at the floor beside me. The child—I don't know why I think it was a child, for it was taller than I was by a head—inched forward, raising its own hands, reaching for the doll I held. I weren't going to shoot. Monster or not, man-eater or not, I wasn't going to gun a child down. Fighting for the Empire was better than letting these monsters eat us, but I knew where I draw the line. I glanced at the helmet I'd left on the floor, then back to the creature. It looked me in the face, eyes narrowed, teeth bared.

And then it had no face. Only smoking ruins.

I don't think it were Larai who shot it. I think it were one of the others. One of the bone-colored Legionnaires in their red tabards looking like the enlistment posters. Faceless as the creature were now.

But they was a human kind of faceless.

※   ※   ※

Christopher Ruocchio is the author of The Sun Eater, a space opera series from DAW Books, including novels *Empire of Silence* and *Howling Dark*. He is the assistant editor at Baen Books and a graduate of North Carolina State University. He lives in Raleigh, NC, with his family.

A TALE OF THE GREAT TREK WAR
ABOARD THE STARSHIP *PERSISTENCE*

Brendan DuBois

There are big ships. Then again there are really big ships. Imagine a vessel so huge that terms like "port" and "starboard" denote not just sides of the ship, but sides of life, of culture. Given enough time in the dark between the stars, might they not also become sides in a war for precious resources? Victory often goes to those who dare, and in such a situation the most daring of all might be the warrior who can literally think outside the box. Or, in this case, outside the bottle. Outside, where the distant stars shine on the just and unjust—and on Port and Starboard alike.

In Year 219 of the Starship *Persistence*'s voyage from Earth to Destination, I found myself one late watch in a wide access tube once designed to be used for automated deliveries from one division to another, following the squad ahead of me by the flickering lights from the battle lanterns strapped to their waists. It was hard to tell how long this access tube had been used—the railings were still shiny and looked like they were ready to move along transport drones at any moment—but one of the armed members of our squad was a rating in logistics and said this tube hadn't been used in decades, especially since it eventually transited to Port.

I was desperately trying to keep notes of what we were doing and where we were going, but after two hours of travel, it was pretty hard to do much except note "Bulkhead 4-G-14 successfully passed," followed by "Bulkhead 4-G-13 successfully passed." The squad consisted of fourteen members of the crew and myself, Avery Conrad, yeoman in the Public Affairs Office, which consisted of me, me, and . . . me. But the captain wanted a firm recording of what was going to happen during this war, and that was my job. As she had told me earlier, "We still don't know what happened during the Event, years back. A lot of the computer files were overwritten, scrubbed, or bleached. What scraps of paper writings and notes that survived say still doesn't make sense. Yeoman, your job is to record a good, accurate story of this conflict, so future generations will have a clear idea of what happened."

With that, I had given the captain a snappy salute, and said, "Aye aye, ma'am," which was why I found myself in this wide yet smelly and dark access tube, tagging along during one of the first clashes of this war.

Up ahead there was a sudden bunching of lights and some harsh whispers, and I swallowed hard, mouth dry. I had gone through the usual weapons and hand-to-hand combat training when I was younger, but I was lax when it came to working out during my regular duty. I had no illusions of my bravery or my strength. I was just there to witness, and secretly, I was also there to run away if a battle were to break out.

I'm no hero. Just a guy who writes things.

I moved ahead and pushed my way through, and three battle lamps were aimed to the deck. There was a smooth joint on the deck and on one side was a line of blue paint, and on the other side—to where we were headed—was a line of gold paint.

Our squad's leader, Petty Officer Blake, whispered, "There you go, shipmates. We cross that line and we're passing from Starboard to Port. We're officially going into enemy territory. Be ready, now . . . and spread out!"

So we spread out in a line and I remained in the rear, along with a cute electronics specialist named Mary Young, and she whispered to me, "I'm so scared. How about you?"

"Stick with me," I said. "It'll be all right."

She nodded, holding a lance in her hand that was almost as long as she was tall, and I didn't bother telling her that by sticking with me, I would ensure her safety by making sure she would run back with me once fighting broke out.

The squad had on the usual blue jumpers and helmets, and the weapons were a mix of lances, swords, and a few power guns. Being stretched out like this, I could almost enjoy the curious sight of seeing bobbing lights ahead of me, stretching out in one long chain. Electronics Specialist Young, walking along with me, whispered, "It looks like a test strip line up there."

I was going to ask her what a test strip line was when we were hit.

The end of the access tube collapsed and spotlights flicked on, and somebody yelled out "Ambush!" and the fight was on.

I was at the rear and I'm ashamed to say that Electronics Specialist Young reacted better than me, and with lance in her hand, she yelled and raced forward. The sudden light blinded my eyes but after a few seconds, I was able to make out what was going on.

The access tube had been sabotaged somehow so the Gold Crew knew we were coming, and could collapse decking and bulkheads to open us up to an attack. They were above us on support beams, in a curving line, and they sent down arrows, long spears, and there were two powered weapons that chattered at the crowd of Blue Crew members.

Most didn't have a chance, dammit, and there was a cry of "Retreat! Fall back! Retreat!" and that's what we survivors did, running back down the access tube, heading back to Starboard, the light from the ambush fading behind us, the bouncing battle lanterns only lighting our way, until we ended up at the Bulkhead 4 terminal, where there were corpsmen and others stationed to help us.

I think maybe there eight survivors, including me.

And not including Electronics Specialist Young.

A few hours earlier I had been called into Captain Quinn's quarters as she was having a meeting with her department heads, from astrogation to propulsion to hibernation maintenance to farming and about a half dozen others. When she noted me she asked me to take a seat in a far corner, which I did, and with notepad in hand along with stylus, I sat there and waited to see what the captain needed.

Which was direct and to the point.

She unfolded a tiny sheet of paper and said, "At oh-eight-hundred this morning, we received a final message from Captain Xi following the cessation of negotiations. The message says, quote, *Qù sǐ ba*, unquote, which, I believe, roughly translates to 'go to hell.'"

There was a sigh and some whispered words as the impact of those words settled in.

War.

I had been about six or so when there had last been war between Blue and Gold, Starboard and Port, Yank or Han—take your choice. I don't remember much about that conflict, only that it was over water rations and I spent most of the time hidden in one of the storage chambers in my family's quarters, and so I wasn't sure how this latest conflict would shake out.

Who would?

Captain Quinn noted the reactions from the department heads and said, "Come now, people. Stout hearts and stout minds, all right? You are all descended from those who made the big leap back at the Start, and our ancestors then were brave and strong. We all have strong spirits and strong genes. Number One."

Commander Rex Chambers, sitting at her right side, said, "Ma'am."

"Execute War Plan Beta immediately. Send out runners to pass along the word."

"It will take a while for the runners to get where they're needed. Since we—"

The captain raised a hand. "I don't need a replay of recent history. That's what got us into this war. Send out the runners and make adjustments to execute Beta at the appropriate time."

"Aye aye, ma'am," he said.

The captain said, "Department heads, take note of Number One's actions and respond accordingly. Dismissed."

She stood up and the department heads stood up as well, and they started bustling out and I was pulling up the rear, when she said, "Avery."

"Captain."

"Stay behind, please."

"Yes, ma'am."

When the room was empty, she said, "I want you at my side, as much as possible, to record what's going on as this war commences. I want a clear record so future gens will have no doubt as to what happened, and who was to blame."

"I'll need an increase in my paper ration."

She nodded. "You've got it. Follow me, all right?"

"Yes, ma'am."

Out in one of the main corridors, members of the food production crew were pushing ahead a herd of swine. I moved past them and kept pace with the captain as she briskly walked to Starboard Cafeteria

Two and entered the low-ceilinged room. Beyond the fixed table and chairs, and near the shuttered ports where food was served, a number of troops were lined up, draftees from the various departments. They had on dark blue jumpers with gold piping, face masks, and helmets, and carried pikes, spears, and a few powered weapons. The captain looked to me and made writing motions with her hands, and I knew what she was looking for.

I sat down at one of the fixed stools and wrote rapidly as the captain spoke to one of our first raiding squadrons. Overhead some of the lighting flickered. There was not one tube, passageway, or compartment that didn't have dead or dying lights.

"I'll make this quick," Captain Quinn said. "You've trained over the years as a fine fighting force, you and the other raiding parties. You and your comrades will be dispatched shortly to do what has to be done for Starboard, for our honor, our families, and our future. I know I can count on all of you."

She then walked forward, shook everyone's hand, and then turned to me.

"Yeoman Avery," she said.

"Yes, Captain," I said.

"Gear up," she said. "You're joining them."

Later that evening, after I had taken part in the disastrous battle, the captain called together another department head meeting.

This one was grim.

Two of the department heads were missing, replaced

by their subordinates. Three others—astrogation, waste management, logistics—had bandages on their arms or heads.

Captain Quinn said, "It seems we've had a rough time of it. Number One?"

Commander Chambers looked at a scrap of paper. "Ma'am, all three raiding parties were beaten back. Casualties . . . were heavy. Twelve dead, twenty wounded, at least six taken prisoner. Two of the wounded will probably die later tonight."

The room was quiet, only the general low hum of the *Persistence*'s machinery and life-support systems being heard.

Captain Quinn looked to us all and said, "Not a first good day."

A pause.

"Very well," she said. "You're dismissed. Maintain guard posts and quick reaction forces where necessary. We'll meet again at oh-eight-hundred tomorrow."

I didn't want to talk to anyone, or be with anyone, but it's hard to do that aboard the *Persistence*. Eventually I crawled into my personal tube and managed to fall into a fitful sleep, until my tube hatch cycled open and in the dim light, I spotted one of the older male chief petty officers looking in.

"The captain's compliments and you're to join her at Docking Port Able."

I got out of my bunk and started getting dressed. "Where . . . what's Docking Port Able? I've never heard of it."

"You'll find out, soon enough," he said.

Finally dressed and woozy over the lack of sleep and the images of that Port ambush, I followed, stumbled, and again followed the chief petty officer up as we climbed, walked, took a powered elevator, and went closer and closer to Surfaceside.

Twice we went past hibernation chambers, where members of hibernation maintenance kept view on the hundreds of colonists who were in DeepSleep. A gigantic letter *T* and the Han symbol marking "Taboo" were painted outside the hatches leading into the hibernation chambers. No matter what conflicts, wars, and disagreements have taken place between Port and Starboard over the years, there has been one consistent agreement, that the hibernation chambers throughout the ship were never to be threatened or damaged.

Some years before my parents were born, one of our captains went insane and threatened the Gold Crew that he would destroy one of the hibernation chambers unless the Gold Crew and the entire Port submitted to Blue Crew rule. That threat didn't last long. At the Neutral Park in the center of the ship, members of his own command staff bound him to a metal pole in front of the Gold Crew and burnt him alive. He was so reviled that his remains weren't even later Recycled.

There's never been another threat against the hibernation chambers since then.

We were now in parts of the ship I had not visited, and would probably never be in again. The way got narrower, with struts and conduits and power cables overhead and underfoot, and then we were crawling, with flickering light tubes guiding us along.

Then the chief petty officer halted and said, "The captain's up ahead, waiting for you."

"You're not coming with me?" I asked.

"Not going to happen, shipmate."

I crawled ahead and came out in a wide but low compartment. The captain was there, as well as a dozen other crew members, and from their bulk and quiet look, I knew they were Marines, the hardest fighters we had. But wars with Port were rare enough that Starboard couldn't afford the logistics to keep a large standing force of Marines just lounging around, training and training.

Captain Quinn spotted me and said, "Over here, Yeoman."

The upper deck was low enough that we were all squatting, and as I got closer, Captain Quinn said, "We're waiting for another squad to arrive, and then we'll move out."

I nodded. "Where to, ma'am?"

"To Port," she said. "Where else?"

As we waited the Marines talked among themselves, ignoring me—a lowly yeoman—and the captain, who was, well, the captain. She took me to a corner of the compartment and said, "The raid you were on today . . . it was a disaster. Correct?"

My chest was tight, remembering the lights, the screams, the blood, the organized way the Gold crew had ambushed us. "Yes, ma'am, it was."

"Well . . . sometimes you need to make a demonstration, just to show your opponents how serious you are. That's the way of wars. Do you know how wars break out?"

I was surprised that in the midst of what was going on, the captain was in a lecturing mode. Her nickname among some decks—but not the ones I trod—was the Professor.

"There's a variety of theories, and—"

"Scarce resources," she said, slapping the bulkhead for emphasis. "That's all it is. Wars in the past on the *Persistence* have been over water, cattle, pigs, wheat . . . resources. And now it's high-technology time. Port has technology we need. It wouldn't agree to a compromise, an agreement to share for the good of the ship, so it had to come down to this."

Rattling noises some distance away. It sounded like another squad of Marines was coming toward us. The captain said, "You did a good job, trailing a raiding party. I've read your personnel file, Yeoman. Pretty adequate job, but you're a curious sort. I've seen three requests filed by you in the past four years to gain access to the Captain's Archives. Care to tell me why?"

"Uh . . ." On the spot. My immediate supervisor, an old CPO perpetually a month away from passing away and off to Recycling, had sent the requests upstream without her recommendation.

What to say? The captain was a fair sort, as captains go, but she's got ship's steel in her blood and spine. I've been to four Captain's Masts where she sentenced fellow shipmates of mine to Medical and then Recycling for offenses against regulations.

She was staring at me, and I knew she wanted an answer, and now.

Why not the truth?

"I'm curious, ma'am," I said. "I want to know the history of the ship . . . the past, what went on, how we got here."

The captain nodded. "Fair enough. Tell you what, you're coming with me on this raiding party. We all get back, and if you write up something satisfactory, I'll open up all the archives to you. No restriction. How does that sound?"

I just nod, speechless. The Captain's Archives . . . some supposedly going all the way back to Light Off . . .

She slapped the bulkhead again. "Here's a secret, just to whet your appetite. Maybe it'll encourage you to do a good job. The name of our big home, it didn't start off as the *Persistence*. I think it was a joke made about a hundred or so years back, during the Event, and the joke stuck. When she was launched, there was an agreement that for half of the journey, she was going to be called for some Yank politician, and at Flip, she'd be called for a Han politician. Supposedly."

Then she caressed the smooth bulkhead. "But I like *Persistence*."

The new squad entered our compartment, bowed over because of the cramped quarters, and the captain said, "Stand ready, Yeoman. We're off to Port."

"Through a corridor, or a system tube?" For that was what I was thinking, that perhaps the captain or one of these Marines had discovered an old approach to Port, a way that won't be defended by the Gold crew.

She smiled. "Nope."

And then I nearly collapsed in terror for what she said next.

"We're going out."

Going out . . .

I had heard of crewmates in the past who have gone out, but never had I ever spoken to one that claimed to have done it.

And now my captain was about to do it.

And I was expected to go along.

"Um, Captain," I stammered, and she said, "Later, Yeoman, we don't have time. Just follow my lead, follow my orders, and you'll be all right."

She stood away from the corner and went to talk to the Marines, and we went through another access hatch and tube that meant lots of crawling, hand-to-feet work, and as we scurried through the dirt and dust, I thought of the legends and stories about going out. How one could fall forever. How the cosmics out there would strike you dead. Or how one would go insane by just looking out . . . and out . . . and out . . .

The tunnel we were in opened up into a large compartment, and I was startled, thinking people were in a line, waiting for us, but no, it was shelving and hooks, and hanging off them were spacesuits.

Spacesuits.

Scores and scores of them.

My mouth was agape and I was still shaking with fear, but I stepped forward, having only seen one suit in my entire life, during my first term in school, and that one had been worn from years of touching and rubbing and examination.

These looked nearly brand-new, as if they had just come off some factory line in long-ago Earth.

Captain Quinn said, "This location . . . is one of the closest secrets we have in Starboard. There's always been rumors, twice-told tales here and there, but when I assumed the captaincy, I was determined to find out if there was some truth to the tales." She reached out and gently touched an empty sleeve. "And there was. Here's a storage facility for those suits used in going out."

The Marines went ahead and the captain said, "There are more suits farther down, but these are the ones we'll be using. From what we've learned, these are the basic models, to be used with little or no training. These suits also contain limited resources and . . . just to be clear . . . no sanitation arrangements. But we shouldn't be gone more than an hour, so that should be fine."

She took a suit down with its clear head flopping to one side, and then removed her boots. The captain said, "You step in like so . . . and put your arms in like this . . . and bring this section forward . . . and then the helmet goes on like this . . ."

The suit hung limply off her but her voice was still clear. "There's an ability with these suits to use electronic communication. We won't be doing that . . . in case the Han have the means to listen to those assigned frequencies. I will maintain the lead . . . we will be hooked together by lines. Marines, carry your weapons but make sure they are secured to the outside of the suits. Any questions?"

No one was brave enough to ask anything.

The captain pointed to the lower waist of the suit. "The green rectangle starts the suit's operation. The red triangle ceases the suit's operation. Simple, but that's how it was designed. When we get to our destination, I'll signal when it's time for us to de-suit. Then it will be time to strike fast, and strike hard. Again, any questions?"

The bravery of the Marines and myself still wasn't tested.

"Go on then, choose a suit. And don't bother looking for any particular size. The suits adjust to your mass and shape."

There was some bumbling and chaos when we got to the suits, and I had to dodge between two tall Marines before grabbing one for myself. The captain must have secretly practiced before, because I fell on the deck three times before I got everything in place, but at least nobody laughed at me. Too many others were doing the same thing, falling over and over again on the deck.

As I reached to the waist, looking for the green rectangular switch, the oddest feeling came over me, thinking that this suit had been built by my ancestors, back home on Earth, and that whoever worked this suit and put it together . . . heck, even his or her grandchildren were probably dead.

I pushed the switch in and yelped in surprise. There was a combination hissing and whirring sound as the open flaps and swatches on the suit seemed to "reach out" and get connected, and then the suit . . . it moved around me, and settled in. My ears popped for some reason, and then

the hissing and whirring noises stopped. Odd, but if I
shifted my head one way or another, green words and
symbols appeared like they were being displayed on the
clear helmet, giving me information such as OUTSIDE
PRESSURE and ZULU TIME and AIR EXPIRATION and other
stuff I couldn't make out. I took a deep breath. The air
was sharp and cold, and there was something else. It
smelled old, I mean, really, really old.

I was jostled by somebody and I turned around, and it
was a fully suited Marine, fixing a long line to my belt.
Others ahead of me were hooked up as well. Their
weapons—swords, lances, powered weapons—were either
being carried or were fastened to the sides of the suits.

This was . . . something.

I felt important.

I felt invincible.

Then there were noises, yells, screams.

I turned around, a bit clumsy because of my suit, and
there were two Marines, writhing on the deck, slapping
at the triangular red button, punching at their helmets,
trying to get them off . . . and it struck me that something
must be wrong with the air system in those two suits. They
couldn't breathe. They were suffocating and dying in front
of us. There was a sudden scream behind me and a
Marine was flat out on the deck, reaching down to his
knees, where his lower legs had been cut clean off by the
suit clamping too hard.

I didn't feel invincible anymore.

We'd lost three Marines already and I was shaking with
fear inside my suit, but being roped in, I was forced to

follow a line of spacesuited crewmen, led by Captain Quinn, as we went down an adjacent passageway, and there was a heavy-looking door that gave us access into a larger compartment, much bigger than the one with the suit storage. We huddled in and there was a lit panel, and the captain pressed a number of switches, and the door closed behind us. I felt the *thump* vibrate in my boots and up my legs. Something seemed wrong with the lights and they dimmed, and I felt more vibration as machinery in this compartment began operating. My suit felt different, somehow, and then there was tugging on the rope, and two more Marines were struggling, struggling . . . and then they settled down on the deck.

Two others were dead because of something wrong with their suits. This attack force had already been depleted before we'd even left Starboard territory. But the lines were refastened and I was hoping Captain Quinn was going to cancel this mission, and I turned and the compartment shuddered, and then a bulkhead fell away and—

Stars.

I saw stars and blackness and stars that seemed to go on forever.

The line tugged and we moved out, and in a few moments, I'm Outside, on the exterior surface of the *Persistence*, and I'm not ashamed to say that my bladder cut loose and I soiled myself.

We stood as a group and I think maybe the captain was giving us a moment to orient ourselves. My breathing was ragged and my heart was thumping along so hard I could actually hear it in my suit.

My God, the stars . . .

I looked around me, and around me, and my knees shook at seeing at just how huge the *Persistence* was. The low light from the open compartment we just left was still illuminating the surrounding area, and the hull of the *Persistence* and the adjoining structures just went on, and on, and on . . .

I knew how large *Persistence* was, for the number of sleepers we carried, and the farms, and the hydroponic tanks, and storage, and quarters for both the Blue and Gold, Port and Starboard, Han and Yank . . . but to see it from the outside.

I closed my eyes. Opened them again.

And the stars . . . we've all seen the stars via the different viewscreens and monitors—including the one hosting Destination—but to see them now . . . everywhere we looked, there were the stars, so many stars, against the blackness and emptiness of space.

Someone tugged the line.

We started moving.

We moved in a ragged line, being gently kept on the hull's surface because of something called "the Field," which also protected the *Persistence* from the constant hammering of debris that we'd encountered over the decades. As we moved along, sometimes the stars were just too much to look at, and I kept my gaze to my slowly shuffling feet. There were openings here and there, struts and antennas, and once in our parade line, the huge hull seemed to dip down and then come back up. There were also paint schemes, numbers and letters outlined on the hull, and I got a tingling feeling at the base of my skull, knowing that these paint marks were made by our ancestors, who built this ship and sent it to the stars. As hard as it was to believe, my breathing eased some as we moved along, yet I still hoped the captain knew where we were going.

And what we would do when we got there.

The slope in the hull rose up and there were dish-shaped structures scattered across the hull, again stretching off forward and aft, blurring out at the length of my vision. My breathing was loud and there was a sudden tug and jostle at my rear, and I fell down on the hull.

I slowly tried to get up, the line wrapped around my legs, and I fought and struggled to free the line, and then I was able to get back up.

I looked to the rear of the line.

And instantly wished I hadn't.

Two Marines at the very end had broken free. Their end of the line must have parted, and one or the other must have panicked and pushed off the hull, strong enough to pass through the Field.

They wiggled and struggled, like two carp being pulled out of one of our ponds, until I couldn't see them anymore as they drifted off in screaming silence.

Another tug on the line.

Time to move.

And I felt like laughing hysterically, thinking so far, the *Persistence* has turned out to be more of an enemy than the Gold Crew.

Some long time later—and I was wondering just how

much air was left within my suit—we came to a halt. Two figures were huddled together up ahead, helmets pressed against each other, and I thought that maybe they could hear each other through the conductive materials of their helmets.

One slapped the other on the shoulder, and we went just a few more meters, and stopped.

There was a large, rectangular shape outlined in faded yellow paint extending along the hull, and we were jostled and pulled to line up nearby. One spacesuited figure—and I was almost sure it was the captain—knelt down. Two battle lanterns were lit off, and it looked like the figure was searching for something with her gloved hands.

Then the hand came up and down, twice on the hull.

A vibration began against my feet.

Light flared out from the hull, and it got brighter, and the outlined shape revealed itself to be a large hatch, just like the one we used to leave Starboard.

A tug of the line, and now we were entering Port.

We gathered in the large compartment and the hatch slammed shut, and there were more vibrations and thudding of machinery against my feet. The lights in here flickered and then grew in strength, and then the thumping and vibration slowed down and ended.

What now?

One figure untied its line, and then pushed down at the red triangle at the waist. The suit changed shape and then a figure emerged, and it was the captain, her face sweaty, her red hair matted down. The rest of us followed her lead, and the suits collapsed in piles on the deck, like cast-off vegetable peelings in the galley.

Murmurs and orders and without warning, a side bulkhead slid up, bringing in more light.

And two curious Gold crewmen, gazing in shock at what they saw before them.

They don't stand long.

Our Marines moved forward and the Gold Crew members were soon dead on the deck, and with shouts and yells, the attack commenced.

I stayed with Captain Quinn as she led the raiding force into the heart of Port, and it was a slaughter. Most of the Han crew we encountered turned and ran at our approach, and only a few stuck behind to fight, and they were overwhelmed. The captain shouted, "Move, move, move!" and she must have known where we were going, for we fought our way up a ramp, and from there, through two passageways, until we reached a spot where about a dozen Han fighters were making a stand. There was the hum of powered weapons, screams, shouts, the clash of swords and lances, and the captain moved four Marines to guard our rear, as shouts and ringing bells sounded off in the distance.

The fight didn't last long.

The compartment was forced open and it was crowded, with viewing screens, desks, and another, smaller adjacent compartment, where an elderly Han man was dragged out of his bunk, wearing loosely fitted light yellow trousers and blouse. He was bald and had a droopy moustache, and Captain Quinn moved forward, lifted her sword up, and placed the point of it under his chin. His eyes were tired-looking and sad.

"Captain Xi?" she asked. "I demand your surrender and that of the Gold Crew."

He managed to nod his agreement, even with the point of a sword dimpling his skin.

There was laughter, a few triumphant yelps and whoops, and two corpsman got to work on our wounded, and even the Han wounded.

And I realized that I hadn't taken a single note.

Then I went to the side of a near bulkhead and threw up.

The official surrender ceremony took place the next day, at Neutral Park. The grass was a fine green and miniature trees and shrubs were scattered here and there, save for an area in the center of the park, a ditch dug a long time ago, back during the Event. A short bridge made of struts and steel spanned the ditch, and that's where the ceremony was held.

Lines of Port crewmembers in their gold jumpsuits were on the Han side of the ditch, while our own Yank crewmembers in blue jumpsuits were on the Starboard side. There were flags and banners held up on poles, and after the slaughter and fighting these past two days, it was all so damned civilized and ordered.

Captain Quinn made a short speech, and then Captain Xi did the same. They shook hands.

Then the Han line parted and a single Han officer came forward with the technological spoil of this brief war, and bowed, and turned it over to Captain Quinn.

I strained to get a good view, and I was impressed with what I saw. It had two spoked tires fore and aft, and a frame with a saddle where a crew member would sit. Two pedals—one port, the other starboard—were connected to a complex chain system that propelled the velocipede.

The paint was faded but the name of the person who made it, back on Earth, was still visible along one of the metal tubes.

T R E K.

At one time there were supposedly scores of these machines aboard *Persistence*, but this was the last one, and it was used for all sorts of courier and messaging services, and whichever crew held the Trek was at an operational advantage.

I looked down at my pad and stylus.

I had neglected to jot down the words of each side's captain, but in seeing the triumphant smile of Captain Quinn, and the look of hate on Captain Xi, I had no doubt that this was not going to be the last war for me to witness on the good ship *Persistence,* and I would have plenty of opportunities to record our bloody history for the crew and our sleeping inhabitants in the future.

But at least, for now, Starboard was victorious.

❄   ❄   ❄

Brendan DuBois is the award-winning author of twenty-one novels and more than 160 short stories. His short stories have thrice won him the Shamus Award from the Private Eye Writers of America, and have also earned him three Edgar Award nominations. He has recently collaborated with *New York Times* best-selling author James Patterson on three novellas for Patterson's Bookshots as well as two upcoming novels. Brendan lives in New Hampshire. A former *Jeopardy!* champion, he also appeared on—and won—the game show *The Chase*.

1636: Commander Cantrell in the West Indies
978-1-4767-8060-3 • $8.99

Oil. The Americas have it. The United States of Europe needs it. Enter Lieutenant-Commander Eddie Cantrell.

1636: The Vatican Sanction
978-1-4814-8386-5 • $7.99

Pope Urban has fled the Vatican and the traitor, Borja. But assassins have followed him to France—and not only assassins! The Pope and his allies have fled right into the clutches of the vile Pedro Dolor.

STARFIRE SERIES
(with Steve White)

Extremis
978-1-4516-3814-1 • $7.99

They have traveled for centuries, slower than light, and now they have arrived at the planet they intend to make their new home: Earth. The fact that humanity is already living there is only a minor inconvenience.

Imperative
978-1-4814-8243-1 • $7.99

A resurrected star navy hero attempts to keep a fragile interstellar alliance together while battling and implacable alien adversary.

Oblivion
978-1-4814-8401-5 • $7.99

It's time to take a stand! For Earth! For Humanity! For the Pan-Sentient Union!

"[T]he intersecting plot threads, action and well-conceived science kept those pages turning." —SFcrowsnest